1st VISION

THE NOSTRADAMUS LEGACY

Book 1 of the Visions series

V. RAY

CONXM PUBLISHING
Lakewood Ranch, Florida
www.CONXM.com

Illustration credits:
1. Cover artwork licensed from CanStockPhoto, Artist Jetrel, and edited by V. Ray.
2. Fort Detroit site layout, Detroit, Michigan USA, by RMHermen / Wikipedia.
3. Eiffel Tower photo, Paris, France, taken and edited by V. Ray.
4. Notre Dame Cathedral photo, Paris, France, taken and edited by V. Ray.
5. Sacré Coeur Basilica photo, Paris, France, taken and edited by V. Ray
6. Oil Rig on Fire photo, Deepwater Horizon, Gulf of Mexico, taken by United States Coast Guard for the public domain and edited by V. Ray.
7. Winter Palace photo, St. Petersburg, Russia, by Craig Nagy / Flickr and edited by V. Ray.
8. Alexander Palace photo, Pushkin, Russia, by Alexei Troshin / Wikimedia and edited by V. Ray.
9. The third Antichrist symbolic drawing, Rome, Italy, by Michel de Nostradamus and edited by V. Ray.
10. Capitol Building photo, Washington DC, USA, by Kevin McCoy / Wikimedia and edited by V. Ray.

CONTENTS

Main Characters

Andrew Vandevelde: Chairman of the Joint Chiefs of Staff in 2012.

Bruce Cullens: Promising new member of Secret Service Advance Intelligence (SSAI) team in 2012.

Cecilia Lawley: Candidate for executive role at Starr Aerospace.

Darrell "Dime Time" Tracewski: High school bully in 1981.

Dennis Flynn: County Sheriff for Macomb County/Shelby Township in 1981.

Donald McMillan: High school teacher in 1981.

Greg Rutledge: CIA Director in 2012.

Halbert Curry: Serial killer in US working for Russians in 1981.

Helen Tyson: High school teacher and mother to Tyson children.

Jessica O'Neill: ER doctor and Trey Tyson's love interest in 2012.

John Hinckley, Jr.: Historical figure. Attempted to assassinate President Ronald Reagan in 1981.

Judith Tyson: Promising young member of SSAI in 1981, and leader of SSAI in 2012.

Karl: Highly secretive Knight of the First Order and financier of privatized Russian espionage.

Katarina Krostov: Russian assassin and visionary.

Khan: African Prince.

Lou Sanchez: Shuttle commander in 1999 and president in 2012.

Marino "Reno" De Santos: Leader of the Democratic National Committee in present day.

Maximo "Max" Medici: SSAI leader in 1981. 2nd Holy Warrior, famous in Washington, DC inner circles for eliminating Adolf Hitler, the 2nd Antichrist. Also a key figure in attempt to stop the third Antichrist.

Michel De Nostradame (Nostradamus): Historical figure. Prophet and visionary.

Paka: Khan's servant in 1981. Leads Somali Pirates in 2012.

Paul Tyson: Trey Tyson's twin brother and computer genius.

Ronald Reagan, President: Historical figure. US president from 1981-1989.

Roy Starr: Billionaire owner of Starr Aerospace and several other ventures.

Samantha "Sam" Fox: Trey Tyson's best friend in 1981, and senior member of SSAI in 2012.

Sarah Tyson: Trey Tyson's younger sister.

Steve Berman: Candidate for executive role at Starr Aerospace.

Tecumseh, Chief: Historical figure. Chief of Shawnee tribe spanning parts of US and Canada.

Tenskwatawa "The Prophet": Historical figure. Younger brother of Chief Tecumseh and source of the Presidential Curse.

Trey Tyson: Promising young visionary in 1981 highly sought by both Americans and Russians. Heads international executive search and consulting company in present day.

Viktor Krostov: Leader of a private Russian espionage group.

William Casey: Historical figure. CIA director in 1981.

Prologue

MICHEL DE NOSTRADAME
SALON-DE-PROVENCE, FRANCE
JULY 1, 1566

Holding my breath, I listen intently for the distant sound of echoing hooves before stumbling through the entrance to my home. The cobbled streets of Salon are devoid of people this late at night. Some have been taken by the Inquisitors, while many more have fallen to the plague, leaving the Mediterranean village dark and destitute.

Villagers have learned to burn the plague-ridden corpses outside the village walls, but not far enough away. The stench of death still permeates the air.

"Master Nostradamus, you return so soon from Paris."

My secretary, Jean de Chavigny, frail yet reliable, seems not the least bit surprised to see me. Only my young son, Cesar, standing next to Jean and staring at me with palpable sadness, is dearer to me. Just thirteen years old, Cesar has been asked to grow up too soon. I've given him far too much responsibility, but I've had no choice.

"I am being hunted and had to draw them away from Catarina."

"Father," starts Cesar. "You are too familiar. The people already whisper that you are responsible for King Henry's death. It is unwise to give them any reason to suspect you further."

"I only foresaw the King's demise. I did not cause it."

With a growing scowl, Jean says, "You published your vision describing the King's death in your 1555 almanac, four years *prior* to his actual death. The prophecy was far too accurate, almost as if you *wanted* to draw the attention of the Inquisitors."

"I knew Catarina would protect me."

"Father," Cesar scolds, "you should use her proper name. Queen Catherine de' Medici."

"Today, of all days, I need not worry about formalities. Remember when I had you transcribe this for my book:"

"On my return home from the embassy, having secured the royal gift,
I will be no more, having returned to God.
Nearby will be my closest family and friend.
I will be found dead near the bed and the bench."

The *royal gift* for my queen and closest ally, has been to draw this danger away from her and her children. It is the least I can do to repay her and the Medici family. They saved my daughter, Lucrezia. My first wife and son were taken by the plague. My daughter survived, but I foresaw she would have been taken by the Inquisition if she had stayed with me. Duke Medici offered to protect my daughter, even marrying her to his son, Giulio de' Medici. The long line of descendants of Giulio and Lucrezia will bear the three Holy Warriors. They will be my descendants, as well, and carry the curse of responsibility for the safety of all the people of the world.

Cesar and Jean do not know of Lucrezia's existence, or that she is the source of the line of the Holy Warriors. It is better this way, and safer for them all.

Because my gout prevents me from climbing stairs, Cesar and Jean have moved my work table, bench, and bed to this entry room on the main level of my house. The arrangement of furniture matches my vision from so many years ago; the vision of my last day of life on Earth.

"Who chases you? The Inquisitors again?" asks Cesar with a trembling voice. "The queen has always protected you from them. Why distance yourself from her now?"

"This hunter is not with the Inquisition. He intends to kill me and anyone near me. I have one final preparation, otherwise I would have never led him here."

Shaking his head with grief, Cesar says, "You have seen this man?"

"Seen him? No. He remains veiled in my visions. I only see the ripples of his wake."

Taking a moment to reflect upon my most recent visions, I say to Jean, "Go now, dear friend. I have an important quest for Cesar. You will not find me alive at sunrise."

Jean's dark eyes grow moist as he bows his head and hastily departs.

Taking a deep breath, and knowing I have few remaining, I grasp Cesar by his shoulders.

"Cesar de Nostradame, my son, you were not given the inner voice by Almighty God. I remember my first vision clearly. Hell on Earth. Wars. Fires. Plagues. Mass starvation. Rotting corpses. All dead or dying. God shows me glimpses of the future and sometimes the past. Some call it a gift. *A gift?* This ability runs through family lines, but will often skip several generations before rearing its hideous head. Thank Almighty God that he did not bestow this horrific gift upon you. I foresee a long and prosperous life ahead of you, my young son. However, I require one last task."

"Father … I have no desire for your gift or your task. Let me stay with you. Let me protect you." Since my last visit, his round face has narrowed, causing his nose to appear longer and more hooked. He looks more like me than ever.

"It is too late for that, my son. You must help me prepare the Holy Warriors."

Taking a moment to gather his strength, Cesar asks, "Have we not done enough? You spent years learning every alchemist trick so you could forge the amulets from that strange metal you found. Every night, you enter a trance and peer through the far reaches of time. Every morning, you code your quatrains and draw your pictures. *Enough*, I say. The amulets are in place. Your prophecies are published. You have foreseen three Antichrists, and you have left the clues necessary for the three Holy Warriors to combat them. You have even trained your successor. What more can you do?"

It is my turn to gather what little strength I still possess. So many nights hunched over and reading the distant future in flames has left my body feeling as though it has been stretched well beyond its limitations. The stagnant Mediterranean air and sweltering summer heat offer no relief. I have *tried* to train my successor, but can he do what must be done? He is gifted beyond belief, but his arrogance and recklessness may be his undoing. And his undoing may be the doom of all throughout history.

Death approaches.

Squeezing Cesar's shoulders tighter, I say, "The Warriors still need more guidance. Take the Vatinicia Code to Rome. Find Uncle Pierre. He will know what to do with it. You must ride tonight and you cannot fail. The fate of the world depends upon you."

Cesar reaches behind a burgundy tapestry and retrieves the large manuscript of painted prophecies from a hidden shelf.

"Your visions span many centuries into our future. Have you not foreseen a victory for each Warrior?" he says, begging for a glimmer of hope.

"I have seen each Holy Warrior find the amulet I have left them. Each will have the necessary clues. But, only God knows if they will succeed."

"How can they fail when you are helping them?" Cesar forces a smile.

"Would that they only require my help to defeat the Antichrists," I answer. "There are forces at work against us. Forces of great power."

"The Oracle of Delphi?"

"Yes, but a millennium has passed since the Oracle was last seated in Delphi. She hides somewhere I cannot see. And, I fear, she is controlled by the First Order."

Cesar's face grows grim and dark. He is about to speak when we hear a muffled cry in the distance.

"Go now," I urge him. "You must use the west gate to avoid the hunter."

After one quick embrace, my son departs.

I will never see him again. Never hear his voice. Sadness and fear threaten to overcome me, but knowing my time is short, I quickly compose my final codicil for Jean to find in the morning.

Heavy footsteps approach from the narrow road leading to my house. Part of me wants to flee, but my aching body would make for slow, easy prey. This is my last day on Earth. Avoiding this doom is not possible.

After hiding my codicil on the shelf behind the tapestry, I sit on the edge of my bed and wait as the footsteps draw near.

A large cloaked figure pushes through the entrance.

"At long last I have found the troublesome Nostradamus," a woman's voice utters with no emotion.

She lets her cloak drop, revealing cropped black hair and a strange distant look in her eyes. She carries a crystal skull in her left hand and a dagger in her right.

The crystal skull is an ancient and powerful talisman I have only seen in the most terrifying of visions. The crimson glow from the skull's sockets paints the entire room a shade of blood red.

V. RAY

"You are a stray sister?" I ask.

"I am," the emotionless woman answers.

Germanic scribes have written of the Oracle and her sisterhood fleeing a Fourth Century Roman invasion into Greece. They escaped to join the barbarian tribes of Germania. Some say they simply wanted to hide from the Romans, while others say they stayed for several generations, guiding the tribal leaders in their efforts to bring down the Roman Empire.

One scribe noted a Greek council of men and women, known as the First Order, that seemed to control the Oracle and her sisters. This same scribe wrote of a breach in the sisterhood in the late Fifth Century. Part of the sisterhood fled the First Order, going into hiding in Eastern Europe. These stray sisters descend from the line of the Oracle and occasionally make their way into history as advisors to royalty … advisors with the ability to see the future.

"What is your name?" I ask, hopelessly trying to delay the inevitable.

"It matters not," she answers. Still no emotion, but she finally blinks.

"Your ancestors left the Sisterhood of the Oracle many centuries ago. You need not obey her command."

Raising the suddenly brighter skull, she says, "While I hold this, my will is the Oracle's to bend."

With a flick of her wrist so quick as to be barely perceptible, the dagger is gone from her hand and buried in my chest. My heart is punctured and blood spews from the wound, but I feel no pain. Only a strange sense of relief. My struggles are over. My time at an end. Crumpling to the floor, a series of final visions emerge from the depths of my faltering consciousness.

The Oracle grows more powerful and events from eras separated by ever greater time will impact each other.

The 3rd Holy Warrior shall meet his end just as I have, pierced through his heart.

History will become malleable. Hitler — the 2nd Antichrist — may prevail over all.

The 2nd Holy Warrior, Maximo Medici … your abilities are weak, but you must find a way …

PART 1—1963

V. RAY

Chapter 1

The ancient work will be accomplished.
From the roof, evil ruin will fall upon the great man.
They will accuse an innocent, in death, of the deed.
The guilty one is hidden in the misty copse.
(Nostradamus, Michel. <u>The Prophecies</u>. C6:Q37)

MAX MEDICI
DALLAS, TEXAS, USA
SUNDAY, NOVEMBER 22, 1963

"Greg is the only one who knows what room I'm in. If he shows up, sneak out the back door. Okay?"

"I am so glad you let me join you this trip," Katarina nods, smiling seductively. Her impressive height, straight jet-black hair, piercing blue eyes, fair skin, and prominent cheekbones give her an air of authority and her self-confidence knows no bounds. Yet she has her moments of weakness. No, weakness isn't the right word. She has moments where she seems to need *me*. Not from weakness or loneliness. Something else.

I'm the one who must be experiencing some sort of weakness. If I get caught with Katarina in my room when I'm on duty, losing my job would just be the beginning of my troubles. Greg and I have become close and he'd probably look the other way, but I don't want to put either one of us in that position.

"Sorry we couldn't stay in a nicer hotel, but I had to pick a place near the airport. Secret Service protocol, you know."

"Yet you brought me with you. This may be the first time I have ever seen you break a rule. It is exciting." Her Ukrainian accent is just one of the many things I find enthralling about her.

"Pour some wine. I'm on a roll."

The sparse room holds nothing but the essentials. A tiny, dimly-lit bathroom, a worn dresser with a cracked mirror, and a small table with two chairs. The view isn't much to brag about, either. The front door faces the highway with the airport just across the way. The back door opens to a parking lot. I can hear every second tick from the clock hanging slightly askew on the wall. It reads 12:21am.

Katarina pours two glasses of wine and we each take a sip.

What was it my mom used to say when I was a young boy? *When you meet the right woman, you will just know.*

"Do you ever think I'm too old for you? I mean, I'm nearly double your age." It's hard for me to remember that she's only twenty. Her maturity belies her youth.

"Look at you," she musses my hair. "Not a single gray in your dark brown hair. Not a single wrinkle in your bronze skin. The only flaws on your entire body are the scars on your hip and above your eye. And those give you character. No one … believe me, my love … no one would ever guess your true age."

Katerina always finds a way to make me feel good about myself. So different from my past. So hard to believe sometimes.

"Can I ask you something?"

"Anything," she purrs.

"You've told me about your father and your brother, but you never talk about your mother. Is she …"

Katarina fills the pause in my question, "My mother died when I was just a baby. My brother tells me she sacrificed her life to save mine. How or why, he will not say. My father died three years ago. I still have my brother, though."

"We've been together for a year. Why haven't we ever talked about this?"

With a half-smile, she says, "Some losses hurt too much."

Ain't that the truth. My mom would have loved Katarina … if she were still here … if she hadn't been taken from me so many years ago.

Nodding, I say, "I've never considered having my own family, but this past year has been a whirlwind. Everything is different now."

I hold her hand as I drop to one knee. Our eyes lock onto each other, and I see a hint of a tear forming in her beautiful eyes. Reaching into my pocket, I retrieve a ring with a white gold band and single small diamond. It was my mother's ring … the one piece of jewelry she ever owned.

"Kat –" I start.

"Maximo," she immediately interrupts, "what are you doing?"

"I'm asking you to marry me."

The single teardrop turns into a steady flow as I stand to face her.

We embrace and kiss, but she's trembling. She pulls back and looks tenderly at my face with an inexplicable sadness in her eyes.

Pressing my cheek to hers, I whisper reassuringly, "I am hopelessly in love with you and I can't imagine not being together the rest of our lives."

Softly, almost solemnly, she says, "I would be proud to be your wife."

I slide the ring on her finger. The way she looks at it ... *cherishing* it ... shines a light on her feelings that words could never equal.

"Are there any engagement traditions I should know about from the Ukraine?"

"Not *the* Ukraine. You Americans always want to put *the* in front of my country. It is just Ukraine – no *the."*

We both laugh, because she's reminded me of this a hundred times.

Her eyes return to mine. She takes a deep breath, and says, "There is *nothing* I would love more than to spend our lives together. Now, finish your wine. I will change into something a little more ... *intimate* ... and I'll meet you in bed." She flicks her tears away and strides into the bathroom.

Quickly downing the rest of my wine, I undress, and slide into bed, wearing only my amulet. In my possession more than half my life, I almost never take it off.

I can't ever talk about how I found it, not that anyone would ever believe me if I did. I had just turned 16 back in 1945 when the Nazis were getting close to finishing the world's first atomic bomb. During an insane mission to sabotage the German plans, I found this strange, mystical amulet. I don't know how, but I knew I was destined to find it.

With an oval base, the amulet bears an emblem of a two-headed eagle. The emblem is perfectly circular and raised in the middle of the oval – shaping the amulet like a human eye. I never could identify what type of metal it's made from. It weighs far less than it looks like it should. I'll never forget the first time I saw it in the light of day. The amulet appeared to shimmer between bronze and silver, reflecting colors that seemed beyond the normal spectrum. Like something from another planet. Warming to my touch, contact with it brings a sense of calmness that is almost eerie.

11

The back is engraved with four lines of text in a mix of Old French and Latin:

My Son of Many Sons, the Second Holy Warrior
MM 26 MAY 1945
C II Q 24
C V Q 29

The Second Holy Warrior. Is that what I am — a Holy Warrior? A descendent of Nostradamus. MM for Maximo Medici. The most disturbing part of the message, the date, was the exact date I read the text. And, it was engraved centuries before I read it. The last two lines ended up being clues, pointing to quatrains Nostradamus wrote in the 16th Century. Clues that were meant for me to read at just the right time to help me in 1945. Feeling the raised scar on my hip, a memento of my battle with Hitler, I doubt I would have survived that fight without my amulet.

I know Nostradamus made the amulet and that he set in motion the chain of events that led to my finding it, but trying to figure out how he did it is staggering.

The one, most important lesson my father ever wanted to teach me … my heritage. He could recite every man's name in our Medici family line all the way back to Duke Alessandro of the 16th Century. The only woman he would acknowledge was secretly the daughter of Nostradamus and the matriarch of our branch in the family tree.

The Nostradamus Legacy. That's what father said we are. He said it was crucial for me to learn our heritage and would he ever beat me if I stumbled on a name. A small hint of psychic ability from the 16th Century prophet passed through the generations and into me. While he could see centuries into the future, I am limited to dreams of the next day or two that sometimes come true.

Everything changed when I found the amulet. When I wear it, my limited abilities are stronger. I can read people better … predict what they might do. I now have a keen sense into someone's intentions.

As I wait for Katarina, I realize I've had too much to drink. I can't keep my eyes open, even though I'm anticipating the sight of her in something … *intimate.* My amulet suddenly grows hot. A dream takes over my awareness.

V. RAY

I'm standing on a stage behind a large curtain. Someone is holding my hand delicately. A voice speaks into a microphone from the other side of the curtain. It's a voice I know well. Young, strong, sharp, Boston accent. What he says strikes me as utterly important.

"The very word 'secrecy' is repugnant in a free and open society; and we are as a people inherently and historically opposed to secret societies, to secret oaths and to secret proceedings. We decided long ago that the dangers of excessive and unwarranted concealment of pertinent facts far outweighed the dangers which are cited to justify it."

The voice continues to speak, but the delicate hand squeezes mine to get my attention. I look her way and am instantly aware of when and where this dream is taking me.

"Did the president just say something about a secret society?" she whispers. Every syllable Marilyn Monroe breathes exudes sex. Every blink of her eyes. Every angle of her posture. Every tilt of her head. Every clothing and perfume choice. Every breath she takes. The living embodiment of sex appeal.

It's April 27, 1961 in this dream. The Agent in Charge had given me the highly enviable job of escorting Ms. Monroe to the speech President Kennedy is giving to the American Newspaper Publishers Association at the Waldorf-Astoria in New York. The first lady rarely attends the president's political events like this, putting the Secret Service in the position to not only protect the president from harm, but to protect his secrets and indulgences as well.

"Please, Ms. Monroe," I whisper in her ear, *"we must remain perfectly silent."*

She leans over to whisper in my ear again, but just exhales. Warm and moist breath washes my ear and neck, causing my entire body to shudder.

I attempt to make eye contact, but see she's already turned to face the president's voice behind the curtain.

"Today, no war has been declared – and however fierce the struggle may be, it may never be declared in the traditional fashion. Our way of life is under attack. Those who make themselves our enemy are advancing around the globe. The survival of our friends is in danger. And yet no war has been declared, no borders have been crossed by marching troops, no missiles have been fired.

"If the press is awaiting a declaration of war before it imposes the self-discipline of combat conditions, then I can only say that no war ever posed a greater threat to our security. If you are awaiting a finding of 'clear and present danger,' then I can only say that the danger has never been clearer and its presence has never been more imminent.

"It requires a change in outlook, a change in tactics, a change in missions — by the government, by the people, by every businessman or labor leader, and by every newspaper. For we are opposed around the world by a monolithic and ruthless conspiracy that relies primarily on covert means for expanding its sphere of influence — on infiltration instead of invasion, on subversion instead of elections, on intimidation instead of free choice, on guerrillas by night instead of armies by day. It is a system which has conscripted vast human and material resources into the building of a tightly knit, highly efficient machine that combines military, diplomatic, intelligence, economic, scientific and political operations."

Stepping back, spiritually, from my dream, I realize that was the day President John F. Kennedy challenged the American press. He challenged them to stay independent. To not be swayed by false news and false intents. The president declared war on espionage. But, did he mean the Russians or something different?

Everything goes black for just an instant and then, suddenly, sunlight blazes everywhere at once.

A warm day, with the sun almost directly overhead ... I'm running frantically. I can hear the rumbling of a car behind me and, somehow, I know it belongs to the president. I must run faster, but people block my way. I fight my way through the crowd, but the car is closing the gap quickly. Ahead is a shaded area ... a hill with trees ... this seems important, so I focus. As I draw near, the barrel of a rifle emerges from the trees. The president's car is right behind me. Then, the vision goes black ... *nothing.*

I struggle my way to consciousness. My throat is parched. My tongue feels three times its normal size and is so dry that it's stuck to the roof of my mouth. A monstrous headache strikes ... pounding ... more pounding. Something pulls me from the fog, and I can actually hear the pounding in my head.

No ... it's a pounding on a door. A loud crash. My eyes flutter as I try to open them, but can't. Yelling ... then a splash of water on my face. Everything is blurry.

"Max! Wake up! What the hell are you still doing here?" Someone grabs my shoulders and shakes me.

I blink a few times and slowly unglue my tongue.

"Greg?"

"Wake up, Max."

"Greg Rutledge?"

V. RAY

"Yes, it's me."

"What time is it?"

"11:35!"

"Where …" I blink a few more times before I can finally focus.

"You missed morning detail. What the fuck is wrong with you?"

As I frantically get dressed, a dark oval burn mark on the sheet grabs my attention. Maybe Katarina took the amulet off me to keep me from being burnt by its heat. She must have slipped out back when she heard Greg knocking.

"Take me to the airport!"

"Too late. You'll have to catch up to the president in the city."

Greg drove like a madman into Dallas, but we ran into a police blockade around the city center. I leapt from the car and am running down Main Street. A quick turn on to Elm, and I start dodging the crowd gathered to see the president. Looking up at the sky, I recall my nightmare. I lived through the first part … held Marilyn Monroe's hand … heard the president's speech on secret societies. The second part was new, though. A vision of the future. *This* is the day. I suddenly feel certain there is someone hiding in the foliage atop a grassy knoll with a rifle and he is going to shoot President Kennedy.

I need to warn someone – to stop this somehow. Reaching into the deepest wells of my reserves, I push myself to run faster. Scanning the horizon, I try to match the moving scenery with the images from my dream.

As I cross the lawn within the center of Dealey Plaza, I see a few of the signs people are holding. Some are favorable, like "All the Way with JFK" and "Hooray for JFK." Most of them are negative. The signs with "Yankee go home!" and "Wanted" posters with JFK's face on them remind me that I'm in Texas, and the president is not well liked by most Texans.

A young boy in a cowboy outfit and bright red shirt steps into my path and I barely dodge past him. He's holding a toy gun in one hand and a "Wanted" poster in the other. Shaking my head, I try to clear the cobwebs that are slowing my thoughts. In the image from my vision, I could make out a cluster of trees along the slope of a hill. A rifle barrel emerging. The sun was almost directly overhead, with stunted shadows in front of me all pointing slightly to my right. Based on the shadow size and angle from my vision, I have to approach the shooter from the northeast, and the time of the shooting is close at hand.

My lungs are starting to burn. With each breath, I take in as much air as they can hold. Thinking about the choices the shooter made – the hiding spot, time of day, crowds of people, multiple escape routes – someone did his homework. A professional assassin.

A shadowy hill … dark and dense trees … a shot about to be fired …. The critical moment plays out as a picture in my head and I need to find that picture in the real world before it's too late.

My vision never revealed the shooter, who managed to stay in the shadows behind leafy branches. I must stop him, but without more detail from my dream, the odds are stacked against me.

Anxiety builds throughout my body and I fight against an unnatural drowsiness that muddies any chance at clarity in my mind. I feel a pang deep in my gut as I think about the potential consequences of my mistake. Sensing I'm closing in on the cluster of trees and the shooter, a sour taste begins to rise in my throat.

Approaching from the northeast, I parallel the motorcade, just as I had in the dream. Fewer people are gathered here, so I need to run closer to the tree line to hide my approach. I envision the rifle protruding from the shadows … a shot ringing … a puff of smoke from the end of the barrel.

Then I see it. The elm trees and hill in front of me match my clouded vision. Just as I hear the rumble of the motorcade closing in behind me, a rifle barrel juts out from the trees.

Running as quickly and quietly as I can, I leap along the tree line to a position in front of the shooter, prepared to take the full force of the shot with my chest.

Staring at the wrong end of a rifle, all I can do is use my body to shield the president. Adrenaline courses through my veins as the shooter presses the barrel against my chest. The midday sun burns warm and bright, but the sniper hides within shaded foliage near the top of this grassy tree-lined knoll.

Hundreds of crows sit atop and within the trees, their caws muffled and hesitant, as if they sense something terrible is about to happen. The roar of the motorcade is closing in. With the top removed from the presidential convertible, the president and first lady wave to the crowd, both exposed and vulnerable.

The only way for the assassin to get to the president is to kill me first. The only solace left to me … my final hope … is that the sound of the rifle gives the other Secret Service agents enough warning to get the president and first lady to safety.

V. RAY

Crack! The echoing blast of the shot reverberates off the buildings surrounding Dealey Plaza before I feel the bullet rip through me. I barely notice the crows scattering as I wait for the searing pain of a hole through my torso ... then terror suddenly drives a frozen stake through my heart when I realize I'm not hit. Whipping my head to the side, I see President Kennedy grasping his neck, trying to cover a gaping hole.

There's another shooter!

Crack! A second shot misses and sparks fly off the road next to the presidential convertible.

Crack! A third shot. The right side of Kennedy's head explodes. He slumps over, shattered pieces of his scalp sprayed about the car. Jacqueline Kennedy tries desperately to gather the skull fragments ... to somehow salvage a life so dear, yet so beyond saving. Wearing a pink suit that is now soaked red in blood, she climbs onto the vehicle's trunk, reaching for pieces of brain and skull. An agent leaps from the road onto the rear of the convertible, and urges her into back into the seat as the entire motorcade speeds away ... under the tracks ... away from the shooters ... but far too late to save the president.

The Secret Service is supposed to protect the president, and since the formation of the agency, we've never lost one ... *until now.* Kennedy's assassination is my fault. The mistakes are all mine. I accept them. I own them. When the hidden shooter in front of me finally pulls the trigger, I'll get what I deserve.

Awareness seems to strike the crowd all at once and utter pandemonium breaks out. Some scream. Some run. Some stand stunned and motionless. Others duck and take cover. None of it crosses into my focus now. There's only one thing I want to know before I die.

Who is on the other end of this rifle?

As I slowly lean left and my eyes work from my end to the other end of the rifle, I see a ring on the hand holding the rifle.

White gold band and a small diamond.

From the shadows, Katarina's surprised face stares back at me. Her finger is poised on the rifle's trigger, a mixture of shock and defeat across her face.

What have I done?

I brought her here. Selfishly wanting her with me, I deliberately broke the rules. The assassins knew the president's schedule, because I gave it to Katarina.

She must have drugged me last night and I let it happen.

Nearly dropping from the immensity of the moment, through clenched teeth, I seethe, "If you want to escape, you have to shoot."

Bracing for the inevitable kill shot, the depth of this betrayal hits me. Katarina spent a year setting me up. The assassins knew that removing me from the equation would be critical to their success. Without my amulet, I couldn't see this coming. I couldn't see the second shooter and I couldn't see Katarina …. I've never been able to see her in my dreams.

I look her directly in the eyes, truly understanding her for the first time.

"What are you waiting for?"

"I … I can't," she murmurs as the rifle shakes in her trembling hands.

"You have *no choice.*"

"Maximo," Katarina almost whispers. "I cannot kill the man I love … the father of my baby." Slowly, she lowers her rifle.

"How?" I yell, feeling rage quickly overtaking me. *"Why?"*

Atlas shrugged, and the world as I know it shakes beyond control. I loved her … trusted her … she meant everything to me. The president of the United States has just been killed on my watch. The woman I just asked to marry me is directly involved. And she's pregnant with my baby.

It's my fault. The thought devastates me and I struggle to stay in the moment.

Everything the past year with Katarina has been a lie …. No, not all of it. If it were *all* a lie, I'd be dead right now. She *is* pregnant with my baby. That much is true.

A motorcycle engine roars as it climbs the far side of the knoll. The rider, a huge man wearing jeans, a black leather jacket, black gloves, and a black helmet, pauses on the train tracks.

With quivering lips, Katarina glances over her shoulder. She wants to say something, but stays mute. Silently, she drops the rifle. The motorcycle sprays gravel as the rider revs the engine and rides the tracks west into the bright Dallas sun.

Chapter 2

VIKTOR KROSTOV
SAVANNAH, GEORGIA, USA
MONDAY, NOVEMBER 23, 1963

"Chyort voz'mi!"

After punching a second hole through the wall of this overly fancy American hotel in Savannah, the crumbling plaster falls like the last steps of my plan. Before taking over the private espionage team my father created in Pushkin, Russia, I had been an Olympic middleweight boxer. I even won the silver medal. Now, I crave for someone's jaw to hit … preferably Maximo Medici's.

Driving eighteen hours from Dallas to Savannah, only stopping for gas and food, I feel as though I'm in the ninth round of a ten-round fight.

Pulling in just before sunrise, I try to avoid seeing anyone other than the man at the front desk. The fewer people who see me or notice my Russian accent, the better.

I stumbled into the room just in time for my call. Although the assassination was successful, my client will be livid if he finds out things did not go *exactly* as planned. He expects my timing to be flawless and hates if any detail differs from his plans. In a word, he expects perfection.

This operation had been far from perfect. If Karl finds out the whole truth, there will be consequences. It's obvious the man has resources. He pays well for my services, but will pay much less if he knows something went wrong.

Katarina, my sister, personifies perfection. Our mother passed along beauty, intelligence, and even her sentimental nature to my sister. As for me, I inherited my father's strength and cunning, as well as his imposing height and massive frame. When my father died, he left me in charge of the spy ring he spent half his life building. We're based in Russia and often work for the Soviet military, but have managed to stay independent of the KGB. Father was wise when he built our business. We only employ beautiful women as our agents. They must be able to adapt immediately to any situation and, when necessary, can fight and kill. Luckily, Russia has plenty of candidates to choose from. Our young men all serve in the military, leaving many young women struggling to support themselves.

None of these women compare to Katarina, though. She's my best agent by far, possessing skills like no other. Strikingly beautiful and highly intelligent, men like Maximo Medici are putty in her hands. Yet even with her unique abilities, she failed to carry out her job this one time. She *allowed* herself to be captured. The rage I feel quickly bubbles back to the surface and I punch a third hole in the wall.

It makes no sense.

All the planning … the long hours of training … Katarina and I went over this so often. If she would have just followed the plan, it should have been simple. This was supposed to be the knockout blow to the Americans – killing their president and Medici on the same day.

Katarina was to kill Medici, yet he lives.

At least she delivered his amulet to me. Over time, she got Medici to tell her about it … how it made his abilities stronger. Taking it from him must have neutralized him.

Oswald did his part, killing Kennedy, and his aim was impressive. After years of re-education, Oswald believed he was doing a service to his country. He also mistakenly believed he was included in the escape plan. What a complete fool.

If he had missed, Katarina was his backup from behind the trees.

My role was simple. As soon as I heard gunshots, I was to ride the motorcycle up the embankment and onto the tracks to pick up Katarina. We were then to take the motorcycle down the tracks west across the Trinity River. This would make it nearly impossible for anyone to follow us. All we had to do was abandon the motorcycle and take the car I left waiting in a parking lot near the tracks. The few people who may have seen us on the motorcycle would find it abandoned.

With our initial route west, anyone following us would most likely look in the wrong direction. We were planning to drive the car east to Savannah and report to Karl before making our way back to St. Petersburg.

Almost every step had been perfectly executed. Almost.

V. RAY

Oswald has been kept in the dark. We were careful to always use fake names around him. But he knows our training location and he can identify several faces, including Katarina's. He must be killed.

But, Katarina, what have you done?

All you had to do was follow the plan. I can still see you dropping your rifle and turning yourself in without a fight. Why? You just had to squeeze the trigger. I had no choice but to go on without you.

The ramifications from Karl will be severe. Lying to him might mean a death sentence for me, but the truth would mean death for Katarina.

It's time. As I dial the phone number to reach Karl's secretary, I'm hoping he can't be reached. The more time I have to figure out what happened to Katarina before I talk with him, the better.

"Yes," crackles the raspy-voiced woman, who seems to be always available no matter what time I call this line.

"It's Viktor. I'm at the hotel. The phone number –"

"We know the number. Karl will call you back." Usually she connects me to Karl. This time she just hung up.

Less than a minute later, the phone rings.

"Yesss," I answer.

"Will you get your fucking teeth fixed? You sound like a goddamn snake," Karl says in a hushed tone.

My front tooth was broken during the gold medal match in the Olympics. I should have won that fight, but I let my guard down when I thought I had my opponent beaten. I leave it this way as a constant reminder to never make that mistake again.

"Say nothing," whispers Karl before I can respond. Several people are speaking in the background on his end. "The splendid news has already spread around the globe. Congratulations. We'll discuss this in person the next time we meet."

I can picture his smug face on the other end of the phone. Not a single silver hair on his head out of place. Overly white teeth. Karl is tall, nearly my height, but his love of rich food and expensive vodka has made him soft and weak.

The call disconnects. Karl hates providing any information over the phone, especially when either party is in America.

Exhaling with relief, I feel like I escaped a knockout and survived to fight the next round. Sometimes, that's all a fighter can do ... make it to the next round.

Chapter 3

The prince who has little pity and clemency
after finding peace from upheaval
will come through death to become very knowledgeable.
And with great tranquility, reign again.
(Nostradamus, Michel. The Prophecies. C7:Q17)

KARL

CAIRO, EGYPT
MONDAY, NOVEMBER 23, 1963

Ah, the Mena House, how splendid! The Egyptian desert air forces me to lick my dry, cracked lips as I enter the hotel's lobby. The embodiment of palatial luxury, the hotel sits in the shadows of the Great Pyramids of Giza. The only reason I know the history of the Mena House is because my Alpha Knight made me study royal lineages when I was a young Beta. I hated him for it back then, but I have grown to understand the value of knowing history. I can even admit that I am thankful for this lesson, and the many others he taught me over the years.

The King of Egypt, Khedive Ismail, built the Mena House as a vacation home and guesthouse for visiting royalty. He eventually sold it before it was converted to a luxury hotel in 1869. Built for royalty, and the most appropriate place for me to stay while I tour Egypt.

"Khan! I have an important call to make. Can I trust you to keep an eye on our luggage?" My personal guard, Ozzie, adds the small bags he carried into the hotel to the group of larger bags Khan and Paka have already placed in the corner. Khan sent Paka to park the limousine while he stands next to the luggage, alert to his surroundings.

The pained look on the boy's face causes me to question myself. Khan seems truly insulted. You either trust someone or you don't, but you should never ask the question. It's another of my Alpha's lessons – one I should have learned by now. How stupid of me.

I met the two boys just after I arrived in Cairo this morning. A tall boy was stationed right outside the airport, standing near the limousine and taxi stand holding a cardboard sign with "Prince Tours" written in thick black marker. With a lean build and a smooth caramel skin tone, he looked to be about 12 or 13 years old, despite standing almost 6 feet tall. He told me his name was Luis Khan, but I should simply call him Khan. He spoke nearly perfect English, with a very slight Spanish accent, and made a highly informative and convincing sales pitch. Claiming to have a limousine and driver at his disposal, Khan appeared to cover all my transportation and tour guide needs while in Egypt.

Without hesitation, I hired him to guide my exploration of the Egyptian pyramids, museums, and artifacts. Paka, several years older, was included in the package deal. He immediately brought the limo up when Khan waved in his direction. In his early 20's, Paka is tall, muscular, and nearly silent. His brutishness only serves to highlight the refinement I see in Khan, who is clearly the leader of this two-person operation.

"I am the son of royalty." Khan proclaims while standing as tall as he can with is chest pushed out proudly.

Hmmm, this should be interesting. "I'm not at all surprised. Who is your father? Perhaps I know him?" I maintain a friendly, inquisitive tone. While I never shy away from taking any measure I think is necessary, I often find I can more easily accomplish my goals with simple kindness. This is a lesson from my Alpha that I *did* learn.

The boy hangs his head slightly. "My father is dead. My family is in exile. But you can trust the word of a prince!"

Getting closer to the truth. "I'm sorry, son. So … Luis Khan isn't your real name?" This much I've guessed already. The exiled prince has been so blatant as to take a fake name meaning strong prince. And Prince Tours? There's some real talent here, but the boy has a lot of maturing to do.

"No …. But, I cannot tell you my real name," the prince says with his head hung lower.

"Well, you and Paka have obviously figured out how to succeed with this splendid venture of yours. How long have you been at it?" I smile warmly at the boy.

"A little over two years."

And there it is – the final clue revealing everything I want to know. There was only one African king who fell a little over two years ago. I, myself, ordered the assassination. The king had warmed to my friends in the Soviet Union, and I was supplying advisors and arms to his military forces. He started to warm up to the idea of adopting communism, but the Americans got to him before he would fully commit to me. The contact from the Americans threw so much money at the king that he walked away from communism, taking the foothold in Africa I had hoped to gain. Assassination had been the only clear course of action.

Thinking back to the king's assassination makes me smile. I had one of my agents pretend to be with the CIA and hire mercenaries out of Portugal. Naturally, word leaked, and the Americans were blamed for the whole thing. The prince must surely hate the Americans with all his heart.

"I'm proud of you, son. Becoming tour guides in Cairo was a smart and lucrative choice for you." I put my hand on the boy's shoulder for emphasis. Now, here with the prince, I have an opportunity to take further advantage of the situation I originally created. "I'm going to go make my call, and then I'd like to take some time and learn more about you."

Khan nods politely as Ozzie and I walk off to find a house phone to make my scheduled call to Viktor.

We come back less than a minute later. I'm extremely satisfied with Viktor and feeling on top of the world. Assassinating a king in Africa while throwing the blame at the Americans was something to be proud of, certainly, but assassinating the president of the United States while making it look like the work of a disgruntled American citizen – now that was truly artistic! The First Order council will be ecstatic.

A nudge from Ozzie brings me back to Earth. Looking where my bodyguard points, I simply can't believe my eyes. And yet, maybe I can. We quietly observe as Khan zips closed one of my bags, opens another, and starts rummaging through it. Khan pulls out my favorite Omega watch, places it on his wrist, and stares at it with an odd look of entitlement.

What an amazingly bold boy! I put my index finger to my lips to signal to Ozzie to be quiet. Here is the former prince caught pilfering from the same tourists he's supposed to be guiding.

I've been looking for a protégé for quite some time and had already taken a liking to Khan. Now, I find him to be even more appealing. I nod to Ozzie, who quickly snatches Khan from behind and brings him around to face me.

"Young prince," I pause to make sure I have the boy's full attention. "Petty crime is beneath you. Surely, you must know this. What, exactly, was your plan? You grab our stuff and Paka drives the getaway limo? Not very elaborate as far as plans go. You have much to learn about choosing the appropriate target, time, place, expected outcome, escape route, and persona you want to present when committing a crime." I can barely contain my urge to smile. "Oh, I nearly forgot. You also need a patsy to take the blame."

PART 2—1981

V. RAY

Chapter 4

Mars and the scepter will be found conjoined
under Cancer; calamitous war:
Shortly afterwards a new Great Leader will be anointed,
who for a long time will pacify the Earth.
(Nostradamus, Michel. The Prophecies. C6:Q24)

MAX MEDICI
WASHINGTON DC, USA
TUESDAY, MARCH 24, 1981

Over the years, I've learned that waiting outside the Oval Office is a given when meeting with the president. Sometimes it's a short wait, but other times, such as today, the wait can seem like forever.

I decide to check if my tie knot is tight enough in the mirror on the wall. Every president is different, and appearance matters far more to some than others. Just four days ago, I celebrated my 52nd birthday, but I'm still blessed with a full head of dark brown hair. The military-type training I went through as a teenager has stayed with me. I keep fit by running five miles every morning and mixing in push-ups, pull-ups, and sit-ups most days.

Not looking too shabby yet, old man.

President Reagan's schedule has him flying to Canada soon for an economic summit. I just returned from Ottawa, where I worked with Canadian authorities to ensure a safe trip for the president and all the heads of state attending.

With my scouting duties for presidential travel, I find that learning about a city on foot is always the best way to understand the geography, the people, and any potential threats. Running a different route every morning provides that opportunity, no matter where I am or the weather conditions. Most every major city centers on a body of water – often a river. This is always where I begin when scouting a new locale. I gain my bearings quickly based on the time of day, location of the sun, and the angle of the ground, which almost imperceptibly dips toward the city's primary body of water.

A secretary I haven't seen before interrupts my thoughts. "The president is ready to see you now." She leads me into the Oval Office and closes the outer door after she leaves.

"Max," CIA Director William Casey greets me. As a new appointment by the president, I've only met him a couple times, but have come to realize he's a man of few words. Casey stands about 5' 10", is nearly bald, with thick glasses. He gestures for me to come meet the new president.

"Good morning, Director Casey," I say, stepping to the sitting area.

President Reagan stands and he's a little taller than I am, with perfectly coiffed hair. Like me, he has unnaturally dark hair for a man his age.

I've served many presidents and have been here many times before, but entering the Oval Office always gives me a sense of awe. Starting with my first assignment as a teenager from Franklin Roosevelt to my current position, I'm now serving my 9th president. Each time I introduce myself to a newly elected president is unique, since each comes into office with his own belief system. What I am about to tell President Reagan is not going to be easy for him to understand … or believe.

"Good morning, Agent Medici." The president shakes my hand firmly and then motions for me to sit in one of the office sofas. "Have a seat."

"Thank you, Mr. President."

The president quickly sets a relaxed tone, leaning back into the other sofa. "Maximo Medici," he reads from the file he's holding. "No middle name?"

"No sir. I believe my parents thought Maximo was quite sufficient. But please feel free to call me Max."

Each new president has redecorated the Oval Office to suit his own individual tastes. I find these choices provide some insight into the man's nature. The President and First Lady chose all white seating and all the furniture is very traditional. Very enlightening. The traditional hero … dressed in white … arriving just in time to save the day … just like one of his movies. President Reagan wants to show the world a new

America and strengthen our position of greatness. Very similar to Kennedy in that regard.

"Max," President Reagan begins. "Bill brought your personnel file to my attention, and he suggested we have a private meeting. I must say, I've read quite a few of these files the last couple of months and yours is by far the most intriguing. I've been looking forward to meeting you and hearing about some of your experiences."

"Thank you, Mr. President. I've had the honor to serve my country most of my life. What can I tell you about my service record?" My first reaction to President Reagan is a feeling that I can trust the man. He carries himself with an air of confidence and credibility, and he seems folksy and likeable as well.

"Let me start by saying that I've heard about you and your team. You have quite a history of protecting our country and our presidents. Obviously, most of what you've done for our country isn't known by the public, but other Secret Service agents talk about you with reverence, like you're a true hero. I'm fascinated by the references to President Roosevelt and Adolf Hitler in your file. But first, tell me about your team and your responsibilities."

And so my tale begins. "As I'm sure you know, the Secret Service was originally formed under our Treasury Department to protect the integrity of our currency and was established the same day President Lincoln was assassinated." Even though President Reagan is almost certainly aware of this detail, I think it's important to introduce the history of presidential assassinations early in the conversation. "Congress considered adding protection for the president to our responsibilities after Lincoln was killed in 1865, but it took the assassinations of President Garfield in 1881 and President McKinley in 1901 before the change was implemented. Only after these additional losses did we realize that defending the safety of our key leaders and their families required more than just a simple security detail. So, the Secret Service was the first agency to be given authority by our government to perform covert operations to accomplish our goals."

I gesture to CIA Director Casey, "While the CIA is now more directly responsible for running covert operations, we still maintain a critical role .... I lead the Advance Intelligence division of the Secret Service. We call it AI. AI is responsible for utilizing the unique abilities of our special agents to gain an advantage over our adversaries. We're able to gain strategic intelligence prior to a major event's occurrence. This allows us to avoid undesirable outcomes. We also possess tactical

31

advance intelligence, which is quite useful for dealing with events as they occur."

"Explain to the president *how* you gather this intelligence," Director Casey cuts directly to the critical point. He also seems content to remain standing for the meeting.

"Sir, we use psychic abilities." *There.* I dropped the bombshell, in as calm and professional a tone as I can manage, but I have no idea what kind of reaction I'll get. While President Reagan takes his time to digest this revelation, I quickly recall this same conversation with previous presidents.

Harry Truman was the first president I met after Roosevelt. He initially doubted my abilities ... until the reports came in about my experience with Hitler and the Nazis. Dwight Eisenhower had first-hand experience with my team of spies during World War II, yet he was extremely pragmatic and seemed uncomfortable with me. John Kennedy needed me more than he knew, but refused to believe in any advanced abilities that he himself didn't possess. A victim of the Presidential Curse, Kennedy's assassination was such a devastating failure. Lyndon Johnson was easy to persuade. It was under Richard Nixon that I had both the most autonomy to expand my team and the most scrutiny as to the way to best use our abilities. Nixon had no doubt about my abilities, but often asked AI to focus on issues other than national security. Although Gerald Ford was Nixon's vice president, the two men couldn't be more dissimilar. Ford was thrust into office with no time to prepare. He served with integrity, but never made the time to fully understand AI. Then there was Jimmy Carter. I try not to roll my eyes in front of President Reagan at the thought of Carter. The previous president never believed in AI, and cut the team to the bare bones.

"Well, Max, Mrs. Reagan has been in frequent contact with several psychics for years, and she insists there's something valuable to be gained from them. She sometimes asks me to change my schedule based on their advice. We've both been amazed at the accuracy of some of the predictions. Well ... I'm not all that surprised that we employ psychic abilities to our advantage. Tell me how these abilities work."

The way he says the word *well* allows him to hold on to an empty space in a conversation and gather his thoughts, and it exudes an unusual mix of self-confidence and diffusing humor rolled into a single drawn-out syllable.

This might become the easiest presidential introduction since Johnson's.

"There are three *typical* psychic abilities, Mr. President. Many psychics can see visions of the near future, usually through dreams or while in a trance state. This is the most common psychic ability. Seeing the past is accomplished by channeling a person's ancestors and experiences and is less common. The least likely of the common abilities is a waking vision of the very near future, which can provide an important tactical advantage during a crisis. Beyond those three abilities, my research has shown there are some psychics so powerful that they can communicate with their thoughts or even possess another person's mind. There are also extremely rare cases of individuals with prophetic abilities to see and influence the distant future. Someone like Nostradamus."

I hesitate for a few moments, trying to gauge their reactions. I sense surprise in them, but no shock, so I continue, "Almost everyone has some form of psychic ability – it's usually seen as déjà vu. The strength of an individual's psychic abilities is certainly an important factor, but what really sets someone apart is the processing power of their mind – speed is critical."

The president continues the conversation, not overly surprised at all by my explanation. Shaking his head, he says, "That's not very different from what Mrs. Reagan and I have heard. Max, you need to understand my primary goals while I'm in office. We face two major threats as a nation: one from the outside, with the Soviets trying to spread communism covertly or with open force. The other is from our own Congress. When I was a young man, I was a Democrat, enthralled by Franklin Roosevelt's New Deal. I was convinced that his programs were well designed to take care of our sick, poor, and needy. Well, after seeing the costs of these programs and the stifling effects on our economy and our people, I became a Republican and have fought for smaller government and more freedom ever since."

The president leans toward me to emphasize his next point. "Left to its own devices, Congress would spend away our futures and imperil our children and grandchildren. It's nothing short of *socialism* disguised as *liberalism*. I've been elected on a platform to reduce the burden of government on our people and to keep our nation safe and free. If the economy is bustling and *opportunities* are available, we Americans are the most motivated people on the planet, and we'll make the most of those opportunities. Lower taxes will lead to huge economic growth. We'll

33

have more high paying jobs and well-off people than any other nation in the history of the world. Charities will flourish and the truly needy will be taken care of. However, I'm a firm believer in the theory that you don't give people fish every day. You teach them how to fish for themselves." He leans even further forward. "Max, are you a Republican?"

President Nixon was the only other president ever to ask me if I belong to a political party. And, in time, I discovered Nixon's motives were rarely selfless. Reagan, however, doesn't seem capable of misleading. It's as if substance and quality of character matter more than the end result with him.

"Sir, with all due respect, I don't think it's appropriate for Secret Service agents to be affiliated with a political party —"

"Well," President Reagan jumps in before I can continue. "How do I *know* you and your team will give me your all to stop the threats to our great nation?"

"I don't believe the two primary threats you stated are distinctly separate, sir. I firmly believe that communism must be fought on *every* front, along with any form of dictatorship that's oppressive to a nation's people. And if I may borrow the Martin Treptow quote you used in your inaugural address; 'I will work, I will save, I will sacrifice, I will endure, I will fight cheerfully and do my utmost, as if the issue of the whole struggle depended on me alone.'"

Director Casey nods, indicating his approval of my assessment.

President Reagan smiles broadly. "Bravo, Max! So, you did pay attention to my speech. I believe I *can* trust you to do your utmost." The president hesitates for a moment, and then continues. "There's another matter that seems to fit within your expertise. One of Mrs. Reagan's psychics has told her of a Presidential Curse, and that we should be wary of it. How does a curse fit into the psychic abilities you described?"

He already knows about the curse!

"Mr. President, imagine if a prophet or a psychic had a vision of traumatic events in the future … and say this vision was about an adversary. That vision could be made public and called a curse. And this would make the psychic appear to be the *cause* of the trauma. Throughout history, many of these visions, which have been used as curses, have come true. That's usually the motivation for the creator of the curse. It could be used to cause fear, gain power or respect, or — more likely — to influence someone's decisions."

Director Casey drives to the main point again. "So, what exactly is the Presidential Curse?"

"It's sometimes referred to as Tecumseh's curse. It was aimed at President Harrison long before he was elected to office. Chief Tecumseh of the Shawnee claimed that his brother, known as the Prophet, had seen in the year 1813 that Harrison would eventually be elected president of the United States. Tecumseh cursed Harrison and every US president elected every 20 years after his election to die while in office. Harrison, in fact, was elected to the office in 1840, and died in 1841 of pneumonia. Abraham Lincoln was elected in 1860, and was assassinated in 1865. James Garfield was elected in 1880, and was assassinated in 1881. William McKinley, elected 1900, was assassinated in 1901. Warren Harding, elected 1920, died from poisoning in 1923. Franklin Roosevelt, reelected 1940, died of a stroke in 1945. In 1960, John Kennedy ...."

Just saying his name makes me flash back to that fateful day in Dallas. I need a moment before I can continue.

President Reagan seems to understand why I paused and decides to jump in, "Max, I'm not supposed to discuss previous presidential remarks in personnel files, but I'm going to make an exception. I want you to know that President Johnson was very explicit in clearing you of any responsibility in President Kennedy's assassination. He wrote that he was in the room when you urged Kennedy to not go on that campaign trip to Texas. He also wrote that there was video from someone in the crowd showing how you heroically tried to prevent the assassination. Well, he couldn't go into the details, as that information was sealed away in the Warren Commission findings. But Max ... it seems to me that you did everything you could."

"Thank you for saying so, sir." I can't help but look to the ground for a moment, trying to gather my strength. "I failed President Kennedy horribly, but I will *not* allow myself to fail you."

"A lot is riding on the success of this presidency for our country and for the world. What can we do to break this curse, Max?" Director Casey asks. He finally seems to become more at ease, and sits in the remaining high-backed chair.

"I have two young recruits I'm hoping to get to join AI. One is a direct descendant of Chief Tecumseh. I'm hoping she can help me learn more about the curse so we can discover a way to end it."

"And the other?" asks Director Casey.

"The other, Trey Tyson, is the younger brother of my most talented special agent in AI," I smile at the thought of this young prospect. "Not only does he have the bloodline to possess strong future vision and rare tactical abilities, but his mental processing speed is the fastest we've ever tested. The problem with this recruit is that he has a uniquely rebellious nature and I'm not sure we can convince him to join the Secret Service. Still, I believe he may be critical to stopping the third Antichrist."

Director Casey was about to ask another question, but President Reagan cut him off. "Wait. Didn't I see a reference to Adolf Hitler as the second Antichrist in your file?"

"Yes, sir. I'm sure that reference is there."

"So, there's another human being capable of causing the devastation Hitler caused?" presses the president.

"There are a few very credible prophecies claiming there will be. Someone even worse than Hitler," I speak cautiously, not knowing yet how much I should divulge.

"What are the sources?"

I've heard the president is a religious man, so I'm concerned that my answer to his question might not go over very well, but the truth is what it is. "Mayan priests, the Nostradamus prophecies, and the Bible."

"*The Bible?* I read it quite frequently, Max. Where are these prophecies in the Bible?" asks President Reagan with sincere curiosity.

"The Book of Daniel, Chapter 7. Interpretation is everything, of course, but when the Bible prophecies are correlated to those from Nostradamus, the picture of this great threat in the future starts to take shape. Daniel writes about four great beasts. Nostradamus predicts three Antichrists and mentions another evil entity that may be the force behind the third. Each prophet points to the third Antichrist taking dominion over ten nations before dominating the rest of the world."

"Do you know who the third man is, or when he'll come to power?" Director Casey jumps back in, as the president seems to be recalling his knowledge of the Book of Daniel.

"There's a Nostradamus reference to the birth – or possibly an emergence – of the third Antichrist in 1999, and there are several Armageddon prophecies pointing to the early 21st Century. The Mayan culture, for example, has a very intriguing view of the period. The Maya were remarkably gifted at astronomy and they produced the most accurate calendars of their time. And that's where the intrigue lies. This period of their long count calendar starts at the date they believe to be their origin, and has what many consider to be an ending in the year 2012."

I know I'm pushing the limit of what the president would consider a reasonable explanation, but I truly believe the future of the planet depends on what we do now. "If I'm still alive when the third Antichrist comes to power, I'll be very old. Because the previous administration greatly reduced the resources allocated to AI, we're down to just me and one other special agent with tactical psychic abilities. So, it's even more important that I land these prospects to help stop the Presidential Curse now and to prepare to face the evil I anticipate in 2012. With your approval, Mr. President, there may be times I advise you to change your schedule. And there may be times where it'll be critically important for me to be the agent in charge for a public appearance you make. I'd also like to put myself or my special agent at your side when necessary."

"Max, you have my approval. And, Bill, see to it that AI gets the resources it needs." President Reagan rises from his seat and once more vigorously shakes my hand.

"Thank you, and *stay safe*, Mr. President!"

Chapter 5

TREY TYSON

SHELBY TOWNSHIP, MICHIGAN, USA
WEDNESDAY, MARCH 25, 1981

"*That* was a mistake," I say calmly, trying to hide my heavy breathing. I just grabbed a rebound on the other end of the basketball court and raced my twin brother Paul to this end. Then I paused at the top left of the key, but continued dribbling.

"You coccydynia. Why would you stop here?" Paul is also struggling to catch his breath.

It takes me a moment, but I figure out his meaning, "Did you just call me a pain in the ass?"

Smiling proudly, he says, "Why, yes."

"Using big words that nobody knows is why you get the shit kicked out of you when I'm not around to protect you. Why the hell can't you just say, 'pain in the ass' instead?"

"Should I be responsible to elucidate my meaning to the less intelligent, or should they perhaps be responsible to develop their vocabulary?"

"Dumb it down. You should think 'dumb it down' before you ever say a word like *elucidate* again. Can we continue now?" I ask.

"We should take advantage of the temperate weather, yes."

Shaking my head, I realize he'll never dumb it down. That's just not his nature.

Late March in Michigan can bring any kind of weather. At this time of year, we're usually facing snow and temperatures well below freezing. But today is a rare sunny and warm day, and Paul and I decided to take advantage of it with a one-on-one basketball game. Although the court is clear, the surrounding trees, mostly oaks and pines, are still covered in melting snow.

"The next point wins. I'm just surprised you let me to get to my favorite spot on the court." I continue to dribble, deking to my left once to see if Paul is still paying attention.

Paul moves with the deke to his right, but he quickly adjusts back. "Dullard. You could have driven for a layup. It's one-on-one. There was no one else here to stop you."

"True, but you'd have fouled me."

"That *was* the plan," Paul admits.

"So, here I am at my favorite spot on the court. I could take a fade-away jumper. It's difficult to block and I'm about 60% from this spot."

"By all means – take your shot."

"Or a quick crossover dribble, drive the left side, and take a layup. The odds are about 75%." I smile, seeing that Paul's starting to get annoyed, but he's not fully distracted yet.

"Whatever it takes to silence you." There's a hint of anger in Paul's voice.

"*Or* …" I pause for dramatic effect. "I could simply dribble to my right, and take my patented hook shot." Paul rolls his eyes in disgust. "The odds of it going in are also about 75% and you can't block that shot."

"Then go –"

The time is right and I take a quick half step back.

Paul is momentarily caught off-guard, but he manages to stay with me. He prepares to leap to block my fade-away, but he doesn't jump.

I then quickly deke to my left.

Paul takes the bait this time. He over commits to his own right to protect against a drive for a layup.

Just the opening I need.

I drive to my right with two dribbles, then take the hook shot. Paul recovers almost immediately, stays close to me, and leaps almost at the exact same moment to block the shot – but he can't. My shot appears to be a line drive with little arc and tons of backspin.

Paul turns to the basket, trying to block me out so he can get the rebound.

The basketball hits the backboard almost directly in the middle. The backspin forces the ball to bounce straight down and the ball goes cleanly through the rim and chain-link net. You can't get the *swish* sound with a chain-link net, but it's still a cool sound. Kind of like chainmail armor being hit by a sword.

Paul turns slowly back to me, with a disgusted look on his face. "That shot defies the laws of physics. It shouldn't be allowed."

"Right! And they shouldn't allow Dr. J to play in the NBA either, because he's too good."

"Oh, you're Julius Erving now, are you? Your arrogance is off the charts, Trey. Besides, that hook shot is *ridiculous*. There's something wrong with the backboard. Too soft or something."

"Is this how you handle defeat? Let me guess. The sun was in your eyes, right?" I wink at Paul, but he's still angry.

We both briefly shoot a glance at the sun to the southwest. Paul returns his gaze to me, ready to continue the argument, but I'm struck suddenly by a sharp pain in the back of my head. I'm forced to look down at the ground, leaning over and hands resting on my knees.

"Hey, old fart! You alright?" We're both only 16 years old, but I have a white streak on the right side of my otherwise black hair that started coming in shortly after I turned 13. Paul, ever the antagonist, reminds me of it any chance he can.

I feel so light-headed, it's as if my blood pressure has suddenly dropped.

"I just need a minute," but, I think I'm going to need a few minutes as the migraine hits hard. Still looking at the ground, I can see white squiggly dots floating around. This is always my precursor to a migraine. The pain starts at the back of my head and quickly spreads to the top.

Maybe it'll pass. I wish I knew what brought these damn things on. A 70-degree day in March here in Michigan is truly unusual. Paul and I didn't hesitate to take advantage of it. Most years, we can't start playing basketball outside until at least late April. Melting snow surrounds the court, as four inches of it fell just two days ago. We're playing full court, so the contest is as much about conditioning as basketball skills, and I have a slight advantage in each. I'm 6' 1" to Paul's 5' 11", but we both hate to lose. Paul's trusty fade-away jumper from either side of the basket keeps him in the game, but I get most of the rebounds with my height and better anticipation.

"How do you think Mom is processing everything?" asks Paul.

"She's not one of your computers. She's *handling* it well. At least she's acting like she's handling it well. But really, how can she be?"

"I know," Paul nods. "She's really trying."

"Mom told me she didn't want either of us to worry about college, but I can tell she's *very* worried about it. She thinks you'll get an academic scholarship – that should help." Anything that would ease our mother's mind is a good thing right now. She's been a wreck since Dad died. I have to give her credit, though, she always appears to have everything under control.

"You could have your choice of scholarships, football or academics."

"I hope you're right." Thinking about Dad's death isn't helping my migraine, so I decide to change the subject. "It's too bad Eric and Dave couldn't play. Two on two would've been more fun. Did you call 'em?"

"Are you kidding?" asks Paul.

"No, why?"

"Jeez, Trey, let me think back to the last time we all played basketball. Eric ended up with a broken ankle and had to wear a cast for two months. Dave somehow managed to only get a sprain. Playing basketball with you is like walking through a mine field. Every time someone goes for a rebound, you're already standing there. Plus, your legs are like frick'n tree trunks. I'm surprised you haven't broken anything on me."

"You're still young," I tilt my head up just enough to let Paul see me wink. "And you have plenty of bones to break."

Paul seems to have tired of this idle chitchat. "Are you stalling? You *are* getting old. I wore you out that game, didn't I? Come on, we don't get this *nice* weather at this time of year – *ever*. Let's go again!"

I don't know if I'm ready yet. Paul has no idea what I'm going through. Complaining doesn't help, so I never talk about my migraines. Still, I can't let his comments go unanswered.

"Old? Worn out? You're the one who should be too tired from another ass kicking, dweeb!" While both of us are into electronics and computers, Paul is gifted with an amazing understanding of the inner workings of computers. So, *dweeb* is my usual comeback to the *old fart* comments from Paul.

"Ass kicking? I led most of the game and only lost on the last shot. This is going to be the game you finally lose, bro. You can't keep sinking those cannonball hook shots." Paul never gives up, and I admire that about my brother. That doesn't mean I'm going to make it any easier on him, though.

Just as I toss the ball to Paul, we both hear a dog barking loudly from across the street. It's enough to make us take notice. The frantic scream we hear next gets us moving. Paul drops the basketball, and we run in the direction of the sounds. On the other side of the street, we find two women, both in their 50's and wearing winter coats trimmed in fur, seemingly unaware of the warm temperature and sunshine. They wave their leather clad hands wildly at us.

"Hurry, please hurry!" one of the women yells.

"What's wrong?" Paul asks after reaching the women. I never slow down, and keep sprinting toward the barking dog. The ground is wet and marshy from all the melting snow, and the trees are tall and thin. It'll be another month or two before they grow new leaves.

"My friend fell in the lake!" She points, and as we run past, she tries to explain, "Her dog fell through the ice."

Reaching the lake, my first reaction is to almost laugh. Now looking at them, I understand what happened.

There, flailing in the water, are a woman and a large German Shepherd. Both are trying desperately to climb out, but the ice keeps breaking away around them.

"What the hell?" Paul joins me at the lake's edge.

I'm standing at the edge of the water staring up at a tree, when I see Paul leap from the shore.

There isn't time to scream at him to stop and my reaction seemed to start before Paul had even decided to jump. I grab him by the back of his shirt, pluck him from midair, and toss him to the muddy shore.

"Don't move!" The ferocity of the command holds Paul in his place.

The dog claws away at the woman in his attempt to escape the hole in the ice, and both look as though they're near the end of their struggles.

I start pulling on one of the thinner trees near the edge of the lake. The muddy ground gives way slowly, and half the roots start to unearth. I estimate the distance from the tree to the ice hole is about 40 feet. If the tree is too short, it'll be useless. If it's too tall, it'll push the woman and dog under water, and that'd pretty much be a bad day for everyone. I keep pushing, almost mesmerized by the way the tree falls in slow motion.

Paul gasps as the tree gains momentum. When it crashes to the ice, luck is on my side. The tree is exactly the right length.

The woman reaches for and clasps the branches from the top of the tree. She seems to barely have enough strength to pull herself onto the ice and yet she pauses halfway out of the ice hole. The dog nimbly climbs her back to escape the water and strolls across the ice over to me as if nothing has happened. The woman half climbs and half rolls her lower half out of the water and lies prone.

"Stay flat on the ice and slowly roll to us," I yell to her in the same voice I used on Paul. The last thing I want right now, is for her to stand up and break through another hole in the ice. She musters enough reserves to roll her way back to shore. With her two friends' coats quickly wrapped around her and 70 degrees of sunshine, she begins to recover from the traumatic event.

"I can't thank you enough," she says. "If you boys will follow us home, I keep a little money there and I'd like to reward you for your trouble."

"That's nice," I answer. "But it was no trouble at all and we have to get home."

As Paul and I make our way back to the basketball court, I try to brush some of the mud off my brother's side, but he pushes my hand away.

"What the hell was that?" Paul yells at me.

"What?"

"You could have killed that woman. How could you possibly know that tree was going to be the right length?" Paul wipes the dirt off his side on his own.

I shrug. "Just got lucky, I guess." I can sense Paul's uneasiness, so I add, "Don't tell Mom. She's got enough to worry about."

"Sure, bro." It was Paul's turn to shrug. "No problem."

With all the action, I almost forgot about my migraine, but I feel some relief in knowing that it's almost over.

Don the new clothes after the find is made.
Malicious plot and machination:
First will die who will prove it,
Color Venetian to entrap.
(Nostradamus, Michel. The Prophecies. C4:Q6)

KATARINA KROSTOV
SHELBY TOWNSHIP, MICHIGAN, USA
WEDNESDAY, MARCH 25, 1981

As the brothers turn and head back home, I slowly lower my rifle. I observed the entire incident from between the trees on the other side of the lake. Dressed in a long white coat with tan boots and accents, I'm perfectly camouflaged for the late Michigan winter. I've been watching Trey and Paul for some time, but testing their abilities has been my priority all along.

I wasn't certain it would work, but I had thrown raw meat onto the thin ice to lure the dog. The fact that the woman followed the dog was fortuitous. Witnessing the events unfold gave me the evidence I need. It's clear that Trey possesses the psychic abilities so strongly sought by both my brother in Russia, as well as Maximo's team in the United States. Paul, on the other hand, clearly does not have the same abilities. He would have joined the woman and the dog in the lake if it hadn't been for Trey. Viktor wanted me to evaluate both brothers, due to their family history. The abilities we seek typically run strongly down certain family lines. The twins' older sister, Judith, who possesses strong psychic capabilities, has already joined the Secret Service with Maximo.

This just doesn't feel right … *none* of it.

Over the time I've been observing Trey, I've witnessed his character. He's extremely intelligent and strong, but overconfident. On the verge of reckless. From his school records, I've seen that he has a rebellious side, lacking respect for almost any authority. I doubt he can be recruited to our cause. If Viktor can't have him, he'll want to make sure Maximo can't have him either. My brother will order Trey's elimination.

After the Kennedy assassination, I had been held in isolation in the United States for nearly a year. I was honest when I explained to Maximo that I had been ordered to kill him the night before our assassination of Kennedy. However, I did not reveal to him that I have a rare trait for a psychic: *Other psychics can't sense me.* Maximo kept asking how I could fool him so thoroughly … how I could drug him the night before the assassination without him seeing it coming. What I couldn't make him understand was that it wasn't all a lie. I *did* love him … I *still* love him. If I didn't, it would have been easy to kill him.

Viktor ordered me to kill Maximo the night before the Kennedy assassination, the first order from him I have ever disobeyed. In my heart, I knew I couldn't do it. Maximo started out as an assignment. I never planned on falling in love with him.

V. RAY

Things became even more complicated when I discovered I was pregnant. In lieu of killing him, I decided to drug him and take his amulet to Viktor. I knew this would neutralize Maximo without causing him any harm. We may have been on opposite sides of the Cold War, but my love transcended that.

During my incarceration and pregnancy, Maximo provided more support than I deserved. It was painfully obvious how conflicted he felt. Even though he was furious with me for the assassination, I could sense he still had feelings for me. He stayed by my side through my long and difficult labor and although he concealed it, he was genuinely excited about the baby's arrival.

Something was wrong, though – terribly wrong. I could get no sense of the baby's life. During the birth, my worries grew. The room was too quiet. Maximo gently cradled our newborn and whispered that he was – *stillborn* – my beautiful son! Taken before I had the chance to hold him, to look into his eyes, or to feel his heartbeat.

I often feel as though I deserve this awful fate. The sadness was unbearable. Life wasn't worth living. My dear Maximo seemed to understand … even to feel my pain … my unrelenting heartache. He made it his mission to have the authorities release me. Letters were written, meetings held, and eventually compromises and deals struck. It came down to one condition. I had to retrieve and return Maximo's amulet to him.

When I finally returned to Russia, I was confronted by Viktor. He gave me the amulet along with an ultimatum: He would not stop me from honoring my word, but *if* I returned the amulet, he would ensure Maximo was hunted down and killed within a year. Without the amulet, he said Maximo was much less of a threat, so Viktor would let him live.

Please forgive my broken promise, my love.

As I wipe the tears from my eyes, I return my focus to the present.

Because Trey's sister Judith is already a member of Maximo's team, Viktor will want to ensure that Trey doesn't join them. Once on the team, it's too late. The potential of having a double agent is too risky. I have no doubt that Trey will become a target. Viktor will be obsessed with eliminating him.

What a waste of potential if we kill him. Still, the Tyson family isn't the only family in the area with a psychic lineage. I'll have to put more time into evaluating the Native American girl. If we can't have Trey, maybe we can get to his friend, Samantha.

Chapter 6

VIKTOR KROSTOV
PUSHKIN, RUSSIA
THURSDAY, MARCH 26, 1981

"Yesss, Karl. I know how important this operation is."

Every time I meet with Karl, I feel like I'm in for a fight. I'm seated at my desk, while he stands, leaning forward, trying to physically intimidate me. Fool. No one physically intimidates me.

He looks more eager than anxious to get started and neither one of us turns away or even blinks.

Without removing his charcoal overcoat, he takes the seat across my desk. Keeping his glare fixed on me, he removes his black mink hat and places it on his lap.

It was odd that Karl had insisted on meeting at my new headquarters. Maybe he wants to see how some of his money is being spent. He'll never admit it, but I know he's impressed with how the location is ingeniously hidden where nobody would expect – close to St. Petersburg, but not too close. Sparse, vast, and vacant grounds for kilometers in all directions allow me to set up training scenarios to cover almost any espionage situation.

Watching my security monitors as Karl walked from his silver Bentley to our entrance, his tongue nearly hit the ground when my newest agent, Dasha, greeted him. It certainly doesn't hurt that the women I choose as my agents are beautiful, and in Dasha's case, exotic as well. Karl may be driven by his cause, but he is a man. And, no man is immune to the lure of my agents.

Still, for Karl to drive here instead of calling … to brave this late winter blizzard … this visit is more than just coming to see my new crop of agents.

"This is quite a splendid new headquarters you have, Viktor. My associates and I have paid handsomely for you to be able to afford this." Vodka is difficult to smell on someone's breath, but quite easy today with Karl. Still, his speech is not impaired.

"We are worth every ruble."

"Are you? I have always stressed the need for perfect execution to you. We can't have any mistakes like we did with the Kennedy assassination," Karl extends the hisses on the word assassination, almost trying to sound like a snake.

Mistakes? What does he know? All these years and he has never brought it up. Could he know about Katarina's arrest in America? I made up a story about her being on another assignment – something for the Soviet military – and I always thought he believed me. However, Karl has often known things he should have no way of knowing. It's as though he has a psychic like Katarina working for him. It makes me wonder about these associates he keeps mentioning.

"The operation was a complete success."

"You don't think I know what happened?" he asks.

I can't tell if he really knows something or if he's just probing, and I'm not about to answer without more information from him.

He continues, "They kept putting Oswald in front of the cameras. He said *on television* that he was just a patsy. The idiot would have talked eventually," says Karl with his arms crossed, waiting to judge my next response.

"He was sssmarter than you expected. But he never talked."

"*I* made sure he never talked," says Karl, his voice rising in anger.

"Fine," I answer, starting to get angry as well. "Either way, he never talked. Why did you come here?"

"I don't like mistakes and I certainly don't like them being covered up. You lied to me about Katarina when she was being held by the Americans. She wasn't doing work for the military."

"She …. Yessss. She was captured by Medici. But, he eventually let her go. What was the harm?"

"Did she tell you why Medici let her go?" Karl leans forward, arms still crossed.

"To trade her freedom for Medici's amulet. But, she has not returned it to him."

Karl shakes his head in disgust. "Did she mention giving birth to Medici's baby?"

"She did." This truly catches me off guard. Katarina reluctantly told me about the birth, but there's no way Karl can know this. "The baby did not sssurvive the birth."

I can almost see the steam rising out of his ears, when he seethes, "Do you know what such a child would be worth? A child of two powerful psychic lineages? Why didn't you tell me about this?"

"Believe me, I know the value. The baby died, though. You are upset and I am just as upset. Yet, here we are today. We're not talking about killing the leader of a backward African country, this was America. You paid us because we were the only organization that could have done it and we sssucceeded in killing Kennedy. Now, you want to kill Reagan. Can we just focus on now … on killing Reagan?"

Karl crushes his hat in his fists and says, "From now on, you will tell me all details of any operation I hire you to do. Or I will not be hiring you in the future. Understood?"

Nodding, I agree, "Fine. I understand."

"Good," he says, smoothing his hat and then placing his hands flat upon my desk. "Now, how can you be certain this Hinckley is going to shoot Reagan?"

"Katarina has foreseen it. Karl, you know she is almost always right with these visions. It's exactly the answer you were sssseeking. A complete nobody is going to take out Reagan. There's no link to us. It's perfect. Hinckley doesn't even know we exist. *All* we have to do is clear a path for him."

"Is Katarina going to be the backup?"

"No!" I shout and immediately worry that I said that with too much force. I take a breath, calm myself, and try to tone down my next words. "I have her personally monitoring another critical situation. To make sure this can't be traced to us, we should let Hinckley do this on his own."

I'm not nearly as confident in the operation as I'm portraying to Karl. As we discovered in 1963, assassinating the president is no simple task. Anyone linked to the event will eventually be hunted down. American authorities found and captured Oswald within hours after we killed Kennedy. Katarina turned herself in to Medici back then, and I want to keep her as far away from this assassination as possible.

"Are you punch-drunk from your boxing days? What assignment, *Viktor*, could possibly be more important than this?" demands Karl.

"Medici has his eyes on a young psychic to join his team. This one appears to be more powerful than most and the timing is critical.

Katarina believes he will never willingly join my team, ssso I am having her kill him."

Karl takes a long moment to consider what I'm saying. Slowly, the tension in his face eases.

He says, "Fine. But, we can't let this opportunity go by without a complete plan – including a backup. I'll find another option on my own."

"Naturally, that is up to you."

Chapter 7

HALBERT CURRY

Shelby Township, Michigan, USA
Friday, March 27, 1981

Who lives in fucking Michigan if they got a choice? It ain't too cold today, but there's slush covering half the ground and the fucking clouds cover the whole fucking state. Is it too much to ask to buy a pack of cigarettes without being hassled?

I can't figure out how they were even able to find me. Yet, somehow, they know everything about me. This group knows about the things I did in Arkansas and they love to use it against me. They can list every girl ... what I did with them ... how I killed them. They even know where I hid the bodies.

I tried to escape from them once, but they knew *exactly* where I was. It was so easy for them to find me. They sent two Russian thugs to bust my chops. The beating left me no doubt that I was owned. They want me to do things for them ... their *dirty work*, as they call it. And I ain't got no choice but to do it. They don't interfere with my habit. Hell, sometimes I think they're even encouraging me.

I have what they call a *handler*. I don't know much about her, other than a name. *Katarina* ... what a knockout! The things I could do with her ... maybe someday when the thugs ain't at her side. I doubt she's that stupid, though.

In the end, I don't mind hurting or even killing someone, but I want to decide who ... how ... when ... and *where*. The fuckers made me move to Michigan. Don't they know it gets cold here? There just ain't as many pretty young girls that go wandering off on their own in the middle of fucking winter! At least it's warm'n up sooner than usual this year.

I'm getting a new assignment today. That's what they call someone they want me to kill, an *assignment*. No one would believe how they get ahold of me to get me my assignment, not that I got anyone to tell. It's fucking weird. Every morning I have to buy a pack of cigarettes at a 7-11, go to the pay phone, look at my watch, then look at the number on the pay phone. It don't matter what 7-11 it is, or even the time. Somehow, when Katarina wants to talk, that phone rings and it's her on the other end.

So, here I am at a 7-11 in overcast fucking Michigan waiting at the pay phone, and I ain't the least bit surprised when it rings.

"Y'ello," I answer.

"Halbert?"

"Yup."

"I have an assignment for you."

The way she says *assignment*, her accent is so fucking hot. I'd like to—

"I figured as much. What is it?"

"There's a young man named Trey Tyson. He attends a high school near where you are now …"

Katarina goes on to explain how I need to go through an odd series of events to set up the kill. It seems like a complete waste of time to me, but she tells me that the steps are necessary. At least I got a better idea why they moved me to Michigan and why they been encouraging me to keep up with my habit. The details of my victims are making the Michigan newspapers, and that was always part of her plan.

"Now, y'all dragged my ass to Michigan – that's bad enough. But when comes to killin' folks, I know what I'm doin'. Why can't I just shoot this guy? Why kidnap his sister first?" I know it's probably stupid to question Katarina like this, but I don't like the way this is going.

"We *wouldn't need you* if that's what we wanted." I can hear the threat in her tone.

I stop asking why and move on to how. "So, I'm s'posed to drug this girl and get her in my car. You're sure he'll show up just then to try to save her?" I seen firsthand how they could predict things like this, but still want to hear it directly from the bitch's mouth.

"You know you don't have to ask that, so get to the real questions."

"After I kill the boy, what am I s'posed to do with his sister?"

"I don't care what happens to her, but make sure Trey dies."

"If I can't just shoot him like y'all say, why do you think that takin' his sister makes it any easier to kill him?"

"His desire to save her will make him ignore the risk involved and blind him to the gun. Now, get busy, you have some preparation to do, and you need to have everything in place for Monday."

I hear a click as she hangs up the phone.

Fucking bitch.

Chapter 8

TREY TYSON
SHELBY TOWNSHIP, MICHIGAN, USA
FRIDAY, MARCH 27, 1981

My Advanced Electronics class could be cool, but the teacher is a total dick. Donald McMillan gets some sick pleasure from berating his students. And, he really gets off on insulting me. Most kids would find that reason enough to not take his class. Me? I like a challenge. There's not much I enjoy more than getting under his skin and seeing the frustration as he fails to break me.

Tinkering with electronics is fun … almost as much fun as messing with McMillan.

This project has taken longer than most of the others, as I finish running it through its testing. Don gave us a week to design and build a light display that would react to sound. During the first two days of any project, I can design the circuit board and figure out the components I need. The third day is all I usually need to solder in all the resisters, diodes, capacitors, and transistors, then build the display box and test the project.

With the extra days, the other kids spend working on their projects, I come up with ways to piss Don off.

But, we had a sub yesterday, and I decided to add some custom upgrades to my project. The single color original design was a bit too simple, so I built it with multicolored lights that react to sounds. Each color lights to a different frequency range, which puts on quite a show with music.

Even with the customization, I'm the first one done and I take the finished project up to the front of the class to run through the final grading test with Don, who always spends at least twice as long poking and prodding my projects as he does for the other students in the class.

This jackass is hoping to find something wrong. But even with the extra scrutiny and testing, the project performs perfectly.

"Tyson, you need a haircut!" He belts out as he grudgingly scribbles an A on my project plan.

Shaking my head in disbelief, I walk slowly to my workstation. I'm not the only guy in class with long hair, but he harasses me more than anyone else. As an ex-marine, maybe he still thinks he's in the service.

Now that I have my grade recorded and am situated at my workstation at the back of the class, I connect my project to the station's variable power source. I'm guessing 25% should be a good place to start and I turn the amperage dial up. I often like to put my project through my own personal and more challenging series of stress tests that are designed to melt, incinerate, or detonate the project – *after* it's been graded.

"Don't do it," my buddy John whispers to me from the next station.

"You may want to step back," I whisper back. I understand fully that I'll be caught and that I'll also be kicked out of class, but I don't care.

Don forms a cone with his hands around his mouth to yell, "Tyson, is that you burning your project again?"

The electronics lab layout has six groups of workstations, each with four individual stations. Our workspaces are set at counter height so we can either stand and work on our projects or sit on stools. They wisely used a black countertop material that has been impervious to electrical current, projectiles, and flames … at least so far. I chose the station furthest from the teacher and closest to the door. John has the station next to mine, with Steve and Bill across from us. They all start backing away, probably because the last project exploded instead of just burning.

"Tyson! Button your shirt up, on the double!" Don yells, in his typically abrupt voice.

"Look around you, *Don*. We're in high school! This isn't a marine base, and there's no military dress code here!" Several of my classmates laugh, spurring me on. I turn up the amps to 50% and now there's a small wisp of smoke emanating from my disco light box.

"You'll call me *Mr. McMillan*. And if you don't button your shirt in the next ten seconds, you can get your ass out in the hall again."

"I'm not buttoning my shirt and I prefer the hall to your class." I raise the amperage to 75%, generating a low-pitched hum.

"What the hell are you doing, Tyson? I can hear that all the way up here."

This is one of the reasons I always take the back row in class. I like to keep any action in front of me and having access to a quick exit can be handy. Pushing the amperage to 90%, I suspect this will be plenty.

"My ten seconds are up. I'm going to the hallway." I exit quickly and listen intently. After about five seconds the mini light bulbs explode in a rapid series of firecracker pops, then a *whoosh* sound. *Flames!*

"Son of a bitch," McMillan curses, and that's followed by a louder *whoosh* noise. *Fire extinguisher!* Then comes the all-out belly laughs of my classmates.

Days like this make all the headaches from having Donald McMillan as a teacher seem worthwhile.

Normally, he would come out after extinguishing the fire and launch into a steady barrage of insults, but today is different.

Instead, Max Medici comes walking down the hall. I try to squash my grin.

"In the hall again, Trey?" Max slowly shakes his head, but I think I see a hint of a smile from the man.

Trying my best not to laugh, I only nod. I'm sure Max knows the commotion in the electronics lab is my doing.

"Take a walk with me," he says.

"Hey, Max. Sure, but what brings you back to Eisenhower High School? How's Judith doing? She's always too busy to come back home – or even call."

Max and my mom are cousins and the only family either of them has in the country, so he's always been close with us. Max is a few years older than Mom, but he looks ten years younger and he stays remarkably fit for his age. They both have dark bronze skin and brown eyes. For work, he very selectively recruits high school kids into what he calls a *unique* government agency.

My older sister Judith apparently has the skills Max is seeking. She decided to join his team right after she finished high school and has been so focused on her career that she almost never makes it back home. Even for Dad's funeral, she only made a brief appearance before heading back to DC.

Max has also taken a special interest in me. He never really tries to sell me on joining his agency. It's always been more of a mentoring relationship. Max likes to present options and suggest areas of study that would be of use for the government – or any career. He also seems to ask just the right question at just the right time to get me to open up about subjects I normally wouldn't discuss with anybody.

Placing a hand on my shoulder as we walk, he says, "Judith is fine, but I'm here to talk about you. I know you've been through a lot. Losing your father was tough on you and your family. I also know that you're holding a full-time night job and squeezing in college courses while you're still in high school. With football, basketball, and the night life I hear you have, when do you ever find time to sleep?"

"There'll be plenty of time to sleep when I'm dead." It's my standard response to the question, but the truth of the matter is that I avoid sleep as much as I can. I've even tried to convince myself that I'm able to get much more done by limiting my sleeping hours.

However, the real reason is to avoid the dreams I've been having lately. The dreams started as simple déjà vu. They seemed to focus on events that would eventually come to be. One dream seemed somewhat silly, but kept recurring. I would dream I was seeing a large rock in a street … a rock that seemed out of place. But the dreams have become more detailed over time and the events more real.

The latest recurring dreams are truly disturbing. Last night I dreamt my younger sister, Sarah, would be kidnapped – right on our own street. *It was so vivid.* She was riding her bike a few houses down, when a large, dark-haired man with a bushy mustache suddenly jumped out of the neighbor's shrubs, grabbed Sarah, and drove off in his rusty, light blue Nova. I've had the same dream every night this week. I'm so spooked by it that I snuck into our garage two nights ago and popped the inner tube of the rear wheel of Sarah's bike so she can't ride it anymore. I figure I'll fix it once the dreams stop.

Max is trying to maintain a reasonable tone in his voice, "I know after all this time of constantly battling Mr. McMillan you're not going to suddenly become best friends. But is there any way you can try to find some middle ground where you two can get along?"

"He still thinks he's a Marine, and I don't think Marines believe in compromising. It's not enough that I get an A on every project and every test. The only way he's going to be happy is if I get a military haircut, start buttoning my shirts up all the way to my neck, and drop and do 50 pushups if I forget to say, 'yes sir' after each sentence. It's ridiculous."

"It's obviously not ridiculous to him," Max reasons. "Look, maybe you could at least stop destroying your projects after getting your grade? It's becoming dangerous. You're lucky your grades are what they are or this conflict with Mr. McMillan would get you suspended. Maybe even kicked off the football team."

"Coach wouldn't let that happen to his star player."

Max shrugs, "No. I suppose he wouldn't. Anyway, I'm taking Samantha to Detroit after school to try a little experiment and I'd like you to join us."

"You're experimenting on Samantha! Maybe we can attach one of my electronics projects to her?"

"I don't think she'd let us. Have you been doing the meditation exercises?" he asks.

"Yeah, I'm getting quite good at clearing my thoughts and breathing deeply." I can see Max catch and ignore the sarcasm in my response.

"Great. Just meet me after your government class in the parking lot."

"We could get Sam and leave now. I don't think we'll be missed by the teacher."

"It just so happens that I've been invited by your teacher to guest lecture for your class."

"Mom called you?"

"Well, she *is* your teacher for government class."

"That should be fun. Max Medici, secret government agency recruiter and now high school teacher as well. Can't wait to see this."

Chapter 9

HELEN TYSON
SHELBY TOWNSHIP, MICHIGAN, USA
FRIDAY, MARCH 27, 1981

I hope inviting Max to my class turns out to be a good idea, but I feel like I might be inviting the wolf to speak with the sheep. My twin boys are juniors in high school and they'll soon be making some very serious decisions. Their father, Thomas, was a professor at the University of Michigan. Thomas and I dreamt about having our four children in our respective classes for years to come. His car accident took away those dreams along with so many others. Life has a way of throwing wrenches into the works of the best of plans. I hope you're watching over us, Thomas. You'd be proud of the kids. How each has handled the devastation of losing you. How intelligent they are. The great friends they have. And, their values. You taught them well, my love. Rest easy.

I'm certain now that growing up with two educators as parents affected my children in different ways. We've encouraged them to read, become conversant in many subjects, and to be able to formulate and defend a position or opinion. Family dinners often evolve into spirited debates on subjects ranging from the weather – with Paul convinced computer modeling will eventually be able to predict weather patterns far into the future – to the normally taboo subjects of religion and politics.

The twins, Trey and Paul, along with their younger sister Sarah, have flourished in this environment. Trey, with a gift for picking up languages quickly, is fluent in Italian and French. He's also conversant in Spanish and Russian. They are all fluent in both English and Italian, and the debates often flow from one language to the other. The oldest, Judith, however, has always been uncomfortable with debating the rest of the family and refuses to speak in any language other than English. Both Paul and Trey have a strong understanding of logic, giving them an advantage in debating. On the rare occasions when Judith participates, the twins often successfully twist her own arguments against her.

Another aspect of growing up with educators as parents is that attending a university and pursuing a higher education has always been a given in the Tyson family. Judith seemed to be sending some sort of message when she refused to take my class in high school. And when she was offered a job with Max in Washington right after high school graduation, she jumped at the opportunity. Thomas and I were proud of her choice to serve her country, but disappointed she didn't go to college first.

Now, with Trey and Paul at the age of deciding their futures, I was thrilled when they both signed up to take my class. It's a college prep class and it seems like a very positive step along a natural progression to deciding on a university.

Asking Max to speak in my class will certainly benefit my students. He's done it before and has always been a hit with previous classes. Max has a rich history working for the US government and can intelligently discuss many of the topics in my class. But the other reason is to have Max see what Trey and Paul have to gain and have to offer in a classroom environment. I don't want either of them to be lured from a university education as Judith was. And I think it might be best to have Max come to the same conclusion on his own.

"Hey Mom, where's Trey?" Paul almost always arrives in class after Trey because he's coming from the computer lab on the opposite side of the school. With this rare opportunity, he doesn't hesitate to take Trey's favorite seat in the back row by the door.

"Hello, Paul. How are you?" I try, subtly, to remind Paul of his social graces.

"Marvelous, but where's Trey?"

"I'm sure he'll be here shortly."

Paul has something important on his mind and the social graces lesson will have to wait. Even though the boys are the same age, Paul has always seemed like the younger brother, living in Trey's shadow. They're so alike in some ways … both so bright … but, Trey has always been more adventurous. He's always testing his limits. Paul, on the other hand, is focused on computers and nothing else.

Ah, there they are. Trey and Max enter the classroom together, in the middle of a conversation. It's so difficult to stand by and watch. Max has always been a positive role model and even a mentor to Trey. With Thomas' passing, that relationship is more important than ever. But, the career path Max represents … the same choice Judith made … it goes against everything Thomas and I wanted for our children.

Before making his way to the front of the classroom, Max whispers something to Trey.

Then, I watch as Trey stands next to Paul, makes sure he has Paul's attention, and then methodically looks at *his* desktop and then back to Paul.

Paul sheepishly grins, "What? Look, bro, I need a favor. Then you can reclaim your precious seat."

"What is it?" Trey seems more amused than annoyed by this.

"I started programming a weather-event tracking system and have a problem I can't quite solve."

Trey's eyebrows raise a full inch as he says, "You have a computer problem, and you need *my* help?"

"For a football jock, you can actually be quite intelligent … when you apply yourself."

Trey shrugs, "Alright, lay it on me."

"I need to identify when the coordinates for a weather event are within the borders of a country or state in a computer model. It must be something that can run quickly on a computer. Any ideas?"

"Hmmm, and you need to consider the potential for separated land masses like Michigan or Hawaii," Trey says after thinking for a few seconds. "So, you want me to come up with this solution in the next 60 seconds before class starts or you won't give me back my seat?"

"You can have your seat, bro, and take as much time as you need." Paul stands up dramatically, bows toward the chair, and takes the next seat over.

"Let me ponder it for a while and let you know if I can come up with anything."

"Hey, Trey …. Yo, what was your Poindexter brother doing in your seat?" asks Samantha Fox as she takes the last available seat in the back row. When I think about her complete lack of social graces, I shouldn't worry about Paul.

"What's up, Sam." says Trey while Paul just glares at her for a moment before going back to writing down some notes.

"Are you on for Detroit tonight?" asks Samantha as she leans forward to see around Paul and make eye contact with Trey.

"Detroit?" asks Paul, leaning forward to forcibly interject himself into the conversation. "What're you two doing in Detroit?"

"Take a chill pill ... can't talk about it," replies Samantha. And before either of my boys can follow up with another question, the school bell rings.

"Class, please settle down quickly." I announce as I walk slowly to the front of the class to let the last few conversations die down. "We have a special guest today. Please welcome Mr. Max Medici, who is in the United States Secret Service and one of the people responsible for protecting our president."

Another pause, but this time for a brief and polite round of applause while Max stands and waves to the class. He then walks to the second podium the class has set up for debates.

"Now, can anyone summarize for Mr. Medici the focus of our studies in AP government and politics?" I ask from the first podium. About half of the students raise their hands. "Samantha Fox."

Samantha stands up confidently. She's such a beautiful and composed young lady in those rare moments when she wants to be. She and Trey have been best friends since they were little, but my mother's intuition tells me there's some mutual attraction stirring between them.

She answers, "We're comparing and contrasting the government structure and politics between the United States of America and other countries. We've started with the Soviet Union, and will continue with China and Cuba later in the term."

"I see that you're comparing our government to three different *communist* governments," notes Max. "I'm curious, though. With what form of government would you classify the US?"

Samantha, still standing, answers, "We're a democracy, of course."

"I'm not sure the ancient Greeks would agree with you, nor the Romans, or even our founding fathers," replies Max. "We certainly have aspects of a democracy within our government, but we're a *republic* — similar to the government in place for the first 500 years of the Roman Empire. What are your thoughts on this, Mrs. Tyson?"

I must give Max some credit, he certainly does add value to the class.

"The definition of a republic, in its most basic sense, is a government without a monarch. And while we don't have a direct democracy, we do have what many have called a representative democracy. Therefore, I believe we're both a representative democracy and a republic. However, we should remember our founding fathers' motivation to separate from England and what their circumstances were at the time. The primary goal at the onset was to ensure we weren't ruled by a monarch. Perhaps we should start calling it a democratic republic instead of a democracy," I posit.

"I like that," adds Max. "So, can anyone explain the differences between our *democratic republic* and the Soviet Union's communist state?"

I raise both of my hands and say, "Let's assign a spokesperson for the US and another for the Soviet Union." I need to maintain control of the conversation before it turns into a class-wide open debate. "Who would like to speak for the US?"

Trey stands up, just as confidently as Samantha had. "I'd be glad to speak for the US."

"Excellent. And who would like to speak for the Soviet Union?"

Paul stands up. "I'll represent the Soviet Union."

"Okay, we'll split the class in half. Take a few minutes to come up with the benefits of your type of government and the failings of the other. We'll have our spokespersons present your findings then."

As I walk over to Max's podium, I stumble. Max's reaction time is remarkable as he nearly dives to keep me from hurting myself.

"Careful, Helen. You nearly took a bad fall there," Max says in a hushed voice. And he holds my arm to support me as we make our way back to my podium. The students are too busy with their assignment to notice the near accident. "Did you trip on something?"

"No," I say in a matching hushed voice, while looking down. "My foot just didn't move the way I wanted it to."

"That didn't look very natural. I think you should talk with your doctor about this." Max is quite serious.

"Thanks for your concern. I will."

"Very intriguing." He nods in the direction of the students, who are still discussing their respective positions.

"In what way?"

"To see Paul and Trey both so easily take on a leadership role in such a challenging subject matter is impressive. But the intriguing part was how the rest of the class expected them to. Has it been this way all year?"

"It's been more natural for Trey, as people just tend to gravitate to his personality. Nevertheless, Paul has really grown in the last year or two. He was shy when he was younger, but I think he's starting to realize his strengths."

I take a moment to gauge how the two groups are progressing before continuing, "Now Max, let me ask you a question. I'm concerned that Trey or Paul will follow in Judith's footsteps. Please don't misunderstand me. I'm very proud that Judith chose to serve our country, but I would have preferred that she attend and finish a university education first. Now, it's time for the boys to make some important decisions that will affect the rest of their lives. With Thomas' passing, I would completely understand if the boys started looking to you for the advice they would have sought from their father. They respect you immensely …. I think you know how strongly I feel about the twins getting an education."

"I completely agree with you, Helen. It took years of night classes at Georgetown before I got my masters. Now, I'm not sure if she would share this with you, but I encouraged Judith to finish her education prior to joining my agency. She's very bright and talented, and she may still make that decision in the future …. I don't know if Paul and Trey are a fit for my agency. But in either case, I want what's best for them, and I believe that to include a higher education."

"*That's* a relief!" I say quietly, before turning to the students and raising my voice. "Okay class, it looks like you're ready. Let's get back into our seats and begin the discussion." I give the students a few moments to settle back into their seats before continuing. "Paul, what did your group come up with as the key components of Soviet communism?"

Paul stands and takes the podium before somewhat uncomfortably diving right into his first point.

"The goal of communism is to put government decision-making power into the hands of the working class instead of the rich," he starts. "And with a one-party system, once a decision is reached by the majority, everyone is expected to abide by it. We see many similarities to the US system, including a legislative body, a head of state, and management of transportation, military, utilities, borders, foreign relations, monetary systems, and law enforcement. There's a difference in taxation. The Soviets do tax at a much higher rate, which allows them to distribute the wealth of their most fortunate people to the less fortunate within their society who really need it."

He glances at his brother, then clears his throat. "The primary difference we see is in the economy. The US system encourages and rewards greed. Resources go to those who can afford them. The rich keep getting richer, and the poor get trampled on. However, the Soviet system *manages* economic activity. Critical resources can be intelligently deployed to the areas that can best put them to use. The needs of the people are gauged, and organizations are established to meet those needs. Communism provides a simpler, less wasteful, and much fairer method of governing." Paul quickly sits down to indicate he's finished and the class follows with a polite round of applause.

"Well done, Paul! Now, Trey, what do you and your group have to say about the democratic republic we have in the United States?" I ask.

Trey stands up slowly, almost as if he's a tiger that has been prowling through the high grass, stalking some unaware prey and is eager to pounce. Instead of taking the podium, he moves about the classroom. "I have to commend you, Paul, for volunteering to speak for the Soviet government even though you *knew* you were representing a flawed system. You and your group have put together a clear and concise comparison. Sure, you may have glossed over some of the major problems with communism. But, hey, maybe we wouldn't notice, right?"

Many in the class laugh at this, even those from Paul's group, sensing that Trey is about to go off on Paul with his usual blend of logic, passion, and humor.

"Decision-making power is in the hands of the working class?" Trey asks the question rhetorically and doesn't wait for any answer. "So, you believe Gorbachev was elected by the working class? It's a *one-party* system, as you pointed out. The party leaders decide who will be in power and the workers get to vote for *what?* For that one political party! Here in the US, we have a *choice*. It may not be a pure direct democracy, but we have an open system where anyone meeting basic requirements is eligible to run for office. We then can vote in primaries to decide who we want to represent our political party of choice. And then we have general elections, and again get to choose between candidates without the requirement of following party lines."

Trey pauses for a moment, seemingly to let the class digest the political differences, before continuing, "Distribution of wealth – the Robin Hood form of government at its finest! Take from the rich to give to the poor. It makes sense, doesn't it? Everyone should have the same amount of everything, right? It's only fair! Well, let me give you an example we can all relate to."

Trey takes a few casual steps, and stands between Paul and Samantha. He places one hand on Paul's shoulder. "Paul, say you get 100% correct on a test and get an A." Trey then places his other hand on Samantha's shoulder. "Samantha, here, gets 50%, and she is about to fail with an E. *So,* in an act of kindness and an effort to be fair, the teacher decides to give you both a C. No one fails and you each get an equal score. *That's* the communist way. And isn't that the *fair* thing to do?"

Paul doesn't respond, but his face takes on a sour look.

"What's wrong, Paul? You're thinking you *earned* your A through ability and hard work, right? Samantha probably never even studied." Trey shakes his head in mocking shame at Samantha. "So really, what's her motivation to work hard if we're all going to get the same grade anyway? *That's* one of the biggest problems with communism, socialism, and the distribution of wealth."

Trey moves to his next point with a strong hint of cynicism, "And then there's the *economy.* The Soviet government owns the land, controls where resources go, and decides what goods and services will be made available to the people at whatever locations and consumption rates *they* decide. The government runs healthcare, banking, housing, manufacturing – you name it – even agriculture. Everyone has the same wage, regardless of education level or career. You can work as hard as you want, strive to be as successful as you can, but it doesn't mean you get to eat better food, buy a new car, or live in a nicer home …. So, what's the motivation there to be productive? What defines *success* for a Soviet citizen? That, today, the government didn't decide to strip you of all your possessions, or even to kill you, for voicing a dissident opinion? That's a *good* day for you?" Trey directs the last question squarely at Paul.

I'm as mesmerized as the rest of the class as Trey takes a couple of deep breaths while he turns slowly, making eye contact with each of his classmates. He nods as, one by one, they return his eye contact and nod their agreement with him. He's looking for, finding, and converting anyone he thinks is on the fence.

"Here, in the United States of America, we have a free market capitalistic economy. The government doesn't decide market winners or losers. *We the people* do. Basic supply and demand set pricing. Moreover, there's competition. *Don't be afraid of it people* – competition is what drives us! It's because of competition and the rewards that go with success that we innovate! And that's the key outcome difference between our economies. We work hard and *we innovate*. An idea to lower costs ... a new product or service ... those can lead to a patent or increased sales. Or, how about better food, a new car, a big house on a lake, and dressing to the nines for a hot date on Saturday night!"

He pauses for a minute, grinning broadly, to let the class burst into laughter. Trey again turns slowly, making a connection with the few individuals who aren't nodding in agreement with him.

"What if your dream is to be an artist ... an engineer ... a designer ... a doctor ... an entrepreneur ... or –" he places his hand on Paul's shoulder. "– a computer dweeb? The Soviet government doesn't care about your silly dreams. They tell you that they need more ditch diggers and that's to be *your* job for the *rest of your life*. How motivated are you by that? Is that the way you want to be governed?" Another pause for effect. "America is more than a country; it's an idea. If I were *there*, or anywhere else, I would do whatever it takes to get *here*. Thank you all very much."

As Trey takes his seat, the class breaks into claps, cheers, or both.

Paul stands and the roar in the class dies down.

Straightening his shirt, he says, "I have to admit that you've made some impressive arguments. You've strayed a little from Communism against Democracy to liberalism versus conservatism. And, your focus has been on communists or liberals giving away things to control people. But, in the end, either group is giving something away. Liberals give away food, money, shelter, clothing, and jobs. They do it to grow their influence ... to increase their followers. Conservatives do the same thing. They're just giving away something different."

"What?" asks Trey, still seated.

"Protection. Conservatives give away protection through a larger military and stronger police force, but they do it to increase their influence and their followers."

Trey stares at him for a while before finally answering, "Wow. I can't disagree with that. Both sides have their flaws. Good point." And the entire class applauds again.

I'm so utterly impressed and I can see that Max is as well.

After the roar dies down, Max jumps into the conversation, "Very well done by both groups and especially by both presenters. Communist governments are like monarchies, with an individual or group of individuals trying to rule the masses. Their only real goal is to have as much power for themselves as possible at the expense of the people they rule .... Some of your parents or grandparents served our country in World War II. And, maybe you've heard stories about Adolf Hitler, and how he radically turned young Germans into soldiers. One of Hitler's best strategies was to indoctrinate the Hitler Youth *before* they were experienced enough to form strong opinions of their own ... opinions that most likely would have differed from his. So, I encourage you all to *read* more, *learn* more, and keep forming your *own opinions.*"

Paul raises his hand to ask a question.

"Yes, Paul?" Max acknowledges him.

"How do you know about Hitler's strategies and how well they worked?"

Max smiles at Paul. "I studied everything about him when I was young. It can be quite revealing to learn about the background and strategies of historic leaders."

Paul nods, but doesn't seem fully convinced of the answer.

After a brief pause, Max continues, "I have worked for our government most of my life – testing and recruiting some of our most talented young people. There's a very basic dynamic that helps me see the difference between our people and the Soviets. Through all the testing we've done over the years, we've seen this ratio repeatedly. Roughly 10% of people will find a way to be successful no matter what challenges they face ... another 10% will find a way to fail no matter what advantages they're given. *It's human nature.* The *real* question is how to treat the other *80%* of the population. Is it better to tell them there's no sense in achieving an education or working hard, essentially pushing them down into a minimalistic and unmotivated life as communism does? Or, does it make more sense to provide the opportunity for growth and success that we offer here in the US?"

Paul raises his hand again. "That does make sense for individuals, but what about for the whole country? Communism does seem to offer better control for the government."

"Governments have to be careful when it comes to control," Max replies calmly. "Our founding fathers were ruled by a monarch who was thousands of miles away, had never set foot on our soil, who wanted to control them and tax them, but didn't offer them any voice in how they were governed. Putting their lives on the line for all future generations, the colonists formed an army and started a revolution. Against the most powerful nation at the time, they fought for and won our freedom. And even more amazing was the thoughtfulness and care they used in forming a government. We have checks and balances that keep the power and control in the hands of our people. Freedom defines us ...

freedom to vote … freedom of speech … freedom to choose whatever religion we want, or even none at all … free markets … freedom to choose our own paths in life. We're a *free* society!"

Max looks at the students, and seems impressed by their attentiveness. "However, the success of our society poses a grave threat to communist states. Their people want the freedom we have, even if *we* often take it for granted. America started with a revolution. And a *revolution* is the single largest threat to any communist regime. Because they're so threatened by our success, they will try to bring us down or convert us at almost any cost. And we have to be *vigilant* and ready to defend our very way of life!"

"But how can the Soviets really affect *our* freedoms?" asks Paul.

"The first and most obvious way would be for the Soviets to attack us openly by declaring war. But, from my experience, they are trying to be stealthy, attacking from within our borders and taking advantage of our free society. *That* may be the more difficult challenge to deal with. If they can get enough people with communist or socialist views elected into key offices within our government, they could slowly convert America into a socialist state. Think about it …. What if we had communists in our Supreme Court or Congress? What if our president was secretly a communist?"

"I don't think you have to worry about that with Reagan!" Samantha answers the question even though it had been rhetorical. "You're in the Secret Service. What if the president really was a communist and maybe even did something to hurt our country? How would we ever stop him?"

"Hmmm … that's a very intriguing question, Samantha." Max thinks about it for a few moments before answering, "Impeachment by Congress would be the proper route to go if there wasn't an immediate threat to the country by leaving the president in office while the trial progressed. If there were an immediate threat, other measures would have to be taken. In theory, the president is subject to being arrested for committing a crime just like you and me. However, any police officer trying to place him under arrest would be stopped by the Secret Service. You'd have to –" The bell rings, cutting him off abruptly.

"Thank you, Mr. Medici, for joining our class today," I almost need to yell to be heard above the growing noise of my students packing up to head home.

"It was my pleasure! Thank you for inviting me," answers Max. Before leaving the class, he leans over to whisper something to me, "Stay safe, Helen, and see a doctor – it's important."

"Okay, Okay. I will," I reply. I then walk over to my sons, intending to congratulate them on a great job on their debate. But, as is often the case, the twins are locked in a conversation I don't understand.

Trey leans over to Paul, "I have it."

"You have what?" Paul asks.

"I have your weather system algorithm."

"Already? What are you waiting for? Let's hear it."

"If you look at a two-dimensional map from above, you have a point representing a weather system and a polygon representing borders of a country or state. And you want know if the point is within the polygon?"

"That *is* the basic question." I can tell Paul is having difficulty being patient.

"Okay," Trey continues. "You can draw a ray from the point directly east. That's an easy and quick equation, right?"

"Yes, it sure is," answers Paul slowly, with a confused look.

"And you can easily and quickly determine if the ray crosses any of the line segments of the polygon, right?"

"Again, that's easy. Yes."

"Well, if the number of segments crossed by the ray is odd, the point is inside the polygon. If the number is zero or even, the point is outside of the polygon." Trey pauses, watching Paul's eyes grow wide open as he seems to gain an understanding.

Sparks of recognition flair in Paul's eyes as he says, "That's it, Trey! You did it! It'll be easy to program and extremely fast to execute the code. How on Earth did you figure that out so quickly?"

"It just came to me. But I need to run. You have fun with your computer, bro."

"Thanks, I will!" Paul runs out of the classroom, heading in the direction of the computer lab.

Chapter 10

TREY TYSON
SHELBY TOWNSHIP, MICHIGAN, USA
FRIDAY, MARCH 27, 1981

As Samantha and I walk together toward the back of the building where the faculty and visitors park, I can't help but notice how well her black jeans fit. She runs some of the longer races on the track team and is captain of her basketball team. With long jet-black hair, she's tall and athletic, yet still has curves in the right places. Too bad we're such great friends.

While trying to think of something witty to say, I start to see the squiggles again. *Damn* – another migraine. I need a few minutes to meditate before getting in a car for a long drive.

"Sam, you go ahead. I gotta hit the john for a minute. I'll meet you and Max in the parking lot."

"Cool beans," she says with her trademark swink – a combination of smiling with half her mouth and winking. She then looks at me … lingering with her smoldering black eyes … and I wonder if she's thinking we should be something different than just friends. Something more. She sees my pain, somehow, and asks, "You okay?"

"Absolutely. See you in a few." I head toward the bathroom in the computer and math lab area, knowing it will most likely be quieter there.

The high school is mostly empty, as few students or faculty stay long after the final bell, so I'm a bit surprised to hear some sort of commotion around the corner near the computer lab.

"It's dime time!" a voice yells from around the corner. It's a gravelly voice I easily recognize as Darrell "Dime Time" Tracewski. He plays defensive tackle on our football team and is the most aggressive player I've ever seen. During the off-season, Darrell seems to need to be in a fight at least once a week just to satisfy his aggressions. It's bad enough that he's a senior, and at 6' 5" and 270 pounds, he's easily the biggest kid in school. But Darrell got his nickname by always carrying a roll of dimes in his pocket in preparation for his next fight. He likes to hold the roll in his fist, taking away the natural cushion in an empty closed hand, to really do some damage with his punches. I wonder what fool would have upset Dime Time, especially after the entire faculty has left the building.

I turn the corner and there, being held by Dime Time's left hand and about to be punched by his right, is *Paul*.

"What's up, Dime?" I ask in as firm yet calm a voice as I can muster. At the same time, I quicken my pace without breaking into a full run.

Darrell glances briefly at me before returning his attention to Paul. "This nerdy brother of yours came runnin' around that corner a minute ago and ran right into me. The dickwad almost knocked me over. He needs to be taught a lesson." Darrell pulls his right hand back ready to let loose, but he always likes to pause for a second to see the fear in the face of whoever is about to receive the blow.

"I'm sure he does need a lesson in manners," I almost yell, causing Darrell to stop and return his attention to me. "But why not just give him a warning this time? He didn't mean to run into you." I've managed to close the distance between us to only a few more steps.

"Back off, Tyson. Unless you want to take his place?" Darrell's father had been a defensive tackle for the Ohio State Buckeyes and with the Tyson family ties to the University of Michigan, the rivalry seems even more important than the fact that both Darrell and I are on the same high school football team.

I'm either going to have to fight Darrell or let Paul take what would be the worst beating of his life. And I have a better chance than Paul does.

"Fine. Either let him go and fight me, or you'll have to take us both on."

Darrell was accepted at Ohio State for his football skills not his intellect, but he is smart enough to not want to fight both of us at once. So, he releases Paul, keeping his right hand in a tight fist around his roll of dimes. "If you really want to get busted up, *let's go.*"

I use my left shoulder to shove Paul out of the way, taking his place against the wall facing Darrell.

And then the strangest thing happens.

My migraine squiggles suddenly disappear, time seems to almost stop, and my vision expands and splits into four views. The current

71

situation — *what's happening now* — occupies a split view on the bottom right of my vision and there are three additional views that I can focus on with some concentration.

What the hell is going on?

My concentration seems to be drawn to the top left view. It shows what looks like a movie of Darrell throwing a wild right hand punch in the direction of my head. It connects directly with my jaw, forcing the back of my head against the wall with a loud crack. Even though it's only a glimpse of a vision, I can feel some of the pain that such a blow would cause. Is this some sort of alternate reality?

Then, my concentration moves to the second view. It shows me trying to block the punch with my left hand, and throw a counter punch with my right. In this vision, Darrell's punch is deflected up, but still connects with my nose. The force of the punch is far less than in the first view, but it's still enough to break my nose.

In the third view, I don't try to block the punch. Instead, I swipe at Darrell's left hand with enough force to break his hold on my neck, freeing myself to duck. Darrell's punch misses me in this reality, and it connects squarely with the wall.

The third alternate reality is easily the best. I sure hope there's a connection between these visions and what really happens!

Just as Darrell starts his fist with the dime roll in the direction of my jaw, I swipe my right arm up into his left. As I foresaw in my vision, Darrell's grip is broken and I'm free to duck. The next thing I hear is a loud cracking noise above my head, followed by a high-pitched yelp and 50 glimmering dimes bouncing around on the tile floor.

I could let this end now, but this fucker tried to hurt my brother. He's staring stupidly at his hand when I drive my knee into his groin.

"Oooof." Darrell buckles over.

Grabbing him by the shoulders, I'm about to drive my other knee into his face when a hand squeezes my shoulder. It's Paul.

Shaking his head, Paul says, "That's enough. Take it easy."

Dime raises his left hand in a form of surrender and slowly stands.

"You broke my hand!" Darrell looks more affected by embarrassment than pain.

"You broke your own hand, dumbass."

"If this messes up my football scholarship, I'm going to make you regret it."

"You know, Dime," I say as my anger begins to defuse, "the next time you want to pick a fight, you really should think about the consequences beforehand. If I were you, I'd get that looked at and set as soon as possible. It'd be a real shame if your finger bones fuse the wrong way."

"Arrogant asshole." Darrell mutters as he runs off in the direction of the front of the school where the students park.

"You gonna be alright, bro?" I ask Paul.

"*Me?* Are you kidding? First, you do the thing with the tree at the lake and now you teach Dime Time a lesson. What's going on with *you* lately?"

"I don't know what you mean," I say with an exaggerated shrug and a healthy dose of sarcasm. "I have to run. Max and Samantha are waiting for me out back. I'll see you later."

"Okay, later, and thanks!"

Paul heads to the computer lab as I make my way to the men's room. My migraine is completely gone, but there's a strange feeling in my head. Better blood flow, new connections firing, almost electric. I don't know, but something happened. I feel different.

As soon as I open the door to the bathroom, I know something's out of place. Turning around the corner, I see that out of place feeling take human form. She's holding a plastic container of Tylenol and smiling at me.

"What took you so long?" Sam says as she takes a single step in my direction.

"My, uh … my headache is gone. I don't need the Tylenol."

"What *do* you need?" She takes another step.

"Need? I don't know what you mean." But I do.

She strides right to me, dropping the pills on the way, and kisses me. A quick darting kiss, at first, but then I find my mouth has opened and we're fully making out. Putting my arms around her, my body reacts to hers almost instantly. I want her. She wants me. All these years as friends, and this has been brewing underneath all along.

Pulling away, I take a deep breath before saying, "Max is waiting for us."

Sam's tongue finds my neck and works its way to my ear. Then she whispers, "This won't take long."

I pull away again. "Samantha. We can't. We're –"

"Don't give me that *friends* bullshit. You want this as much as I do."

"It's not bullshit. We aren't just friends. We're best friends. This would change everything. I don't want to risk it."

She glares at me for a long moment, angry, and unable or unwilling to say anything. It's the fiery part of her personality that I'm most drawn to, and my body is begging me to cave in.

She turns around, stepping away, then stops. Kicking off her shoes, she pulls her shirt over her head quickly, and unbuttons her jeans. Sam's facing the mirror and she notices in the reflection that I'm not complaining anymore, so she slowly slides her jeans down to her ankles, bending over seductively. No bra. No panties. Naked and scalding hot.

Her body is as sexy as I always imagined. Hands on the counter, back slightly arched, she waits for me. Confidently smiling at the mirror, Sam sees my resistance crumble. Removing my clothes isn't a conscious act on my part. It just happens.

As I ease up behind her, throbbing, I mention, "I don't have a rubber."

Sam licks her hand, coating it with saliva, then spreads it on me as a lubricant.

"We'll be careful," she says. "Now shut up and fuck me."

Arching her back more, she watches me in the mirror intently as I push her hair to the side and plant my lips on her neck. Sucking gently, I reach around and cup her tits. Her nipples are as erect as I am and she moans as I circle them with my fingertips.

"Just this once," I say. "After this, we're back to being friends."

"I said shut up and fuck me."

Lifting her leg on the counter, she gasps as I enter her from behind. We're not making love. This is raw, primal fucking. As we both approach climax, she pushes me away and turns around to face me.

"I need to see this," she says between heavy breaths.

With her elbows on the counter, Sam wraps her legs around me and pulls me back in, matching my pumping with her legs squeezing me in faster and harder. Rapture.

The lights suddenly dim and the air seems to thin out. I struggle to get oxygen into my system. A slow trickle of blood drips from her nose as her eyes roll back. The lights flicker and then return to full power.

At the last possible moment, I pull out. Both of us shuddering, I spray everything I have over her stomach and breasts.

After we clean up and get dressed, I say, "That was amazing. But, remember … from now on, just friends."

"Friends." And with that one word left hanging in the thinned air, she stomps out of the men's room.

V. RAY

Chapter 11

MAX MEDICI
SHELBY TOWNSHIP, MICHIGAN, USA
FRIDAY, MARCH 27, 1981

Clouds have rolled in and it looks like a storm is brewing. The temperature hovers just above freezing, so this could end up being rain, sleet, snow or a combination. Trey and Samantha finally make it to the parking lot.

"What took so long to get here?"

"I had to, uh, use the bathroom. Sorry about the wait." Trey climbs into the back seat, as Samantha has already claimed the front passenger seat.

"Same here," Samantha replies.

Noticing a dried trail of blood from her nose, I pass her my handkerchief. "You had a nosebleed, Samantha. What happened?"

With a confused look, she dabs her upper lip and stares at the red flakes contrasting with the white handkerchief. "No clue. I think maybe I blacked out for a little while."

"Should I take you home?"

"No," she shakes her head angrily. "I'm fine."

"I was planning on telling you both more about the agency and doing some additional testing to see if you might be a fit later in the year. But things have changed and we need to move up our timetable. This is very important, and for national security reasons, what I'm about to tell you *cannot* be disclosed to anyone else. Are you both able to honor that?"

In unison and without hesitation, both Trey and Samantha reply, "Yes."

"I'm not a typical Secret Service agent. In fact, I run a division of the Secret Service called Advance Intelligence and, along with other responsibilities, we handle *covert* operations." I can see that Trey and Samantha are hardly shocked by this revelation. "We've learned that there's a credible threat to President Reagan's life and I'm hoping through our efforts today that we can find a way to keep him safe."

"What?" asks Trey with thick incredulity. "Are you saying Sam and I are somehow supposed to save the president?"

"Actually, this is a situation where Samantha may be the only person alive who can help. Trey, I want you to just observe today. You'll both finally understand why I've asked you to keep up with the breathing, meditation, and internal focus exercises I've taught you. Samantha, have you kept up with your exercises?"

"My great uncle taught me the same exercises he taught you. I take them very seriously."

"Your Great Uncle Johnny was my first mentor and a truly amazing man. I wish he were here to help us now. But, we'll find out soon if we've been able to learn what he so desperately wanted to teach us. Let me start by asking if you've ever experienced déjà vu?"

"Yes, all the time. Doesn't everyone?" Samantha replies with a little more enthusiasm in her voice.

It's good to see her get excited about this. Johnny taught me much about their family line, which includes a rich history of visionaries. Suspecting that Samantha has some of these abilities, I've kept an eye on her over the years.

"It's my belief that we all have the ability to see the past or the future to some degree, but a few people have greatly magnified abilities to do so. Déjà vu is the simplest form. Some people can see future events with great clarity, with this ability being more prevalent in men. Other people can channel the past. This is more prevalent in women. With either skill, it helps to be close to the person or event in the vision."

I watch as they glance briefly at each other. This isn't nearly as shocking to Samantha as it is to Trey, but she's been exposed to it already. "Again – this cannot be disclosed to anyone." I make eye contact with each of them in turn. "Advance Intelligence, or AI for short, employs agents with these abilities for both strategic and tactical purposes. At the top of our list of responsibilities is to ensure the safety of the president. That's where Samantha comes in."

"Why are you two so quiet?" They barely spoke the entire drive to Detroit.

Trey just shrugs as we make our way into the lobby. Samantha stops and looks around as though she recognizes the place. I wonder if she senses the significance of this location.

"Whoa Max – a room at the Pontchartrain Hotel? I didn't think they paid government employees that well," jokes Trey.

Samantha chuckles and this jars her into motion again.

"I chose this hotel for a reason and it's related directly to Samantha's ancestry. We are presently standing on the site where Fort Pontchartrain du Detroit was originally built by French settlers in 1701."

As we reach the front desk, I turn my attention to the clerk. "Hello, my name is Maximo Medici and I'm checking in."

"Mr. Medici, welcome to the Pontchartrain Hotel." The clerk takes a moment to locate the reservation. "I have you staying with us for one night and I see a special request for the first-floor Southeast corner, which we were able to accommodate. Are you certain you wouldn't prefer a room on a higher floor? The views of the river and Canada are quite spectacular at night."

"No, thanks. I'll keep the room I requested."

"Very well, Mr. Medici. I see the room is prepaid. Will you need help with your bags or require a wakeup call in the morning?"

"I can manage with the bags, but I have an early flight to catch. Please make a wakeup call for 5:15 tomorrow."

"Yes, sir. Your room is on the first floor, up one level from here, turn right out of the elevator, and it will be at the end of the hall on your left. If there is anything else you need, don't hesitate to call or visit the front desk. Enjoy your stay with us." The clerk hands me the room key and a hotel map.

"Thank you." I return my attention to Samantha and Trey as we take the elevator up a level. "The French held the fort until 1763 before turning it over to the British after losing the French and Indian War. It remained in British hands until 1796, when it was finally handed over to the Americans long after the end of the Revolutionary War. The original fort burned down in 1805, but an adjacent fort was renamed Fort Detroit."

As we exit the elevator and walk down the hallway, I continue, "Then came the war of 1812, with the British trying to reclaim their colonies from America. The British still held much of what is now Canada, which put Fort Detroit on the front line of the war."

"This is all very intriguing history about Detroit, Max, but why are you telling us this?" asks Samantha.

"If our experiment is successful, you will need to know *all* this information, as well as the rest of what I'm about to tell you." I hand Trey one of my bags as I open the door to the room.

"This weighs more than just clothes for a couple of days. What's in the bag?" asks Trey.

"You'll see when you open it. Can you set it up on the desk?" I toss my other bag on the bed.

Trey opens the bag and pulls out a very large brass object that resembles an open lantern. The bottom is a wide triangle and holds a short thick ivory candle. The middle consists of three brass arms that taper in to a point on the top. He sets it on the desk. "Okay, now what?"

"You seem to like setting things on fire, Trey. Why don't you do the honors and the light the wick?" I point to the bag Trey had placed on the floor.

Trey laughs, and then finds a lighter in the bag and lights the candle. "I'm guessing this is where our breathing exercises come into play?"

"Exactly. Except there are a couple of more steps for Samantha to take, and remember, you'll just be observing this time." I reach into the bag that had held the lantern, unzip the front pocket and pull out a long, carved pipe and a packet of tobacco. I proceed to stuff some of the tobacco into the pipe and offer it with the lighter to Samantha.

"I've only smoked a couple of times before," Samantha says with a hint of trepidation in her voice.

I nod my understanding while sliding the desk chair to the side and pulling the reclining chair from the corner to the desk. "Samantha, I want you to get comfortable in the recliner, start smoking the pipe, and then clear your mind and focus on the flame from the candle."

After Samantha lights the pipe, I shut off all the lights in the room. The candle becomes the only focal point. I stand behind Samantha and motion to Trey. "Trey, you can sit or stand, but don't make a movement or sound until I tell you it's okay."

As Samantha takes a few puffs from the pipe, Trey chooses to sit on the end of the bed.

"Samantha, you're a direct descendant of Chief Tecumseh of the Shawnee tribe of Native Americans. He was a famous leader known for building coalitions between different tribes and fighting for the rights of all Native Americans during the United States' expansion west from the original thirteen states. This pipe belonged to Tecumseh's brother Tenskwatawa, who was known by many tribes simply as *the Prophet*. The pipe was passed down through the generations of your family all the way to Johnny Fox, who gave it to me many years ago. Johnny taught me the history of Chief Tecumseh and the Prophet. Back in 1811, the Shawnee fought and lost a key battle at Tippecanoe to a United States force led by William Harrison. Then, with the War of 1812 between the British and the United States, many Native Americans saw an opportunity to aid the British and perhaps regain some of their lost land. Detroit was a key battleground as it stood as the gateway to all the fertile land in what is now the Midwest."

To aid Samantha's transition into a trance state, I'm carefully keeping my voice low and monotone. "The British, along with Native Americans who were led by Tecumseh and Tenskwatawa, captured and held Fort Detroit early in the war. But the United States also understood the importance of the location. The Americans built a superior force, to be led by none other than William Harrison. Are you getting all of this, Samantha?"

"I know my family's history," Samantha replies. She sounds relaxed as she continues to smoke the pipe and stare at the flame.

Samantha's long black hair and prominent cheekbones remind me of her great uncle, yet her skin is fair compared to most of her family.

"Excellent," I still maintain an even voice, trying to sound relaxed. "Tenskwatawa was said to have foreseen a fate for Harrison: he would be elected president, but he would die in office. The Prophet also saw that every president elected every 20 years after Harrison would also die in office. This came to be known as the Presidential Curse. I believe the curse originated at Fort Detroit just before the arrival of Harrison. Samantha, you've shown potential to possess some of the same abilities as Tenskwatawa. I want you to use the meditation and internal focus exercises I taught you. This will help you to look back in time to this location in 1813, to *see* Tecumseh and Tenskwatawa in Fort Detroit. You may even be able to focus enough to communicate with the Prophet. He may well be aware of your presence."

I pause, gauging how close she is to a trance state. "Samantha, President Reagan was elected in a curse term and every president elected in a curse term prior to Reagan *has* in fact died in office. If you can communicate with the Prophet, I need to know the circumstances of how he sees President Reagan's death happening and if there's any way to prevent it. Being that you're a descendant of Tecumseh and that we're in the same location where the curse originated should give you the best chance possible to succeed."

1ST VISION

"I think I understand," Samantha utters as she gently places the pipe on the desk and then slowly falls into a trance state.

Chapter 12

SAMANTHA FOX
SHELBY TOWNSHIP, MICHIGAN, USA
FRIDAY, MARCH 27, 1981

Max thinks I'm just some stupid teenager, but he doesn't have a clue. He's not the only one Great Uncle Johnny trained before he died. I spent years with him in the Canadian wilderness and he taught me about my family history and so much more. To track an animal even after a heavy downpour. To know where the fish will be in a lake. To know where to hit a man to knock him down and where to hit him if you need to kill him. To throw a knife. To shoot exactly where I aim with a gun. And, he taught me about dreams and visions.

I've had a few visions over the years that have allowed me to see my family's past, but the visions have seemed random and with no specific meaning. This is very different. Max gave me a goal. I just wish I knew how the hell to make it happen.

"Where do I begin?" I try to speak, but it's more of a thought that extends beyond my mind.

"I can help you." I hear this strange voice in my head, seemingly in answer to my question. I've never heard a voice in any of my previous dreams, and until now, I wasn't even sure I had entered a trance state yet. Great Uncle Johnny told me, years ago, that I may have a guide appear in my dream. It hasn't ever happened, though, till now.

"Kick ass!"

The voice asks, *"What does kick ass mean?"*

"Who are you? Is that you, Max?" I try to project my thoughts as though they work the same as my voice.

"I am your vision guide." The voice is unrecognizable, yet eerily familiar.

"That's not an answer."

"It is an answer. Just not the answer you may have sought. But I will guide you, nonetheless." A man's voice. Deep, yet gentle. It seems trustworthy.

"How do I see a specific event in the past?" I ask this guide.

"First you must come to accept that time and space are connected. They are dimensions. The first three, length, width, and height, make up space and are easy for anyone to perceive. Time is the fourth dimension. All of time has played out, but only the gifted few are able to perceive anything beyond the present of space-time. You possess this gift."

"But how do I use it?"

"You must focus on the place and time you desire to perceive and allow your mind to take you there."

I've heard Max say the same thing before … something about Einstein's theory of relativity. *Okay, time is the fourth dimension and has already played out.* I'm going to make this work, so I force my mind to focus even harder on the key points I think will get me where I need to go. *Tecumseh's curse. Fort Detroit. 1813. Tecumseh's curse. Fort Detroit. 1813. Tecumseh's curse. Fort Detroit. 1813.* I start to feel a floating sensation, and everything around me turns black. *Tecumseh's curse. Fort Detroit. 1813. Tecumseh's curse. Fort Detroit. 1813.*

Stars emerge into my view and they begin to spin into a crazy violet swirl. I feel nauseous from the spinning almost instantly. I squeeze my eyes shut, but the spinning sensation continues. There's no sound and the silence seems louder than an explosion. Just when I think I can't bear it any more, the spinning wanes. And when it stops, I slowly open my eyes. The stars are gone, only blackness remains. But even that is fleeting. Light returns gradually. I want to rub my eyes to clear the blurriness, but can't.

Tecumseh's curse. Fort Detroit. 1813.

A river and then a grassy field emerge into my view. Clarity is starting to return.

Tecumseh's curse. Fort Detroit. 1813.

The grassy field and river become completely clear. I turn around and see a familiar looking Shawnee chief in traditional attire. Tecumseh is far more handsome a man than I imagined. He looks to be in his upper thirties and stands about 5' 10", which would be tall among our people of his time. He's thin, with a light copper complexion, oval face, and blazing hazel eyes. Hanging from his prominently hooked nose is a string of three silver crosses.

I can only watch as he starts walking away from the river. His gait is energetic and decisive.

A figure approaches the chief from the north ... a Shawnee warrior, running wildly. The warrior only slows when he is within a few feet of the chief.

"Chief Tecumseh, your brother, the Prophet, wakes from his deep sleep and asks for you," the warrior blurts between heavy breaths.

"Focus, Samantha." The voice of the guide has softened a bit, but is still forceful.

"I wish your father, Blue Jacket, was here. He was a very wise war chief and we have an important decision ahead of us." I can hear Tecumseh speak to the warrior as they walk briskly toward an encampment. It's surrounded by a tall wood fence with guard towers on the corners. This must be Fort Detroit.

"I am certain, my chief, that you will lead us to victory. You have always done so." The warrior's shrill voice reveals his youth.

"I have led our people as wisely as I can. Only the Shawnee and some of the Creek still resist the white man's advance. We are fighting a losing battle and it does not have to be so. If only all the tribes would unite as I have so strongly urged other chiefs, we could stop the white man from advancing any further .... With any luck, we could even retake some of the land other chiefs have simply traded away. *The drunken fools!* What *right* do they have to trade the land? Can you trade the air? Can you trade the sea? The land belongs to *all* the tribes, and no one chief should be able to trade it away .... Your father might have helped us get more allies."

"We have the British as allies because of you," praises the warrior.

"The British are no better than the Americans. We are allies now, but they wanted to take our land just as the Americans are doing. For now, they are our only hope .... I cannot remember what white man said it, but they have a proverb that says *the enemy of my enemy is my friend.* I can see the truth in it. This war alongside the British has gone well so far. The British General Brock had a good plan to take Detroit. And now we will gather our forces from the west and from the north here to launch an attack. But what is Moneto's will? Will I live to see our people safe and free again? And what will become of my enemy, General William Harrison?"

"Harrison has earned your anger," the warrior says solemnly, and I guess he may be trying to be the trusted advisor Chief Tecumseh seems to crave. "As governor of Indiana, Harrison was cunning with the other

Chiefs, trading for huge tracts of land with nothing more than barrels of whiskey and tobacco. Now, as a general for the Americans, Harrison's army has chased our people off much of the most fertile land, even though we refused to agree to any land trading. He killed and wounded many of our people, including women and children."

"I will have my revenge!" The great chief seems inspired by the warrior. "Now that we have Detroit, Harrison will have no choice but to come here to fight. However, Harrison is not a fool. He will not come to Detroit until he has enough men to retake the fort. I need an advantage."

I so want to communicate with Tecumseh, perhaps the most famous Shawnee in all our history – and *my* ancestor. But I fear his reaction to my presence and I have not yet found the Prophet or the crucial information I need.

"Perhaps the Prophet will have an answer," says the warrior.

"I hope so," replies Tecumseh.

After passing through a large field of tall grasses and sparse oak trees, keeping the river to our right, we come upon the large fort surrounded by a tall wooden fence.

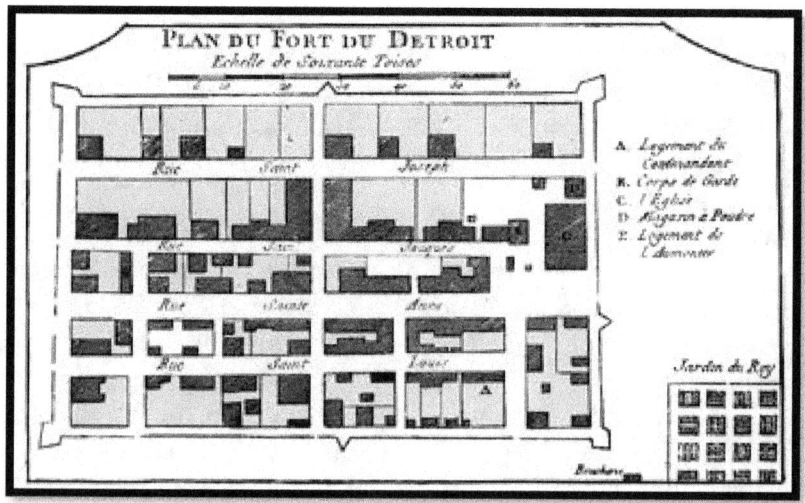

I don't know if it's my choice or if my spirit is tied to my ancestor, but, somehow, I float alongside Chief Tecumseh as he enters the fort. I then accompany Tecumseh through the eastern gate, past the first tower, and into a small building while the warrior heads in another direction. There, resting on the ground, is the Prophet. Lying next to him is the exact pipe that I just smoked.

"Kick ass!"

"Again, with this kicking of the ass. Calm down and pay attention," comes the guide's voice, sterner this time.

"Tenskwatawa, you awake my brother! You must tell me – has Mishe Moneto shown you the way of Harrison?" asks Tecumseh.

"Yes, my great brother. I have been shown that in time he is to become president of the Americans."

"That is a very bad omen," Tecumseh takes a deep breath before continuing. "It can *only* mean that *he* will prevail in our upcoming battle."

"Yes, I fear it does mean that. But there is more I have seen. Harrison will die as president shortly after he is elected. And every president the Americans elect every 20 years after Harrison's election will also die in office for the next 200 years."

"Who are these other men you have seen?" asks Tecumseh.

The Prophet looks up into the air, pauses for a moment, and then says, "Abraham Linkin ... James Garfield ... William Mikkenly ... Warren Harding ... Frank Lynn Rosepelt ... John Kennedy ... Ronald Raygum ... George Bush."

"Those are strange names to me," says Tecumseh. "What will happen after these 200 years?"

"I know not. Moneto shows me nothing after the year 2012."

"What do you think that means?"

"I believe there will be something of major importance to happen in 2012 ... something that will change the future beyond the event, and that future is not clear."

"Brother, this is very important." Tecumseh looks about, almost as if he can sense my presence in the room. After seeing he is alone with his brother, he returns his attention to Tenskwatawa. "If the coming battle should claim my life, I want you to deliver this prophecy to the Americans. Let *Tecumseh's curse* be our revenge upon them for centuries to come!"

"I will, my brother." Tenskwatawa is stoic. I can only guess what he's feeling, knowing that their tribe is about to lose a major battle, as well as their chief. *Yet he shows nothing!*

"We must prepare to leave Detroit. Harrison is coming soon. Ready yourself, Prophet." Tecumseh hurries off, but I will my spirit to stay behind ... to stay and try to learn more from the Prophet.

"Young one … tell me what brings you here?" asks the Prophet, but no one else is in the room.

"Can you see me?" I try to speak, but I'm not sure if my spirit will be heard.

"No, young one … but, Mishe Moneto said you would be here at this moment."

"Is that who has been guiding me, the Great Spirit … Mishe Moneto?"

"I see you have much to learn yet. Moneto has told me it is important for me to help you …. What help do you seek?"

"I heard what you told Chief Tecumseh about the fate of the American presidents who are elected every 20 years after Harrison. I know how important this revenge is to your brother, but the world in my time is a very different place than in your time. It is critical that we do not let the current president die in office as you have foreseen. It could have dire effects on the entire world. It is President Ronald Reagan and the year is 1981. Any details from your vision that you can share may be important. What can you tell me about it?"

"I do not understand *why* you would want to save the American president when they have done so much to harm our people. Yet Mishe Moneto said I should help you and so I feel compelled to do so. Perhaps Moneto seeks to avoid these dire effects you speak of …. I have seen two differing visions for this President Raygum of your time. The date is the 30th of March in 1981 and Raygum is to meet with a large gathering of important people …. If he arrives *before* the rain starts, he will be killed. If he arrives *after* the rain begins to fall, he will survive the day and the rest of his time in office."

I repeat the message in my head to be certain I can retain the memory of it after I wake. *"March 30, 1981, large gathering of people. President Reagan must not arrive until after the rain starts."*

"Thank you, great uncle. I believe you have done the people of my time a great favor." I can feel my concentration starting to falter. I don't think I can maintain it much longer.

"Which people are yours, young one? *Which* people?" The Prophet's words hang in my thoughts as I let go of my focus. I know I'm about to begin the journey back to my own time, hoping it is much more brief and easy on my spirit.

Everything goes black again. I struggle to find myself, searching for the empty vessel of my body. I try to open my eyes, but my eyelids seem too heavy. I try again, and there's a small point of light trying to break through the blurry fog.

"Samantha, are you alright?" comes a man's voice through the fog.

"Is that you, Great Spirit?" My own voice seems shallow and raspy. "Tell me what you have seen."

The point of light is starting to clarify. "The Prophet has given me the answer I sought. March 30 of 1981. President Reagan is to go to an important meeting with a large group of people. If he arrives at the meeting before the rain, he will be assassinated. If he arrives after the rain starts, he will not." I hope I remembered everything the right way.

"You've done it, Samantha." The voice is excited. "Today, you have done your country a great service." More clarity returns and I can now tell it is *Max's* voice and not Mishe Moneto after all.

My country? After seeing the great Chief Tecumseh and hearing his words … after communicating with the Prophet … Is America truly *my* country?

Chapter 13

KARL

ST. PETERSBURG, RUSSIA
SUNDAY, MARCH 29, 1981

My private line rings at the appointed time, exactly the way I expect.
"Yes."

"The woman you call *Rogue* is on the line, sir." My personal secretary is my constant link to the First Order. Even though she's assigned to assist me, I'm certain her duties include reporting on my activities to the council. When I was chosen as a Knight, I took a new identity, leaving my family and all other connections on Pythos behind. I report to the council, yet I know they don't fully trust me. My secretary – I don't know her real name and she hasn't bothered to give me a fake one – is keeping tabs on me. At least I know *exactly* where her priorities lie.

I can't blame the council for taking precautions, as I have vast funds – First Order funds – at my disposal. As a Knight of Economics, my task is to grow those funds, and no one in the history of the First Order has been able to make a profit the way I have. The more I make, the more they give me to invest, and now I control billions. Some of it is invested here in Russia. I keep this apartment in the heart of St. Petersburg to stay close to my Russian connections. America, however, is the true land of opportunity.

"Connect the call now," I answer, waiting for the usual clicking sound that signals the connection has been made.

"Hello," is all I say at first, wanting to make sure the person on the other end is who it should be.

"Are we still a go?" asks the caller.

"Yes," I respond, now convinced I have the right person. I've relied on Viktor for so long that perhaps he feels a sense of empowerment, thinking I have no other options. It's time to create another option. "I want to confirm that you understand what you're to do?"

"I got it the first time we talked," the caller says confidently.

"I have no faith in Hinckley and want to make sure there is a solid backup. You are certain you will be in position at the proper time?"

"Yes. As you instructed, I'll wait for Hinckley to make an attempt. If he fails, I'll step in."

"And you understand that it's imperative that only Hinckley can be implicated in this? That's an even higher priority than the successful completion of the assignment."

"Relax. I get it. I already found an excellent vantage point where I'll be able to keep an eye on Hinckley." The voice on the phone pauses for a moment. "Are you going pay me in person?"

"No. You and I will not meet," I reply. "This is your first assignment. If you prove yourself on this one, there may be additional business we can do together. Were you able to get into Hinckley's home and inspect his gun?"

"Yes. All is cool on that front. But, there's another issue. I found a pile of letters showing Hinckley's been exchanging notes with at least three people about his plans. Is that anything we should be worried about?"

"Not as long as the authorities cannot connect him to us. They can spend all the time they want tracking down false leads once this all comes to fruition. You were careful to not leave any traces at his home, right?"

"Of course."

"And you know you should try to avoid Medici – at least until the assignment is over." I cannot stress this point enough.

"I can't promise we won't cross paths, but I'm cool with it if we do. I'm not worried at all."

"I'm not suggesting you should be worried, but I'm telling you to be cautious. He's quite good at what he does."

"Then I'll be cautious."

"Very well. Someone from my organization will be in contact with you after the assignment to arrange final payment."

VIKTOR KROSTOV
PUSHKIN, RUSSIA
SUNDAY, MARCH 29, 1981

"We need a change our plans, Katarina. I want you to monitor the operation in Washington."

It was good that Katarina called me. I've been thinking about the two operations and how Karl responded when I told him Katarina would not be going to DC. The benefits of ensuring success with killing the Tyson boy do not outweigh the risks of losing Karl as a client.

"If I'm not in Detroit, I won't be able to back up Halbert. That will make his chances of success much less likely," replies Katarina.

"Karl is acting like he has a new source for the type of work we do. He won't tell me who it is and I don't like the idea of having competition for our services. If you can find out who this new competitor is, it could be quite useful."

"Then I'll be in Washington, stay close to Hinckley, and see what I can discover."

For some reason, she seems happy with this change of plans. I can't imagine why, but don't have time to pursue the issue with her.

V. RAY

Chapter 14

The noise will be vain, the faltering ones bundled up,
The Shaven Ones captured: the all-powerful One elected:
The two Reds and four true crusaders to fail,
Rain troublesome to the powerful Leader.
(Nostradamus Almanac)

MAX MEDICI
WASHINGTON DC, USA
MONDAY, MARCH 30, 1981

Rawhide – our Secret Service codename for President Reagan – sits comfortably on the white sofa in the Oval Office, discussing the conclusion of his speech with Special Assistant, David Fischer. The speech is to be delivered to leaders and key members of the AFL-CIO union. The president has consulted Fischer to leverage his experience in running manufacturing and packaging operations with a unionized labor force.

Rawhide reads his closing paragraph, "I know we can't make things right overnight, but we *will* make them right. Our destiny is not our fate; it is our choice. I'm asking you, as I'm asking all Americans in these months of decision: please join me down this new path. You and your forebears built our nation – now, please, help us rebuild it. Together, we will make America great again."

Fischer says, "It sounds incredible to me, Mr. President. The only suggestion I have is to change join me *down* this new path to join me *as we take* this new path. Down sounds negative."

The president scribbles on his speech and says, "Perfect. Thanks for your time, David."

As Fischer and the president shake hands, I begin to focus on the upcoming meeting.

I'll let no distractions into my life on *this* day. Today will be a day of redemption. I've never forgiven myself for President Kennedy's assassination. I never will. But *atonement* and *redemption* ... those are possible. This is my chance to keep President Reagan from becoming the next victim of Tecumseh's curse. If Samantha's vision was accurate, she may have provided me with the exact opportunity I need. President Reagan is headed to the Washington Hilton today.

March 30, 1981. An important meeting with a large group of people.

"Mr. President, may I have a word?" I ask, keeping the president in the Oval Office a bit longer than he would like. The president reluctantly closes the door behind Fischer and faces me. "Sir, I believe very strongly that there's going to be an attempt upon your life today at this conference. I think it's wise for you to cancel or at least postpone the event."

"Max, this is not an event I can reschedule."

"Then don't go, sir. The Washington Hilton is too accessible. With hotel staff, reporters, and hotel guests, an assassin can easily get close to you."

"I have to be there. The building and construction trades conference is being hosted by the AFL-CIO, and I don't need to tell you they're the largest union in the country. This conference offers a unique opportunity at a critical juncture for our country."

"But —"

"Max, I trust that you and the rest of the Secret Service will take every precaution to ensure my safety." President Reagan has a way of making you feel like you're right, even while you're being convinced to agree with him.

"With all due respect, sir, I don't need to remind you of Tecumseh's curse. This isn't a risk you should take for your own sake or for the sake of this country." I believe the only way to dissuade the president will be to convince him that not going will be better for the country. Yet I have an odd feeling that the president does, in fact, need to be at this luncheon.

"Max, I need to know more before I can make the decision to sacrifice this opportunity. And you only have a couple of minutes before we go."

"I've spent some time with the two recruits we discussed when we first met. One of them had a vision where she was able to gather some intelligence about today's events. The vision was of someone attempting to kill you and the time of your arrival was the deciding factor in whether you live or die. She said if the timing is right and you survive the attack, we'll break the curse. But the prudent action would be to avoid the situation altogether."

Even though I want to convince the president not to go, I'm sensing a long-term gain can be made from this short-term risk. There's so much at stake today. The real question is *can Samantha's vision be trusted?*

"Well, that doesn't sound exactly clear-cut to me. Very few people know about this, Max. But we have evidence of large sums of money flowing from the Soviet Union to several key union leaders. They think they can influence the union through bribery and I *can't* let a socialist agenda of this magnitude go unchallenged. I need to be there." The president, dressed in a navy pinstripe suit, white shirt, and navy tie, seems resolute.

The more I think about it, the more I'm starting to be convinced that the risk involved is worth the potential gains.

"Mr. President, I will do everything in my power to ensure your safety. Judith Tyson, my top agent, is scouting the location and I'll be at your side for the duration."

"We need more people like you, Max. Did you manage to land either of the recruits for your AI team on your trip to Michigan?"

I shake my head. "I don't have a definitive answer for either yet. With the vision warning about today's event, I came back so I could be at your side. I'll be heading back to Michigan as soon as possible to continue evaluating both recruits, and see if I can get them to join AI."

"I hope it goes well." President Reagan checks his watch – a gold Rolex. "Well, it's time to head to the conference. I don't expect a warm welcome, especially if I'm late."

ROGUE

Rogue. That's what Karl calls me. It's a kick-ass name! From this position, I'll be able to see everyone entering and leaving the Washington Hilton. If Hinckley fails, I won't.

MAX MEDICI

Walking just behind and to the right of President Reagan as we exit the White House, we approach the presidential limo. I look up, searching for dark clouds. No rain yet. And it's a very short drive to the conference.

The Prophet said if the president arrives at the meeting before the rain, he will be assassinated. If he arrives after the rain starts, he will not.

"Mr. President!" I need to find a way to delay the president long enough for the rain to start.

President Reagan stops walking, but only turns his head in my direction. "Yes, Max?"

"Sir, I noticed earlier that you're wearing a Rolex. And, well sir, you're going to a union conference with almost all blue-collar workers."

After glancing at his watch, President Reagan turns to face me. "Goodness Max, you're right! There's no sense in giving anyone a reason to initiate a class war. The rest of you wait here. Max, you're with me." The president looks up briefly at the sky as we turn back toward the White House to switch watches. "There's a storm coming."

ROGUE

The skies suddenly darken.

Thick clouds roll in and a steady rain begins to fall. Hmmm, that could help hide a weapon from the sight of the Secret Service agents, but could also mess up Hinckley's aim or mine. I wonder if he'll take the shot while the president is going *into* the hotel or *leaving* it. I'll have to be ready for either possibility.

The president's limo, along with another, arrive at the southern entrance to the Washington Hilton, the only place where there's cover from the rain. As the car pulls near the entrance, police are forced to move the waiting crowd of about thirty onlookers out from under the protection of the large white porte-cochere so the president and his party can enter the hotel unimpeded.

This could be a problem. Casually folding my arms, I place my hand near the gun I'm carrying in a shoulder holster. The gun has a silencer and has been altered to create nearly identical bullet markings to those produced by Hinckley's gun. Even if the FBI performs ballistics testing, the results will match so closely that an expert would find it nearly impossible to identify any differences.

Be calm and be ready. Initially, two Secret Service agents exit the first of the two limos to arrive. They move about, surveying the area to ensure the path is clear and there are no immediate threats to the president. Once they're certain all is clear, they signal to the driver of the first limo, and the president and several others exit the two limos and make their way toward the entrance of the hotel.

Now's the time! Reagan is walking right in the direction of the crowd of onlookers. And Hinckley has himself positioned perfectly. With only one man in front of him, Hinckley is shielded from the view of the police and Secret Service. He just needs to push by the one man to get a clean shot. He won't get a better opportunity than this. Focusing on Hinckley's eyes, I watch as his gaze stays fixed on President Reagan while his hand moves to his weapon. I tense up, ready to draw my own gun should the need arise. Just as Hinckley is about to draw his gun, the one man between him and the president opens his umbrella, completely blocking Hinckley's view of his target. Frustrated by his unsuccessful efforts to look past the umbrella, Hinckley wisely doesn't draw his weapon. As the umbrella is finally fully open and raised above the man's head to expose Hinckley's view, the president is already walking through the entrance of the hotel.

Patience. If it weren't for the idiot with the umbrella, the president would have paused to talk to the crowd, and might have even offered to shake a few hands. It would have been all too easy for Hinckley to kill Reagan, and I wouldn't have to risk exposure. But, now, we'll both have to wait until after his speech.

MAX MEDICI

Pressing the button on my earpiece, I transmit, "Tyson, what's your status?"

I can finally take a moment to contact Agent Judith Tyson now that we have successfully passed through the entrance to the Washington Hilton. With rain being such an important factor in the Prophet's vision, I'm certain that any attempt on the president's life would have to be taken some time during the short walk between the limo and the entrance to the hotel.

Her voice buzzes in my ear, "DC's finest are here in numbers. We had the hotel staff and all the conference attendees pass through a metal detector, as you instructed. There are agents at every entrance to the hotel and the roof is clear. I'm with the hotel security guard in the back office monitoring the security cameras. Do you want me to join you in the conference hall as an extra set of eyes?"

"No, use the security cameras to help us. Stay there, and keep your focus on the hotel entrances and grounds. Notify me if you see anything out of the ordinary. Remember – the Soviets prefer to use a man to do their dirty work, but they'll probably have a woman managing the situation here. Keep an eye out for a nervous man in the crowd and an attractive woman on high ground."

"Yes, sir."

The speech, itself, was uneventful. I hope it was well received, considering all the risks we've taken. After the president finishes shaking hands with the union leaders, I organize my team for the exit.

"Everyone be alert." I direct this message to all agents with transceivers. Now comes the *real* challenge: getting the president out of here alive. Our team is fully briefed on the potential threat against the president, but I save one surprise for our exit. This is just in case the attackers are aware of how the Secret Service would normally escort and protect the president, and there's plenty of pictures and video of just how we do it for them to scour through. The surprise might be just enough to cause them to hesitate and any advantage we can gain could prove pivotal. "Protection pattern *delta.*" It's a rarely used formation, but I trust my team remembers their training.

"Tyson, give me an update." Judith has overseen the situation outside during the speech.

"The press has been told there'll be no comments from the president and no questions will be taken. It was blamed on the rain. They've pretty much dispersed, but there are a few reporters still here. The crowd is about the same. Nothing out of the ordinary."

"Excellent. Keep your eyes on the area around the exit and let me know immediately if you see anything."

"Yes, sir."

ROGUE

Any moment now! Hinckley moves subtly to the side of the man with the umbrella, so that won't get in his way again. I must be ready for anything and I move my hand to within an inch of my gun. Positioned between two large evergreens just northwest of the exit Reagan will be using, this high ground provides an excellent view.

Here they come through the door near Hinckley ...

They're not stopping for comments ...

Wow, Medici's instincts are amazing – just as Karl warned. He's positioned exactly in my line of fire to Reagan, and he has another agent right between Reagan and the crowd. They're not making it easy.

Someone in the crowd yells a question to Reagan, and he's pausing a moment to wave to them ...

Hinckley's opening! He shoves his way past the one man in front of him, draws his gun, and starts shooting.

The first two shots hit other people – looks like a cop and someone walking next to Reagan. Everyone's scrambling and hitting the ground. Here's his chance, but he'll have to hurry. The cops are converging on him ...

Holy shit, the agent in front of Reagan is staying in Hinckley's line of fire, using his body to shield the president. He's been hit. What! He's still standing. I grip my gun, ready to join the fray.

Only another moment or two, and then I see Medici grabbing President Reagan from behind and pushing him into the back of the limo, never giving me a clear shot. The cops have Hinckley and are dragging him down. He's still trying to shoot on the way to the ground.

I have *one* chance at this. I draw my silenced gun, take the only shot I have, and holster the weapon, hoping no one has seen me. I start running away from the scene at the same pace as the few onlookers near where I was hiding. The timing was impeccable, with my shot coinciding perfectly with Hinckley's last errant shot as he was being dragged to the ground. With Max in my line of fire, I had to try a ricochet shot off the limousine. It's armored, so the bullet would bounce instead of embedding in or passing through the metal. I hit where I aimed, but it'd still be a miracle if the bullet struck the president. I can't wait around to see if it connected or not.

I'm sure I won't have to wait too long to find out, as the news of this will be on TV in minutes.

MAX MEDICI

"Max, is the president okay? Are you *both* okay? I'm on my way to you now." I hear Judith scream through the earpiece.

Once the limo doors are closed, I transmit back, "Rawhide is okay. Rawhide is okay."

I yell to the driver, "Get us back to the White House, immediately!"

Turning my attention to the president, I have him secure, lying face down on the back seat of the limo.

"Sir, are you alright?"

We literally dodged a bullet. I pull myself up and off the president, and help him get horizontal and into the seat as the limo pulls away from the hotel.

Reagan grimaces.

"What's wrong, is it your heart?"

In a pained voice, he says, "I think you broke my rib."

The president reaches into his jacket pocket and pulls out a paper napkin. After wiping his lips, the napkin is bloody.

"I must have cut the inside of my mouth," he utters, and then suddenly coughs up frothy blood, indicating a lung injury. The president is in *mortal danger*.

"Mr. President, we're going to G.W. Hospital!"

"Now!" I yell to the driver.

I help the president lean forward to check his back and see blood starting to soak his jacket.

"You've been injured, Mr. President, but we'll get you fixed up in no time." I try to sound as confident as possible as I apply pressure to the wound to stop the bleeding. "Don't move, sir. I'm sure it's painful, but the less you move, the better."

"Tyson!" I yell into my earpiece microphone, "we're going to George Washington University Hospital. Have four agents meet us there, and prepare for our arrival. You stay here to help secure the scene. And get me the tapes from all the security cameras and the press cameras that were there. Stay safe – that shooter may not be working alone!"

Chapter 15

Through hunger, the prey will imprison the wolf,
The assailant outside in extreme distress:
The heir having his youngest sister before him,
The big one does not escape.
(Nostradamus, Michel. The Prophecies. C2:Q82)

TREY TYSON
SHELBY TOWNSHIP, MICHIGAN, USA
MONDAY, MARCH 30, 1981

Another migraine?

The skies directly above me are mostly clear, but dark clouds are rolling in from the south and I see a distant lightning strike. I barely miss a pothole that would have easily blown my tire. Gotta love the roads in Michigan.

My head hasn't started to hurt yet, but I've already gone through a low blood pressure episode, and the white squiggly dots are visible. I'm driving home from school alone. This is the first time the onset of a migraine is starting while I'm driving, and I realize the potential danger if it suddenly hits hard. Usually both Paul and Samantha would be driving home with me from school, but Paul wanted to work late in the computer lab and Sam wasn't at school.

Sam was silent on the drive home from the Pontchartrain Hotel Friday night. She didn't return my calls over the weekend and didn't show up at school today. I hope she's okay. Having sex in the bathroom at school may not have been the brightest idea, but *damn* it felt good.

I have the strangest feeling I should be hurrying home, especially with a potential migraine forming. My 1970 Olds 98 is completely rusted out and has more exposed foam than vinyl on the seats. But it also has a 455 engine and a 4-barrel carburetor, so getting somewhere fast isn't a problem. Paying for the gas, however, *is* a problem. I can see my gas gauge moving toward empty while driving. It's like the Olds should be measured in gallons per mile, not miles per gallon. This thought makes me chuckle aloud and provides a brief distraction from my coming migraine.

I turn on my radio, hoping some music will soothe my head. The five saved stations on my stereo include three that play rock, one for the latest hits, and the one I want now that plays oldies. I press the fifth metal button, hoping to hear one of my favorite Beatles songs, but instead the announcer is reading an urgent news report.

"—been confirmed. There has been an assassination attempt this afternoon at the Washington Hilton. President Reagan was rushed to George Washington University Hospital in Washington, DC. It's not known yet if he's been shot, or even sustained an injury of any kind. Vice President Bush has made no comment, and there's been no comment from the White House yet. Stay tuned, and we will provide updates as they come in. Again, this report has been confirmed. There has been —" I shut the stereo off.

An assassination attempt on the president. Holy shit! This is what Max was worried about and why he had Sam visit her ancestors in the past. Could these abilities Max thinks we have be real? The visions I saw when I had the fight with Dime Time have been playing in my head ever since. And Samantha actually *connected* with her ancestors.

I pull into my driveway and park my car in front of the garage. I'm about to run to the side door nearest the driveway, but am struck suddenly with an odd sinking feeling. *The garage door was left open.* I run back to the garage, make my way past Mom's car, and quickly look to the back of the garage where I last left Sarah's bike. *It's gone!* With a sense of dread, I know right away where to look for it.

I run out of the garage toward the line of shrubs from my dreams. *I'm too late!* I see Sarah's bike on the sidewalk near the shrubs and wonder who fixed her tire. I also see a rusted blue Chevy Nova, the one from my dream, is parked on the opposite side of the street ... near the bike. This *can't* be really happening. My adrenaline kicks in and I break into a full-out sprint.

Suddenly, just as in my dreams, a large man with a thick mustache emerges from behind the tall line of shrubs, and he's carrying Sarah over his shoulder. She isn't fighting him, or even moving. *That can't be good.* It's easy to calculate that the man will be in the car and driving away before I can reach them. I push even harder, hoping the kidnapper will trip, or Sarah will find a way to break free or at least stall him. Just about halfway between my house and the Nova, I see it. A grapefruit-sized rock in the street that seems too big, too out of place, to be real. I don't think I have time to stop or even slow down to pick up the rock carefully. The man will be gone with my sister if my timing isn't perfect.

My vision morphs suddenly into four views again – reality, along with three alternate realities. Time slows around me so much that the man with the mustache seems to almost stop in place as my views of the alternate realities play out in my mind.

I scan through them. This time starting with the third reality, hoping I guess at the best one. I see myself sprinting along the road, angle left toward the rock, and reach down with my left hand to grab the rock on the run. This is the most direct path, but I fumble the rock and instantly know I've lost my only opportunity to save my sister in this reality.

The middle reality is almost identical. However, this time I take a slightly larger angle away from the car, so I can get my dominant right hand around the rock. *A clean scoop!*

I don't bother to focus on the first reality, and alter my angle of approach to allow my right hand to scoop the rock up cleanly while I maintain full running speed.

I bend over and grab the rock without slowing my pace. *It worked!* Now comes the throw.

My vision morphs again, but into just a primary view of the real-time world around me and one alternate view of potential outcomes. I hold the rock with both hands as I run, knowing I can't afford to drop it. I'm beginning to trust these visions.

Even while knowing there's a chance the throw could kill Sarah, I have no choice but to take a shot. The man with the mustache must be the person police are seeking related to several missing young girls in the area. The story's been all over the news. *None* of the girls have been found, dead or alive.

I cock the large rock just over my shoulder. He's reached the car with Sarah – it's now or never. Just as I'm about to heave the rock, my vision of the alternate reality grabs my attention. It shows the rock whizzing by the man's head, narrowly missing, and crashing on the street just beyond the Nova. *Wait.* The man looks right at me. There's no surprise in his face when he sees me, but he hurriedly opens the Nova's door and prepares to toss Sarah onto the seat.

The alternate reality view now shows the rock heading for the man's head, but at the last moment he sees it coming and he shifts Sarah around as a shield. I quickly turn my attention away from this reality. *Wait.* Much faster than I could have imagined, the man tosses Sarah's 5' tall, 90-pound body into the car, and jumps in right behind her. *Noooo!*

I quickly return my attention to my vision, desperately seeking some sort of hope. To my utter surprise it shows the result I want. In a leap of faith, I immediately hurl the rock with all my might. My lungs are starting to ache. I'm not sure if I've been remembering to breathe, but I keep sprinting behind the launched rock. A hand comes into view to close the car door. *No wait,* he's not closing the door. *He has a gun.* It doesn't matter. I can't afford to slow down. The man peeks out to aim before shooting, and just as he does, the rock connects with the middle of his face.

The rock hits with such force that the dull, squishy sound of his head crushing inward is worse than the sight of the blood exploding from his scalp. The man falls out of the car and hits the pavement with no attempt to break his fall.

When I reach them, I feel no need or desire to check for the man's pulse. I hurriedly push his legs the rest of the way out of the car to reach Sarah, hoping beyond hope that she's not hurt. Amazingly, she's breathing. She has a pulse, and seems unharmed. The relief … the elation I feel overwhelms me. I hug her to my chest and don't even try to hold back the tears. She's out cold, probably drugged.

Beyond my awareness, one of the neighbors had witnessed the whole event and called the police, while I sat in the car holding Sarah, shaking from the thought of what might have happened to her.

Eventually, several police cars arrive to investigate the crime scene. The police find the gun under the Nova. They search the vehicle next. With shock and horror, they discover the body of another 13-year-old girl about the same size as Sarah. She's wrapped in plastic and duct tape, lying dead in the man's trunk.

"I think we have a name," announces one of the officers who had been looking through the glove box and pulled out what appeared to be a registration slip. "Halbert Curry."

Chapter 16

MAX MEDICI

WASHINGTON DC, USA
MONDAY, MARCH 30, 1981

I've stayed by the president's side from the limousine to the emergency room, the operating room, and now the recovery room. Praying for good news. Waiting and waiting. Finally, at 6:30pm, my hope comes to fruition as the president awakes from the surgery where doctors removed the bullet.

Rainbow – our codename for Nancy Reagan – arrived shortly after Rawhide was admitted and stands on the other side of the hospital bed with her hand placed lovingly on the president's forehead.

It takes a moment for the president to focus his eyes and mine are the first they find.

"President Reagan, you're in recovery here at the hospital. How are you feeling?" I ask.

"How are the others doing?" The president speaks softly, still groggy. We heard about the three other shooting victims on the ride to the hospital. It was the last thing the president said before collapsing near the entrance of the hospital – the same question – *how are the others doing?*

"We won't know about James Brady for some time, but the injuries to Officer Delahanty and Agent McCarthy do not appear to be life-threatening. You should know, sir, that while there were many agents and officers who responded bravely during the attempt, Agent McCarthy purposefully stood between the shooter and you. He took a bullet to protect you, sir."

"Max, I don't think I'd be here right now if it weren't them or for you."

"I'm just glad to have you back with us. You gave us a scare there for a while."

"Nancy," the president turns to face his wife, "from now on, make sure you call Max to confirm anything your psychics say."

She raises her eyebrows a bit and smiles at me noncommittally.

"I'd like some time alone with my wife, Max. Have the other agents wait outside the door and you should be getting home to your family as well …. On your way out, please visit with Jim's family and let them know that he's in my prayers."

"I will, Mr. President. You stay safe." I don't have any family waiting at home, but the president obviously doesn't know that. Challenging times like these are when family is most important. I haven't allowed myself to love or even trust again, since Katarina. After all these years, she still affects me.

Chapter 17

KATARINA KROSTOV
WASHINGTON DC, USA
MONDAY, MARCH 30, 1981

This all seems so wrong. I chartered a flight on a small single propeller plane from Detroit City Airport to Frederick Municipal Airport to the northwest of Washington, DC. The entire trip, I've been wondering if I'm on the right side of this war.

After the assassination attempt, I drove my rental car through a steady rain back to the airport in Frederick. I found a pay phone and established a secure line to my brother.

"I have news about both operations." There is no emotion left in my voice.

"I already know that Reagan has been shot," Viktor's tone gives away his foul mood. "They sssay in the news that he is expected to recover quickly. Karl will not be pleased by this. Is there any way he could know that you were there to monitor the situation?"

"No, I wore a disguise."

"Good. In a way, this failure should make us look better to Karl. After all, killing Kennedy was not perfect but at least we killed him. Without us involved, Reagan lived. Now, tell me what happened with the Tyson boy?"

"Halbert never reported back to me and I don't sense his presence any more. I'll head back to Michigan to find out the details, but I strongly suspect it was a failure." I don't imagine that this news will help Viktor's mood.

"Trey Tyson was the reason we didn't help Karl. And that was a failure?"

"The original plan was to run both operations simultaneously to make sure Medici couldn't be in two places at once, but that also meant that I couldn't be at both places either. *You* are the one who told me to go to DC. I had to leave the fate of the Tyson boy in the hands of a dim-witted psychopath." I've only felt defensive with Viktor once before, when I finally returned to St. Petersburg after Kennedy's assassination and my incarceration. "Do you want me to set up another operation to address the boy?"

"No," Viktor says after a moment to think. "We will leave him be for now. If he decides to join Medici's group, we can deal with him then."

Chapter 18

MAX MEDICI
WASHINGTON DC, USA
MONDAY, MARCH 30, 1981

Judith raps on my open office door as she enters. My best and most gifted agent, she's my cousin Helen's oldest daughter. At 23, she's not only mentally gifted, but she easily passed the Service's physical testing. Tall and athletic with auburn hair, she looks more like her father, Thomas, than Helen.

"How's the president?" she asks.

"He's been shot. Not so great – he nearly died." I'm weary from the long day and shouldn't take it out on Judith, but she's the fifth person to ask me that question in the last hour.

"I need to talk with you," she says.

"Have a seat." While I keep an office in DC, I don't use it very often. I primarily work at the White House or travel for advance scouting, staff recruitment, or intelligence gathering.

My office is very different from other Secret Service agents. Most agents have family pictures or projects from their kids on their walls and desk. I have shelves full of books, a few scattered files, but not one picture. I see Judith glancing at my collection – books in mathematics, history, biographies, chemistry, physics, philosophy – and any other subject that held interest. Her eyes then move to the book in my hand. It's from one of my mentors … the man who helped me to solve my stuttering problem … the man who started me down the path that led to my current position in AI. Amazing that he took the time to help me when he was usually busy solving some of the most complex problems the world has ever known. I wish I could ask his advice now.

"You're reading the Theory of Relativity? For fun?" she asks

"Albert Einstein was able to solve incredibly complex problems with simple thought experiments. He spent the last half of his life trying to find common ground between the two most important theories in physics. Something he said once will always stick with me. 'It's not the knowledge or wisdom we lack, but the *imagination* required to bridge the gap between the Theories of Relativity and Quantum Physics.' I'm hoping his book will give me some inspiration. I don't believe for a second that Hinckley acted alone."

"Do you think Einstein would be able to figure out who's really behind today's mess?" she asks, still standing.

"Oh, I think I know who's behind this." My answer causes her to raise an eyebrow.

"Who, this Karl you keep telling us about?"

"Yes. This is exactly the type of thing he'd do. Why don't you sit?"

"Thanks, Max. But I can't stay. I need to head to the airport to catch a flight. I've seen the reports that the president is already in recovery. What a huge success on your part to get him to the hospital and keep him alive."

"Success?" I stand to emphasize my point. "Are you kidding me? Any time the president gets shot, it's a huge *failure* for the Secret Service. If it weren't for Agent McCarthy, today's events could have turned out very differently. We're extremely fortunate President Reagan survived." I don't want to beat her up too badly over her comment, but I want to be sure that Judith understands the gravity of our position. "I'd like to start reviewing the hotel's video tapes immediately. We need to find out who was behind this before the trail goes cold."

"Unfortunately," Judith says, "the FBI's taken all of the originals for their investigation. The field agent said he'd make us copies, but it'll be a few days."

"A few days? We'll see about that. I'll have them by tomorrow."

"There's a little bit of good news, though. On one of the panning security camera feeds, not long before all of this went down, there was a brief glimpse of a tall, thin woman with dark hair. She was standing between the main hotel entrance and the side entrance the president used. She caught my eye because she was wearing dark sunglasses and you know how cloudy it was. It seemed like she was watching the area where Hinckley was standing. But between the rain and the poor camera quality, the video was too obscured to make any positive identification."

Katarina? My mind jumps to that conclusion immediately and my heart skips a beat.

"Very intriguing." That's as much as I'm willing to share with Judith until I know more. I force myself to relax and take my seat again. "Where are you off to? What could possibly be more important than investigating today's events?"

"It's a family crisis," Judith says, worry in her eyes. "I need to head back to Michigan for a couple of days. Someone tried to kidnap Sarah today. Trey stopped it all from happening." She glances at her watch. "I should be going. I still have to go home and pack."

"Is he alright?"

"They're *both* alright, but I still think it's important for me to be there."

Perhaps the best way to investigate what happened to President Reagan is to investigate what happened to the Tyson family. The two events may well be related if they planned them to occur on the same day, knowing I couldn't be in two places at once.

"Absolutely," I say. "I may only be your mother's cousin, but your family is my family … and I'm coming with you."

Chapter 19

MAX MEDICI
MOUNT CLEMENS, MICHIGAN, USA
TUESDAY, MARCH 31, 1981

After we landed in Detroit, and found Michigan's typically cold weather had returned, Judith and I went in separate directions. She headed straight to her family's house in Shelby Township, while I arranged to meet the county sheriff in Mount Clemens.

"Thanks for allowing me to pick your brain about your investigation, Sheriff Flynn," I say as I sit in a wooden chair across a steel gray desk from the sheriff, squinting my eyes as the morning sun shines through the small single window in the office and directly into my face. If this chair placement isn't on purpose, it's an extremely fortunate accident. I can only imagine a suspect sitting here with that sunshine in his face and being grilled by the large and gruff sheriff.

"We don't have a lot to share yet, Agent Medici. But when you said our case may be related to the assassination attempt on President Reagan ... well, I don't see how they can be related, but I'm glad to help any way I can."

I nod in gratitude to the sheriff. "What can you tell me about the perpetrator?"

"We were lucky to get a name. Hell, we were lucky to get a dead perp, frankly. His name's Halbert Curry. Just sounds Southern, don't it?"

The sheriff pauses for an answer, but I assume the question is rhetorical, so don't offer one.

He continues, "Well, he didn't have any ID on his body, but we found his car registration – and he had Arkansas plates. Curry tried to kidnap Sarah Tyson and he most likely would have killed her if her brother didn't intervene. We found the body of a young girl, the same age and with similar features to the Tyson girl, in the trunk of the car Curry was driving. It appears this freak had a taste for this kind of thing. There are five missing girls reported in the area that fit the same description. And we've already been in touch with Arkansas authorities. They say there are 14 young girls that have gone missing over the last several years in their state. And their caseload stopped growing just before our cases started."

"Does Curry have any known associates?" I ask.

"Not that we've been able to track down yet. There isn't even a record of him being in Michigan. His car is from Arkansas. We found out he'd been staying at a motel and paying with cash."

"Can you make me a copy of the phone records from the motel?"

"We checked that already. The motel operator said Curry had been there nearly a month now. But he didn't use the phone at all. Not once."

A dead end ... *damn.* "Have you checked his room for fingerprints?"

"Not yet," the sheriff replies. "But we have it taped off so no one else can get in there until we can dust it down."

"Who called the police yesterday when all of this happened?"

"It was Mrs. Sandra Nagy. It happened right in front of her house."

"What did she report to the officer at the scene?"

The sheriff locates the report on his desk and reviews it as he answers me, "She reported seeing a suspicious car parked across the street from her house with a stranger sitting in it for over an hour. She said it made her nervous, so she kept checking out the front window, hoping it would be gone. The last time she checked out her window, she saw Curry carrying the Tyson girl to his car. Mrs. Nagy watched him throw the girl into his car. She said she was torn about whether to go to her phone in her kitchen to call the police, or stay by her front window to try to get a license plate number as he drove off. Choosing to stay by the window, she watched as Curry leaned out of his car with a gun. Then she saw a large rock hit him in the face and kill him. She looked to see where the rock came from and it was the victim's brother, Trey Tyson, running like crazy to the car. Mrs. Nagy said that rock throw was one in a million."

Hmmm, *very interesting.*

"Here's my card, sheriff. Please call me after you dust the motel room if you find any fingerprints other than those of Curry or any of the motel staff. Or if you locate anyone who knew this guy that we can question."

"I sure will," he says while standing and extending his hand.

"Thanks, Sheriff."

Chapter 20

MAX MEDICI
SHELBY TOWNSHIP, MICHIGAN, USA
TUESDAY, MARCH 31, 1981

After having dinner with the Tyson family at their home, I asked Trey if we could talk privately and he showed me into his father's home office. I can't help but notice that the office looks as though Thomas is still alive and using it every night. Nearly the polar opposite of my office, Thomas kept his desk organized and stacked his shelves with family pictures. Many are of Trey with his twin brother, Paul, in various sports and activities. There's Paul as president of the school computer club and another of him as president of the school chess club. Trey has a few showing him as captain of the football and basketball teams, and one of him and Thomas on the golf course. Quite a few show young Sarah growing up. Apparently, Thomas and Helen took more pictures of their baby girl than their eldest. I only see one picture of Judith, standing alone in her blue high school graduation cap and gown.

"That was a wonderful dinner, Trey. Thanks for taking the time to talk. From what I've heard, it sounds like you had quite an eventful afternoon yesterday. How is Sarah?"

After sitting in his father's chair, Trey's piercing blue eyes focus on mine. "She's going to be fine. Fortunately, she only remembers being pulled off her bike and having a cloth shoved in her face. When I saw them down the street, I was so worried she'd been hurt or even … killed. Thank God it was only chloroform that knocked her out."

"Tell me, Trey. How did you manage to stop the guy?" I'm studying the boy, trying to learn something from the way he reacts to my questions. There's so much he doesn't know … so much he *can't* know.

"There weren't many options at the time. I saw what was happening and started running, and there was this rock. I scooped it up and threw it at him," Trey shrugs. "It was really dumb luck that it hit him at all. I don't really want to dwell on it, though. Seeing someone die, even if it was someone trying to hurt my sister, was awful."

"I understand and I don't want you to dwell on it either. In fact, I'd like to talk about something entirely different." I suspect it's going to be challenging to get Trey to join my team. I can only show him this option. He must choose his own path. "Trey, I'd like to have a conversation about your future. What do you want to *do* with your life? Any thoughts on a university? What about a career choice?"

Trey seems calm. "Believe it or not, Max, I have given this some thought. While I know my dad, if he were alive, would want me to choose my own path, I have a great opportunity to go to where he taught. The University of Michigan has offered me a full ride football scholarship. Missing Dad's income for our family has made things very difficult for Mom. So even though I was prepared to work my way through college, now that I have this scholarship Mom won't have to worry about helping to pay for my education."

"That's wonderful," I say, but am not so sure it is very wonderful. "What are you going to study?"

"I have so many areas that interest me, but I definitely want to do something in electronics and computers. The potential there is unbelievable."

I should have known he'd be prepared for this. "Football is a high-risk career, but I have no doubt you'll succeed at it. I've seen you play and your coaches think the world of you. Personally, I think you'd make an outstanding running back. I asked your head coach once why he played you at safety instead. He said he could easily play you at running back, wide receiver, or cornerback. However, he said he sleeps better at night knowing you're the last line of defense at safety."

Trey nods, smiling, and says, "That's nice of Coach to say that."

"From what I've seen, your real strengths are your vision of the whole field and that you never give up. Those are the exact same strengths that would help you excel with my group. I can see you've put some thought into your future, but you should take your time with this decision. It will set the course for your entire life."

"I just know when something feels right. You're not going to tell me that the University of Michigan is a bad decision, are you?" Trey asks.

"No," I shake my head, emphatically, while smiling. "Going to Michigan is certainly not a bad decision, but you have another option that you haven't heard enough about yet. And I think it's important for you to consider this before jumping to any conclusions so quickly."

"What are you talking about?" Trey's interest is piqued, but I'm not sure I can sway him from football. Still ... have to try.

I reach into my inner jacket pocket and pull out an envelope. Carefully removing a letter from the envelope, I hand it to Trey to read.

Trey takes his time, reads the entire letter, then starts at the beginning and reads it again. "What's this – a recommendation letter from Senator Levin to gain admittance to West Point? But I haven't even applied to West Point. And I certainly haven't met Senator Levin."

"That may be true, Trey, but Senator Levin is fully aware of who you are. Being Judith's brother obviously helps. People in Washington have had their eye on you for quite some time." He's at least intrigued. I can tell I'm making an impact. "Do you remember the first time we met?"

Trey thinks for a moment before answering. "Sure. I was in seventh grade. My family had just moved, and you started recruiting Judith. Mom told me you're her cousin, but said you never were very close with her."

"That was *not* the first time we met." I pause to give Trey a chance to dig through his memories. "Think back to when you were nine years old. Do you remember a couple of men in dark suits visiting your home? We became acutely aware of you, based on some test results as well as your ancestry. But, I have to give you some background for you to fully understand what I'm about to say."

"Okay." Trey leans back. He's curious.

"When I was your age, America was fighting World War II. Throughout the war, and especially with the race to build the first atomic bomb, the military was reminded that wars could be won or even avoided with advanced technology. We took that lesson to heart. By the '60s, it was anticipated that science, math, electronics, and even computers would be the first line of offense and defense for our country. To meet that challenge, we started introducing these subjects in all our schools. Moreover, we set up comprehensive early testing for kids. The goal of the testing was to identify exceptional students with the potential to move into leadership roles in the military or those with advanced technology abilities. You took the early tests in 1973, and were one of 19 kids in the country to answer every question correctly. Is this starting to ring a bell?"

"Yes! After that, I was taken to Selfridge Air Force Base and was told I was taking part two of the test with a group of other kids. It didn't seem like too big of a deal, and I was glad Samantha was there with me. I always wondered what that was all about."

"Let me tell you, Trey. The part-two questions would have stumped most university professors even if they didn't have a time limit to take the test. The students taking it *did* have a time limit, and you were never supposed to be able to finish it. You not only solved every problem correctly, but you did it in half the allotted time. The test administrators had never seen anything like it. They figured your IQ was off the charts, and they brought me in to observe you more closely. I discussed your situation with your parents, and discovered your older sister, Judith, showed similar traits. I told your parents they shouldn't tell you about your gifts. Our studies showed that if young students know they're gifted, they often end up putting less effort into their education. But I think with your career choices in front of you now, it's important for you to fully understand your abilities and what they could mean for our country."

"Max, can you tell me more about what you and Judith do?" He's intrigued, but he has some reservations.

"I can't get into the specific details of what we do until you join the group and obtain your security clearances. In general, we use all the abilities of our team members to ensure the safety of the president and other key individuals within our government. Trey, I want you to go to West Point, learn from the best, and then join my team."

Trey shakes his head slowly. "There are tons of bright kids in the country. In fact, several students in my school are at least my academic equal. My IQ is no reason to have someone with your background spend so much time getting to know me. Even being my mom's cousin … there has to be more to it than that."

"Don't sell yourself short. I spent some time with Albert Einstein years ago. You're the only person we've ever tested whose IQ would be comparable to his. And it's the quickness of your mind that is most intriguing to me. If you have the abilities I believe you have, then it's your quick mind that will set you apart from anyone else with the same abilities. It comes down to being able to process all the information available to you in time to act upon it. That's what I believe is so unique about you." I pause for a few seconds to see if Trey will open up about his abilities.

Not yet.

He just shrugs, so I'll have to be more direct.

"Trey, I'd like to know if you used any special ability to save Sarah. Something you haven't talked about yet. You saw what happened at the hotel with Samantha, so I think you understand the type of abilities I'm hoping to find in you. Did you have a vision of what to do just before you did it?"

He's struggling with what to say. There's something he's not telling me.

"Max, I know why you're asking me that question. You want Samantha and me to join you and Judith. But I have to tell you that it's not the right path for me."

I look across the desk and straight into Trey's eyes. He didn't actually answer my question. "What you did was nothing short of heroic. Throwing a rock at a serial killer with a gun – what if you missed?"

"At the time, I had no idea he had a gun. But, it didn't matter. I had to do whatever I could to make sure he didn't take Sarah."

"Think about it, Trey. How would yesterday have turned out if you hadn't been here to save Sarah? Don't you think you have too much to offer your country to turn away from your abilities? I need you on my team. Your country needs you. What do you say?"

"I heard about your day yesterday on the radio," Trey responds, his deep voice more serious than usual, "and I'm guessing things would have turned out much worse for the president if you hadn't been there. I understand the importance of what you and Judith do, and I admire your desire to serve our country." He takes a deep breath, running his fingers through his black hair. "When I envision my future, I see my university years. I see myself playing safety on Michigan's football team. And who knows, maybe even having a career in the NFL. If not that, then something in technology. I'd like to run my own company someday. I don't see myself in the government establishment at all. It's just not me. I think, as well as you know me, that you probably understand that about me already. If there comes a day when I can serve my country in some capacity *after* I've completed my education and *without* having to join the government – well, I won't close the door to that possibility."

He's made his decision and he's going to stick to it, no matter what I say. "As I said, Trey. You have obviously put some thought into your future. True success in life comes from finding and enjoying the path you choose to achieve your goals. I'll respect your decision. And I'm glad you've left open the door to the possibility of joining the Service. I have a feeling the opportunity to do so will present itself someday. Before I head back to Washington, I'd like to visit with Samantha. Do you know if she's home today?"

Trey looks to the side for a moment, then says, "I called her house earlier. Her mom said she suddenly packed her stuff and moved to Canada to live with her aunt."

That's odd timing.

"I know her aunt and how to reach her. Thanks, and you stay safe."

PART 3—1999

V. Ray

Chapter 21

KARL

St. Petersburg, Russia

Tuesday, August 17, 1999

August is by far the most splendid month in St. Petersburg. Since moving into an estate outside of the city, I haven't spent nearly enough time enjoying the culture the former capital offers. With today's events, I needed to be in the heart of the city to gauge the reaction of the Russian people.

Ozzie accompanied me this morning on a stroll along the Neva where we passed the Winter Palace and soon found a lovely café where we ate a late breakfast as we watched the news. As a bodyguard, Ozzie has served quite well, but he lacks the intellect and natural curiosity of the world around him to be a satisfactory companion. We ate in silence during the news coverage of the spaceship Cassini's flyby of Earth.

Ozzie barely raised an eyebrow when the newscaster announced how fortunate we all are that the American space shuttle Atlantis was able to nudge Cassini into the proper orbit. Flying off course, the Cassini would have entered the Earth's atmosphere, possibly breaking apart and spreading a toxin in our air that could have killed everyone. Can he truly bet that stupid? Doesn't Ozzie understand just how close we were to being wiped out as a species?

I asked him what he thought about the fact that no one in the news mentioned the Cassini was off course *before* the mission to save our planet had been successful. Ozzie shrugged, chewing his croissant and staring vapidly around for anyone who might attack me. A single task for a single-minded dimwit. The job fits him and he fits the job. I just wish he were less boring.

I miss having Khan with me and Sir Archimedes is away on an assignment in America. Archimedes has been my Beta Knight for three years and he's earned both my respect and my trust with his diligence. The First Order council allowed me to choose between several candidates on Pythos Island. The council puts all Beta Knight candidates through stringent testing, and shares the results with Alphas, like myself, who then choose a Beta. Archimedes wasn't the fastest. Not the strongest. Not the bravest. He's not adept at using weapons. He doesn't even know how to make a fist the right way.

I chose him for other reasons.

And, I gave him his name.

Sir Archimedes. He was the smartest knight candidate we've tested since ... well, since me. And, he's more cunning than most. He understands the importance of details and timeliness.

I didn't need a Knight of War or a Knight of Leadership. A Knight of Science may have served, but I needed someone to take the vast wealth I've built for the First Order and grow it. To be a trusty Beta and to learn from me. I needed a Knight of Economics.

Now that we're back home, I had Ozzie get Archimedes on the telephone.

"Sir Archie, how are my enterprises in America?"

He hesitates for a moment before answering in his nasally voice, "Sir Karl. You mean, of course, the First Order's enterprises."

What's this – his first hint of independence?

"I've been running First Order enterprises outside of Pythos long before you were even born. I founded them, ran them, and through *my* hard work, I made them hugely successful. So, I hardly find it inappropriate to call them *my* enterprises."

"Of course, Sir Karl. I apologize."

Much better tone from a Beta.

"I have a few things I need you to handle. First, when Khan returns from his trip, he'll need his paperwork updated. The details, Archie, remember the details. He'll need an entirely new wardrobe as well. You know how much he hates to wear the same outfit twice."

Silence on the other end of the phone, but I imagine Archie is rolling his eyes.

"Understand?" I ask.

"Yes. Of course. The prince doesn't like to wear the same thing twice. Anything else?"

"There's a software company based out of Detroit called Global Positioning Corporation, or GPC. I want you to acquire it."

"GPC," he says. "I've heard of them. What are my budget constraints – how much are you willing to spend to get them?"

Laughing, I say, "There's no budget on this one. We must have this company and it's even more imperative that the software engineers are part of the deal. Naturally, I trust that you'll make the best deal you can, but do what you have to do to acquire GPC."

"What if the owners won't sell it?" he asks.

Archie has an affinity for classic American movies. He spends all his free time at the movie theatres or renting movies at his house. Our society on Pythos has nothing to compare to Hollywood, so his fascination is hardly surprising.

"You've seen *The Godfather*, right? Make them an offer they can't refuse."

CHAPTER 22

TREY TYSON
TAMPA, FLORIDA, USA
TUESDAY, AUGUST 17, 1999

"I think you got another two or three seasons in you, Trey. You sure you want to do this?" Coach Raphael Wilkins whispers in my ear. He coached defensive backs for the last couple seasons of my career.

With the applause after my college coach, Bo Schembechler, just finished an overly gracious speech about my accomplishments as a Wolverine player and student, my attempt to whisper is closer to yelling, "I'm sure."

"But we just built a new stadium for you," Coach Wilkins says.

Laughing, I say, "I've had a great 13 years in the league, but it's time."

Raymond James Stadium is brand new and it's beautiful, but that doesn't change my mind. We're set up on the corner of the field with a couple of cameras and a few dozen people in the stands. The Florida sun at 10am isn't beating down too hard yet.

While Coach Wilkins walks to the podium, I glance through the small crowd of reporters, former teammates, family, and friends. Mom, Paul, and Sarah are in the front row, but Max has Judith on an assignment in Europe. Samantha joined Max's team at AI after we graduated from university, but she could make it and sits next to Paul. She had taken a year off from high school to spend with her family in Canada in 1981, so she graduated a year after I did.

Bo walks over to where I'm standing and shakes my hand.

"Thanks, Coach. What you said was very kind. After what I did in college, I wasn't sure you'd ever forgive me. Thanks for being here."

"Trey," he says in his raspy voice, "a lot of great players have played at Michigan. Many have had great careers in the NFL. And a few have gone on to do something great after football. Every single one of them has made a mistake in their life at some point. We all do. The best of us learn from our mistakes. That's what I expect from you. We worked hard. We won games. We hung banners. We won awards. Now, it's time to pay it forward."

"I'll do my best, Coach. You going back for the first game?"

"I won't be in the stands," he says, "but I wouldn't miss a game against Notre Dame. Coach Carr says his senior quarterback, this Tom Brady, may be something special. I'll be watching."

Bo shakes my hand again and heads for the tunnel to the locker rooms.

Coach Wilkins, with a group of five microphones facing him on the podium, starts by saying, "In 1995, when we traded for Trey Tyson, we knew we were getting a winner. Big Ten championships in three of his four years at Michigan. A three-time All-American safety for the Wolverines. Drafted in the first round by the 49ers, he went on to win three Super Bowls with them. Overall in his NFL career, Trey has more interceptions than anyone in the history of the league. He's been to 13 Pro Bowls, has been an All Pro 12 of his 13 years, and won the league MVP twice. He brought that passion to win with him here in Tampa. We'll miss him on the Bucs. We'll miss him in the NFL. But, we haven't heard the last of Trey Tyson. He's not the type to retire quietly and stay in the background. You all know I wear my religion on my sleeve."

Turning to me, he continues, "It's been a luxury having you play safety on our defense, Trey. But, God has a plan for you. Find what it is and go do it."

I bow my head briefly and smile as the small crowd erupts in applause again.

Coach grabs one of the microphones and says, "Before you go, Trey, come on up here and say a few words."

As I walk up to the podium, Coach meets me halfway and embraces me.

He whispers, "Don't be afraid to cry, son. They all do."

"Thanks, Coach. You're the best."

I can't count the number of times I've stood at a podium and answered questions for the press about a football game. That was always easy. But, talking about myself is another story altogether.

As the applause dies down, one of Bucs' linemen runs up and grabs a microphone.

Turning to team owner, Malcolm Glazer, he yells, "Pay the man. We need him on our team. Just double his salary!"

A raucous applause breaks out and Mr. Glazer shrugs, saying, "I tried, but he already has more money than me."

When the laughter finally fades, I say, "Thank you, Mr. Glazer for all of your support. I've been truly fortunate in having some the best coaches in the history of football. I've had the best teammates and we've won a lot of games over the years. The fans here in Tampa –"

At this, I pause and let the crowd applaud before continuing, "And, we've had great fans in San Fran and Ann Arbor, too. Most of all, I want to thank my family for always being there for me. Mom, Paul, Sarah, Judith ... and Sam. You're family, too. I love you all. Thank you from the bottom of my heart." I wish Dad could be here. I wish Max could be here, too. I know he would be if he could.

CHAPTER 23

The year one thousand nine hundred ninety-nine, seven months.
From the sky will come a great king of terror.
To resuscitate the great king of the Mongols.
Before and after Mars, to reign in good fortune.
(Nostradamus, Michel. The Prophecies. C10:Q72)

MAX MEDICI

HOUSTON, TEXAS, USA
TUESDAY, AUGUST 17, 1999

What an exhausting day. Eagle – our codename for President Bill Clinton – has had a couple month break in his typically chaotic international travel schedule. He had time to visit NASA's Johnson Space Center here in Houston to witness the flight of the Cassini spacecraft on its historic journey to Saturn.

I flew into the new George Bush Intercontinental Airport yesterday to scout the space center and the president's hotel before Eagle's arrival this morning. While I found no direct threat to the president, I was shocked to learn of a threat to our entire planet. NASA had the Cassini routed to orbit Earth in a slingshot maneuver to use our gravity to boost the spaceship's speed by 12,000 miles per hour. Cassini's orbit was intended to be 727 miles above Earth's surface, well outside of our atmosphere. But, a slight miscalculation had it speeding much closer to our planet and crossing into the outer edge of our atmosphere.

"Is that a problem?" I asked one of the NASA scientists yesterday.

He studied me for a long moment before answering, "Cassini is powered by 72 pounds of extremely toxic plutonium dioxide. If the ship breaks apart in our atmosphere, the dispersal of plutonium would cover Earth in toxic dust and wipe out almost all life on the planet."

That sure sounded like a problem to me.

"What are you going to do? NASA has to have a contingency plan … right?" I asked.

Another long moment went by before he answered, "We have the space shuttle Atlantis out there. Her pilot is establishing an orbit to line up with the Cassini as it flies by and nudge it away from our atmosphere."

I'm not a rocket scientist, but I could imagine the odds against that working.

"How confident are you this will work?"

"We have our best pilot out there," he said with a little hope in his voice.

"Who?" I asked.

"Commander Lou Sanchez."

Earlier today, Sanchez pulled off the miracle and saved life as we know it on planet Earth. He successfully nudged Cassini into the proper orbit and on its way to Saturn. President Clinton called Sanchez a national hero in an impromptu interview on ABC News tonight. But, the hero still needs to get home, and the most dangerous part of his mission may end up being a forced night landing at Cape Canaveral shortly before midnight.

The guy at NASA said I'd be able to see Sanchez pilot the Atlantis into our atmosphere over the Gulf of Mexico at 11:30pm. I set my alarm and figure I'll catch a little shuteye since I have a couple hours to kill.

As I drift into REM sleep, I begin to dream … a dream I haven't had since I was a teenager.

It's a clear day and the sun is high. Looking at the landscape, there's a great clearing surrounded by a dense jungle. Around the edges of the clearing are several large stone structures. One structure commands my attention – a pyramid near the center of the clearing. The pyramid has columns of steps at the center of the two sides I can see. It doesn't end with a point on top like the Egyptian pyramids. Instead, there is a flat stone plateau with a large four-sided stone temple perched on top. This must be the Mayan pyramid temple of Chichen Itza. I remember seeing a picture of it in a book once when I was a child.

Floating toward the top of the pyramid, I can hear voices emanating from within the stone temple. They are speaking a language I don't recognize, yet the words flow easily and understandably through my mind.

"Votan, you cannot do this!" the first voice commands.

"It is necessary, Kukulkan, my king." As they emerge from the temple, I can see that both men are tall, with bronze-toned skin. The king is heavily muscled and wears a bejeweled gold crown that funnels a mass of long feathers and braided hair up through the crown opening. Atop the crown sits a life-size, clear crystal skull. It makes him appear at least a foot taller than Votan, even though they are about the same height.

Votan and King Kukulkan walk out of the temple to the northern edge of the plateau topping the pyramid. Eight Mayan warriors follow them closely, each dressed in only a hanging loincloth and feathered headdress. The warriors carry long spears with obsidian tips. Votan carries a wooden club that resembles a four-foot long baseball bat. It has a round handle just like a bat, but the other end is flat like an oar. The oar end has obsidian blades on both sides that run half the club's length.

The king walks gracefully with long strides, but appears to have his hands bound behind his back. Thousands of people surround the base of the pyramid. Their attention is directed to the top of the pyramid where King Kukulkan, Votan, and the warriors have stopped walking, and now stand facing the people below. Scanning the crowd, I see the people are emaciated, with dark circles under their eyes. Most have matted hair and hollow cheeks. Some wear loin clothes, while others are naked. They stand in stark contrast to the healthy, robust physiques of Votan and the king.

"People, you *must* hear me!" Votan yells, and then waits impatiently for the crowd to be silent. "As your high priest, I have meditated many times to see the future of our people. For 4000 years, our priests have looked to the future. Not one of us has ever seen past the end of our long count! Today, this shortest of days, we are precisely 1000 years from the day the long count ends."

The shortest of days must mean the winter solstice, December 21.

Votan looks to the skies briefly and then back to the crowd. "We have suffered the wrath of the gods for many years now. There is little water and our crops fail. We have sacrificed many of our enemies, and we have sacrificed many of our own. But the gods are very angry, more than ever before!" Votan's voice is deep and rich, and it projects clearly to everyone in the crowd. "We must *appease* the gods. If nothing changes, I see that we will not make it to the next shortest of days. The gods demand something more from us!"

A voice from the crowd below yells, "Sacrifice!" Another voice follows with, "Yes, sacrifice!" The first man starts chanting, "Sacrifice … Sacrifice …" At first, a few people join in, then a few hundred. After the fifth chant, they all join in, "Sacrifice … Sacrifice!"

Votan raises his free hand, and the chant suddenly becomes softer – but doesn't stop.

"Yes!" Votan's voice rises above the crowd's noise and his eyes dart to the king. "The gods demand a sacrifice greater than ever before! They demand a sacrifice of *royal* blood!"

Again, almost in unison, the crowd shouts, "Sacrifice! Sacrifice!"

Votan raises his bladed club as high as his arms can reach, and waits. The crowd falls silent.

"Do you, King Kukulkan, have anything to say to your people?"

The king leans forward, to the point where I think he might tumble down the pyramid steps. Yet he holds his ground. Facing east, he turns slowly to the north and then the west, glaring at the crowd gathered to see today's sacrifice – his sacrifice. "I *do* have something to say to *my* people!" he shouts in the most savage voice I've ever heard. "Votan is our priest and our prophet, but he cannot see beyond our long count! Not one of our priests or prophets has ever been able to see beyond our long count. However, *I* have seen. I have had a vision! You can sacrifice me to the gods. It matters not, as I am already one of them. If you do this, I shall return! I will appear as a *flame* crossing the sky!"

The king makes an exaggerated turn of his head to the northwest sky. The entire crowd, along with Votan and the warriors, follow his gaze. A comet makes its way slowly across the sky, its tail visible even in the bright mid-day, and blazing a fiery trail toward the ocean. Several gasps can be heard, then utter silence.

Kukulkan returns his gaze to the people below. "Your king shall return as the fiery prince of princes! Great famine will be known by all! Great sacrifice will be made by all! When the long count ends, I shall rule all! I am Ku – Kul – Kaaaaaan!"

The king's vehement screaming of his name ends abruptly – silenced, as the blade of Votan's club, swung with enormous force, hits the back of Kukulkan's neck and lops off his head.

Beeeeep … beeeeep … beeeep!

V. RAY

My alarm goes off before my dream could reach the end I remember seeing as a youth.

Hurrying, I open the glass sliding door behind the thick burgundy curtains and the hot and humid Texas air rushes past me. I step out onto the terrace, trying to rub the sleep from my eyes.

Looking to the southeast, an object with a flaming tail flies through the night sky.

Our national hero, NASA commander and pilot, Lou Sanchez, is on his way home.

PART 4—2012

V. Ray

Chapter 24

KARL

A cold front blew in from the west last week and has been hovering over the entire area, with no sign of easing up. My old bones crave a warmer climate. I should have retired a decade ago, not that the First Order has a pension program.

With enough money stashed away to last several lifetimes, I can quit any time I want. But, where would I go? I have property in Florida, Arizona, and a few other warm places, but I would still be alone. I've been separated from my family for 58 of my 75 years and can't remember the last time I was able to picture any of their faces. The First Order council has had me on a nearly continuous mission in the outer world. Always surrounded by people, but always alone.

At least I have a reliable Beta Knight in Sir Archie.

And I have Khan. All these years since I first met him in Egypt I've been treating him like my own son … the only family I have or will ever have.

The council tells me the Oracle has foreseen an extremely high likelihood of success for my plan, and that's comforting, but that success depends upon precise execution.

I've been working more from my offices in America than my estate in Russia, but getting a truly secure phone connection in either country has become increasingly difficult. Archie, is quite resourceful, however, and helped acquire the equipment we needed to make sure I can have a private conversation with Khan.

"Khan, my splendid son, how are you holding up?" I ask.

"You know how difficult it is for me to get away for a private conversation. We should make this as quick as possible." Khan sounds exasperated.

I know his schedule is endlessly hectic, but he always finds a way to make time for our conversations. He's come so far, yet to me he'll always be that young boy in Egypt I caught trying to steal my watch.

"I know, Khan, I know. I just want to share a quick update that all our plans are progressing well. You will soon be the wealthiest and most powerful man on the planet. And together, we will change the path of the world to suit our needs. The First Order council leaders and I are very proud of you and all that you've accomplished."

"Father?" Khan knows how much I enjoy it when he calls me that. "Yes?"

"I don't just want to *hurt* the Americans. It's not enough. I want to *destroy* their very way of life. I want them all to bow to me – or to die. They destroyed my family and my country. And I will make them pay. *All* of them!"

The fury in Khan has been building for decades and it will not be quelled unless all our plans work out successfully.

"I understand, my son. And we are well on our way to doing just that. Do you remember what I taught you about committing a crime?"

"How could I forget?" he starts. "I may have been a naïve young prince when we first met, but you have reminded me of this often over the last, what? Nearly 50 years. I could rattle this off in my sleep. We need the appropriate target, time, place, expected outcome, escape route, and persona we want to present when committing a crime. And you always tell me that we need a patsy to take the blame."

Pride springs forth in the form of a silent tear that Khan will never see. My boy has surpassed all that I have ever hoped he could become, and I always have very high expectations.

How splendid, indeed.

Chapter 25

TREY TYSON
TROY, MICHIGAN, USA
SATURDAY, OCTOBER 27, 2012

It's the path. The thought causes me to pause before walking through the double mahogany doors at the main entrance of my company's offices. I've recently achieved one of my primary goals in life. It took leveraging my career earnings from football, working hard to build Tyson Search into a global leader in executive search and consulting services, as well as phenomenally successful investment strategies. Thanks to the timely buying and selling of shares of companies like Apple, Qualcomm, and Microsoft, my personal net worth now exceeds $1 billion dollars. I knew the day was coming, but achieving the goal is somewhat bittersweet. Even though it's the company I founded and has my name on the door, I've always planned to retire from Tyson Search when I hit this goal. The day is here, and it's come much sooner than I could reasonably expect.

We all have goals we want to achieve. I feel a sense of nostalgia, walking through these doors for the last time as CEO. My business career has been extremely gratifying, but my heart yearns for something more. The competition in sports was very different from the competition of business. In the end, though, the goal in both is to win. The thrill of success seemed to mean everything, and the agony of defeat truly hurt. My football days are long over and I'm about to put an end to my days of running a business.

True success in life comes from finding and enjoying the path you choose to achieve your goals. I'm trying to remember who said that to me as I walk through the doors and into the lobby. My father? No, maybe it was Max Medici.

I've accomplished many of my goals, and have thoroughly enjoyed the path I've chosen. Now, it's time to forge a new path. Something where competing and winning aren't the only goals. It's time to focus more on giving back.

There are usually at least three or four people in the lobby waiting to be interviewed, but today the room is empty. On the wall hangs a large, framed mirror that many candidates use to do one last visual check before their interviews. I linger briefly to do my own self-evaluation.

It's a big day, old man. Many changes are coming. I try to tame my windblown hair by brushing it with my fingertips. Now, at 48 and with as much salt as pepper in my hair, I think Paul's usual 'old fart' joke seems to finally fit. I have a lot on my plate right now, between packing for my trip, putting my house on the market, and preparing for an important conversation with Sarah.

Another variable just *had* to be thrown into the mix. Roy Starr, CEO of Starr Aerospace, told me on the phone earlier that he wants to have an important and private conversation at some point during tonight's Detroit Pistons basketball game. Roy is hiring a new divisional vice president and has the candidates narrowed down to two. Both candidates have been recruited and represented by my executive search company, and they both are waiting in one of the offices for me to prep them for tonight's final interview at the Piston's game with Roy. I normally would never consider letting a client dictate an interview with two candidates at the same time. And with the plans I have for today, I would allow almost no one to alter them. But Roy has a way about him. He gets what he wants, and he makes you feel as though he's doing you a favor, when, in reality, you're doing a favor for him.

I often have lunch and dinner meetings with Roy, and we frequently share stock market advice with each other. Tyson Search has also been responsible for securing almost every executive in Starr Aerospace as well as Roy's other companies. So, we often have important and private conversations. What seems odd is for Roy to request the conversation with me the day before he knows I'm about to leave for an extended period. There must be some deeper meaning to this than discussing some stock tip or the merits of the candidates we represent.

"Trey, you're here." Sarah comes out from the inner offices and into the lobby to meet me. "The two candidates have been here for about 15 minutes. They're waiting in the same room, just like you asked …. We've never had candidates vying for the same position sit together like this. I'm sure you have a good reason for it, but I'm curious why we're having them wait together?"

"Hey short-stuff." Sarah is barely five feet tall and I have various nicknames for her to remind her of this often. I love all my siblings, but with Sarah, I've always felt an extra need to protect her. When our father died, she was so young … so vulnerable. Judith had already moved out, started her career, and was never that close with our parents. Paul and I have always been very independent. Dad's absence left a huge void in Sarah's life. Dad knew she would be his last child and treated her differently from the rest of us. She was his baby … his last baby. He never really wanted her to grow up. Losing him hit Sarah harder than any of us. But something inside her became stronger along the way. She may appear to be timid, but she's tough when she needs to be. Sarah is smart, and loyal to a fault.

I put my arm around my younger sister, gently steering her back toward the door to the inner offices, and say, "They're both interviewing with Roy Starr tonight. Well, I don't know if I can accurately call this an interview. We're all going to the Piston's game together. I'm not sure what Roy has planned, but I think it's best to give them a chance to get to know each other before the game. At least that will eliminate *one* of the variables for tonight. Have you explained to them how they will be at a social event, but it is in fact still an interview?"

"I have," she nods.

"And while it's important they not come across as too stiff, they do need to take this very seriously?"

"I certainly have, and they both seemed to understand."

"Excellent," I smile, trusting Sarah would handle everything perfectly. It's her nature. "I want to give them some more time on their own, and … I need to have a conversation with you before I leave tonight."

"You mean before you leave for the next two weeks?" Sarah peers into my eyes. She's trying to read me!

"There's more to it than that. Let's step into my office."

Once we're in my office, I sit in one of the guest seats, and motion for her to take my chair. "Please sit down for a minute."

"Okay, I'm officially freaking out now." Sarah looks at me with suspicion. "Why do you want me to sit in *your* chair, Trey?"

"I want to see how comfortable you look in it. You may have to raise it up a bit," I tease with a smile on my face.

"Not funny!" She reluctantly sits in the chair and swivels to face me. "What's going on? You're being more odd than usual. And that says a lot!"

"Sarah, I think it's best if I get right to the point. I'm leaving Tyson Search, effective immediately after tonight's client interviews with Roy."

I scratch my signature on a document, and slide it across the desk to her, rotating it so it so she can easily read it.

"What! Trey, this is *your* company. It's not like you can just quit and walk away."

"You know me better than almost anyone and I'm guessing that you knew this would happen eventually."

"I suppose," she says, a bit sheepishly. "But why now?"

"The timing feels right. And, it's not like we're unprepared for this. Over the last few years, I've lined up account executives to handle all our major accounts, except Starr. Roy has insisted that I personally stay involved with his company. I'll break the news to him tonight. So, the client side will be easy to manage. You're the finance and tax expert. I need you to figure out how to make the transition happen while minimizing costs."

"The costs? Trey, I need some time to absorb all of this. Maybe you do, too. Why are you doing this? Things are going so well the way they are."

I know her well enough to know she only has my best interests in mind. This will be a big adjustment for Sarah, but she can handle it.

"It's my opinion that no one should run any individual organization for too long. You get comfortable with what worked in the past and innovation suffers. It's time for new leadership at Tyson Search. And personally, I'm ready for a new challenge. I spent 17 years playing college and pro football, and another 13 years right here building and running Tyson Search. I've thoroughly enjoyed both phases of my career, but I'm ready for something new. I think I've done what I can with Tyson Search and it's time to hand if off to someone else. *You,* Sarah."

"Trey," she sits introspectively for a moment before continuing, "I'm so flattered that you think I could run your company, but I don't know that I'm ready for that yet."

"Let's be honest, Sarah. You've been running the finance end of the business, and you've filled in for me to run the entire company more and more frequently during the last few years while I've been busy satisfying my need to explore the many wonders of our planet. You work well with all our department and satellite office heads. I … I just haven't had nearly the same fire for the business I once had. With *your* energy, I truly believe the company will reach even greater heights."

"But why me? You have other executives who have been with the firm longer."

"You're bright and energetic. You're responsible and conservative, but you know when a calculated risk may be necessary. You know the business and I trust you completely …. Frankly, that's a hard combination to find these days."

Sarah sits a little taller, the confidence building in her, and I see that she's beginning to warm to the challenge.

"I don't know what to say."

"Say yes. It's that simple." I smile and offer her a pen.

"Okay. *Yes.* And thank you so much for believing in me, Trey." Sarah beams with excitement. She then looks at the document I placed in front of her, and laughs out loud.

"What's so funny?"

"Trey Thomas Tyson. Your *T3* signature always cracks me up."

I laugh as well. "Look, when you sign your name as often as I do, you'd come up with a short version, too!"

"Yes, I know, Mr. NFL superstar with all of your adoring fans after your autograph. I just think it's funny that you never changed it once you started Tyson Search. And now … retiring at 48. What on Earth are you going to do with all your free time?"

"I'm moving back to Florida. I fell in love with the Tampa area while I was playing for the Bucs. I'm going to find a nice piece of waterfront property, build a house, and buy a boat. Then I'm going to play golf for a few months."

"*Golf?* You've got to be kidding, right? There isn't a sport that has *more rules* than golf."

"What's *that* supposed to mean?" Now, it's my turn to be a little shocked.

"Well, you've never exactly been one to worry about rules."

All I can do is raise my eyebrows, dismayed, "Who? Me?"

"You *stole* Dad's car when you were 14."

"*Borrowed!* And, he said I could use it in an emergency."

"The police found you, Paul, and your friends at the drive-in theatre. Since when is going to the movies an emergency?"

"I … I …" I don't have an answer for this.

"You were kicked out of every class you ever had in high school … *even Mom's!*" Sarah has her hands on her hips. I'm starting to think she's become a little *too* courageous. Maybe I prefer the timid little girl of her youth.

"She just did that to use me as an example to the rest of the class. I'm sure she didn't really want to kick me out of her class."

"You were an All American on Michigan's football team, and as a senior your coach suspended you for the Rose Bowl, by far the biggest and most important game of the year. You never told me, but what *rule* did you break to make that happen?"

Her memory's a little too good, as well. I did break a rule and an important one. I was betting on sports, and had an uncanny ability to pick winners. Not only was it illegal, but it broke the number one rule of the NCAA … and the number one rule of our coach, Bo Schembechler. I started off small, but the more I won the bigger my bets got to be. There I was, about to fly with my team to Pasadena, and my bookie was so in debt to me that he thought it was better to expose me to my coach than to pay me my winnings. Coach had no choice but to suspend me, even if the timing sucked. What Sarah doesn't know … what she can't know, is that every dime I ever won went to our mom. Judith never went to college. Paul and I won scholarships, but mom could never have afforded to pay for Sarah's education … not with the costs of her medications … not without some help.

With a forced laugh, I say, "Okay, okay … I've broken a few rules along the way."

"I'm having trouble imagining Trey Tyson winding down at such a young age. You've always been out there running a hundred miles an hour. Always finding a way to challenge yourself."

"Hey! I never said I was winding down. Those are your words. Golf is the one sport I can play competitively for the rest of my life. And talk about challenge. It's impossible for anyone to perfect the game. No matter how well you play, there's always some room for improvement."

"It's still a shock. I always thought you'd sell the company, and become a day trader."

"Why'd you think that?" I ask, truly curious.

"Because I've watched you turn a $150 million in earnings from your NFL career and Tyson Search into a net worth now over $1 billion dollars. You rode the Intel and Qualcomm stocks for huge gains, knew just when to buy Microsoft and Apple shares, put most of it into property before the housing bubble, then moved it to gold just before the entire economy tanked. It's been uncanny to watch. I've learned to follow your lead with my own investments. On top of that, I know Roy Starr has been following your investment advice for years. I can't even guess at how much he's made with the resources he has. Trey, you obviously have a gift for this. Just imagine where you'd be financially if you focused on investing full-time."

"It's never been about the money." I fight off laughing at myself. Thinking back to how tight finances were for our family after Dad died, it's easy to say it's not about the money now that I have it.

"I do your taxes, so I know it's not about the money ... not any more at least. You enjoy winning. That's what makes you tick."

I flash my sister my warmest smile. "Actually, I've been competing for too much of my life already. After my little winding down period, I'm planning to start a foundation. I'm going to name it after Mom and Dad."

"For multiple sclerosis?" she asks.

Nodding, I say, "There are too many people with MS who can't afford the medicine they need."

"What size check are you going to write to kick this off?"

"Half," I answer. There's no sense in hiding it. She'll see it on my next tax return. "$500 million."

Sarah's eyes well up, but she holds back the tears. "Can't you run your foundation here in Michigan?"

"I miss the Suncoast. Warm breezes, midday cooling rain, sunsets over the Gulf."

"Have you told Mom yet?" Sarah's a detail-oriented person and likes to remind me to cover all the bases.

"No. I'm seeing her tomorrow morning and will let her know then."

"How do you think she's going to react when you tell here you're moving back to Florida?"

"It depends."

"Depends on what?" she asks.

"I'll let her tell you that after our conversation. I don't want to guess at her reaction to this, but I'm fairly certain she'll understand."

Sarah stands up and walks around the desk to give me a hug. She gestures to the other end of the office. "Can you take the foosball table with you?"

"Ha!" I can't help the laugh that escapes as I hug her back. "I'm going to leave it here with you. It's your office. You can remove it if you like, but some of our best management meetings have come during a stirring round of foosball."

"That's a good point. The one thing I'm going to have the most difficulty with, is keeping the office fun and competitive the way you always have." She smiles.

"You'll do just fine," I wink. "Trust your instincts. I always have."

"You better come back to Michigan and visit often." She stops trying to hold back the tears. "We're going to miss you."

"I will, Sarah. And you know I'll miss you, too."

Chapter 26

GREG RUTLEDGE
WASHINGTON DC, USA
SATURDAY, OCTOBER 27, 2012

As CIA director, I don't mind providing status reports during White House Situation Room meetings. It's a frequent enough task that goes along with my job. What I *do* mind is the inappropriate reaction to these reports that I consistently receive from *this* president. Still, even if the guy is an asshole, it's my job to feed the asshole the latest intelligence updates.

"Mr. President, the Somali pirates captured another vessel last night."

President Sanchez is tall with caramel skin, sharp facial features, and even sharper black eyes.

Merely raising his eyebrows, not even making eye contact with me, he says, "And *that's* why you called this meeting?"

"The pirates ventured beyond the Gulf of Aden and into the Red Sea. The situation is escalating to the point where, in my opinion, we need to step in and solve it, once and for all. It was bad enough when they limited their activities to Somali coastal waters. But now they're recruiting militants from neighboring countries, expanding their territory, and steadily increasing the size of their forces as well as the size of their fleet."

I've served three separate presidents as CIA director. Each of them has had preferred stances and standard operating procedures for dealing with a crisis. This president is unpredictable and frequently very difficult for me to understand.

"Whose vessel was it?" asks the president, still focusing on a briefing document.

His level of concern seems as if I just told him the office printer ran out of ink, and he's asking if we have another cartridge in the supply room.

"It was a Saudi yacht, sir. To further complicate things, two members of the Saudi royal family are among the hostages."

The president finally makes eye contact. He seems to be considering a few options before his next question, "How have the Saudis responded?"

"They don't have the resources to deal with a threat of this nature. Of course, they have publicly expressed concern over the hostage situation. But, sir, they're asking us our opinion on whether they should pay the ransom demands to retrieve the crew members."

"Get the fucking UN Security Council involved. Let them take the lead and advise the Saudis. Has anyone from State been in contact with the UN yet?"

"We have, sir. The UN advised the Saudis to quietly pay the ransom in exchange for the hostages. The pirates won't surrender the yacht. They've been amassing more and more ships. Some are even sophisticated naval vessels, and they have a rather impressive fleet at this point. It's my opinion that they have something more sophisticated and *dangerous* planned with this fleet than simply taking hostages and collecting ransoms."

"My briefings indicate they have a pitifully tiny fleet. Their hostages give them the upper hand, at the moment. Without them, we could wipe the pirates out with an airstrike in no time. So … they've carved out a nice little criminal niche for themselves." He shrugs. "It's financially rewarding, so I don't expect them to suddenly find a need to *expand* their operations. Let's be honest; they haven't overtly tried to hurt anyone. In fact, when paid the requested ransom, they've always returned the hostages. Hell, they're more reliable than some of our allies. It's a nuisance. I understand that. However, not so much so that I want to commit our military forces to correct it. If we raise the stakes, we may very well end up with a much bigger problem on our hands."

I was afraid this would be his response. The guy was a pilot and shuttle commander, with almost no political experience. His concept of compromising means you have to do it his way, but you don't have to like it. Thank God he's so far down in the polls, and doesn't seem to have much of a chance for a second term.

"Respectfully, sir, they're *already* raising the stakes. The Saudis have been our most stable relationship in the region and they're asking for our help. Beyond that, the Somalis now have vessels from every major naval fleet on the planet, including ours." I still can't tell if the president is taking this seriously. I have to assume he is as I continue, "Sir, this is much bigger than just the pirates. My operative there reports that the government is controlled by one man — the same man who leads the Somali pirates at sea and the militants on land. I'm concerned if we don't step up militarily right now, there may be dire consequences later."

The president finally places his briefing document on the table and gives me his full attention, "With the coming elections, Greg, this is *not* the right time to initiate anything militarily."

"The pirates don't give a shit about our elections. They're not going to sit idly by waiting to see who wins the race. Our intelligence leads me to believe they're going to do something before the election. What then?"

He shrugs again, then asks, "Barring any overt action against these pirates prior to the elections, what would you have me do?"

"I think we should move a carrier battle group to the area, sir. We'll have options by sea and air. If nothing else, it will at least pressure the pirates into thinking we *may* have plans to act against them. That could prevent them from taking any more vessels or hostages while the US Navy is looking over their shoulders."

"Will our presence there be enough for them to give up the Saudi royals?" The president seems concerned finally.

"We've never taken this step before, so I don't know how the pirates will react. I can comfortably say that the Saudi's will appreciate the move. And when they owe us a favor, they always come through."

The president deliberates for a moment before making his decision, "Greg, you're a wise man and you provide solid counsel. I think it's best to follow your advice here. I'll need the latest intel and satellite imagery of the area, and we should get frequent reports from your person on the ground there as well. Is it someone you trust?"

"Yes, sir! Arthur Sumner is one of our best agents. I'm certain he'll provide whatever we need."

Hmmm. Maybe this president isn't so naïve after all.

Chapter 27

VIKTOR KROSTOV
PUSHKIN, RUSSIA
SATURDAY, OCTOBER 27, 2012

Curse my sister for retiring. Katarina was always a steadying influence on me, a voice of reason when I need it most. I could use her vision ... her advice. She inherited her abilities from our mother. Abilities I've never had or fully understood. In my time of greatest need, Katarina has left me ... just like my mother so many years ago. It almost seems like history repeating itself.

It was 1941, when the Germans invaded Russia. My father never thought they could reach us in Leningrad. I was only two years old, but I still remember my mother from before she disappeared. A tiny and beautiful woman, and she had the voice of an angel. I remember her warmth ... her kindness. Father and I loved her so much. Mother never chose to leave. She was taken against her will. Taken when the Germans surrounded and set siege to Leningrad. Anyone they could capture was taken to work camps back in Germany. When mother was captured, the fury in father was instant and boundless. He rallied forces in the city to fight the Germans, and they delayed the German advance for months and months, until more Russian forces from the East could reach the city and send the Germans running back home.

The city celebrated, but we'd lost so many of our people, taken by the Germans as work slaves ... or worse. My mother was gone and my father would do *anything* to get her back. As the leader of the Leningrad forces that held off the Germans, he was promoted to General and given command of a tank division of the Russian army. When the tides of war had turned, and it was our turn to invade Germany, father insisted on going first. I don't know if it was because he had no one to leave me with, but he took me to war with him.

I turned six in 1945, and our tanks reached Berlin from the East just ahead of the Americans from the West. We surrounded the city and there, in Berlin, father found mother. She was not in a work camp, but roaming free in the city. She wasn't alone when he found her. She was with a man, and had a daughter with her that father had never met. The child was Katarina, and she was only two years old. *Too young to be my father's child.* When he figured that out, he had some soldiers take away the man she was with. The woman he sacrificed so much to find ... the woman he fought so long and so hard to save ... she had betrayed him ... so he killed my mother. He made sure I watched. It was a lesson he wanted me to learn, the harshest of the many lessons he taught me. He claimed young Katarina as his own, and brought her back home. She was my sister, he explained, and we were to be a family again.

Father was a war hero and made many friends in both the army and the government. He started a private espionage organization that was outside of both, yet could service both. When he retired, only a year before he died, he left me in charge ... with all the lessons he taught me over all the years to guide me.

As I study Karl's weathered face on the main monitor in the massive control room at my headquarters, my staff is working around me all the time, but the place feels empty without my sister.

As if reading my mind, Karl asks, "Where is Katarina?"

Do I tell him the truth? He'll *know* if I don't. "My sssister has left. She ... retired."

"Retired? Why didn't you tell me? Go to her. Tell her we need her," Karl almost pleads with me in a gentle, persuasive voice. It's the voice he uses when trying to get what he wants. He can sound like a kind old man when he wants to. But, if that doesn't work ....

"Believe me. I have tried. When she understood what we were planning, she told me she wanted nothing to do with it. She quit. She's out. Worse than that, she assured me this operation will end very badly."

On the monitor Karl's face turns from friendly concern, slowly, to fiery anger. "The bitch! I'll —"

"You'll what?" I cut him off. Karl and his secret friends are the money, but I'm the muscle of the operation. I can tolerate direct threats to myself, but *not* my sister.

Karl tries unsuccessfully to regain his composure. "Fuck it. My friends have relied on women like her for far too long. Fucking oracles will tell you a tale. Sometimes it helps you, but more often it just helps the bitch telling the tale. We don't need her or her kind any more. Everything is set up. There's nothing that can stop us now. It's time for the First Order to step out of the shadows!"

"First Order?" I've never heard of this before. Perhaps, in Karl's fury, he finally let the name of his group slip.

Karl closes his eyes for a moment before speaking. "*Nothing.* It's nothing for you to worry about." He smiles warmly, back to being the kind old man. "Your biggest concern, my old friend, is what to do with all the money you're going to have when this is done."

"How much do you think we'll get?" I ask.

"This is the ultimate terrorist scenario. The entire world will be trembling, and we'll be able to demand and receive whatever we want. They will have no choice but to pay any price we name. We can demand *anything* we desire from *any* government around the globe." Karl's laugh is loud, long, and sinister.

I'm not one who worries about my place in history, but I can imagine the devastation that Karl plans will be a first in the history of the planet — if we're not paid what we want. All his actions have been in preparation for this moment.

Karl continues, "This is the culmination of everything the First Order has strived to achieve over millennia! This will be my crowning achievement. The splendid sweetness of success lies before us, my friend. We just have to stay the course!" Just the thought of his plan succeeding makes Karl sound young and energetic again.

"You know you can count on me." With Katarina out of the picture, I feel a need to assure Karl that I *will* in fact stay loyal to him.

"Yes, of course. Were you able to get Paka the proper munitions and communications devices?" Karl asks.

"I had to call in every favor I could from my Russian military contacts, and convince them this was a project that would benefit all of Russia. Fortunately, the explosives required were sssimple. The challenging part turned out to be the communications equipment. These were from the Russian government's most current technological advancements. My contacts claim they cannot be hacked. Not even by their inventors."

"Very good! That's precisely what we need," says Karl.

"Yes, but that only accounts for the receiving end of the communications chain. We'll need to transmit a sssignal that reaches most every part of the planet. The timing must be perfect. I don't trust using the Russian military sssatellites. First, they are not known for their reliability. But even if they were reliable, our communications would not remain *private*."

"Don't worry about that, Viktor. You'll be running point for the entire operation, with the hub being at your headquarters. You send me the receiver frequency and encryption software, and I'll provide the link protocol and arrange for private satellite transmission. You'll be able to communicate with Paka and his men in virtual real-time."

"But where did you find this Paka fellow?" Bringing in someone new always concerns me. "Can we trust him?"

"We can trust him, because *I say* we can trust him. Don't start second-guessing me!" Angry Karl is back. "Now listen … Paka will lead the crew at the first site, and record the message to go out to the major news agencies. The packets will be delivered in such a way as to be untraceable."

"What about the payments?" I ask.

"Viktor, *you* set up the accounts. They *are* set up properly, right?"

"Of course, but you've always taken in and distributed any funds for our operations."

"After all these years, Viktor? Really? I know I can trust you to distribute the funds appropriately." Karl uses the warmest voice and sincerest tone I've ever heard him use. Naturally, this makes me suspicious.

"And you're sure that we'll only need to detonate one?" I ask.

"Completely. The *last* thing we want is to take it to the next level. When will Paka's men be in position?"

"If I can trust him, as you sssay, his crews are well on their way. Without any problems, they'll be ready in three days."

"Perfect! So will I." Karl sounds nearly gleeful about this operation.

Chapter 28

TREY TYSON
AUBURN HILLS, MICHIGAN, USA
SATURDAY, OCTOBER 27, 2012

I'm walking with the two candidates from valet parking at the Palace of Auburn Hills toward the nearest stadium entrance. The night sky is clear and the lot is well lit.

Speaking to both, I say, "I've been recruiting executives for quite a few years, and this is a first for me. You've probably heard plenty of rumors that Roy Starr is as eccentric as they come. They're all true! That being said, he is dynamic and extremely successful. His request to hold a joint interview with his two top candidates is a new approach, but I'm certain he has a good reason for it. Part of the process may well be to see how each of you adapts to this unique situation. So, take it seriously. The candidate he chooses will have a very promising future with Starr Aeronautics."

Both Cecilia and Steve seem at ease with the group-interview-at-a-basketball-game concept, even if I'm having trouble figuring out Roy's reasons for it.

"When we meet Roy inside, I'll introduce you, and then I'll try to stay out of the way and let Roy lead the process. I don't know what to expect any more than you do, but I do expect the unexpected." I pause to make sure I have their attention. "One bit of advice, though. If he offers you a drink, accept it. However, don't get drunk – or even tipsy. He'll want to know that you can conduct business effectively in a social setting."

Both Cecilia and Steve nod their understanding.

Just inside, I spot Roy walking toward us. It's amazing how great the man looks for his age. Straight posture, a youthful and confident gait to his walk … almost like he owns the world.

Roy quickly closes the gap to meet us. He shakes my hand warmly. "Trey, so good to see you again. I'm glad you all could make it to the game. It's the first game of the season, and I have high hopes the Pistons will have a great year. Now, who do we have here?"

"Roy, so good to see you as well! How have you been?"

"I'm above ground. At this age, that's doing well. How have you been lately?" Roy replies.

"I'm above ground, too. And at any age, that's a good place to start!" We all chuckle briefly. "Roy, let me introduce you to Cecilia Lawley and Steve Berman." Roy shakes hands with both. "As you know, they've both made it through the first three rounds of interviews with Starr. Would you like a quick review of their employment history and education?"

"That won't be necessary. I've done my research." Roy turns his attention to the two candidates. "Thank you both for your interest in joining Starr Aerospace. From what I understand, either of you would be a strong fit to take over our Engineering lead. Educated, driven, and successful – each of you has also received glowing evaluations from the rest of the team involved in the interview process. It appears ..." he pauses for effect, "that the decision will come down to *intangibles* and *personalities*. So, let's enjoy the basketball game, and get to know each other!" Roy hands each of us a ticket.

I look at my ticket and read aloud, "Section 222, row 19, seat 1. What happened to your midcourt suite?"

Roy gives me a sly smile, waggling his eyebrows a few times. "Follow me." He starts walking at his usual brisk pace, and we follow closely.

After winding through the Palace concourse and locating the stairs leading up to our section, I start counting rows as we keep climbing. Row 19 ends up being the top row of the top level of the Palace, and our seats are just off to the side of one of the backboards. I'm about to make a joke about the seats, but Steve beats me to it.

"Roy, is the company doing alright financially? These are the worst seats in the stadium." Steve laughs aloud after joking about the obvious.

"These are the perfect seats," Roy replies coyly. He takes the fourth seat in, followed immediately by Steve and Cecilia. I end up with the seat at the end of the row.

"Roy, what's going on?" I ask.

Before Roy can reply, a cheerleader reaches our row at the top of the stairs and hands me a stack of red and white sheets of paper.

"Please keep one, and pass the rest down your row," she says to me. She then does a double-take, winks at me, places her hand on my arm, and says, "I know who you are! You were on the Tampa Bay Bucs. You played safety, right? My dad followed your career from Michigan to the NFL ... and into the Hall of Fame. Those shaving cream commercials were hilarious!" She glances at my left hand, smiles, and then says, "Tyson? Trey Tyson, right?"

I hold up my index finger to my lips. "Shhh. We football players aren't recognized nearly as much as baseball or basketball players. I think it's because we wear helmets."

She pulls a pen from somewhere I can't guess due to the skimpiness of her outfit, and I'm worried she's going to hand it to me to sign something. Instead, *she* scribbles something on one of the sheets, hands it to me, then says, "*You* can have two."

"What are these for?" I ask, noticing that she still has her hand on my arm and isn't letting go.

"New to this section?" she winks.

"Yes, is it that obvious?"

"It's pretty simple." She finally removes her hand from my arm and takes a single sheet in her right hand. "Wave these around like crazy when the opposing team is shooting free throws on this end of the court." Emphasizing her point, she jumps up and down as she waves the sheet around. I can't help but notice just how shapely she is.

"Ah, to try to distract them." I state the obvious.

"I knew you'd get it. And they say football players aren't too bright." She winks at me again, then turns around.

The cheerleader gives a similar stack to each person on the end of the rows on her way back down the stairs. The announcer has just finished introducing the visiting Chicago Bulls team, and starts to introduce the Pistons. I read her note and discover I now have her name and phone number. After a moment's hesitation, I keep a blank sheet, and hand the stack to Cecilia. She is about to take just one, when Roy holds up his hand.

"Cecilia, please keep all of the white sheets in the stack and give the red sheets to Steve." She glances at me for affirmation, but she complies without question.

Steve stuffs the top red sheet – the one with the cheerleader's name and number – into his pocket, and keeps the rest of the stack on his lap.

"Now," Roy continues once he sees that they each have their own stack of paper. "I'd like to know that the head of engineering at Starr

Aerospace actually understands aeronautics. What I'd like you to do is design and build paper airplanes from the stack of paper you have. Whenever a Chicago player is shooting free throws on this end of the court, and the crowd is flapping their sheets of paper around, I want you to throw your paper airplane from here to the free throw shooter. Whoever lands their airplane anywhere in the free throw circle first will also *land* the job at Starr."

There is a long moment of silence. Both candidates look to me, and I just shrug.

"Best of luck to you, Steve." Cecilia extends her hand to Steve, but he ignores her and starts building paper airplanes. One by one, fold by fold, they are all identical.

Cecilia thinks for a few moments, and then folds her first plane. Steve continues to build more and more paper airplanes until he is surrounded by them. Cecilia only builds three airplanes, each with a distinctly different design, and then waits patiently for the Bulls to get to the free throw line.

"What a great idea, Roy!" Steve says with genuine excitement, and he goes back to folding more airplanes.

"Mr. Starr, can you share your background with us?" Cecilia asks, placing her three airplanes on her lap. "I'd like to learn more about the founding of Starr Aerospace."

"Thanks for asking, Cecilia," Roy answers. I can tell from his voice that he likes that she asked the question. "Starr Aerospace is probably the most notable company I own. If you've read up on us, you know we got our start in the mid '80s by providing components for military aircraft. As our capabilities grew, so did the scope of the projects we took on. We moved into satellite components, entire satellites, and the rocketry necessary to launch them into space." He's obviously proud of himself and his company. "With the scaling back of NASA by the government, we became the leading provider for the US space program. We hold several key patents, primarily for components used on the space shuttles and satellite communications systems. Now, we continue to provide satellites, rocketry, military aircraft and components, and we're even helping with the International Space Station. Our growth has always been strong, but with the current administration, we've almost quadrupled our revenues in the last three years. Starr's various projects are all well run by our project managers, but we still have a need for someone other than me to coordinate all of them. That's why you and Steve are here."

"I couldn't find any personal information about you and how you got your start. I'm always curious when a company is as successful as Starr Aerospace has been to find out how the founder started it?" Cecilia's sincere interest is starting to win Roy over, at least as far as I can tell.

"Well, I'm a fairly private person ..."

I intended to stay out of the conversation, but I can't help but jump in when he says that. "Fairly? You should see what he does if someone tries to take a picture of him." Cecilia and Trey enjoy a good laugh, while Roy smiles a bit broader than usual.

"Not all of us are professional athletes with movie star looks, like you, Trey!" They all three start laughing.

"So, while I don't enjoy personal publicity much," Roy continues. "I don't mind telling you that I was very fortunate to have been given quite a nice head start by my parents. They came to America in 1942 and started a small café in downtown Detroit. My mother was an amazing cook, and brought many of her favorite recipes to America. My father loved people and loved entertaining. He insisted on greeting and seating everyone that entered their café. If they were slow, he would go into the street and sing to draw attention and get people to come in and try their food. They never wanted anyone to leave their place hungry, so they provided their customers with *huge* portions of whatever they ordered. The café quickly gained a great reputation and a loyal customer base, and my parents were able to expand."

He leans back, a look of satisfaction on his face. "First, they added space, and became a complete family restaurant. Then came a second and a third restaurant the following year. My father wanted the best people he could get to manage each restaurant. He'd put candidates through IQ and personality testing, and did thorough background checks before hiring anyone. Many of the restaurant managers had no experience at all in restaurants, but he could spot someone with talent and determination. His methods proved to be enormously successful. They soon expanded into other regions, and then started franchising them all over the country. It became a *true* American success story."

He looks at me and grins, and I think his story is intended more for my benefit than Cecilia's. Roy continues, "My mother insisted I get an extensive education, and that I travel the world to learn about other cultures. As I got older, I was worried about their entire net worth being tied up in one industry. So, I kept trying to get them to diversify. And I still remember how my father always replied whenever I suggested he do something else. 'People gotta eat' is what he always said. 'People gotta eat.' I found it difficult to argue with his simple logic." Roy shakes his head for a moment, and takes a deep breath. "They died in a car crash, leaving me with an expansive restaurant empire. I was able to leverage the restaurants into founding Starr Aerospace and several other ventures."

An attendant appears suddenly carrying a tray with four glasses of wine that Roy must have arranged to be sent. He also hands each of us a menu, giving us a moment to review it before saying, "Would anyone care for anything from the menu?"

"People gotta eat," I quip immediately, getting bursts of laughter from Roy and Cecilia.

Before we can place our food order, there's a loud whistle from the court.

"Foul on the Pistons! Bulls shooting two!" belts the announcer.

Cecilia pulls out her smartphone so she can record the results of her first flight attempts. By the time she stands up, Steve has already stood and thrown two of his paper airplanes. One made it ten rows before plummeting into the crowd. The other did a loop straight up, went two rows forward, and landed in a woman's hair.

Cecilia throws her first airplane, and it flies straight and carries almost halfway through the rows of seats in the direction of the basketball court. She then keys in a few notes on her smartphone.

"Not bad for a first try," says Roy. A few people around us have noticed what we're doing, and start making their own paper airplanes. Roy looks about him and laughs aloud, seeming to find the number of people joining in our task to be highly amusing.

Steve has thrown another two planes with similar results to his earlier efforts by the time Cecilia picks up and throws her second plane. This one flies with remarkable height and distance, but veers to the right from a draft in the upper air of the Palace. Again, she pauses and types some notes in her smartphone.

Within ten seconds, Steve throws three more planes. But all his planes have the same simplistic design, and none of them travel very far. It reminds me of an Albert Einstein quote that Max Medici has often repeated to me: *The definition of insanity is doing the same thing over and over again and expecting different results.*

More people in the crowd catch on, and begin throwing paper airplanes from the same section. One airplane flies all the way to the lower level, passing right in front of a Palace security guards. The guard quickly locates where the plane came from, and stomps his feet as he climbs the stairs from just a few rows above the basketball court all the way to our section. The guard, breathing heavily, stops five rows from the top, so he can address us as a group.

"No more airplanes, people!" he yells as loudly as he can. "If one of these hits the court, the refs will call a technical foul on the Pistons. Is that what you want?"

He abruptly turns around, and storms back down the stairs to the lower level.

The Bulls are no longer shooting free throws, so Cecilia decides to build two more airplanes. One is very similar to her first design, and the other is almost exactly like her second.

I turn to face Cecilia. "May I see the last plane you built?"

"Certainly. But why?" She reaches down from under her seat to retrieve the plane.

"I think your design is right on target, but the conditions may not be ideal," I say.

While Cecilia's paper airplane is rather intricate, I'm still able to quickly fold my one sheet of paper to match it identically. Just as I finish folding it, the security guard has reached the front row and commences screaming at two kids about their feet being too close to the court.

"This guy needs to get a lesson in humility!" I say loud enough for several rows in front of me to hear. I pause for a moment, then sense the timing is perfect. "This plane is going to hit him right in the middle of the forehead!" I dip the nose of the plane in my wine to add a small amount of weight to the front to keep the plane flying a bit lower than Cecilia's last flight. I then dip the left wingtip in the wine to counter the draft that had pushed Cecilia's plane to the right. Standing up, I reach back, and flick my arm and wrist forward to launch my plane.

"Ha! I think it has a chance! The initial trajectory seems perfect," says Cecilia excitedly.

Roy, Cecilia, and Steve all stand to watch the flight.

The plane starts turning slightly to the left and Steve can't contain himself, "Oh no! It's headin' left!"

Fans seated around us and several rows below start to stand and root for the airplane. The security guard is so intent on yelling at the two kids in the front row that he seems oblivious to the action in the sections above.

When the plane enters the area with the draft, it slightly over-corrects the plane's trajectory. It's now heading a little to the right of its target.

"It was a great try, Trey, but it looks like it's going to miss after all," says Steve.

"Don't give up on him yet, Steve." Roy says while not taking his eyes off the airplane. "I've learned to trust in Trey's ability to do almost anything."

The paper airplane is now flying halfway over the section below ours, and word is spreading almost as fast as the plane is floating downward. Row by row, people are yelling about the flight and its target. Then row by row, they stand to watch.

Something one of the boys in the front row says appears to be the last straw for the security guard. He yells, spraying spittle in their faces, "Stand up! You two are coming with me!" And just as the guard stands up straight, the paper airplane curves slightly to the left, and pops him right in the middle of his forehead. The guard stumbles backward and falls onto the basketball court. At the same time, the Bulls point guard shoots and makes a three-pointer as the clock expires to end the first quarter. Even though the shot went in, giving the Bulls a two-point lead, several hundred Pistons' fans stand and cheer wildly.

Roy applauds with the nearby crowd, then turns to face us. "Wow, after a huge aeronautical success like that, I guess I have to hire Trey for the job!" Roy is on the verge of being boisterous, but there's a hint of hesitation I see. There's something on his mind ... something important.

"That was incredible!" Cecilia yells to be heard above the still cheering crowd in our section. "How did you do it?"

"It was your design I copied. I could tell you put a lot of thought into it," I reply.

Roy looks down the stairs, then back to me. He seems worried about something. I follow Roy's gaze back down the stairs, and see that the security guard is stomping his way back up. He seems as furious as anyone I've ever seen before. His face is bright pink with so much blood pressure and anger built up, but the color still can't hide the indelible red dot on his forehead where the paper airplane struck.

Suddenly sensing what might be bothering Roy, I offer a quick solution, "Why don't you three head down the other stairs to the VIP Club, and I'll meet you down there after working things out with the guard."

"Wonderful idea, Trey!" Roy seems relieved. "Cecilia, Steve, please follow me."

I turn back to look at the guard's progress up the stairs, but don't see him. At the midpoint between the lower and upper levels, people are required to briefly enter the concourse before turning back around to head up the second flight of stairs. While I figure I'll likely be tossed out of the Palace once the guard reaches me, I'm pretty sure I'll be able to find a way back in, even if I need to buy another ticket.

Chapter 29

Judith Tyson
Washington DC, USA
Saturday, October 27, 2012

"President Sanchez?" I often feel like I'm disturbing the president, even when he calls me into a meeting. Looking around the Oval Office, a new statue catches my eye. A large gold obelisk, sitting right where a replica of the Washington Monument once sat. Gaudy and phallic, the obelisk is at least a few inches taller than the replica was. When do men ever grow up?

"Yes, Judith?"

"Sir, I'd like to introduce you to Agent Bruce Cullens." The president doesn't stand up, but reaches to shake hands with Bruce. "He's relatively new to AI, but he's competent. He'll be AI's representative agent responsible for your protection while Samantha and I are out of the country."

"It's an honor to meet you, sir." Cullens is on the verge of gushing. "I watched the shuttle entry from 1999. It was remarkable! Do you mind, sir ... telling me about it?"

This gets the president's attention and he smiles broadly. "It wasn't *that* big of a deal."

Oh, no ... not this story again!

"It was to me, sir. What you did …. You saved the world. And, then we were all worried about you making it back alive. The news said several heat shield tiles had been lost on the nose of the shuttle, and the odds of you bringing it back safely were slim. The shuttle came in so hot that it looked like a blazing meteor in our sky. We all thought you and everyone on board were toast."

I glare at him for showing his youth with that analogy.

"Thank you for your concern," the president patiently responds. "But I could rotate the section with the missing tiles just far enough to avoid burning up, and still keep a proper trajectory for entry."

"The whole world was listening and your voice was so *calm*. I think that's why so many people wanted you to go into politics, because of how cool you were under pressure." Bruce is still gushing, and I don't think he's going to stop any time soon.

I can only take so much of it, though, "If you're done, Bruce, the president is a very busy man."

The president shoots a quick glance at me, showing his annoyance at having one of his stories cut short. I'm not sure if he's going to go on bragging about himself, or move on to the reason we're here.

"Agent Cullens, Judith has overseen AI for almost 20 years, and Samantha has been her top agent that entire time. While I've been president, at least one of them has always been by my side, giving me peace of mind. I *trust* them. Their departure cannot be avoided, as their assignment is critical. That being said, I trust that you understand how *uncomfortable* I am with their leaving." The president briefly makes eye contact with Bruce. "No offense, Agent Cullens."

"None taken, sir." Bruce stiffens a bit, more formal now. He may be embarrassed by his lack of professionalism, and he's suddenly uncomfortable. His voice has become more ... robotic. "I've seen both Judith and Samantha in training, and I've never seen anyone aim, shoot, or react as quickly as either one of them. And they're both deadly accurate. I would want either one of them by my side if I were you, too."

I need to move this meeting along and get on to my assignment, "Sir, we have some intel on a risk from abroad that in my opinion will require both Samantha and me if we're to have any hope of containing the situation. I wish I could leave Samantha here with you, but Agent Cullens will be available as you need him."

"Alright," the president seems resigned to the situation. "But does Agent Cullens possess the same skills as you and Samantha?"

"To a lesser extent, yes," I answer. "Males don't typically have the same level of waking psychic abilities as females. Yet, he shows promise. You're certainly better off with him at your side than the standard Secret Service agents."

The president stands and faces me directly. "Keep me informed of your progress and best of luck to you and to Samantha."

"I will, Mr. President. And thank you."

Chapter 30

TREY TYSON
AUBURN HILLS, MICHIGAN, USA
SATURDAY, OCTOBER 27, 2012

It took me a while and I did have to buy another ticket, but I finally made it back into the Palace. I'm in the VIP club with Roy about to have the private conversation he requested.

Roy seems relieved to see me. "Trey, I arranged for transportation for Steve and Cecilia. I know it may have been awkward to send them on their way at halftime, but I need to speak with you alone for a while."

"I saw them outside and it's no trouble, Roy. I think they were okay with a limo ride home after nearly being tossed out of the arena." We both chuckle at the situation. "How are you going to handle the hire though? Neither one of them met your airplane challenge."

"Who would you hire if you were me?" asks Roy.

"Their education and work experience are very similar, but I think your paper airplane idea did show something of their personalities that probably couldn't have come out in an ordinary interview process," I concede. "Based on what I saw today, I'd hire Cecilia. She was problem solving out there, not just trying to use brute force. I also think her interpersonal skills are quite good. But I'm not the one pulling the trigger here. What do you think?"

"I couldn't agree more."

"Well, then, that decision is made. So ... I have some news of my own to share."

"This sounds a little ominous." Roy half-jokes.

"I'm getting out of the executive recruiting business, Roy. I'm leaving Tyson Search in the hands of my sister, Sarah, and moving on to something else." I try to read Roy's reaction, but can't gauge how he feels about it. "I believe you and Sarah have had a good working relationship, and trust that will continue without me."

"Trey, I have *one* more job I want you to fill for me." Roy smiles ruefully.

I laugh. "I just explained, Roy, that I'm getting *out* of the business. My passion for it has been waning for quite some time. I need to head out for a long vacation. In fact, I'm off to Europe. It's time to kick back and enjoy life. My mind is made up. I'm not coming back to Tyson Search. Sarah will be leading the company going forward. She is more than capable to help you find candidates for this new position –"

Roy cuts me off with a wave of his hands. "I don't think you understand. I don't want you to *recruit* an executive for me. I have a role that I want *you* to take on personally."

"What?"

"One of my companies needs a CEO. As much as I'd like to, sometimes, I can't run them *all* myself. I need someone talented and with vision to run this company. I think you're ideal for the role."

"Trying to recruit the recruiter?" I jest.

"In a word, *yes*. We've had a highly successful business relationship and friendship, Trey. I think the timing is incredible, if you're moving on from Tyson Search just as I need someone to run what's becoming the most important company in my portfolio."

"Roy, I'm extremely flattered you'd want me to run one of your companies, but I have another path I plan to follow. Besides, you already have my twin brother working for you, isn't that close enough?" I smile, trying to lighten the mood and change the subject.

"You're *both* brilliant, and I'm glad we already have Paul in the fold."

"How has Paul been working out so far?" I ask.

"You know him better than anyone, Trey. We tried, but we couldn't get him to commit to working in our offices. He's one of those rare talents, however, that I find is worth accommodating his *unique* personality."

"Oh, he's unique alright." I laugh.

"Many geniuses have social issues. But, it's his talent I need. His software is ubiquitous to all satellite-based tracking systems. He's been working with our programmers to get them up to speed on his systems, and we learned of the algorithm to pinpoint locations of events within geographical borders. Paul said *you* came up with the idea when you were in high school." Roy smiles, having successfully returned the conversation to me. "It didn't surprise me a bit. So at least hear me out before you say no."

"Of course, I'll hear you out. I just want to be fair, and set a reasonable expectation. Enlighten me with the details of your new company. Do I know any of the management team? Maybe even placed a few of them over the years?"

"No, Trey. This company has been flying under the radar, and for a very good reason. There aren't many employees yet. Naturally, as the CEO with recruiting experience, you're a perfect fit to bring in the necessary additional staff. It's called Modern Agriculture and Biofuels, US division. The US division is the only division right now, but I expect it will grow and acquire international divisions very quickly. My investments in international farming conglomerates will grease the skids to buying some of these companies."

"Modern *Agriculture* and Biofuels? This sounds like a bit of a tangent to my areas of expertise. What does the company do?"

"Up until now, we've been mostly acquiring farmland." Roy seems hesitant to tell me too much.

"Roy, I know technology, engineering, manufacturing, sports, staffing, and have some expertise in related fields. But farming? Acquiring land? I wouldn't know where to begin."

"You wouldn't be starting from ground zero, so to speak. Very quietly and under several holding companies, I've acquired almost 50 million acres of the richest farmland in the United States. And I have options on another 100 million acres. I've also invested heavily in the largest international farmland holding companies. When the real estate market tanked, and so many properties went into foreclosure, I started selling my gold holdings that *you* so wisely talked me into buying. The land deals were incredible. I could buy huge tracts of foreclosed land for prices as low as 10% of value. Here in Michigan, plus in Iowa, Illinois, Indiana, Ohio, California and Florida. It was a once-in-a-lifetime opportunity that I couldn't let pass. I'm looking at the Niagara area in Canada next, and then I'd like you to start looking for land in Ukraine and Argentina."

"But why farmland?" Roy must have had a plan in place. He's too intelligent not to. Nevertheless, I can't imagine what it could be.

"Well, the biofuel component is certainly important. We don't have an endless supply of oil on the planet, and biofuels will be an important part of any strategy to become energy independent in the US and for other nations. But really, in the end, my father had it right. *People gotta eat.* And we'll be the country's leading grower for almost everything."

"Farmer Roy Starr. I'm still having trouble picturing you in overalls!" Roy always dresses well, and the mere thought of him on a farm makes me laugh. "Why haven't I heard of this before? Why so secretive?"

"I'm glad you find the thought to be so humorous." Roy allows himself to laugh at his own expense. "But let me tell you that acquiring 50 million acres of land is a daunting task. Can you just imagine how foolish I'd have been to announce that I wanted to buy up land before I did it? I'd drive the prices through the roof."

That part of it makes perfect sense. "I can certainly understand that. But why me? I have no experience in farming, distribution, or real estate. If I were recruiting for this role, I wouldn't recruit *me* for it."

"Trey, you have talent and determination. You're a competitor … no, not just a competitor, you're a winner. You won at every level of football imaginable. I've also seen you turn a one-man business operation with Tyson Search into one of the leading executive search and consulting firms in the country. Not to mention what your investment advice has done for my pocketbook. Plus, I *trust* you. And that's hard to find these days" I have a quick flashback to my earlier conversation with Sarah. Trust is so critical when it comes to finding a successor … for all of us. "Name your price, Trey. I want *you* to lead MAB."

I can't believe the temptation Roy's offer presents. My mind has been made up for quite some time, but this twist causes me to hesitate … to think.

"Wow, Roy. You'd make one hell of a recruiter. It's no wonder you always land the most talented executives at Starr. And there's no doubt you'll find the right leader for MAB. I'm *hugely* flattered. You've been a client and a friend for years. Nevertheless, I *know* I don't want to run a company any more. My heart leads me in another direction."

Roy looks down for a long moment, then back at me. "I could read your response before you gave it."

"That's why I don't play poker with you anymore." I smile.

"You're too honest to be an effective poker player. But that same honesty inspires trust from your staff, your clients, and everyone else who knows you. So, what is your heart telling you to do with your life?"

"I'm going to take a few months off and just relax and play golf."

"*Golf?* Are you kidding?" Roy lets out a hardy laugh. "I remember the first time we met. It was the Starr Aerospace company golf outing. Our head of human resources asked you to fill in for another golfer who was too ill to make it. You warned us you had never golfed before, but we didn't really believe you." Roy pauses. "We should have. Your practice swing looked quite odd, so I stepped closer to see how you'd ever be able hit the ball with that odd swing. You told me to take a step back just as you were about to tee off. I thought my shadow might have been distracting you, so I obliged. Next thing I knew, you take this crazy, shifting, Happy Gilmore type swing with your driver. The ball launched perpendicular to the direction you were aiming, and literally parted my hair down the middle as it whizzed a millimeter over the top of my head. I truly believe the golf ball, at that speed, would have killed me if I hadn't taken the one step back you insisted upon. I hit the ground from trying so hard to duck, and the next thing I heard was a burst of laughter from the crowd followed closely by stunned silence."

Roy takes a deep breath, obviously remembering the details of the moment. "The ball flew over the practice area and onto the 18th green, bounced a couple of times, hit the flagstick, then fell straight down into the hole. You let the crowd's silence sit for a moment, then smugly declared – wait, what were your *exact words* again? Oh yeah, you said, 'That's 18 holes in one shot. Who can beat that score?' And the crowd burst into laughter again, even louder. You're a cocky son of a bitch, but miracles seem to be waiting to happen around you."

I'm about to protest, but Roy just keeps going, "Now I know you've improved your game dramatically in the last ten years, and you can hit the ball a country mile. But Trey, your short game is, well, I don't quite know how to say this politely. Your short game needs a lot of work. And your putting is an absolute nightmare."

"I'm glad you found a *polite* way to say that." I roll my eyes, pretending my feelings are hurt. "After a break in the action, I'm going to start a foundation for MS. Guess who I'm coming after for a few bucks for a good cause?"

Roy shakes his head, "Multiple sclerosis is as good a cause as any. I'm sure Helen will appreciate it. Although I'm losing out on my first choice to run MAB, you're blazing your own trail, Trey, and I respect that. I have no doubt you'll be successful. You always are. I wish you all the best with this new adventure of yours, and you know I'll support you."

"Thanks for understanding." I'm not sure how to phrase a question I want to ask, without possibly offending him. "I have to ask …. Roy, you're well into your eighties. You have all the success and wealth anyone could ever dream to achieve. Why –"

Roy cuts me off, "Why is an old bastard like me still working so hard, when I could easily afford to spend the next hundred lifetimes relaxing on the beach?" He doesn't wait for me to have to answer that question. "I have a son, Trey. And I want the best for him. His future means everything to me, no matter how much longer I'm around."

"Wow! I'm surprised this is the first time I'm hearing about a son. What's his name?"

"Never mind. He's … well, he's adopted. I don't want to talk about him."

"No worries, Roy. You know I wish you nothing but the best in all that you do. I'm sure we'll stay in touch after I return, too." I extend my hand to him.

"Of course, Trey." Roy shakes my hand warmly. "I'm going to head home. Are you staying for the rest of the game?"

I glance at the bar and a woman catches my eye. "I think I'll have one more glass of wine before heading out. Have a good night."

"You, too, my friend."

Chapter 31

GREG RUTLEDGE
WASHINGTON DC, USA
SATURDAY, OCTOBER 27, 2012

Approaching my office, I see my Deputy Director, Jim Fritz, waiting in the hallway at our Langley headquarters. Jim has a jovial demeanor, but knows when to get serious. I've been grooming him for my job over the last few years and he's ready to take over as soon as I'm ready to retire. I have a strong feeling this Somali pirate crisis will be pushing that day sooner.

"Come on in," I say as I unlock and open the door.

"Director Rutledge … you wanted to see me?"

"Jim, when it's just the two of us, you know you can call me Greg. Save the formalities for when we're with the president."

His disarming smile may well be his best asset. Using it, he says, "No problem, *Greg*. Why did you want to see me?"

I close the door, but I don't sit or offer him a seat. This isn't going to be a long conversation. "I want you to stay on alert 24/7 while this Somali pirate crisis is in high gear. The CIA is in a position to provide a huge advantage for this operation. I want to make Desert Storm look like a long, tough battle compared to this. The pirates won't have any idea our fleet is moving into the area. We control the satellites, so we control the advance intelligence. We'll have surprise on our side, along with a vastly superior force."

"I agree with all of that, Greg. So, what are you *really* worried about?"

"Ever since Homeland Security was introduced, we've been counted on less and less. They take credit for any of our wins. And they're all too happy to point a spotlight at any mistakes we make. We can't be sloppy. We can't afford a mistake here. The whole world is watching how we respond to these pirates. This time, their hostages are Saudi royals. That spotlight will be bigger and brighter than ever. I want at least one of our satellites on the pirates at all times. Have our best analysts study their movements. Sumner is our only asset in the arena. Make sure he understands that I want to know where they're holding the hostages before the fleet gets there."

"Consider it done, Direc ... I mean Greg."

Chapter 32

Trey Tyson
Auburn Hills, Michigan, USA
Saturday, October 27, 2012

As I walk toward the bar, I once again focus on the tall, lithe redhead I noticed while speaking with Roy. She's facing the bar and has two men standing to her right who seem to be offering to buy her a drink. She shakes her head, turning them down, yet they persist.

I approach on her left where there's a small opening at the bar. Reaching my arms around, I gently place my hands over her eyes.

"You're quite a stunning young woman," I say confidently. "I can see why these fine gentlemen have offered to buy you a cocktail. Looks aren't everything, though. I believe there's so much more involved in attraction than just how one looks. I also believe our other senses help define what's attractive to us. Much like a fine wine doesn't need to be seen to be appreciated. First, its aroma should be inhaled *deeply*. Then just a sip, swished *slowly* around the palate. So, without looking at me, let me test your other senses. How would you like to share a bottle of a deep and rich Bordeaux?"

"No thanks!" she says glibly, but I think I can feel her face smiling under my hands.

The two men to her right start to laugh.

I give them a minute before continuing, "But I didn't finish my offer. How would you like to share a bottle of a deep and rich Bordeaux while dining in Paris on the Eiffel Tower?"

"Aye, the Bordeaux region does produce my favorite wines ...." Speaking with a slight Irish accent, she seems to be considering the offer. "Not that I'm committing to anything, but how would we get there?"

"We could leave on my private jet tomorrow night."

"That's quite a tempting offer. I'm a doctor, however, and seeing my patient is critical to making a proper diagnosis. Do I get to *see* you before I decide?" She seems intrigued, yet the two men seem to be waiting around hoping she'll reject the offer.

"This time, doctor, I think you should trust your other senses," I say, not releasing my hands.

"*Okay*, I'll go. Sounds like fun!" I finally remove my hands slowly and she turns around to face me. I smile my best toothy grin, like I just made an interception during the Super Bowl and ran it back for a touchdown.

I expect to see her smiling back at me, but she's grimacing instead. "Hmmm. Perhaps I spoke too soon. Now that I see you, well I can't exactly *ignore* my sense of sight."

The two men, now behind her, do a quick high five and burst into laughter.

"*Really?* It's a limited time offer. Perhaps I should make this offer to that woman at the end of the bar?" I gesture to the end of the bar and the two men can't help but look to see if there's another beautiful woman there.

"Oh, alright. Maybe your hideous looks will eventually grow on me," she jokes. Then she slowly and deliberately reaches her arms around me, and pulls me in for a long, passionate kiss. About halfway through the kiss, the two men give up and walk away.

"So kind of you to ignore my hideous looks, doctor." I produce a fake pout.

"Just kidding! You know how attracted I am to you, Trey."

"I may need another kiss like the last one to be fully convinced, Jess."

Jessica obliges, this time with even more passion than the first.

Chapter 33

TREY TYSON

SHELBY TOWNSHIP, MICHIGAN, USA
SUNDAY, OCTOBER 28, 2012

"Mom, I'm off to Paris tonight with Jessica." I'm pushing her wheelchair along the bike path at Stony Creek Metropark. It's a cool day, but when we find a spot along the path like this one, where the clearing in the trees allows the sun to shine through, I like to stop and let her soak up the warmth. "She *may* just be the one."

We're taking part in the MS Walkathon and our stroll through Stony Creek has been quite pleasant and relaxing, but Helen definitely perks up at that comment, "Dr. Jessica O'Neill? *The one?* I've always heard that Italian men shouldn't marry Irish women, because there would be too much passion for the relationship to last. It's like burning a candle at both ends. But personally, I don't know if you can have too much passion in a relationship …. Wow, it's about time! You've lived the bachelor life for far too long and I want some grandkids!" She's more excited about this than I ever imagined she would be.

"Slow down, Mom. I'm just saying that she *may* be the one."

"I know you'll be a great husband and father."

"Mom, tone it down. You're embarrassing me. Let's not get ahead of ourselves. I haven't even asked Jessica to marry me yet and who knows if she'll say yes. We haven't known each other for that long."

"You've dated quite a few women over the years, son, and not one of them compares to Jessica. She'll say yes. I've seen the way she looks at you when you don't know she's looking. A mother always knows …. Even though it's a bit old-fashioned, have you spoken to her parents about this proposal?"

"Yes, it *is* old-fashioned, but perhaps I am as well. I took them out to dinner last week when Jessica was working late at the hospital. I was so concerned that they'd spill the beans before I could ask her that I didn't really want to mention it yet. But then I decided I really want to do this the right way and I took the risk by asking for their permission."

"How'd it go?" she presses for details.

"Her mom just started bawling, and they both gave me a big hug and welcomed me to their family." I reflect on the moment and shrug. "I guess that means it went well."

Helen reaches her hand over her shoulder to gently pat my hand while I continue pushing her wheelchair. "The best thing I can say about you and Jessica is that I think you're *both* lucky to have found each other. That's pretty rare these days."

"Thanks, Mom. You know I wouldn't have ever met her if it weren't for that fall you took."

"You mean my multiple sclerosis has finally proven to be beneficial in some way?" she says with a healthy dose of sarcasm.

"If you hadn't broken your leg and ended up in the hospital …." My mom's comment replays in my head and my train of thought quickly shifts. "Mom, how are you coping lately? Will you be okay while I'm gone?" We pause again where the path starts heading uphill at a steep angle. A small group of people wearing "Walk MS" tee shirts walk past us. With a somewhat chilly Fall day for the MS walk, most of the participants are wearing their tee shirts over a sweatshirt or hoodie. I wrapped a large wool blanket around my mom before we started the walk and I take a moment to tuck it around her legs again.

"I'll be just fine, Trey. Obviously, Judith is in Washington, still very focused on her career there. Paul and Sarah are both available if I need them, but I can still get around okay on my own. Don't worry about me. I just want you to enjoy your trip."

"How do you do it?"

"Do what?" she asks.

"You lost Dad to a car accident, had to raise four kids on your own, and have had MS for three decades. I know how much you dislike being in a wheelchair, and you're always dealing with pain and all the medications. I've *never once* heard you complain about it. You're always so upbeat and optimistic."

Thinking about Mom's bravery facing a disease that has disabled and shortened the lives of so many people, I feel a sudden mix of both pride and sorrow sweep over me. I wipe the tears that silently roll down my cheeks with my right sleeve while still pushing the wheelchair with my left hand. Taking a deep breath to try to check my emotions, I put my sunglasses on. "I'm simply awed by the way you face this disease and refuse to be a victim." The words almost catch in my throat, and my glasses don't hide my tears very well.

Mom takes a moment before responding. "While I don't wish MS on anyone, I was extremely fortunate to have caught it so early. I remember when Max insisted I see a doctor way back in the '80s. It was as if he *knew* something was wrong before any doctor possibly could have. I've had very good medical care, Trey. And you kids have always been there for me when I need you."

"Your doctors say you may soon reach a point where you need more care than the weekly visit to do your shopping and handyman chores. They say – *eventually* – you'll be spending more and more time in a wheelchair, and far less time being able to walk." I take a deep breath and slowly release it. "So, I have a proposal for *you,* as well."

"What are you talking about, Trey?"

"You know how much I loved the Tampa area when I was playing for the Bucs. Well, I'm going to ask Jessica to move with me to Florida. It would mean she'd have to make a career adjustment, but I'm hoping she'll be open to it. I want to fly down there with her and find a nice piece of property on one of the barrier islands where we can build a home. And I want you to spend the winters with us when it's done."

Helen applies her wheelchair brake softly to signal for me to stop. "Now *you* are moving way too fast," she says.

"Sorry, Mom. I'll slow my pace."

"No, *not* with the wheelchair." She lets out a quick laugh. "Come around here so I can see you."

"Okay." I make sure the wheelchair brakes are locked. Then I walk around to face Mom, and crouch down so she can speak with me without having to crane her neck up.

"I think you and Jessica make a beautiful couple, and I can't imagine why she would hesitate to marry you or move to Florida with you. However," she shakes her head, "I don't think it's wise to have a parent living with you so soon after you've been married. She may not be comfortable with that. I'm not even sure I'd be comfortable with that arrangement."

"Mom," I smile warmly and confidently. I've thought this through and am certain my plan will work well for everyone. "We're going to build a guest house on the property. A beautiful, *close,* but *separate* living space. And I'll have my architect make sure the entire home is wheelchair-friendly."

Mom's face turns from doubtful, to introspective, then to somewhat excited. "That would certainly work from my point of view. It's so kind of you to plan ahead like this, and you ... well ...."

"What is it, Mom?" More doubts, something very important is on her mind.

"Nothing. I just ... I just think you better get engaged, and then married, *before* we have any more conversations about me moving in."

"Well, if your wishes for grandkids come true, we're going to need someone we trust to babysit on occasion!"

"Now who's getting ahead of himself again? Why don't we take this a step at a time? You go have a great time in France with Jessica, and come home with her as your fiancé. Once this dream home of yours is built, I'll be happy and grateful to spend a few weeks there. If it's comfortable for everyone, we can look at extending the time the next year."

"That sounds like a great plan." I kiss her cheek, stand up, and walk back to the other side of the wheelchair. We've reached the summit of the hill and I can see the tallest buildings in downtown Detroit, even though they're 30 miles away.

Suddenly I experience a quick flashback to the night Max, Samantha, and I went there to see if she could connect to her long dead ancestors.

The third Antichrist rises. The third Holy Warrior must awaken. Was that my thought? *No* .... I didn't just think that. That was a voice. Something like what Samantha described from her vision of her ancestors. I shake my head and am back in the moment.

"Mom, why did you name me Trey?"

"After 48 years with that name, you're asking me that now? Why?"

"I don't know. It just hit me that my name means three or third, but I'm a twin. It would make more sense if I were the third of triplets."

She takes a long few seconds before answering, "I wanted to name you Thomas, after your father and grandfather. Your dad wanted you to have your own name, though. Your own identity. You would have been Thomas Tyson the third, so Trey seemed to fit. It just felt right."

Chapter 34

TREY TYSON
PARIS, FRANCE
MONDAY, OCTOBER 29, 2012

It's a sunny and breezy day in Paris. The choppy river Seine rocks the taxi boat and Jessica snuggles up to me, intertwining her fingers with mine.

"Sweetheart," she speaks quietly and seductively into my ear, "you're truly one of a kind. What girl gets taken by private jet to Paris to indulge in the finest French cuisine? True enough … banana-chocolate crêpes are my new favorite breakfast!" She smiles, then nibbles gently on my earlobe before continuing, "A romantic day spent at the Louvre – the masterpieces took my breath away. And now we're traveling along the Seine, off to dinner at the Eiffel Tower!" She stops and stares at me, but my attention is focused inward. Not one to be ignored, she nudges me. "Hey, are you alright?"

Startled, I blink a few times before answering. "Yes, fine."

"Do you have jetlag? We can always postpone the Eiffel Tower and pick up something at a Bistro."

I look at her … truly taking in the person she is, and realize I'm the luckiest man in the world. At 48, I had begun to wonder if I'd ever find my one true love. Oh, I've had my fair share of short relationships, and way too many blind dates set up by family and friends. For me to not get bored quickly, I need a woman of substance; well read, educated, with a quick wit. I've always had a constant desire to learn as much as I can about history, religion, politics, technology, science, and different cultures. It's my addiction. A woman who's able to hold a stimulating conversation about several different topics is not only critically important, it's … *sexy*. It's even better if she can bring to the conversation some base of knowledge I don't have.

As much as I'd like to convince myself that physical beauty is a minor factor, there's no denying chemistry. Simply put, my body should want her body. It may not be very *evolved* of me, but so be it. Nature is nature.

Shortly after meeting a woman, I can sense if she's basically good-natured or not. A woman who can roll with life's curveballs is also important. Ironically, I wasn't looking to meet someone when Jessica crossed my path. Yet, when we did meet, sparks were flying. Her physical beauty was obvious, so I worked at getting to know her. The way she cared for Mom after her fall was more than just professional. She's emotionally invested in her patients and possesses a warmth and kindness that radiates to those around her. Initially, I was captivated by her intelligence, striking good looks, and inner beauty ... a combination of characteristics that struck me as truly rare. The more time we spent together during Mom's recovery, the more I thought about Jessica. I started to get the feeling that she enjoyed my company, so I asked her out to dinner. The conversation was everything I hoped it would be. And then I saw her smile. It was simply ... *breathtaking.*

After a few short months of dating, I can't imagine life without her. I can only hope Jessica feels the same way about me. Yet, as the taxi boat glides along the Seine, quickly approaching the Eiffel Tower, I start to feel nervous about proposing and can feel my pulse quicken. I'm accustomed to having all the answers and this time I don't. Having no sense as to whether she'll say yes or no is unnerving.

"Are you kidding?" I finally respond. "Postpone a romantic dinner with the most amazing, kind, and absolutely stunning woman on the planet? In the most beautiful city in the world? Not a chance."

"Aye. Flattery will get you everywhere! I can't imagine anything that would top today, but what's the plan for tomorrow?"

"Plan for tomorrow? Let me see .... Well, for tomorrow I thought we'd head to an important site – a place that intertwines religion, politics, architecture, and centuries of history and romance." I give her a sideways glance and raise an eyebrow. "Enticed?"

"True enough, Trey. You have my full attention. I'm enticed! But, I can think of a few places in Paris that might fit that lofty description. What did you have in mind?"

I look down, shaking my head in feigned distaste. "As much as it pains me, I know we couldn't come to Paris without visiting Notre Dame Cathedral."

"Of course! Why didn't I think of that?"

"Perhaps it's due to your inferior education." I smile and wink at her.

This dig draws an immediate flared response from Jessica, "*What?* I've never heard anyone call a degree from the University of Notre Dame inferior. Only an unruly *Wolverine* would even consider such a thing. Just because you made a poor choice in universities and you're jealous of our rich college football history, doesn't mean you should disparage the fine education Notre Dame provides."

"Rich college football history? Jealous?" I'm speechless for a moment. I look at her, then across the Seine, and back to Jessica. She can take it *and* dish it out! "Okay, I'll concede one point. You Irish have the *second* richest history in all of college football. It's impressive, really. In wins and winning percentage, you're behind only one team in history. And, you have a winning record against everyone you've ever faced ... oh ... except that one same team – *Michigan.*"

These collegiate jabs at each other are fun, but they sometimes escalate out of control, kind of like how Mom warned me about an Italian man and an Irish woman – maybe we can be too passionate. Jessica is about to turn around, faking being upset ... or possibly *truly* being upset. Before she can turn, I put my arms around her, and pull her in for a kiss. Our bodies gel so tightly together, I can feel her heartbeat up against my chest. Jessica's heart rate quickens at the onset of the kiss, but after a few moments her heart relaxes into a steady and strong beat. With just a brief hesitation she surrenders fully to me, until finally, breathless, we separate a few inches. I gaze into her glimmering green eyes, and my uneasiness fades.

Chapter 35

GREG RUTLEDGE
WASHINGTON DC, USA
MONDAY, OCTOBER 29, 2012

What a day. With back-to-back Situation Room meetings, my head is pounding, and I desperately need a drink. This time, the president's flanked by the Secretary of Defense and the Chairman of the Joint Chiefs of Staff.

"Director Rutledge, what's the latest intel from the ground in Somalia?" President Sanchez barks in my direction.

"We don't have any, Mr. President." I look down to the ground, unable to mask the disbelief I feel. "Our local asset, Arthur Sumner, has gone dark. We sent another asset in, and he was detected and detained shortly after arriving. I'm concerned that someone tipped off the Somali government about Sumner, and warned them that we'd be moving someone else. Once we found out about the detainment, we reached out to the Somalis requesting cooperation, especially given the nature of the situation with the pirates. They refused to help us, sir, saying brazenly that we should've been more up front instead of trying to sneak around in their country."

The president taps his fingers annoyingly on the large table, pondering his next move. "How soon before we can get another asset in place?"

"I'm not sure we *can* get someone else in place before the Navy arrives. The Somalis will be looking for us now. Sending someone else in would be unwise. I think we're stuck having to rely on our satellites for intel."

The president glances briefly to Chairman Andrew Vandevelde, and then stands up and glares down at me. "Are you confident we're doing the right thing? We're moving two carrier battle groups into the region."

"*Two?* Sir, my suggestion was *one* battle group. Taking two into the region will leave significant holes along our eastern seaboard."

Andrew leans forward to address this point. At 45, he had been the youngest Chairman ever appointed, and only the second from the Marines. He's known to be brash and aggressive, which is why, I believe, the president chose him in the first place. "Mr. President. If we're going to the region, we need to go there in *force*. With two battle groups, we'll scare the living shit out of the Somali pirates. We need them to think we *can* and *will* squash them, sir. On top of that, we need to retrieve the Saudi royalty without harm. If push comes to shove, we can wipe out their fleet in 15 minutes."

Being confident in my own assessment of the situation, I stand to meet the president eye-to-eye. "I would agree with Chairman Vandevelde *if* it weren't for the hostages being held, not to mention the change in attitude we've seen lately. The Somalis have become quite bold, to the point of being fearless ... even reckless. If they see an overwhelming show of force, they may just decide to kill the hostages and scatter."

Again, the president glances quickly to Andrew before addressing me. "Let's stick to Andrew's plan, and go with two."

Chapter 36

TREY TYSON
PARIS, FRANCE
MONDAY, OCTOBER 29, 2012

Darkness settled on Paris as we rode the Eiffel Tower inclinators up to Altitude 95, the restaurant perched amid the tower at 95 meters above sea level. I catch the singer's eye and wink at her. She winks back to confirm she understands. On cue, our waiter visits our table.

"Tout est prêt?" I ask the waiter if everything is ready, in French, hoping Jessica doesn't know what I'm saying. The buildup to this moment has me anxious, and I can't wait any longer.

The waiter nods.

"Merci." I wait as patiently as I can as he clears our dinner table, removing the empty Bordeaux bottle. The waiter then pours two glasses of their finest champagne.

Jessica takes a sip from her glass. She seems both content and relaxed. "Trey, this band is terrific. I have to pinch myself. Dinner at the Eiffel Tower. The diagonal elevator ride was an event in itself. The food, the ambiance, and of course, the company – all fine enough."

My heart skips a beat in anticipation. She is utterly enchanting.

Pointing out the window, I say, "It's quite an amazing view, isn't it?"

We have the center table beside the windows. It's dark out, but the lights reflecting off the gentle waves of the river are mesmerizing. As Jessica turns to look out the window, I wave my left hand toward the singer for the piano quintet. They've been watching for my signal and start playing *Time to Say Goodbye*, Jessica's favorite song. I reach into my jacket and pull out the ring. Jessica is still looking out the window as I subtly step back from my seat, close my right hand tightly around the ring, lower to one knee, and wait quietly for her to notice.

"Oh, my, it's *Time to Say Goodbye?*" Jessica turns back to my empty seat, and her eyes then dart to where I'm kneeling. She gasps just loudly enough for me to hear. The corners of her mouth curve up into a warm smile that ever so subtly quivers, and her eyes begin to well up.

V. RAY

Reaching out for her hand, she eagerly places it into mine. "Jessica," I nearly whisper her name. "I've traveled much of the world, and experienced so many things. But I've done it all on my own." I squeeze her hand a little tighter, and she squeezes back. "It's time to say goodbye to that way of life. My life is richer and fuller because you're part of it. I want to spend the rest of our lives together. *Always*. I love you more than words can express." I pause for half of a heartbeat. "Will you marry me?"

Jessica leans over and puts her arms around me. "I love you, Trey!" She starts in for a kiss, and I meet her halfway. It was the start of another long kiss, when suddenly Jessica pulls away slightly. "Is that a ring in your hand?"

"Yes," I reply calmly.

"Are you going to show it to me?"

"Of course." I raise my hand with the ring still tightly held and hidden from view. Opening one finger slowly, I watch as Jessica's eyes get bigger with excitement. Then I quickly close the finger again. "You know ... you haven't actually answered my question."

Jessica laughs. "Yes! A million times, yes! Of course, I'll marry you."

"Then close your eyes, and hold out your hand." I'm beaming with such joy that I can barely contain myself. Yet there's also a sense of relief. A light-headed sensation begins to overwhelm me, but I recover quickly and find my balance.

I gently slide the ring onto her left ring finger, and watch her eyes open abruptly, bursting with excitement.

"Oh, Trey. It's beautiful ... absolutely perfect." She holds it up, and we're both able to see the overhead light glimmer off the large diamond. She leans in for another long and deep kiss, but this time doesn't pull away.

Chapter 37

GREG RUTLEDGE
WASHINGTON, DC, USA
MONDAY, OCTOBER 29, 2012

As I approach my Langley office, I see Max Medici waiting patiently outside my door. I wouldn't be where I am today if it weren't for Max's training. His thoroughness, professionalism, and humility are traits so many of our younger teammates lack. Max is revered by the few people who know his record, and his retirement was a huge loss for AI. It's amazing how young and fit he looks for a man of over eighty years.

"Maximo Medici, my old friend! It's been too long. Good to see you." Shaking Max's hand enthusiastically, I lead him into my office. "I have to tell you how surprised I was to get your call. I figured once you retired, I'd never hear from you again. What's so urgent?"

"Greg, you're a busy man, so thanks for taking the time."

"Care for a cup of coffee or anything?" I ask.

"No, thanks." Max seems to be in quite a hurry to get to his point. "Greg, I'm here looking for some information that's probably classified. But it's critical to our nation and, frankly, everyone else as well."

"Max, are you kidding me? Your security clearance was always at least as high as my own and I know you always do things for the right reasons. What's going on?"

"I fear the time of the third Antichrist is upon us." This is a subject that Max rarely broaches and it's been at least a decade since the last time I can remember him mentioning the third Antichrist. "I don't know who it is, but I'm certain it's related to the Somali situation. The media has downplayed the crisis, yet my intuition tells me there's far more to this."

"We've discussed this in the past, Max. I'm not sure I even believe in Christ – let alone an Antichrist." Assessing my old friend, Max seems to have his wits about him. He's *dead serious* about this threat he perceives. That doesn't make him necessarily right, but I can't discount Max's intuition either. Over the years, it's proven to be quite an effective tool in fighting threats to the president and the country. "You name it. What can I do for you?"

"I've heard some rumblings of some action being taken in the Gulf of Aden. What can you tell me about it?"

As Director of the CIA, I must consider if I should tell Max the details, but that consideration only takes a moment before I conclude I have to trust this man completely. His lifetime of service deserves nothing less.

"Max, your intuition may be on target here. This whole situation stinks to high heaven, if you ask me. The Somali pirates have gone far beyond the nuisance stage. They've become a top priority now."

"Okay, but what have they done *now* that they haven't done before?" Max shrugs. "The news hasn't mentioned anything out of the ordinary. From what I see on CNN, it seems like just another day in the neighborhood ... at least the Gulf of Aden neighborhood."

"They took two members of the Saudi royal family as hostages," I reveal.

Max becomes instantly agitated, as if he expected something like that. "What's our response?"

"We're moving part of our Atlantic fleet into the arena. We need to retrieve the hostages and put an end to this problem, once and for all."

"Who do you have in the field there?" Max presses.

"We had Sumner in place. He'd been embedded there for years, but he's been captured by the Somalis." I bow my head briefly in respect, knowing Max and Sumner were friends.

"How? You know Arthur, and he's one of our best."

"You're right. He *is* one of our best. There's no way he did anything to give himself away. I sent in another agent. When he landed, he was instantly picked up at the airport and detained."

Max raises his eyebrows in disbelief. "That's all the evidence we need – we're dealing with an insider. Who knew Arthur was there?"

I quickly think about the five or six people who knew about Sumner, and if any one of them is a spy, there will be serious ramifications. "Not many, I'll tell you that much."

"Any way to get someone else in place?"

"I don't honestly know *who* I can trust right now. We're relying on satellite surveillance for our intel 24/7."

189

"We don't have any live contact with anyone in the arena? And we don't know where the hostages are being held?"

I wish I had better answers, but can only shake my head. "No and no."

"I'm sure you know this," Max pauses for just a moment. "But, this is going to be a far more serious problem than just the two royal hostages."

"Max, give it to me straight. As an administration, we have a noose around our necks. Anything that can loosen the grip would be welcomed …. Wait, you don't think the infamous *Karl* is involved, do you?" I was a young CIA agent training under Max and assigned to help interrogate Katarina Krostov after the Kennedy assassination. Max and I worked together for months trying to get as much information as possible out of her. We learned the mysterious Karl was the financier for Viktor Krostov's Russian team. Karl and Viktor are an ongoing threat to the United States, and a constant thorn in my side.

"I don't know yet, but I can tell you is that this is going to get *far* worse than anyone can imagine right now."

Knowing there may be an enemy spy deep within the Agency or the president's administration, I can think of no one I'd rather have suddenly appear at my office door than Max Medici. "What do you need from me?"

"First, we need to limit the people who know about my involvement to only essentials. I have no desire to be snatched by the Somalis or anyone else for that matter. Second, I'm going to need to be able to reach you from anywhere in the world on a moment's notice. Do you have any of your new-fangled high-tech communications devices that you can let me use?"

"Hmmm … I wish you could tell me more about your plans, but maybe it's better to keep those to yourself. I'll help you any way I can, Max, especially if you can get me some intel on the situation beyond what our satellites can provide." Picking up my phone, I speed-dial two numbers, and wait a couple of seconds for the other side. "Yes." I speak into the phone, but project my voice Max to hear me. "Q, this is important. Max Medici will be there to see you in a few minutes …. Yes, he is …. Listen, he's going to need temporary full clearance, 30 days, starting today. Get him a firearm and arrange for any transportation he needs. Oh, and he's going to need the new ComWatch …. Yes, and no one else is to know about this. And, I mean *no one*. Understood? …. Good."

V. RAY

Max looks perplexed as I hang up the phone. "ComWatch?"

"Yes …. Go see Q. He'll show you how to operate the ComWatch. But in a nutshell, it will use cell towers, satellites, or even hack into private Wi-Fi networks if necessary to automatically set you up with a secure connection."

"This is what happens after I've been retired for a little while? You're calling the CIA's head of Research and Development by the same name they use in the Bond movies?"

"Oh!" I let a quick chuckle escape me. "I forgot that you haven't met Q yet. So, we bring in a new head of R & D, and his name is Jason Quincy. I mean, come on … how do we *not* call him Q?"

"Does this Q have a British accent, too?"

"No," I let out another chuckle, this one a little hardier. "He's from San Antonio – pure Texas drawl!"

The almost always serious face that Max projects cracks a smile. But he quickly becomes serious again. "One more thing, Greg. I may need some assistance from Judith or Samantha in AI; will I be able to reach them with this ComWatch thing?"

"Yes, just make sure to ask Q to program those connections into the device." Wait, aren't they on assignment? "Max, come to think of it, I believe they're both on a direct assignment from the president. In any event, you'll be able to reach me, them, or any phone number you need to from nearly anywhere on the planet."

Max stands up, extending his hand. "Stay safe, Greg. I can't begin to thank you enough."

"Yes, you can." I shake Max's hand, wondering if the old man is going on his last mission for our country. "You can find out what the hell is going on over there, before this gets really messy."

Chapter 38

MAX MEDICI
WASHINGTON, DC, USA
MONDAY, OCTOBER 29, 2012

Q arranged to get me on the next flight to Detroit from DC and had a rental car waiting for me. I drove to Shelby Township and now stand waiting outside a front door. I knocked on the door nearly two minutes ago, but I know the occupant will need some time to get here. Ah, here she comes. The click of the door unlocking is soon followed by movement. Eventually, the door swings open to the inside. Helen Tyson wheels her chair closer to the opening and then rubs one of her eyes.

"Maximo? What brings you here at this hour? Is Judith okay?"

"Hi, Helen. I'm sorry to disturb you, but I need to talk. Can I come in?"

"Of course," she says warily, not trying to hide that she expects me to bring bad news.

"Can I help?" I ask, gesturing to the handles on Helen's wheelchair.

"That would be lovely ... thank you."

I push Helen's chair to her living room, angle her chair to one of the two wingback chairs, and sit down to face her. "Helen, I'm trying to reach Trey and I can't find him anywhere. His mobile phone is off. I get nothing but his answering service at his home and office numbers. It's extremely important that I find him as soon as possible. Any idea where he is or how to reach him?"

Helen pauses tentatively before answering me, "You could have called me, Max. Why is the personal visit necessary?"

She's on to me. No sense in beating around the bush. It's the reason I came personally, instead of calling. I need for her to know just how critical this is. "The time has come, and I need Trey's help."

Helen bows her head to shield the tears building up in her eyes. "There must be some other way! Trey can't be the only one who can help you. Judith signed up for this, not Trey. Why can't she help you?"

"Judith has a role to play as well. Nevertheless, Trey is destined for this. He always has been. You don't have to believe me, but he's a Holy Warrior and the future of everyone on this planet is at risk. I'm sure you know where he is and I need to find him right away."

Helen looks around her, almost as if she's seeking some sort of way to escape. She soon focuses her attention back to bear on me. "Your timing couldn't be worse, Max. He's finally found the love of his life. In fact, you'd be interrupting a marriage proposal. Can't you find someone else, or at least give him some more time?"

"That nice doctor, who has been caring for you?"

She nods.

"Knowing Trey, he's not going to do this halfway. He'll want to make an impression. He took her to Paris, didn't he?"

Helen shakes her head, no, but her eyes reveal the truth.

I stand up, having ascertained what I needed to know. "Thank you, Helen. You've always favored Trey. He has an important role to play that may have an impact on all of us. But you know you can trust me to do my utmost to keep him safe."

"Please let him be. *Please* ... find another way."

"I wish I could, but we both know what's at stake. The risks are too great for me not to involve him. Stay safe. I can see myself out."

Chapter 39

TREY TYSON
PARIS, FRANCE
TUESDAY, OCTOBER 30, 2012

Jessica slows her pace as we're crossing a bridge over the Seine to reach the Ile de la Cité and Notre Dame Cathedral. "You know; it would have been easy enough to take one of those taxi boat things down the Seine to get here this morning." Jessica says as she tugs my hand, signaling for me to slow down with her. She tries, in vain, to cover a long, drawn-out yawn.

"What? Are you bored after just one day in Paris?" I ask in a sarcastic tone.

"A bit tired, maybe, but how could I be bored?" And with this, she perks up a bit.

"Why would we take the Batabus, Dr. O'Neill?"

"Dr. O'Neill?" Jessica seems to be taken aback when hearing me address her that way. "I'm going to have to get used to being referred to as Dr. Tyson at some point. Might as well start now."

"Really? You know, I've never even thought about you changing your name once we're married. I figured it might be challenging to make the change, given your profession."

"Of course, I'm going to take your name. I may be old-fashioned, I guess, but that's who you're marrying. I'm not the only one, apparently. I called my parents while you were out getting coffee. They weren't surprised at all. Sure enough, Dad tried to deny that you asked them first, but I can always get the truth out of Mom." A breeze pushes Jessica's hair over her face, and she pushes it aside. I love the gracefulness of her every gesture. "I think it's important for our family to all share the same last name and even more so should we be blessed with children. It provides a sense of tradition … unity … maybe even family pride."

I grin, feeling a sense of calmness. Even though Jess and I have only dated a short time, this decision just seems so right. I'm already looking so forward to starting our lives together as a family and hearing her talk about children warms my heart. Then, I remember my original point, "I'd expect anyone in the medical profession to appreciate a healthy exercise regimen, especially someone as athletic as you."

"Aye, most days, to be sure. But, I may have had too much to drink last night to feel good about a five-mile hike through Paris this morning. And I certainly didn't get enough sleep, thanks to you!" She winks at me, then continues, "You got even less sleep than I did. But you average, what, five hours a night?"

"I think of sleep as my personal holy grail; an ever-unachievable goal. And yet I wonder what I'd do with it if I ever did get any."

"You startled me when you woke up. I think it was around four. You were dreaming, weren't you?"

I'm not sure what to say to Jessica. I've never discussed my dreams with anyone. But, if we're to be married, I certainly don't want to begin by hiding anything. "It was a very odd dream. Well, more of a *vision* that was followed by a picture in my head. I just couldn't figure out what it was or why I was seeing it."

Jessica reaches over and grasps my hand. "Something disturbing enough to startle you to wake? Can you describe it?"

This is what it's going to be like to be married to a doctor. She'll always be eager to care for me, but I think I'm being diagnosed. The thought makes me smile. "The dream was brief. It was a vision of a massive fire on top of a body of water …. The picture to follow was quite vivid." Searching momentarily through my thoughts, I consider how best to describe the picture. "It was a hand-painted picture. On top, there was a wheel, and right below that was a crescent moon. In the middle was an archer, with bow drawn and arrow aimed at a woman. The woman held the bow, as if they were connected somehow. And she seemed concerned, but the concern on her face seemed far broader than just for her own wellbeing." There's more about the woman that I should be grasping, something important, but I don't know what it is. "And on the bottom of the picture were a white bull on one side and a lever scale on the other. The two sides of the scale were in perfect balance, but the implication seemed to be that a threat from above or from the bull would cause one side or the other to move out of balance." Trying to remember if there was anything else of importance in the picture, I'm drawing a blank. "I'm not at all sure where the picture came from, or why it was in my dreams last night. What do you think, Doc? Am I going crazy?"

"What a vivid picture. And with so much potential for symbolism." She keeps her gaze fixed on me, almost *studying* my face. "No, I don't think you're crazy. As an emergency room doctor, I've heard of some unique dreams and visions from my patients; especially the ones who are experiencing a traumatic event. Then, there are the people who have come back after being pronounced dead. You want to talk about some descriptions of odd and vivid pictures! I think we should explore what this means, Trey. Any ideas where to start?"

"I wish I did." Where is my old friend Max now? I bet he'd have an idea. This level of probing is a little uncomfortable. Time to change the subject. "You know … I find walking through a city to be the best way to truly learn about it, and the fresh air will do us some good."

Jessica takes a deep breath, quickly adjusting when I increase my pace slightly as we approach the entrance to the cathedral. "What's the hurry? I'm having a hard time imagining a stern Wolverine such as you, acting so anxious to visit Notre Dame."

Just outside the entrance, I take a long moment to appreciate the beautifully crafted, circular, leaded glass window above the center double doors. I point out the ongoing construction, with the odd chute running almost the entire height of the front left facade that ends abruptly in a dumpster. "They must be trying to *restore* Notre Dame's tradition."

Jessica glares at me, "Ha Ha. Very funny! Are you trying to stir it up again about my Fighting Irish?"

I sense Jessica's lack of desire to engage in another Notre Dame versus Michigan debate, and decide to change the subject again. "Not today, my dear …. You know how much I appreciate historical sites such as this, even with the religious aspect."

"Aye. *Speaking* of religious aspects, what are your thoughts about getting married in a church?" That's a doozy of a question. She's been waiting for an opening, and I just gave it to her. Jessica is a devout Catholic and she knows I'm not particularly fond of any organized religion.

Still, I'm happy to segue from college football to religion. We'll need to have this conversation at some point, and here in front of Notre

Dame Cathedral is as appropriate as any place I can imagine. "I don't have the same appreciation for the church that you do."

"I know that. In fact, I think you may be an … *atheist.*" Jessica looks down, almost embarrassed to say that.

I gently put my hand under her chin, coaxing her to look back into my eyes. "While I can't find a solid argument to disagree with an atheist, I don't consider myself to be one. My views are far more in line with agnostics. Barring a verifiable miracle, I believe it's simply impossible to know whether God exists. That is, of course, until we die …. So, I'm in no hurry to find out." I try to finish deep thoughts with some humor to lighten the moment, but I'm not sure it's going to work this time.

Jessica finally brings her gaze back to me. "There are so many wrongs that happen in life to cause doubt. I get that. But there are also so many miracles – life itself, for example – that simply couldn't *be* without a guiding force."

"The existence of a single god or multiple gods has been debated over millennia. It seems to me, looking at the issue through the long history of humankind, that many gods have been created and worshipped to answer questions we couldn't answer for ourselves. Across several ancient cultures, there have been gods to move the moon or the sun. Gods to make it rain or cause lightning to strike the Earth." I shrug. "But as we discovered how each of these things happen, our reason for that god went away, and the god was no longer worshipped. Now, most major religions worship one God. Seemingly, to answer the remaining unanswerable questions in life …. *Do* we have a *soul*? Is there an afterlife? *How* did we come to *be*? And we could debate these questions endlessly without empirical proof for either side of the argument."

"So, you think gods have always been created by us, *just* to answer questions we couldn't answer?"

"That's not the only reason. Religion has been used to control the masses, usually, but not always, for good reason. It's also been used as a means to take money or possessions from the masses, often against their will."

"Now you're talking about religion and I'm talking about God. Very different subjects!" Jessica's intensity for this subject shines through clearly.

"You're right." I concede the point. My beliefs differ from hers greatly, but we've always respected our differences. "Listen. I believe the debate about the existence of God must eventually focus on space and matter." I pause to let her absorb the slight tangent in my line of reason. "Once you establish a foundation in the universe of space and matter, then science can explain the elements, the compounds, and the many forces that shape the stars and planets. Through science, we can even understand how an environment capable of sustaining life comes to be, as well as the series of genetic mutations that eventually lead to the evolvement of humankind – life! *But,* everything and everyone in existence must reside in the realm that is space, and come from some form of matter …. So, I believe it comes down to two simple options when considering the existence of God. Is it easier to believe that space and matter have simply always existed? *Or* … is it easier to believe that an all-powerful being has *always* existed that could *create* the universe and everything in it from an empty void, and *guide* the evolution of humans?"

Jessica's smile evaporates instantly. "But what about *faith?*"

"Faith in what?" I ask gently.

"Faith in God!"

"How do you know about God?" It seems like a ridiculous question, initially, but it's important in my logic stream.

"What do you mean?"

"Well, do you know about God because he or she has spoken to you directly?"

"No, of course not."

"Well, then you must have learned about God from another person, right? Most likely your parents?"

"Aye," she reluctantly admits.

"And they were taught this concept from other people, most likely their parents?"

"Aye, true enough, I suppose."

"Then your faith is more accurately placed in the long line of people who have passed down this concept over time …. I believe there are two ways to look at that: one is that this many people over this duration of history *can't* possibly be wrong." Jessica nods slightly. "The other is that maybe they *are* in fact wrong. And then you have to consider the motives for those who first started the concept of one God."

"I don't even want to go there." Tears start to well in her eyes.

I gently put my hands on Jessica's cheeks, and make sure our eyes meet and stay focused on each other. This may just be an intellectual exercise for me, but it is extremely important to her. "I just want to be honest with you, and explain my thoughts and feelings about it." I smile warmly at her, and she responds with her own warm smile. "Theories are great, but I don't *know* any of this for certain. I do know I want to spend the rest of our lives together. If you want to get married in a church … well, I'm more than happy to." I take a deep breath so she can fully take in that statement. "Just because I can't logically make a case for the existence of God, doesn't mean that he or she hasn't always existed."

I think back to when Max and I watched as Samantha experienced her vision of Tecumseh's curse. She probably saved President Reagan's life with her vision. Now, *there's* a good reason to leave open the possibility of the existence of God.

JESSICA O'NEILL

Did I just hear what I think I heard?

I let the tear that had been growing in my eye finally escape, now that it's a tear of happiness. Oh my, what a relief! I finally let out a breath that I didn't even realize I was holding in.

"Have I told you how much I love you yet today?"

"Yes," Trey replies, "but you can say that as many times as you like. It'll never get old to me."

I've known we have very different views on religion, but I always thought it was a moot point … because I never expected Trey to propose marriage. Last night was a whirlwind of emotions. First, I couldn't believe he was on his knee about to propose. Then, when he did propose, my heart instantly wanted to jump for joy. But, my head started to take over as we went back to our hotel. I fell in love with Trey early on in our dating, but I never thought it would lead to marriage. He's a gorgeous and wealthy playboy; a former pro athlete who keeps his 6' 1" body in shape. In his upper 40s and never married, it seemed much more likely that he would be a permanent bachelor. True enough, probably just playing the field. So, I braced myself for the eventual breakup I was sure would come as soon as any conversation of commitment came up. But the more time I spent with Trey, the deeper my love for him grew, and the more I secretly hoped it would be lasting.

He's 12 years older, but his energy and quick wit often make me feel like I'm the older one. Trey's a rebel at heart, yet he's always honest with himself and everyone around him. It's a bit scary just how perfect he is for me, balancing my conservative nature, and my heart would break if I ever lost him.

I'm a bit shocked and at the same time overjoyed at knowing how happy my family will be to see me get married in a Catholic church. It's been the one worry I've had about marrying Trey. We're so compatible in so many ways, but religion is important to me and it isn't to him.

"Trey, can you tell me some of the history behind Notre Dame? I'm very intrigued."

The sun is shining brightly in the Paris morning sky, so as I turn southeast to examine the cathedral, I'm forced to squint a bit. I love that his knowledge of history and historical sites is both so broad and so deep. Hard to imagine for a football jock.

Trey gestures to the cathedral. "Well, I suppose we start with the original decision to build it by Bishop Maurice de Sully during the reign of King Louis VII. They demolished the previous Paris Cathedral, and chose to use the same site on the Ile de la Cité, the center of Paris and one of the two natural islands along the Seine within the city. Groundbreaking started in 1163 and they used portions of the old cathedral during construction. The new cathedral wasn't completed until the year 1345. It's gone through several renovations. And, as can be seen by the construction chute here, there's often a need for minor restorations." Just as Trey finishes that sentence, a large object crashes into the dumpster below. The sound of debris clanking against the metal reverberates over the entire island.

Trey continues, not distracted in the least, "Notre Dame has been the site of many royal coronations, perhaps the most famous of which was for non-royalty."

"Aye, you mean Napoleon?" I ask.

Trey grins. "Right you are, my dear. Napoleon Bonaparte was a brilliant military and political strategist. After aiding the American Revolution, the French were inspired by America's success at gaining independence from the British monarchy and forging a new republic. The French people had grown weary of their own monarchy, and especially the privileges bestowed upon aristocratic and religious leaders under the reign of King Louis XVI. The French Revolution began, and the king was soon forced to face the wrath of the people."

He looks up at the edifice in front of us. "Having ousted and executed their king, the French formed a new government called the Consulate, and declared France to be a republic. What they never anticipated, however, was Napoleon's sheer lust for power. He rode a wave of anti-monarchy sentiment during the French Revolution to a leadership role in both the revolution and the new government. After a mere seven years as a republic, Napoleon succeeded in a coup d'état, establishing himself as First Consul of the Consulate. He marshaled the

French military and started the hugely successful Napoleonic Wars over much of Europe. And, in 1804, Napoleon had himself crowned as Emperor of France right here in Notre Dame Cathedral. He became the *very thing* the French Revolution was inspired to destroy."

"Amazing!" I love his mind. "The architecture of the cathedral is simply beautiful. Has it changed much since Napoleon's time?"

"From what I've read, the structure has stood mostly the way it is now since 1345, other than minor renovations and repairs."

"What a rich history. I'm surprised that it made it through all those centuries; what with the French Revolution and two world wars fought in Europe where France was heavily involved in the fighting. The Germans took Paris in World War II. Why didn't they destroy it, or at least loot it for its valuable artworks?" I ask.

"Oh, it's been looted a few times in history and Hitler did in fact order its destruction along with the burning of all of Paris in August of 1944." Trey shoots another glance at the cathedral before looking back at me. "Thankfully, Allied forces were able to liberate Paris just before the order could be executed."

"Incredible! Let's go and see the inside." I'm hoping the inside will be as beautiful as the outside. "I want to see how those leaded glass windows look with the sunlight passing through them."

Walking through the large double doors centering the western facade of Notre Dame Cathedral leaves me with a sense of awe. As I take a few steps inside, I can't help but notice the difficulty the sunlight is having as it tries to pass through the leaded glass windows and make a dent on the darkness of the cathedral. That's my first impression of this place – *darkness*.

A horrible memory takes over my mind before I can stop it. *Dark ... alone ...* I was four years old ... my parents went on a weeklong vacation and left me with Grandma. Day one was wonderful, as no one spoiled me like Grandma. I had my favorite doll, Grandma always made me my favorite foods, and she played with me all day. The tiny, two-bedroom home was cozy and comfortable. A small, burgundy velvet couch, thick shag carpeting, and a black piano were in the main room. There was also a black and white TV, but Grandma never watched it. The small kitchen had green and gold Formica flooring and a table just barely big enough for two people to share. The bedrooms were small, with oversized red and white quilts Grandma had made on each of the beds. I remember going to bed in warm flannel pajamas with a small glass of chocolate milk. Only Grandma did that for me.

V. RAY

The morning of day two started great as well. Grandma made hot oatmeal with a dab of honey in it and it smelled *so* good. She was getting me a spoon, when the lights suddenly went out. "Must have blown a fuse in the basement. I'll be right back," she said. Grandma found a candle and lit it. She went down the creaky steps, slowly in the dark, only the candle to light her way. Then there was a long minute of silence, a scuffling noise, and the lights came back on. A sudden loud pop was immediately followed by the lights going out again … and I thought I heard a *thud*. "Grandma?" I yelled. Silence. "Grandma?" I tried again. Nothing. I tiptoed to the basement steps, not wanting to make a noise. I was so afraid I wouldn't hear her. The stairs were dark, but there was a faint flickering light coming from deeper in the basement … the candle was still lit! "Grandma?" I yelled from the top of the stairs. Still nothing.

It was so dark down there and I was afraid. But I had to check on Grandma. I went down the steps as quickly as I could, squeezing the railing. Once I reached the bottom, I could see the flickering candle in the back corner of the basement, but I couldn't see Grandma. Running to the candle, I saw her lying motionless on the floor. "Grandma?" No response … no movement at all. I tried to shake her awake and that's when I saw her left hand, fingers blackened. I hugged her with all my might … and then realized she wasn't breathing. Terrified, I ran upstairs, found my doll, and hid in the bedroom. The rest of the week was a blur. I ate sometimes … sometimes I slept … I cried day and night for Grandma and for myself … and I held my doll in the darkness of each night … alone.

A hand touches mine suddenly and my whole body shudders, breaking my stream of memories. It's Trey. Somehow, he must have sensed how much I needed him.

Then a feeling of foreboding takes over, and I fight an urge to turn around and run. So much history has happened right here.

"You okay?" he whispers in my ear.

I try to steady myself and squeeze his hand. "Aye … thank you."

"Any time." He gestures back to a small group forming near a table of candles. "I arranged for us to join a tour group that is going to climb the stairs of the north tower."

Pulling myself fully into the present, I force a laugh. "Oh, great! You *know* I've never been a professional athlete, right? First a five-mile hike and now we get to climb a hundred stairs."

"A hundred stairs?" Trey grins. "My dear doctor. It's over four hundred stairs to the top! But don't despair. The reward for this climb is to see some of the history behind the cathedral's construction. Not to mention a view of the tower bell in the southern tower."

Starting to truly feel better, I gain strength from his hand and his smile. "You mean the same tower bell rung by Quasimodo?"

"Indeed, my love. Victor Hugo's *hunchback.*"

"Okay, let's go!"

"That's the spirit!"

MAX MEDICI

The Charles De Gaulle airport looks the same as the last time I was in Paris. Of course, the last time I came here, I didn't need to take a nap on the flight. Thankfully, I slept on the flight from Detroit, though. A sense of trepidation almost overwhelms me, knowing the third Antichrist will soon strike. And I have no idea how or where. Trey is in Paris, it's just a matter of finding him.

He must be the third Holy Warrior. The chosen one. And he may be the only person able to help me stop the third Antichrist.

Using my ComWatch, I dial Trey's mobile phone. However, the results are no different from my previous attempts – an immediate jump to voicemail – meaning his phone is turned off.

Hmmm … If Trey is proposing marriage, he would only do so on the Eiffel Tower. I'll start there.

Dammit, Trey, *turn on your phone!*

TREY TYSON

Just as Jessica and I reach the top of the circular stairs of Notre Dame Cathedral's northern tower, I feel my thigh vibrate. Reaching for my phone is my natural instinct after that vibration. *Wait.* My phone's not even on. Jeez … I can only shake my head in disbelief. Pavlov would be pleased! Part of me wants to turn the phone on, but I decided before this trip that I wouldn't accept any interruptions. I left Sarah in charge and she has the expectation that she'll have to make any critical business decisions herself from now on.

The English-speaking tour guide can see everyone still needs a moment to catch their breath after the climb, so he stops the group near the top of the stairs. "As I said on the main level, much of the facade outside was added after the original walls had been up in order to strengthen the structure. Inside, however, the renovations have been more cosmetic. Looters ravaged Notre Dame during the French Revolution and much damage was done to the inner walls. This," he points at an unfinished portion of the renovations as the group ascends the final few stone steps, "clearly shows the original structure along with the renovations that came long after the Revolution was over. Above us are the smaller bells of the north tower, now controlled by an electric, motorized system. To reach the south tower –"

Oh no, not now! I can't believe one of my migraines is coming on. I hope it passes quickly.

"Look!" Jessica grabs my arm, urging me up the final steps. She tries to whisper, but a few of the other tourists around us hear her and look to where she's pointing.

"What is it?" I whisper back. Looking at the tops of my shoes while I attempt to will the pain away, I can't imagine what would be so exciting about seeing the original wall here in the northern tower. Jessica probably thinks I need to catch my breath. And while it may hurt my ego a bit as a former athlete, it might serve well to buy some time.

"We can't delay here. The next group is right behind us." The tour guide works to get his group to keep moving forward.

"Just look." She isn't even *trying* to whisper anymore. We're the last in our group to reach the top of the stairs. The rest of the group has

already spilled into the north tower. Jessica stops in her tracks, pressing to get my attention.

"Okay, okay." I lift and turn my head, trying to ignore the blast of pain, and then do a double take. "Huh? That's odd."

"Weird enough, isn't it? That's why you had to see this. It's your signature on the original wall within Notre Dame Cathedral. It's just unbelievable."

"There are lots of random scratches and carvings on the wall. It's just a very odd coincidence."

"No, Trey. I don't think it's a coincidence at all. It's not a random carving either. It's the *exact* way you sign your name. It's *T3*, and it's identical to how you write it."

"It does look the same, but what of it? Perhaps I have a crazy football fan in Paris, who decided to chisel my autograph for me."

"This doesn't look recent. It looks more like it was chiseled out centuries ago …."

JUDITH TYSON
AMSTERDAM, NETHERLANDS

"Hello?" My caller ID simply reads *"blocked"* in its attempt to identify the caller. That often means someone from the Agency is trying to reach me.

"Judith, is that you?"

"Yes … Max? Is that your voice? Max Medici! How are you? *Where* are you?"

"Judith, yes it's me. I'm fine and I'm in Paris. Where are you right now?"

"I'm in Amsterdam. At the airport. I'm here with Samantha on an assignment for the president. Max, what's wrong? You sound stressed out and you almost never sound stressed out."

"Sam's with you? Wonderful! How soon can the two of you be in Paris?"

"We're on a *very important* assignment, Max. We can't just drop everything and head to Paris. What's going on?"

"It's the time of the third Antichrist. I need to find your brother, and it's imperative that you and Sam help me as well." Max sounds exasperated, yet there is also a hint of excitement in his tone.

"What makes you think it's time for the third Antichrist to appear? And what does *Trey* have to do with this?"

"I'll tell you what I know once we're all together here in Paris. I need you to trust me on this. Whatever important assignment you two are on ... well, it's not as important as *this.*"

"We have some flexibility in our assignment that would allow for a meeting there," I give in. "We'll be there as soon as possible. I'll reach out to you once we land. Can I call your mobile when we arrive?"

"Yes, it's linked to this new com device. By the way, any idea how to reach your brother?"

"Sorry, Max. Nothing better than trying his mobile number, but I'm sure you've already tried that."

"I have. Okay, thanks for changing your plans. I'll see you soon."

"Max. If you believe it's the time of the Antichrist, then I believe you. See you in a few hours."

TREY TYSON
PARIS, FRANCE

"This was much more enjoyable when you were the one doing the posing." I wink at Jessica.

"Hold still!" she exclaims.

"Come on. I watched him drawing you and you hardly held still. Between chewing gum, flipping your hair, and watching people walk by,

I'm surprised he could capture you at all. But your part came out fantastic. I can't wait to see the finished product."

Jessica laughs boisterously, but quickly stifles it. "Trey! You *have* to hold still!" She winks, and then forces her eyes to cross. I look at her curiously, but guess she's just trying to make me laugh. After seeing the rest of Notre Dame, we visited a café for lunch and then hiked through the Paris theatre district to reach the top of Montmartre to visit the Sacré Coeur Basilica.

I insisted on stopping on the way down Montmartre to get one of the local artists to do a sketch of us as a memento of our engagement. The artist we chose is originally from Japan and speaks very little English. But we discovered the artist's French is worse than his English.

After a while, we stopped trying to include the artist in our conversations. He refused to give his name, getting the message across that he's an apprentice and will not share his name or sign any of his sketches until he achieves a professional level of skill. I think his skills with charcoal and chalk are nothing short of remarkable, and can't imagine how he can improve.

"Did you enjoy the two churches today?" Her mood is so much better here than it was at Notre Dame.

"They're beautiful enough, aye." Jessica moves behind the artist as he pauses to study me before continuing the sketch. He had drawn her first in the foreground. Then I sat down to pose and the artist is drawing me standing up behind Jessica. "The two churches were built in very different periods and are architecturally like night and day. Notre Dame was *so dark* like the night, but the Basilica of Sacré Coeur seems to represent the opposite. Pure white … bright … sitting on the highest point in all of Paris. So beautiful … it's like the warm sunny day after a long dark night."

"The Montmartre district is beautiful," I agree.

"I'm guessing you can tell my why this district is called Montmartre?"

"Yes, of course." I try to remain calm and still for the artist, but I'm excited to discuss the history of the region and the martyrdom of Saint Denis. "There have been so many great artists who have worked in this community; Monet, Picasso, Van Gogh, just to name a few. Montmartre gets its name from the first –"

"Finished," the artist interrupts.

By now, I'm accustomed to his one- or two-word sentences. I stand, and walk over to join Jessica and see the final work. After what he had drawn during Jessica's session, I can't wait to see it.

I smile, taking in just how well the artist captured my fiancé's beauty. Then my focus moves to my own rendering and I fight with all my willpower the overpowering urge to laugh. "It's wonderful! It's kind of a *cross* between Henry Yan and Omar Rodriguez. Wouldn't you agree, sweetheart?"

Jessica lets out a snort of a laugh, but quickly controls herself. Everything is perfect with the drawing, except that my eyes are looking in two distinctly different directions. They appear to be crossed. It's one of the funniest things I've ever seen.

"You like?" asks the artist, but it sounds as much like a command as a question.

"I love it!" Jessica replies. "Except ... is there any way to fix Trey's eyes?"

"His eyes ...." The artist glares into my eyes for a long few moments. "They see many things at once – no fix." With that said, he sprays something over the entire drawing meant to keep it from smearing. Then he rolls it up, slides it into a cardboard tube, and extends his hand for payment.

I don't hesitate to pay the artist's requested $200 fee plus an additional $100 as a tip. "Thank you. Your work is just incredible."

The artist accepts the fee and compliment, bows quickly to us, and hands me the tube.

"Our first art purchase together." Jessica and I start the downhill walk back toward the Seine.

"What do you suppose he meant by that remark about your eyes seeing many things at once?" she asks.

"That was a bit odd, wasn't it?" I can't imagine how the artist could know about the visions I've experienced or how to explain any of this to Jessica.

Chapter 40

The ships have sailed to hide their gallery,
The great fleet will come to be the lesser one:
Ten ships near will turn to attack,
The great one conquered is forced to return.
(Nostradamus, Michel. <u>The Prophecies</u>. C10:Q2)

GREG RUTLEDGE
WASHINGTON, DC, USA
TUESDAY, OCTOBER 30, 2012

The Situation Room is abuzz with activity. Once again flanked by chief advisors and analysts, one end of the long conference table is headed by the president. "I've called you all back in as our fleet has arrived at the Gulf of Aden. The two battle groups are positioned just out of reach of any weapons the Somali pirates have. Director Rutledge, your assessment?"

"Thank you, Mr. President." I clear my throat and then take a sip of water before continuing. "The formation of the Somali fleet has not changed since this incident began. While we don't have anyone on the ground there, we have maintained constant satellite surveillance. We've seen no vessels joining or leaving their fleet." I point to a satellite image on a large display on the wall. "There's one vessel that seems to be protected in all directions by other vessels and our analysts believe that the Saudi royals are being held on it."

"So, the question is how do we recover the Saudi royals and put an *end* to the Somali threat?" The president directs this question directly at me.

"Indeed, sir. We've analyzed the two operational plans presented by Chairman Vandevelde." I pull a document that had been second in my stack to the top so I can refer to it. "The primary plan, our analysts believe, is too aggressive." Looking directly at Andrew, his jaw clenches, indicating he'll stand firmly with his recommended course of action. "Sending in both battle groups in an attempt to surprise the Somalis may drive them to kill the hostages before we're close enough to try to prevent it. The secondary plan of sending in three smaller ships to negotiate with the pirates makes much more sense. They'll never know that we've loaded the ships with SEAL teams, until it's too late. In addition, we can begin negotiations while we maneuver the main fleet into place. I can't stress enough that we don't want to alienate the Saudis by letting the hostages get killed. All that being said, I strongly recommend we go with the less aggressive, stealthier approach of Andrew's secondary plan."

"Andrew, what do you have to say?" The president's tone doesn't reveal how he's leaning on this issue.

"Thank you, President Sanchez. I'll begin by saying that *our* analysts believe the primary plan was the *only* plan to consider. Frankly, we only bothered to put together a secondary plan due to protocol. The Somali pirates haven't abandoned their methods in any skirmish with any nation, no matter how the odds were stacked against them. Not ever. We don't think there's a reasonable possibility they'll do so now, either. Our assessment is that we want to present an overwhelming force where they will have no choice but to surrender or die. We think that's the *only* way to end this threat quickly, and to give the Saudi royal hostages their single best opportunity to get out of this alive."

The president takes a long moment to consider his two options and apparently isn't ready yet to decide. "Do we know if the Somalis are aware of our presence yet?"

"We've seen no change of any kind with the Somali fleet. I would expect them to show signs of preparing for a battle or to flee if they were aware of our presence." The president seems responsive, but I need to cover all the bases. "We don't *know* if they have the capabilities to be alerted to our fleet, but based on our observations from previous situations and this current situation, I'd say they have no idea we're there."

"If that's the case, either plan is still viable."

"Sir," Vandevelde continues his argument for going in force, "I'm *extremely* concerned that if we only send in three ships, those three ships and those SEAL teams will be easily destroyed or taken as additional hostages. That would only complicate this situation further. *And –*"

"Mr. Chairman?" An analyst interrupts him.

"Yes." Vandevelde doesn't even try to hide his annoyance.

"Sir," the analyst nervously continues, "we're getting reports that a group of ten ships have split off from the Somali fleet and are heading directly for our fleet."

Vandevelde pounds his fist to the table. "Mr. President, we need to decide this immediately. We don't know the extent of the Somali capabilities. This could be a suicide run with explosives. Those ships pose a real threat and we need to put them down before they get too close to our fleet."

"Then *put them down!*" The president emphatically leaves no room for further debate.

Chapter 41

The heat of the sun will be above the sea
In Negrepont, the fish are half cooked,
The inhabitants will begin to eat each other
when food will fail in Rhodes and Genoa.
(Nostradamus, Michel. <u>The Prophecies</u>. C2:Q3)

TREY TYSON
PARIS, FRANCE
TUESDAY, OCTOBER 30, 2012

Paris nights are even more beautiful than the days. Darkness settled in during our hike back from Montmartre and Jessica has been holding my hand tightly since the sun went down. The Eiffel Tower is now aglow with lights, sometimes flashing and changing colors.

"I wonder what that's all about." Jessica points to the café just to our left where a large group of people are huddled around a television.

"I don't know, but let's find out." We walk to the café and find an opening where we can see the screen.

It's the BBC channel and the report is in English, so Jessica will be able to understand the report without interpretation. A waiter walks over with a remote and turns the volume up loud enough for us to hear the report over the sounds of the small crowd.

"We need to show that video again. In case you have just joined our broadcast, we at the BBC have received a recorded message from a self-proclaimed leader of what was once thought to be a very small group of Somali pirates. The video we're about to play is rather disturbing, so those viewers in our audience with young children may want to switch to another channel …. Roll the tape …"

Jessica and I shoot a quick glance to each other and then return our attention to the TV.

"I want you all to pay attention. Your lives depend upon it ..." The recorded voice is deep and guttural, and the spoken words scroll on the bottom of the screen. *"You call us Somali pirates. You think we take some boats, someone pays us, and all is fine. But you don't know Somalia at all. Our people are not just poor, they* starve *to death by the hundreds of thousands. You let this happen.* Your governments *let this happen! No more! You don't think it is important until we have someone or something you care about! We now have something* you *all* will care about ... *By the time you see this, we will have thirty oil platforms under our control on every major body of water around the world! There are explosives above the water that will destroy each platform. More of a concern to you, however, is that we have explosives below the water as well. These will create thirty oil spills and we will paint the oceans black! If anyone comes within sight of any of the platforms, we will all know, and we will destroy them all. There is no price too high to save your oceans. Your governments* must *understand we are serious. You* must *understand we are serious ... We will prove our intentions with one platform in the Aegean. When you try to clean up this one mess, you will see the damage that thirty will cause. We have sent our demands to the major governments of the world. You need to petition your governments to meet our demands by noon tomorrow in Washington."*

A sense of dread comes over me while listening the Somali man's recorded message.

"Do you think it's real?" Jessica whispers, not taking her eyes off the TV.

"My gut instincts tell me it's very real. Let's see what else they have to say."

After giving the audience a moment to digest what we just heard from the leader of the Somali pirates, the BBC reporter is back on the screen. *"We have already verified much of what you just heard. We take you now to the current situation in the Aegean Sea where the Somali terrorists have in fact destroyed an oil platform. Wallace, what are you seeing there?"*

"Yes, Olivia." It's a British man's voice, obviously in a helicopter and in great distress. The camera shows a monstrous blaze on top of the water. *"It's an utter disaster here. Flames have engulfed the platform. Beyond the*

smoke, there are visible distortions in the sky from the sheer heat being generated from the burning oil. There are several ships surrounding the platform, spraying steady streams of water on it. But they don't seem to be having any impact at all on the fire. Below the surface of the water, one can see a huge trail of black, spewing from the drill site and leading away from the platform. This, of course, meaning the terrorists have most likely detonated explosives at or near the bottom of the sea .... I'm told there are containment vessels on the way, but there's no telling how much damage will be done before this can be contained and hopefully, someday, cleansed."

The screen flashes back to Olivia in the BBC newsroom. *"Wallace, have you had any conversations yet with Greek or Turkish authorities? What effects, long-term, do they anticipate from the oil slick?"*

We wait impatiently the seemingly long second it takes for Wallace to hear what Olivia has just asked before responding. *"Indeed, Olivia. Greek authorities have expressed grave concern over the health of the local fishing industry as well as tourism. Seafood is so important to the Greek diet that they have over-fished the Aegean. The fear here is that the remaining fish in the Aegean will be essentially wiped out if this oil slick is not contained immediately .... I should remind our viewers; this is just one oil spill from one oil rig. The Somalis say they have control of thirty of these."*

"This reminds me of your dream, with the fire on top of the water." She squeezes my hand.

"Yes, the vision from my dream matches this so well, it's got me a little freaked out." My leg suddenly vibrates again. It's a conditioned response. Hell, my phone isn't even on. I can't stop myself any longer. Reaching into my pocket, I find my iPhone and turn it on. Within moments, it's vibrating out of control with text messages all in caps and urgent voicemails. "Jessica, keep watching, okay? I think I better check my messages." I take a few steps away from the growing crowd around the café and, just as I'm pulling up the first urgent text message, my phone rings. Hmmm. Blocked number. I normally would let a blocked number go to voicemail, but not today. "Hello?"

"Trey! Finally. This is Max. We must meet *right now*. Where are you?"

"I'm in Paris, Max. What's going on?"

"I know you're in Paris, but *where* in Paris? Are you near the Eiffel Tower?"

"Only a couple of blocks away, on the right bank. At Café Valentin."

"I know the place. Okay, don't move. We'll be there in 10 minutes. And keep your damn phone on."

"We?" The timing of this call with the newscast about the Somali terrorists can't be a coincidence. But Max had already hung up before I could find out who was with him.

Chapter 42

GREG RUTLEDGE
WASHINGTON, DC, USA

"What news? Keep the status updates coming!" demands the president.

"Yes, sir," began the analyst. "The ten ships that broke off from the pirate fleet were all destroyed or disabled almost immediately. Our battle groups moved in and boarded the remaining ships in their fleet with no resistance."

"No resistance?"

"None, sir. We found the Saudi yacht, and unfortunately .... Well, the hostages were all dead when we got there."

"*All* dead? Even the royals?" The president's anger at this news is evident.

"Sir, we haven't found anyone alive. Not one Somali pirate. Only sixteen dead hostages. Two of the bodies match the pictures provided of the Saudi royals taken with their yacht. They're all dead."

Just then, my phone vibrates with an urgent message from my deputy director. I quickly read it. "There's more, Mr. President."

"What is it?" The president's glare is now directed squarely at me.

"Our embassy in London received a package from the Somali terrorists that seems authentic. It has a list of demands which includes —"

"It's on the news now." Vandevelde cut me off mid-sentence and directs everyone's attention to another large screen on the wall.

"I want you all to pay attention. Your lives depend upon it ...."

After viewing the recording of the Somali terrorist leader's tirade, the president returns his attention to me. "What, *exactly*, are their demands?"

My email is a condensed synopsis of the original, but I begin to read it. "They start by saying if we attack any one of the oil rigs they hold; they will blow all of the rigs. There's an onsite trigger for each bomb and a remote trigger for all of them. The onsite trigger must be held closed. Shooting the triggerman will cause him to release the trigger and set off the bomb. They're all in constant communication with each other. If one bomb goes off, they will set them all off. The following amounts are to be wired by their respective governments to an account to be designated later. Ten billion US dollars. Ten billion euros to be paid by Germany, France, and Italy. Fifty billion yuans from China. Seven hundred million yen from Japan. Ten billion pounds from the UK. Ten billion reais from Brazil. Four hundred million rupees from India. And ten billion Canadian dollars. Sir, we have until noon tomorrow our time to make this happen. Wait a minute. *That's* odd …."

"What?" the president yells.

"Well, first, the numbers are all fairly equal per nation and ten billion dollars is a relatively low number for each nation when considering the devastation of having the planet's oceans destroyed along with the ensuing global famine that would follow. But, second, the combined funds are so vast that it will be virtually impossible to hide the transactions for anyone other than a government. And, third, it strikes me as extremely odd that they haven't asked for an equivalent number of rubles. Why aren't the *Russians* being asked to pay anything?"

"I'll leave it to you to figure that out." The president stands and scans the faces of everyone in the Situation Room. "What I need to have is some intel from the field. How many oil rigs have they captured? What's the status of the people who were working those rigs? I want an assessment of the effects if all the oil rigs in terrorist possession *are* in fact blown up. I want State to get input from the other governments whose currencies were in the terrorist demands. Are they prepared to pay these terrorists, should it come down to that? I want a video conference set up with the appropriate leaders from all affected nations in … Greg, how long to get the field update and effects assessment?"

I've never seen the president act so assertively, or seem so well prepared to deal with a crisis. "At least two, maybe three hours."

"I want that conference call set up in three and a half hours. How are we supposed to communicate with the terrorists?"

"They've left instructions for us to broadcast any communication to them over every major television station in the country. The other governments have been given the same instructions, sir."

"What! *Dammit.*" President Sanchez literally throws his hands up in disgust. "They're putting us in a tough position. So, we have no way to pay them quietly and still save face with the public." The president looks down, and shakes his head a few times. He looks back up, now more determined than ever. "Let's get on it, people! We need to step up and face this challenge. I want everyone back here in three hours, with some goddamn answers!"

Chapter 43

MAX MEDICI
PARIS, FRANCE
TUESDAY, OCTOBER 30, 2012

On the short walk from the Eiffel Tower to Café Valentin, it's been a good opportunity for Judith and me to catch up on the latest with AI. Samantha, however, hasn't said anything beyond the most basic of pleasantries. I wonder what's bothering her. As we enter the café, I quickly locate Trey and a very fetching redhead, who is most likely his fiancé by now. They haven't been dating that long, or I would have met the young woman before today. I hope Trey knows what he's doing. My own experience with proposing to someone after a short courtship didn't work out so well. *Katarina ... are you involved in this terrorist mess in any way? I don't sense that she is ... but then I've never been able to sense what she's up to.*

"Max, my old friend! You brought Judith and Sam!" Trey, who *was* able to sense our presence, stands, turns around to face us, and shakes my hand vigorously. "Jessica, this is my dear friend and mom's cousin, Max Medici."

Jessica hugs me, catching me off guard. "I've heard many good things about you, Max. I'm so glad to finally meet you."

"What a striking couple!" I look at her, then Trey, then her again. They obviously love each other. This is the sacrifice I've made since Katarina. The core of what I missed out on in life. It's not a sacrifice I can allow Trey to make. There's a lot at stake with the third Antichrist, but if he's going to be a hero, he should have a *something* in his life worth saving. I continue, "I've heard so many good things about you as well!"

Keeping my eyes on Jessica, I direct my voice to Trey. "My dear boy, you do have good taste. Did she say yes?"

Jessica answers before Trey can, "Of course I did!" She shows me her new engagement ring, and the only thing beaming more brilliantly than the huge diamond in the middle of the ring is Jessica herself.

TREY TYSON

"Jess, this is my sister Judith." I give Judith a hug, and she returns it … uncomfortably. She's never been much of a hugger, though. "Judith, my fiancé, Jessica."

She also hugs Judith, and Judith seems more relaxed with Jessica. "I finally get to meet you. Your schedule is busier than an ER doctor. It's so good to put a face to a name!"

Judith smiles as warmly as I can ever remember. "My future sister-in-law. Congratulations to you both!"

I then give Samantha a big hug and again sense just how uncomfortable she is in returning it. "And this, Jess, is my best friend from all the way back to grade school, Samantha Fox."

Jessica goes in to hug Samantha, but Samantha offers a hand to shake instead, and Jessica very formally shakes it. "You're the *Sam Fox* that Trey is always talking about? Funny that he never mentioned that you're a woman."

"Enough of the pleasantries," Max tries to corral our group. "We have an international crisis on our hands and we need to react to it immediately." Max points to the table we've been reserving. "Let's sit down and figure out how we can best work together to stop these Somali terrorists."

As soon as we sit down, Jessica jumps into the conversation, "What exactly can the five of us do to stop an international crisis, from a café in Paris, no less?"

Max and Judith exchange a quick glance with knowing smiles. "Forgive my sidestepping that question, Jessica, but I have to ask Trey something before I can answer you." Max turns his attention to me. "You know that I've wanted you to join AI since you were in high school. Your sister decided to serve our country early in life. Your best friend made that same decision. You chose a different path. I respected that decision and have watched you do great things with your life. However, the time of the third Antichrist is here and I believe *you* are the key to stopping him. Are you going to help us?"

Part of me has always expected this day would come, but just didn't know when. I've followed my own path all my life, but I have a strong feeling that's about to change. "Max, I will do anything I can to help. I just don't understand how I fit into all of this. *How* can I help?"

"I don't think you've ever been fully forthright about your abilities, Trey. Let me be very direct, so we can figure this out quickly. Have you ever had a dream or vision of an event that has later come to happen?"

"Yes, I have." As soon as I answer Max, Jessica's focus turns to me. She looks dismayed.

Max continues, "Have you ever had a dream of an event from the past and heard a voice guiding what you were seeing?"

"No, nothing like what Sam went through in Detroit."

"Hmmm …. Have you ever experienced an event where you could preview multiple outcomes in your mind and actually influence how the event turned out?"

I flash back to Sarah's near-kidnapping back in 1981. "Yes, that's happened."

Max doesn't seem surprised by my answers in the least. "So back to your original question, Jessica. We have some abilities, which if applied properly, may very well be able to help stop the Somali terrorists and the third Antichrist. There are two other people we need to discuss. *Viktor Krostov* is the head of a private espionage group in Russia. I'd be shocked if he's not involved in this in some way."

"And then there's *Karl,*" adds Judith.

"Yes," Max agrees. "The man we know only as *Karl* is the primary financier for Viktor's activities. These are very dangerous men. And we're potentially going to be exposed to very dangerous situations." He let that sink in for a few seconds. "I believe Trey is crucial, but I think it would be very wise if Jessica were to fly back home."

I'm about to nod my approval, but Jessica has a very different point of view she voices, "Are you kidding me? I'm a doctor in the *ER* ... in *Detroit*. There's nothing we're going to come across that can top that. I'm not going to go home and hope you're all okay while trying to save the world. The more dangerous it is, the better the reason I should be included."

Judith's phone rings, "I have to take this, but my two cents are that we need to stop arguing about who's in and who's out, and get busy working on our next steps." She steps outside to take her call.

"Max," I begin, "as much as I want Jessica to stay out of harm's way, I get the feeling we will very possibly need her help. And I don't think we're going to be able to convince her to leave, anyway. She's very headstrong and determined." I think back to my mom's comment about an Irish woman.

"Aye, I'm not quite sure if that was a compliment or not, but I'll choose to take it as one." Jessica smiles at me and then directs a question to Max. "What or who is this Antichrist?"

"We're pressed for time, but that certainly deserves an explanation. The term Antichrist appears several times in the Bible and may have been derived from the term Anti-Messiah found in early Jewish writings. An Antichrist, in the most basic sense of the word, is the opposite of Christ. If Christ is the ultimate representation of *good* in humankind, an Antichrist is the ultimate representation of *evil*."

We intently listen to every word as Max continues, "Michel de Nostradamus, a 16th Century prophet, predicted three Antichrists in parts of many quatrains he first published in 1555 in a book called *The Prophecies*. You have certainly heard of the first two. The first Antichrist was Napoleon Bonaparte, and the second was Adolf Hitler. In their times, the previous Antichrists were easily identified, but with dominant armies supporting them, they were extremely difficult to stop. The third Antichrist is a very different situation. While it may be that fellow from

Somalia we heard on TV earlier, I think the real challenge may come in *identifying* just who the true Antichrist is."

Max focuses on me with his next point, "I am certain that Nostradamus, in his time, found a way to get a message to us to help our quest. The trick will be to *see* and *understand* the message in time."

"But *how?* He died centuries ago." asks Jessica.

"Primarily through his book. He foresaw many things and wrote about them in the form of quatrains."

"Did the quatrains tell us who the Antichrist is and how to stop him?" I ask.

"It's not at all that simple, unfortunately. You see, back in the 16th Century there were the Spanish, Portuguese, and Roman Inquisitions to worry about. They targeted followers of Islam and Judaism, as well as anyone that might be a threat to Christianity. Nostradamus' family converted to Christianity from Judaism to avoid persecution. But being able to see the future would be considered a major threat, punishable by death. He walked a very fine line, as he personally counseled Queen Catherine de Medici of France, and was rewarded quite nicely for his services. To avoid the wrath of the inquisitions and because he knew people reading his quatrains may be able to use the information for both good or evil purposes, he intentionally obscured his writings. Nostradamus rarely provided specific dates or locations of events and often altered or coded the names of the people he saw. Yet he had to be seen as accurate enough so his book would stay relevant and survive the centuries."

"Accuracy is critical if we're to trust his writings," I point out. "Is there any evidence his prophecies have been accurate?"

"Let me give you some examples, and you can all judge for yourselves. Queen Catherine of France asked Nostradamus to tell her about the future of her family. With regards to the king, Nostradamus wrote a prophecy that translates to 'The young lion will overcome the older one on the field of battle in a singular duel; In a golden cage, his eyes will be pierced. Two wounds become one, causing a cruel death.' Well ... King Henry II ignored the warnings of Queen Catherine, entered a jousting tournament in 1559, and faced the younger Comte de Montgomery. Both men bore a lion on their shields. Montgomery's lance splintered on contact, sending two shards through the king's golden visor and into his brain. One shard went through his eye, the other through his temple. The king survived for ten days in utter agony before dying …. I think we can all agree that would constitute a cruel death."

Max let us think about that prophecy for a moment before continuing. "Nostradamus foresaw Napoleon as the first Antichrist, Hitler as the second, as well as both world wars, the nuclear destruction of Hiroshima and Nagasaki, the French Revolution, the great London fire, the September 11 attacks, De Gaulle, Franco, Pasteur …." Max pauses for a moment, eyes drifting downward. "Even the Kennedy assassination."

"Amazing," is all I can say in response. If Max believes all of this to be true, I trust that it is.

"Nostradamus even wrote a quatrain that seems to apply to our current situation. It reads, 'The heat of the sun will be above the sea. In Negrepont the fish are half cooked. The inhabitants will begin to eat each other when food will fail in Rhodes and Genoa.' If you think about a 16th Century man trying to describe a burning oil rig in the Aegean, it starts to make sense. And, this is just the beginning. If the terrorists blow all the oil rigs they control, all sea life will be imperiled. It would cause a *famine* the likes of which the *world has never known."*

Judith walks back into the café and seems to be in a hurry. "Something else has happened. It's related. And I must attend to my assignment from the president. I'm leaving Samantha with you. I believe you'll need her help more than I will. Samantha, keep them safe."

Samantha nods.

"Trey, I need to have a word with you." Judith walks out the café door, holding the door open just long enough for me to slip through and join her outside. Her auburn hair is cut shorter than ever, pulled straight back, highlighting her intense eyes. "Listen, little bro." She makes sure our eyes meet. "First, this isn't some millionaire playboy adventure, this is the big leagues. There may be dangers ahead for you all, as Max said. I've been in this role using these abilities for decades.

You need to take this seriously. We're not the only people in the world with these abilities and others may have *very different motives*. Watch your back."

"Okay, I will," I agree.

"And second, keep the marriage and lovey-dovey stuff to a minimum while you're with Samantha."

"What?" I shoot a quick glance through the café's window to Samantha and find her eyes already focused squarely on me. "Why?"

"You know," she shakes her head, "Max thinks you're going to be the most gifted visionary to walk the planet since, well, ever. But after all these years you *still* haven't noticed that Samantha has had a crush on you since you were teenagers."

I'm about to protest, but think back to the day Max took us to Detroit. We had sex that day. Just that one time. Samantha spent a year in Canada after that. When she came back, we went back to being best friends. We haven't seen each other much the last few years, but that's how it goes sometimes with best friends. You can be separated for a while, but pick up right where you left off when you reconnect.

"A crush? Maybe some interest at times, but we've always been too good of friends to mess with that."

Judith isn't buying that argument for a moment. "*Whatever* ... but there's no sense in rubbing it in her face."

I don't want to concede the point, but can't deny it either. "Okay, fine, but I'm still not sure you're right about this."

She hugs me again, before leaving. "I *am* right and you be careful."

"You take care, too."

She yells over her shoulder as she runs to catch an available taxi. "I'll call you as soon as I can."

When I walk back into the café, I try to quickly gauge if there are any feelings Samantha isn't sharing. She seems so unhappy, but that could easily be due to the fact that we have terrorists about to destroy our oceans. I smile at her, hoping to cheer her up, but she quickly looks away.

"Trey, tell Max and Samantha about your dream last night. It could be the sign from Nostradamus that Max expects us to see," says Jessica.

Sitting back down with the group, I'm not sure what to say to Samantha, if anything. I can't let any hurt feelings be a big concern right now with everything else going on. "Well, I basically had a dream of the very fire on top of water we saw today in the Aegean."

Max raises an eyebrow as I've seen him do on occasion when his interest is truly piqued. "How alike was the dream to the actual event?"

"They were identical. Unless there was some sort of a trick of the mind."

"I don't think that was any trick of the mind. I think you could see a glimpse of the future. Did you dream anything else?" asks Max.

"Yes, but it was extremely odd. I'm not sure what it means or if it can help."

"What was it?"

I recall the picture from my dream again. "The second part of the dream was really just a picture. I'll try to describe it. On top was a ship's wheel with a crescent moon just below it. The middle showed an archer, aiming an arrow at a woman next to him. And on the bottom, there was a white bull on the left side and a lever scale on the right."

Max takes just a moment to put the picture puzzle together in his mind and then announces, "Trey, I know that picture."

"How on Earth is *that* possible?"

"It's from a book of watercolor pictures that Nostradamus created, titled The Vatinicia Code. It was meant to show major events during the tenure of future popes and César brought it to Rome after his father died. It went unnoticed in the Rome Central National Library for centuries, but was discovered in 1982."

"*The Vatinicia Code*? But what does the picture mean?" Jessica asks Max.

"I don't know yet. That's something we need to figure out. There must be something else we're missing. *Any* other signs of any kind that you've experienced, Trey?"

"Yes, there was one more thing … T3." Jessica nods her agreement as I bring up what we found earlier in the day.

"T3? Like your signature?" asks Samantha, *finally* breaking her silence.

"Yes," replies Jessica, looking quizzically at Samantha. "It was just like Trey's signature. We saw it in Notre Dame Cathedral this morning."

"*That* could be the first clue we need!" Max seems energized. "Tell me about it."

"We were in the north tower and Jessica found it carved into one of the stones of the original inner wall. I didn't really think too much of it, but we both thought it was eerily similar to the way I sign my name."

Max's intensity level goes up a notch, "This is *very important*: Nostradamus was not only a prophet, alchemist, and physician, but he was a member of the Freemasons. In 1548, the cathedral had been damaged during riots, and underwent major alterations and repairs. Nostradamus could easily have been involved in the project. Look, you all may have trouble believing this, but I believe he has seen our future and is trying to guide us to stop this threat to humankind. Sometime in the 16th Century, Nostradamus left a clue for us to find in our time." Max checks the time on his strange looking watch. "The cathedral will be closed soon. We'll have to break in and find out what's *on*, *in* or *behind* that stone."

Jessica won't like the idea of breaking into any cathedral, especially Notre Dame. So, it comes as no surprise when she protests, "Don't you and Samantha work for the government? Why can't we just tell French authorities what we want to do and ask for their help?"

"Too risky," replies Max. "The French are very … well, *French*. They're highly unlikely to let us damage any part of one of their most treasured structures; even if we're convinced it means saving the oceans of the world. I'm afraid we'd just put them on alert to what we're up to. We don't have much time and we're going to have to figure out how to get into the cathedral. Plus, we need some tools to break open that wall."

I stand up and the others follow my lead. "The tools we need are already there. They're being used for the renovations currently underway. And I think I know how to get into the cathedral unnoticed. But it's going to be very physically challenging." Quickly assessing Samantha, I see she's kept herself in good shape. "Sam and I can get into the cathedral. But, we'll need some help …."

Chapter 44

MARINO "RENO" DE SANTOS
WASHINGTON, DC, USA
TUESDAY, OCTOBER 30, 2012

I've been the head of the Democratic National Party for over a decade and I always enjoy coming to the White House to meet with the president, especially a Democrat I helped get elected. But, with the current elections looming and the polls not looking promising for our party, I have no idea what to expect from this sometimes-volatile president. Looking around the Oval Office, I can't help but notice some of the new gaudy furnishings he's chosen.

"Have a seat, Reno."

"Thank you, Mr. President. To what do I owe the pleasure of an invitation to the White House?"

"Fuck you and your pleasure. I want to know what you're going to do about the election. The polls, the press, and the pundits all agree. According to them, I can't win a second term."

"I understand completely, but things can change very quickly in an election. This Somali terrorist issue, for example. Of course, it's a terrible threat to the world, but it might help us. People tend to want to clean house when there's a domestic crisis. However, they tend to want to keep incumbents in place during an *international* crisis. If it had to happen, it really couldn't be timed any better."

"What's your view on how this will affect the polls, Reno?" the president asks as he straightens his bright red tie.

Reno is a nickname that has stuck with me because I'm extremely good at determining the odds for almost anything pertaining to politics.

Not only can I pick winners and losers reliably, but I'm usually within a point or two of the margin of victory. This same ability led to my rise in the party. "I'm sure it will be a positive influence for us across the board."

"Can you be more specific?"

The president's chances to remain in office were in doubt, but the terrorist situation has changed that in his favor. Surely, he's aware of that already. "Perhaps. What exactly do you want to know?"

"We currently have a solid majority in the house and a filibuster-proof majority in the senate. What I *exactly* want to know is, come next year, will that still be the case?" The president seems a bit testy, but he's got a lot on his plate right now.

"Sir, we have a 27-seat lead in the house, and we hold 61 seats in the senate. With complete certainty, I can say we will lose seats in both chambers this election. This is primarily due to the current state of our economy. I'm 90% certain we will no longer hold a filibuster-proof majority in the senate, but 75% sure we will keep a majority. Unfortunately, I expect that we'll lose our majority in the house."

"Even with the international crisis?"

"Without that, we'd be in far worse shape," I reply.

"That's what I feared." The president takes a few moments to think before continuing, "I have some legislation I was planning on introducing next year, but I have to do it before we lose the house. It's critical to America and it's critical to our party."

"What is it, sir? And how can I help?"

"This country is going to hell and I have to stop it. Corporate greed. Individual greed. We're involved in everyone else's business. Being despised by other countries. Being a target for every whack-job terrorist group out there. The free market has run amuck. People vote the way they do and they have no idea why. There's a *total* lack of control. We need to create a new society in America." He pauses, flashing a toothy grin. "Holy shit, that's it!"

"What?"

"*A New Society!* I've been trying for weeks to come up with a name that would sound similar to and more powerful than Roosevelt's New

Deal, and it reminds me of Johnson's Great Society. Dammit, write that down. A New Society!"

I'm not even sure if the president is serious at first, but his fervent attitude quickly convinces me that he is. In my portfolio, I find my pen and write A NEW SOCIETY in all caps. "What's this *New Society* legislation going to include?"

"It's a broad ranging bill, just like the New Deal. First, we're going to raise taxes on the rich, *significantly*. We need to pay for this shit and this will excite our base. Then we're getting rid of capital gains tax loopholes. If we need it, we'll play the class-war card to work public sentiment. We're going to truly regulate the banks, insurance companies, and Wall Street. They've had far too much power in the past and we need to be stronger as a government and a nation. An enhanced national healthcare system is incorporated. We simply can't continue to fall behind the British, Canadians, and almost everyone else when it comes to caring for our sick and needy."

"These are fairly core Democratic party concepts," I note. "If we're ever going to pass legislation like this, we need to do it while we have a Democratic president and congress."

"Exactly," the president grins. "Transportation and logistics are too competitive, and there's too much overlap. Why can't we offer next day service with the post office and get rid of private services? And why are all our people having dropped calls and poor cell phone reception. We're supposed to be the technological leader of the world, yet we have two different cell phone broadcast methodologies. The mobile corporations are hoarding and fighting over frequency ranges and bandwidth. It's ridiculous how inefficient that is. We just need to pick one system and go with it. Even if we need to nationalize that industry, too. Cell phones will just *work*, anywhere in the country."

"You just won over most of Generation Y and half of Generation X!" I point out, excitedly.

"And we need to better care for our unemployed, our weak, and our homeless. We're going to introduce a national welfare system that won't stop providing benefits after six weeks or even six months. It's going to be permanent. As long as anyone needs it."

I ... love ... it. Finally, a president with big enough balls to go for what we in the party really want. "That'll create a much larger and more loyal Democratic voter base!"

"Yes, I'm well aware of that. And lastly, we'll provide amnesty for all illegal aliens, offering an opportunity for them to register to get a photo ID so they can enjoy some of the basic necessities of living in America. A democratic nation should welcome participation. With this ID, we can even allow them to vote."

"It's a liberal utopia kind of concept! I love it, *but* I'm not sure we can pass it, even with the majorities we hold. So many congressional Democrats are in precarious positions with their elections. The centrists and conservatives are going to have a very hard time with this. How can we modify it to sway their votes?" I ask.

"It includes a provision to bolster our military and intelligence operations to specifically address terrorism. The message will be that the only real way to deal with terrorism is to prevent it."

"Very well thought out, sir." I quickly run through some names and calculate the numbers. "I do believe that will do what it takes to get it passed. We'll have a few holdouts who will want some special earmarks built in. But as long as you're open to some compromise there, I'd put us at 80-85%."

"I like those odds, Reno!" The president walks to his desk, grabs a large folder, and hands it to me. "Here's a hard copy. I'll have it emailed as well. I want you to start lining up votes right now. Get it in the hands of Democrats tonight. I'll make sure the Republicans get a preview tomorrow morning before I introduce the bill. I intend to address congress *directly* tomorrow to ensure this gets voted on and passed by the end of the year."

"By the end of the year?" I estimate the bill has to be at least three inches thick. "With the terrorist crisis? Sir, with a bill of this magnitude, they're going to need some time to read and digest all of this. Not to mention negotiations and modifications."

"Read it? They need to just trust you and more importantly, they need to trust me. The last day of business this year is December 21. I expect to sign a passed bill that day or sooner. I *know* you can make it happen, Reno." The president puts his hand on my shoulder and steers me to the door and out of the Oval Office, closing the door quickly behind me.

I'm truly excited. This is easily the single most important moment in my career. As I'm rounding a corner, I glance proudly at my portfolio and marvel at how much the legislation I'm carrying will transform the country. I lift my head just in time to see Greg Rutledge's face, but not in time to stop from crashing right into him. My portfolio drops to the ground and the folder holding the legislation bounces to the side.

"So sorry, Greg." I'm a bit embarrassed by my carelessness.

Greg quickly bends over to help me pick up my belongings. "No worries, Reno. Everyone's always in such a hurry around here that we could use some mirrors hung up so we can all see around the corners." We both chuckle.

GREG RUTLEDGE

On my way to the Situation Room, I take a moment to pull out my smartphone and text my deputy director, *"Put a flag in the monitoring system to check for anything containing NEW SOCIETY right now."*

Chapter 45

TREY TYSON
PARIS, FRANCE
TUESDAY, OCTOBER 30, 2012

Max and I came up with a plan. He insisted on just the two of us working it out and after a brief discussion I understood why, even if I didn't agree with his reasoning.

Having sent Jessica in her own taxi to the left bank of the Seine, Max, Samantha, and I came to the Hotel de Ville on the right bank. We didn't speak much during the taxi ride. The tension of the situation and not knowing what to say when a driver could hear every word left little to discuss. Max started to talk about how much he liked Jessica, but one glance at Sam's face confirmed Judith's concerns, so I changed the subject quickly to the weather. As we're walking the short distance to Pont d'Arcole, the silence is deafening and I decide to break it.

"What do you think we're going to find, Max?" I suspect Max is holding back something important. What or why, I can't guess.

"Always the rebel, Trey!" There's a new level of excitement in Max's voice.

"What do you mean?"

"How many times did you get kicked out of class when you were in school?" asks Max.

"Too many times to count," Sam chimes in.

I laugh, thinking it's probably better if I don't mention getting kicked out of the Piston's game recently. "I don't see the connection," is all I say.

"Well, you don't seem the least bit concerned with breaking and entering into one of the most famous and prestigious cathedrals in the world, or the consequences should you be caught."

"Trey's never been one to think the rules ever apply to him ... *or* to worry about consequences," adds Sam.

Great. *This* is the topic that brings her out of her shell. I'm not sure if it's a compliment or an attack on my character. I suppose it doesn't really matter either way.

I try to take the high road, "Breaking rules *or laws* and the consequences that follow are fairly meaningless when you weigh them against the devastation the terrorists are threatening."

"Very true," Max admits. "Very true, indeed .... I have a suspicion that what you will find will be in written form. You must be very careful not to harm the stone with your T3 signature on it. Are you confident you'll find a hammer and chisel at the site?"

"They were there this morning."

"Do you have a camera and flashlight on you?" Max asks, trying to cover all the possible needs for our secret mission.

"My iPhone has a great camera built into it. Plus, I have a flashlight app," I reply.

"What's a flashlight app?" asks Max.

Samantha, who's been so stoic since we met at the café, lets out brief laugh and even flashes me a quick smile. Even though Max looks young enough to be my brother, he's in eighties and unintentionally reminds us of the fact.

"It's a software application that will convert my iPhone into a flashlight when I need it."

Max shrugs, "Well, if you say so."

Having crossed Pont d'Arcole, Max confirms our timing with a brief glance to his watch. "Wait exactly five minutes before making your move. Are you ready?"

I look at Samantha and she nods. "We are."

With that, Max walks briskly off to the south. We chose to approach Notre Dame from the north. According to our make-shift plan, Jessica should have just crossed Pont au Double to the south of the cathedral.

As soon as Max is out of earshot, Samantha gently grabs my arm, surprising me with how close she is before speaking quietly into my ear, "I still don't understand why all the secrecy between you and Max was necessary. We should have *all* discussed this plan first."

"Max has been in close contact with the head of the CIA. Sam, they have reason to believe that someone on the inside has been working with the Somalis."

"So, Max doesn't trust me? Is *that* what's going on?" She's truly insulted.

"I can't speak for Max, but I told him you're beyond reproach. You must understand there's a lot at stake here. Max has been preparing for this his whole life and he's approaching this situation with extreme caution."

As we walk toward the cathedral, Samantha takes a moment to consider what I said. "Well, I'm glad you stood up for me. Let's talk about this crazy plan of yours. How the hell are we supposed to get inside?"

"After all these years, Sam. Don't you trust me yet?" I smile at her.

"Fuck off. You know I trust you. I just like to *know* what I'm getting into. All the entrances will be locked and electronically monitored. And there'll be at least one guard stationed on the inside. So, *how* will we get in?"

"Hope for a ladder." I wink at her.

"A ladder? Are you crazy? You think they're going to leave a ladder outside so we can climb right in?" She looks at me quizzically.

"See, *now* you understand the plan." We can see Notre Dame now and I point to the northeast corner of the cathedral. "See that garbage chute over there?"

"Sure, but how does that help us?"

"I locked myself out of my office once when the building was being renovated and it had the same sort of setup. The chute had a ladder built into the inside wall to allow someone to climb up there and unjam it in case anything got stuck. I was able to climb through the middle of the chute up to the third floor and right into an open window ... Let's hope it's the same here. The guard will almost certainly be staying on the main level. Who, after all, would expect someone to break in from the top opening?" I shrug to both emphasize the point and lighten the moment.

"Okay. *Assuming* for a moment that there's a ladder in that chute, an opening at the top, *and* you're right about the guard," Samantha points to several people standing outside the eastern entrance, "how the fuck are we going to get in without anyone seeing us?"

"We have to time it out right." I reply as I check my watch. "Like *now*. Come on, let's go." I break into a very quick walk toward the dumpster at the bottom of the garbage chute, motioning for Samantha to follow.

She catches up in no time. We're only a hundred yards away when we see Max near the southeast corner of the cathedral hunch over and cough loudly.

We keep moving as Max lifts his head, then yells, "Help! *J'ai besoin de secours!*" Max then grabs his chest, stumbles around a couple of times, and hits the ground with an audible thud.

I estimate quickly that there are fifteen people who might be able to see the chute and dumpster. They all respond to Max's apparent medical emergency.

Samantha follows as I up my pace from a fast walk to jogging, still trying to be as quiet as possible. When we reach the dumpster, I slide open a side door, and we slip inside and close the door.

"How fortunate," I whisper.

"Is there a ladder?" Samantha is still picking herself up off the base of the dumpster.

"I meant we're lucky the dumpster is empty. But yes, we're very fortunate there's also a ladder. After you, my dear." I gesture for Samantha to go first.

"Keep your mouth shut on the way up," she suggests quietly. "Every sound will echo."

I nod and we start our ascent.

Jessica O'Neill

By the time I make it to Max, he's lying on the ground and surrounded by concerned onlookers. I shift through the people, kneel at his side, and take a good look at him. Dark bronze skin with very few wrinkles. Full head of hair and not one of them is white or gray. I studied gerontology in med school and have never seen an octogenarian appear so young. He's been so comfortable being in charge, but he's pushing himself far more than anyone his age should.

In my most commanding ER voice, I grab the attention of everyone nearby, "I'm a doctor. Does anyone here speak English?"

A tall young man with dark hair and glasses looks around, sees that no one else is volunteering, and then speaks. "*Oui ... euh ...* Yes, I do."

"Good. What's your name?" I ask with an urgent tone.

"Luc."

"Okay, Luc." I begin to measure Max's pulse with two fingers pressed against his neck. "We don't have much time. He's breathing, but unconscious. There should be an emergency medical kit at the cathedral. Go pound on that door and tell the guard to bring it here as quickly as possible."

Luc nods, then runs to the cathedral door.

Trey Tyson

Quietly and methodically, Sam and I are making our way up the metal ladder inside the garbage chute. While I have no way of knowing for certain, it seems like we should be near the top.

"There's an angled chute at the end with no stairs," Samantha whispers down to me.

"What?"

"I can see the opening, but there's about four or five feet of no stairs to get there. I'm going to have to crawl through it."

"Wait –" But Samantha already starts just as I get the word out. There's a squeak of rubber sole sliding against metal. Then she hits the side of the chute with a bang. I instantly bring my feet together on one rung and tighten my grip on the ladder.

"Trey!" she yells as she's falling toward me.

In the dark, with only a very dim light coming from the top opening, I can just make out her silhouette. I reach out with my left arm, pluck her from midair, and pull her in against me while still clenching a rung with my right hand. We're both sweaty and breathing heavily from the climb. I can feel every part of her body wrapped desperately around mine. We're now eye to eye and she intently holds my gaze.

"Sam," I whisper.

"What?"

"Can you, um, grab the ladder? My hand is starting to slip."

She smiles and kisses me on the cheek as she reaches around to take her own hold of the ladder.

It's good to see her smile, even in this dim light, and I smile back. "Why don't you wait till I'm up there with you and you can use me to push off with your feet to reach the opening? Then you can help me once you're up there."

"That's a kick ass plan. Might be better than just going for it."

"Yup, might be." We both let out a quiet laugh as she climbs up a few rungs. I follow much more closely now.

JESSICA O'NEILL

Luc returns hurriedly with Notre Dame's night guard – an average height, heavy set man of around forty, who is carrying an emergency medical kit.

"Ah, thank you." Pointing to the guard, I ask, "Do you speak English?"

"No, he does not." Luc speaks for the guard. "I already asked him."

"Alright, I'll need you to ask the guard to squeeze this man's wrist. He should monitor his pulse and let me know if it slows down significantly."

Luc relays the instructions in French and the guard obliges, but only after huffing a few times in passive resistance.

"Great. And Luc, I want you to get the crowd to back up and give this man some room to breathe."

While Luc manages the crowd, I remove a needle from its packaging. Sticking the needle into a liquid I found in the kit, I pull the plunger back, remove the needle, and ensure there are no air bubbles. Then I roll up the sleeve of Max's free arm and inject him with the liquid.

After waiting a few seconds, I pull out a pocket flashlight from the kit, lift Max's eyelids one at a time, and check his pupils for dilation.

"This could take twenty minutes or so before he's stable enough to move," I direct my comment to Luc. "I'll need you to keep these people back. Can you let the guard know that I need him to keep monitoring the man's pulse?"

"No problem." Luc again relays my message, but this time there's talk back and forth between the two men. I don't understand the French, but can tell from the conversation that the guard's not happy. He did end up staying, but he positioned himself so he could see the entrance to the cathedral.

TREY TYSON

With some solid teamwork, we were able to climb into Notre Dame's north tower, and I'm relieved to spot the tools. "The tools are still here," I say to Sam, hoping I sound like I've had no fear they'd be gone. Grabbing a short sledgehammer and chisel, I head to the top of the stairs to locate the T3 stone with Samantha following closely.

"That *is* eerily identical to your T3 signature," Sam points out when we find the stone.

"Look, it's a corner stone. We just need to loosen the mortar around it. The stone should slide out fairly easily once we do," I say.

"You work on the stone and I'll keep a watch on the stairs."

"Perfect." Holding the chisel at the edge of the mortar opposite the stone, I hit it with the sledge with a moderate level of force.

Crrraaacckkkk! The sound echoes through the tower and down the stairs.

"There's no way anyone will miss hearing *that* on the main level!" I'm no longer worried about whispering.

"Don't worry about the sound. Get your ass in gear and get the stone free. Even if the guard starts now, he won't get here quickly, and we've got another way out."

"I agree." Using my full force on the next hammer blow, I break away a chunk of the mortar.

JESSICA O'NEILL

"Avez-vous entendu?" the guard asks Luc after the strange sound echoed from the cathedral.

Luc nods.

"Je dois m'en aller." The guard lets go of Max's wrist and stands.

"Tell him to wait! This man's life depends on *both* of you!" I yell to Luc, as I cling to the guard's sleeve.

Another crack from the top of the cathedral reaches us, and the guard rips his arm free and scurries as fast as he can for the cathedral door.

All the people around us are now watching the guard run and listening to the rhythmic hammer blows from the north tower. Suddenly I feel a tug on my arm. It's Max, and he's upright and motioning for me to follow. I stuff the med kit into my backpack as we make a hasty exit from the island.

———————————————————————

TREY TYSON

"We'll have visitors soon. How much longer?" Samantha yells in my direction, while keeping her focus down the stairs.

"Just about there." I pound the last bit of mortar attached to the stone with another loud crack and the stone shifts noticeably. After jamming my fingers into the openings between the stones where the mortar had been, I start sliding the stone free by shifting it back and forth while pulling.

"He'll be here any minute!" Samantha pulls out something from her bag. It's a gun. She flips the safety and levels it toward the stairs. Her blazing speed with the maneuver surprises me as I stuff the stone into my backpack and head for the opening to the chute.

"What are you going to do, shoot an innocent security guard?" I don't even wait for an answer. "Put that thing away and come on. We need to work together to get back down the chute."

She puts her gun back in the bag and follows me to the chute opening.

"I'll go head first, while you hold my feet," I begin. "Once I reach the top rung and turn around, you come feet first. I'll help you on the ladder and we can make our way down."

Samantha nods her agreement. We complete the maneuvers in seconds and wait quietly on the ladder in the chute just out of sight from the opening. She takes a deep breath and inhales some of the construction dust in the chute. Samantha coughs once, but quickly regains control by holding one of her hands firmly over her mouth.

The guard comes rumbling up the stairs, huffing and puffing from the hurried climb. Using his flashlight, he quickly scans the entire north tower and finds it empty. He then moves carefully in the direction of the south tower.

With the light from the guard's flashlight moving away from us, we start our descent as quickly and quietly as possible.

JESSICA O'NEILL

Max and I ran back to the right bank, and I was shocked at how fast and agile he was. We were nearly silent on our taxi ride to the hotel, as we weren't sure if any news of our activities might become public soon.

"What did you inject into me back there, my dear doctor? I nearly jumped when I felt the needle go in." Max checks the time as he speaks.

"Just saline solution. You'll be fine." I smile because his tone is such that he seems to trust me already ... even though we just met. Or maybe he trusts Trey's judgment and trusts me because of that. "Trey speaks so highly of you, very much like a father figure. How long have you known him?"

"I've known him all his life and am very fond of him as well. Trey's father died when he was young. I can only hope to have filled a small part of that void in his life."

Are there tears welling up in Max's eyes? I didn't know there was such a strong bond between them. "He credits you for motivating him to excel in so many areas. I'd say you did well enough by him."

Trey and Samantha walk into the hotel lobby suddenly, both wearing a layer of grime and dust. I greet Trey with a hug. "You're okay?"

"Did you find anything on the stone?" Max cuts to the chase. "I hope you got some pictures."

"Better," Trey says, flashing his toothy grin. "We have the stone." He pulls his backpack off and places it carefully on the coffee table. We all sit down as he unzips the backpack, pulls out the large rectangular stone, and places it on the table with the T3 facing up.

"Flip it over!" Max says anxiously.

Trey lifts the stone, turns it over, and carefully places it back on the table. "There's writing! It's in French, but I can read it ..." He's still out of breath from the run to the hotel, so takes a moment while he dusts off the back of the stone and then begins his translation. "To the land of your father's fathers you must go. The Moor you seek; the Moor you must find. Hmm. Moor is spelled M-O-O-R in both instances." He shrugs and shakes his head. "I have absolutely no idea what it means."

Max stands up abruptly and turns away. His left hand rubs the stubble on his chin while he ponders the message. The rest of us just watch him, afraid to speak or ruin his flow of thoughts.

Eventually he turns back around to face us. "See if there's anything on the other sides of the stone."

Trey turns the stone a quarter turn and uses his shirtsleeve to rub off the remaining mortar on that face. He stares at the writing for a moment, visibly disturbed by what he sees.

"What is it?" I ask.

"It's ... It's *today's date*."

Max is so calm, as though he expected that tidbit. "Nostradamus either had a strange sense of humor, or he's trying to prove to us that he *has* seen our future so we'll stay on the path he's laid out. Possibly a bit of both. And the next side?"

Trey rotates the stone and again rubs off the mortar with his shirtsleeve. "Not much on this side. It just says *4:87*. Hmmm. I wonder if that was meant to be some odd representation of the time."

"No, Trey," Max seems to draw a conclusion and he holds out a hand to keep the rest of us from speaking while he finishes his train of thought. "I'm fairly certain that is a reference to one of Nostradamus' quatrains."

"Do you know what it means?"

"I believe I understand the first part of the first side you read. We're to go to the land of your father's fathers, Trey. *Florence, Italy*. We need to get into the Florence Cathedral tonight. *This* time, however, let's try to go through proper channels. The Italians can be more practical than the French. Samantha, can you work through your leadership to make that happen?"

Samantha beams, seeming almost giddy to break into a second cathedral. "Fuck yeah!" She steps out to make the necessary phone calls.

"Perfect," Max continues. "Now, if only we can find a bookstore or library open at this hour."

"A bookstore?"

"Yes. I must get my hands on Nostradamus' book *The Prophecies*. I need it to reference his quatrains. Each word could be a critically important clue."

"Hold that thought for a moment." Trey pulls out his iPhone, presses the button, and begins to speak into it. "Search for a book called *The Prophecies* by Nostradamus." Then he waits a few seconds and touches the screen of his phone. Trey locates and downloads a digital copy of the book. He puts the book cover on the screen, and shows it to Max. "You mean this book?"

"My dear boy, that's it!" Max is beaming. "This is vitally important … may I read it on our drive to the airport?"

"Of course!" Trey quickly calls the airport to have his jet prepared.

Chapter 46

GREG RUTLEDGE
WASHINGTON, DC, USA
TUESDAY, OCTOBER 30, 2012

With my slight delay from crashing into Reno, I'm the last to arrive in the Situation Room. The only available chair is at the foot of the table, directly across from a clearly agitated President Sanchez.

"Here we are and it's simply unacceptable," the president says, shaking his head in disbelief. "If we even get close to the oil rigs, the Somalis will blow them all. If we don't pay them what they want – *publicly* – they blow them all. We have thirty minutes to get our shit together before my call with the other heads of state and I want answers." He scans the room quickly, but then settles his attention on me. "Greg, as the *Director of the CIA*, situational intel is your arena. *You* go first."

"Yes, sir." I clear my throat. "The Somalis were able to take 28 of the 30 oil rigs they attacked. The crews of the other two rigs fought them off, killing or scattering those pirates. Our long-range visuals and satellite imagery show some or all of the crews of the Somali-controlled rigs being held openly on the top deck of each rig. Sir, they're making it clear that hostages will die if we strike the rigs they hold. We've spotted trigger men holding devices that fit the description from their leader."

"Not very promising …. How about a projection if the rigs all blow?"

"If *all* the rigs blow?" Is he serious? "It's extremely bleak, sir. We could contain two, maybe three oil spills of the nature we've seen in the Aegean. In time, we could recover from that. If 28 are blown – that's simply beyond our capabilities to manage. The Somalis hold rigs in every ocean and major sea on the planet. Our top environmental scientists tell us that saltwater sea-life will be virtually wiped out. Even if we're able to somehow clean the spills globally, it'll be decades – if not *centuries* – before life returns in any measurable numbers. That's not where it ends, though. Many air and land-based species depend on the sea for sustenance. The world will quickly lose at least 25% of those species – they'll be extinct. Our team predicts about one out of every six people will soon starve to death. Globally, we'll lose at least a billion people to famine within a year and *far* more in the years to come. It's nothing short of a global catastrophe."

The president let that sink in for a moment before continuing. "Andrew, do you have *any* scenario where we might be able to take back control of at least 26 of the oil rigs before the Somalis are able to blow them up?"

"I … sir, I …" It's the first time Andrew has *ever* looked uncomfortable since I've known him. Taking a deep breath, he looks up at the ceiling, seeking an answer that eludes all his analysts. Apparently, nothing comes to him. "Sir, I don't."

"If I may, Mr. President?"

"Yes, Greg?"

"Sir, I believe we're going to have to pay the Somalis what they want." The room bursts into pockets of chatter. It's a long-held belief that submitting to a terrorist demand would result in nothing more than an increase in terrorist activity. "Look!" I manage to get everyone's attention again. "I don't like this any more than anyone else here. But you simply *can't* hide this much money. It *will* be traceable. What we need to do is end this threat, track the money, and make whoever's found holding it pay with their lives in a very public fashion."

Everyone sits silently for a moment, waiting while the president considers his options. "I don't see any other answer, Greg. I think you're right. Now I just have to convince the other heads of state to agree to pay their share and trust our abilities to hunt these bastards down."

V. RAY

Chapter 47

The successor to the Duchy will come,
from much farther than the sea of Tuscany.
The Gallic branch will hold Florence
in its folds, an agreement to reign the seas.
(Nostradamus, Michel. The Prophecies. C5:Q3)

TREY TYSON
FLORENCE, ITALY
WEDNESDAY, OCTOBER 31, 2012

Samantha coordinated with Judith to arrange a flight for us to Florence and a car waiting for us at the airport. We landed shortly before 5am and Max insisted on driving.

"Max, do you believe Nostradamus' message on the stone is directed at me?" I ask. Max is driving us in what seems to be a roundabout way to get to the Basilica of Saint Mary of the Flower, Florence's cathedral.

"I'm quite certain it is." He takes another turn and is now heading southwest on Borgo Pinti.

"I don't really know my father's ancestry. I know there's a Tyson family presence in Rome, but didn't know about any branch of the family in Florence. Are you certain we should be in Florence instead of Rome?"

"Trust me, and be patient, my boy. It will all become clear very soon." Max turns right on Via Sant'Egidio and stops the car abruptly. "Even with the Italians agreeing to help us, we need to be cautious. I think Samantha should approach the cathedral's main east entrance from here. I'll drive Trey and Jessica to the north entrance, and I'll come in from the south. At least one of us has to get into the cathedral and locate the next clue left for us there."

"Are we looking for another T3 on the wall?" asks Samantha.

"That wouldn't surprise me," replies Max, "but we have to be open-minded for other clues as well. Stay safe!"

I suddenly feel one of my migraines coming on, the burst of pain so instant and fierce that I nearly pass out. Knowing how important our timing is and that Samantha won't walk away if she's aware of my pain, I keep it to myself.

"Cool beans. See you in there." Samantha exits the car and walks briskly down Via dell'Oriuolo toward the main entrance of the cathedral. She's about 50 feet away when my migraine disappears as suddenly as it came. *Gone?* I'm not sure how, but I feel perfectly fine again.

Max accelerates the car as Samantha continues walking, but instead of heading to the north entrance, he pulls over to the right and parks.

"What are we doing?" asks Jessica.

"Come with me," Max replies as he exits the car.

"What's going on, Max?" Jessica and I quickly follow him.

Max walks to the intersection where Via Sant'Egidio and Via dell'Oriuolo meet, staying behind the building at the corner. He leans his head out, so I do the same. We can see Samantha about half the distance to the cathedral. "She'll be there very soon," Max whispers.

"All the more reason to get moving." I don't understand why we're just watching Samantha walk to the cathedral when we should be getting in position to meet her there.

"I've been in contact with the CIA Director and there are some extremely convincing circumstances. Someone on the inside – very close to the situation – is working with the people behind this terrorist attack." While Max is still trying to whisper, his voice is rising as Sam gets further from us.

"What is this, some sort of a test?" I ask.

"A test. Yes, exactly."

While we stand two blocks away, we can still see Samantha clearly as she approaches the open courtyard leading up to the cathedral. She never wavers as she heads for the steps leading to the main entrance. Suddenly, sirens start blaring and we see the unmistakable flashing of police car lights. Italian police surround Samantha in moments. She puts up her hands and tries to explain something to them, but they want nothing to do with anything she tries to say. Instead, they handcuff her and push her into the backseat of one of the police cars.

Jessica and I stare at each other, dumbfounded.

"Let's move! We can't afford to get caught." Max quickly makes his way back to our car and we follow right behind him.

"So, she *failed* the test?" asks Jessica as we all climb quickly into the car.

"It certainly appears that way." Max starts the car and we pull away.

"*What?* We just handed Sam to the Italian police?" I'm livid.

"Trey, *she* made the arrangements for the Italian authorities to help us. This was a trap that *she* set up," Max tries to reason with me.

Reasoning is not what I want to hear right now. I simply can't believe Samantha had *anything* to do with the terrorists. "Sam has been my best friend most of my life. I'd know if she were capable of being involved in something so heinous." Yet, Max's words start to sink in … maybe even make a little bit of sense. Sam was the one who made the arrangements. She's been so antisocial, maybe something *is* up with her. Or maybe the terrorists are just using her and she doesn't know how. "Where does this leave us? The police are still swarming around the cathedral. How do we get in there now?"

"The cathedral was merely a decoy. That's *not* where we need to go."

"Where, then?" asks Jessica.

"The Basilica di San Lorenzo. It's just a few blocks away."

I shoot a quick glance at Jessica and she simply shrugs.

"So, you set this whole thing up to test Sam and to create a diversion from our real goal?" I'm not sure if I'm pissed off, impressed, or both.

Max nods. "Trey, it's time to give you all the details you need to fully understand our situation." He pauses. "Pull out your phone, open Nostradamus' book, and read Century 4, Quatrain 87."

"Aye, the quatrain from the stone?" asks Jessica, while I manipulate my iPhone to get to that section of the book.

"Yes," I begin my translation. "It reads: 'The royal son who knows many languages, different from the senior in his home. His beautiful father full of beautiful deeds. His best friend will perish because of him.'" I take a moment to let it all sink in, mesmerized by the words. My world begins to spin as I start to understand the meaning of the quatrain. *"Different from the senior in his home? Max, this quatrain is referencing me."*

Max slowly nods. "Trey …" He pulls over on the shoulder, puts the car in park, and turns directly to face me. "You're of the family Medici. In fact," he pauses, taking a deep breath and slowly releasing it, "you're my son." Tears quickly form and start rolling down Max's cheeks.

I first take a moment to digest Max's words. A Medici? Max's son, not Thomas' son. My first reaction is to dispute it. *How* can it be possible? Wouldn't Mom have told me this by now? And, what the hell kind of relationship did they have? I want to scream that he's lying, but every part of me knows what Max is saying is true. In the end, all I can do is ask, "How?"

"Trey, you're my son." Max's voice cracks with emotion. "You're the product of two visionaries …."

"Wait!" I interrupt. "So, Mom is not my mom, either?"

"Helen is not your birth mother. The day you were born, she gave birth to twin boys – one healthy and one stillborn. I saw the perfect opportunity to protect you and still have you raised by loving family. Helen jumped at the chance to raise you as her own, and she and Thomas raised you beautifully. I couldn't be prouder of the man you've become."

"Then, *why?*" I'm still trying to square away the *how* part, but this question rises to the top of my list of questions.

"Because of who your birth parents are … because we both have psychic abilities … there was never any doubt about the abilities you'd possess. I feared for your safety. Our enemies would seek to recruit you or kill you. You'd have lived your life constantly looking over your shoulder."

"He's a Medici?" Jessica seems to need confirmation as much as I do.

"He is a Medici, from a long line of royal blood."

I don't care about royal blood. There's a more pressing matter. "The quatrain says his best friend will *perish* because of him. What happens to Sam? And why is it my fault?"

"I assure you, I don't know. But she's being held by the Italians now and probably safer there than she would be with us."

"No! Nostradamus has seen that she will *perish*. We need to get her out of there."

"Alright, alright," Max says in a calming voice. "*After* we get what we need here, I'll contact Judith. She can get the State Department involved to make sure Sam's safe."

Jessica beats me to the next most pressing question. "Who is his mother?"

"Her name is Katarina Krostov. She's —"

"*Krostov?*" I cut him off. "As in the same last name as Viktor Krostov, one of the men you think is behind the Somali terrorists?"

"Yes. She is Viktor's sister. Listen, I'm sure you want to know more. But we have a window of opportunity with all the police of Florence at the wrong church right now." Max wipes the tears from his cheeks and pulls himself together in a matter of seconds.

"You're right," I nod slowly. I'm a Medici. My father isn't my father. I've never even met my birth mother, and her brother — my uncle — is a suspected terrorist! Oh, and the terrorist's deadline looms over our heads. This is *way* too much to process. My mind seems to prefer to push that all to the side and focus on our task. "So how do you know we need to be at this church?"

"It's *the Moor* that was the key clue from Nostradamus. You see, I've been taught my ancestry ... well ... *our* ancestry all the way back to Alessandro de' Medici. He was the illegitimate son of Giulio de' Medici, who later became Pope Clement VII. Alessandro was called the Moor because his mother was a servant in the Medici home and was of African descent. When Alessandro became Duke of Florence in 1532, he was the first person of African descent to ever lead a western state."

"You're both descendants of a duke and then a *Pope* before him?" asks Jessica.

"Yes, but there's more to it than that." Max gets out of the car and grabs the tire iron from the trunk. "History tells us that Nostradamus first married in 1531, had a daughter and a son, and that his wife and children all died of the plague in 1534."

"And?" I'm not sure I really *want* to know any more.

"Well, *I* think it happened differently. France was in religious upheaval at the time and anyone with prophetic abilities would've been considered a threat. They'd be burned at the stake and their families may well have been killed as well. Instead of facing that fate, I believe Nostradamus faked his family's deaths and moved them quietly to Florence. There, his prophetic abilities became quite useful to the young Duke Alessandro. What Nostradamus asked in return for his services was for the duke to take in his family and keep them safe. I believe his first wife died either during or shortly after his trip to Italy, but his children lived on and were raised by Alessandro."

Max starts across the street toward the basilica. "Come on," he says and we follow him.

"I have a feeling I know where this is going." Jessica says as she reaches for my hand.

"In 1537," Max continues, "Alessandro went to meet his cousins Lorenzino and Cosimo, even though Nostradamus had a vision of the event and warned him not to go to the meeting. Cosimo, jealous that his cousin was so loved by the people of Florence, murdered Alessandro. At the time, this basilica was under construction. Part of it was complete and Alessandro had commissioned a local artist to design a special tomb for the Medici royalty. Cosimo and Lorenzino were in such a hurry to hide Alessandro's body that they put it in the artist's tomb and sealed it. Cosimo, trying to gain favor with the people, then took in all of Alessandro's family and wards within his own home."

Max pauses the story as he walks up to an old wooden double-door entrance at the back of the basilica. He wedges the tire iron into the small gap between the doors and pries the right door open with a small pop when the latch breaks. "Trey, would you be so kind as to use your flashlight app?" Max asks with a smile.

I don't understand it, but Max's nonchalance may be rubbing off on me. I'm feeling a sense confidence that we'll meet no resistance on the inside as I quickly turn the flashlight app on and walk through the door.

Max continues his story as he and Jessica enter right behind me, "While in Florence, Nostradamus became close with Catherine de' Medici. Catherine ended up marrying Henry II, King of France, and when she moved to Paris to become queen, Nostradamus moved back there as well. At this point, he became a trusted advisor to the queen. His first two children remained in Italy under the protection of Cosimo de' Medici, and when they grew older, Nostradamus' daughter married Alessandro's son Giulio. They lived long and prosperous lives, and had many children and grandchildren, *including* our ancestors."

"I thought so!" Jessica's excitement seems to come as much from Max's story as from the fact they we're breaking into yet another church. "So not only are you a descendant of the royal family Medici and a Pope, but you're also a direct descendant of *Nostradamus.*"

"If that's true, I should have seen that coming, too," I try to make light of the situation, but my whole world has just flipped over. I stop walking and the others stop with me.

"You okay, sweetheart?" Jessica puts her hand on my shoulder.

"It's a lot to take in, but I'm fine, thanks." I turn to face Max directly. "I think I understand what you did and why you did it. When Dad died … well, *you* stepped in. And now I understand that as well. Max, you've always been like a father to me … I want you to know that I'm glad to know the truth."

I extend my hand to shake Max's, but Max would have nothing to do with it. Instead, he embraces me. "Thanks Trey … that means the world to me. Now, let's go find Alessandro."

"Which way do we go?" asks Jessica.

"I've been here several times and believe I know exactly where we have to go." Max leads us to a sarcophagus with two statues resting on top of it.

"These statues are amazing. They remind me of something Michelangelo would create." Jessica reaches out tentatively and touches one of them.

"You have a good eye, my dear. Michelangelo *was* the local artist commissioned by the Medici and he *did* create these." Max positions himself and Jessica on one side of the sarcophagus, and then points to the end. "Trey, if you can use the tire iron to raise this end a bit, we'll push it open. Be careful. We only need it partially open. No need to harm the statues at all."

I move to the end, wedge the tire iron between the base and top of the sarcophagus, and heave with all my weight. There is a slight *whoosh* sound as fresh air enters the sarcophagus for the first time in almost five centuries. The top lifts just enough for Max and Jessica to slide it open about two feet.

"May I use the light?" Max asks, holding out his hand.

"Of course."

Max positions the light and peers inside the sarcophagus. "Ah, this is what we came for."

Jessica and I watch intently as Max feels around with his hand. We all hear the movement of metal against stone in a light scraping noise.

"Thank heavens! Nostradamus must have entrusted this to Alessandro. Cosimo was in such a hurry to hide Alessandro's body that he never took the time to remove any of his valuables. Maybe he just didn't care to do so." Max frees something from the sarcophagus. "I have it!" He's holding an oval-shaped metal object with a chain attached to the two sides. In the center of the shape is a raised circle, and within the circle is a glimmering two-headed eagle.

In all the years I've known Max, I've never seen him so happy. "What, exactly, is it?"

"*This*, my boy —" Max has often called me his boy, but now it means so much more that our relationship is revealed, "is an amulet that works as a catalyst for our special abilities. It's meant for *you.*" He hands the amulet to me.

Shifting the amulet in my hand, I aim my light at it. The metal's colors reflect sometimes like bronze and sometimes like silver. It's warming to my touch and I suddenly feel a jolt of what feels like electric power. It's as though some great weight is lifting from my mind. "Whoa …" I begin to stumble, but Max steps in quickly to support me.

Max smiles, suddenly looking even younger and more energetic. "I believe the reaction to its power is relative to the power of the visionary. And obviously, you possess an extreme talent. It takes a little getting used to. Give yourself a minute before you try to move."

"What is it?" A calmness takes over my mind and body. I can sense the next breath Jessica is about to take. More than hearing or seeing her breathe, I can *feel* when she's about to inhale. Without much surprise, I can also tell when Max is about to speak.

"The amulet is made from a unique metal, unlike anything on our planet. I'm certain it's a new element, in fact. Nostradamus discovered a small meteor when he was young that consisted almost entirely of this metal. The effects when *he* touched it were immediate as well. As an alchemist, he used techniques that, unfortunately, have not been passed down through the ages. He crafted at least three of these amulets from the meteor and wore one of them at all times."

"How do you know so much about this?" I ask. "It's almost like you've lived through this before."

"This isn't the first amulet from Nostradamus I've found." Max hints at a long story, but leaves it untold. He points to the amulet. "I think it's important for you to read the back of it yourself."

Max holds the light for me as I clean the back of the amulet with my shirt before reading it. "*Incredibly*, it starts with today's date again. It's in French." I take a moment to do the translation, "Find your mother where the last Tsar last ruled. She must lead you to where he last lived." I glance at Max to see if there are any signs of recognition in his face. "There are two other engravings. The first is Daniel, chapter 8, verses 23-24. The second appears to be his another of Nostradamus' prophecies, Century 2, Quatrain 62."

"Max, do you know these?" asks Jessica.

"We'll have to look up the quatrain on the ride back to the airport, but I know the Book of Daniel quite well." He pauses before reciting from memory. "The verses read … 'In the latter part of their reign, when rebels have become completely wicked, a stern-faced king, a master of intrigue, will arise. He will become very strong, but not by his own power. He will cause astounding devastation and will succeed in whatever he does. He will destroy the mighty men and the holy people.'"

"What can it mean?" I ask.

Max thinks about it for a full minute before responding, "I believe Nostradamus and Daniel are trying to tell us something about the third Antichrist. He is a rebel, yet he is a head of state somewhere. *Master of intrigue* tells me he isn't who he appears to be to others. He diverts attention away from his true intentions through deceit. I'm very concerned about the reference to the devastation and destruction Daniel says he will cause. This could mean that the terrorists have every intention of blowing up the oil rigs, whether their demands are met or not. Something else to keep in mind … there's someone else who is the power behind the throne, so to speak. I wish we had more to go on. Perhaps the quatrain will clarify things."

Checking the time on my phone, I say, "Sunrise is in a few minutes. We need to go. It's 7am here, which makes it 1am in Washington. We only have eleven hours before our oceans are destroyed and the trip is at least six hours to get to St. Petersburg!"

"Russia? Where in Russia?" asks Jessica. We've gone through the night without sleep and she looks exhausted.

"The Winter Palace," Max and I answer her in unison, then we share a quick glance and a smile.

Chapter 48

JUDITH TYSON
FLORENCE, ITALY
WEDNESDAY, OCTOBER 31, 2012

As Samantha and I walk out of the Florence police headquarters, she doesn't have any interest in talking about what happened. I've never seen her so pissed off in all the years I've known her and it's directed squarely at Max. It was Max who recruited us both and brought us into AI. He trained us in how to use our abilities and he also trained us in espionage, lethal weapons, being aware of our environment, and so much more. When Max finally retired, he named me as his replacement. There was some resentment there on Sam's part. I could always sense it. What I didn't know was if the resentment was with Max for choosing me, or with me for being chosen. I just know it runs deep inside her.

"You okay, Sam?" I break the ice.

"Yup. Thanks for getting me out of there. How the hell did you find me and get here so quickly?"

"I was tracking down a lead on Karl in Rome when Max called and told me where you were. I guess the Italians weren't so cooperative after all?"

"No, but at least they released me without a fight. I expected to be here for a long time."

"I asked the president to make a phone call. Apparently, it worked. Sam ... I think I found out where Karl is."

"Whoa. A legitimate lead on Karl?" Sam perks up at this. "Where?"

I open my rental car door and hand Samantha her bag – a perfect match to my own. They're not exactly Secret Service standard uniform, but with a hidden pocket for a gun, they serve us both well. "Jump in. I'll update you as we drive."

Chapter 49

GREG RUTLEDGE
WASHINGTON, DC, USA
WEDNESDAY, OCTOBER 31, 2012

I'm shown into the Oval Office just as the president is wrapping up his calls with the other heads of state targeted for funds by the terrorists and I'm caught off guard when he slams the phone down suddenly in anger.

"What a complete clusterfuck!" President Sanchez begins pacing back and forth. He pauses at a liquor cabinet, holds up a bottle of scotch, and stares at it longingly for a couple of seconds. He even opens the bottle and inhales the aroma deeply. But he then puts the bottle back without pouring a drink and turns to face me.

"Mr. President?" I ask.

"I thought we had a fucking deal, making it *very* clear that we'd be able to trace the money to find the bastards behind this. The Brits jumped in right away. They had no problem supporting our decision to pay the Somalis. Canada, Japan, and Brazil were right behind the Brits."

He shakes his head and it seems more like an uncontrollable shudder before continuing, "Then came the *fucking* Chinese. They questioned why the Russians were left out of the Somali demands. Their stance was that the Russians should pay an equal share, even though the terrorists left them out, to reduce what the other nations had to pay. I pointed out they were obviously targeting the top economies in the world and the Russians would have been next on the list."

"Solid point. How'd that go over?"

The president's voice skips from overuse when he says, "The Chinese held their ground. They won't pay unless the Russians pay, too. Then, the Indians said if the Chinese *and* Russians wouldn't pay, neither would they. Either we need to convince the Russians to pony up, or we need some leverage against the Chinese."

"Want my help?"

"I'll contact the Russians. I need you to give me something to use against China. I think India will come to the table if China does. Greg, I don't need to remind you that we need to move quickly."

"Yes, sir." My top people have committed to working around the clock until this crisis is over, but I'm not sure if we have enough time or what we can come up with to convince China to pay the terrorists.

Chapter 50

MAX MEDICI
St. Petersburg, Russia
Wednesday, October 31, 2012

"Crowded enough, aye? Max, how will we ever find this Katarina?" Jessica asks wearily. She slept a couple of hours on the flight, but still looks exhausted and overwhelmed.

I understand her concern, though. The square in front of the Winter Palace is huge, with masses of people in all directions. Other than the Alexander Column in the center, it's completely flat.

Trying to sound hopeful, I say, "Nostradamus saw that we'd find her here, so we have to trust that we will. We're looking for a woman in her 60s. She's about 5' 8", thin, fair skin, blue eyes, high cheekbones, and probably still has long black hair. We need to split up to cover more ground."

"Katarina doesn't know who we are," Trey points out. "What should we say if we spot her before you do?"

"If either of you finds her first, do *not* approach her without me. She is far more dangerous than you can imagine. Just call my ComWatch and tell me where you are. Then wait for me to make first contact with her." They've seen me use my gadget from the CIA. During our flight to St. Petersburg, Trey was probing it, trying to see what it could do. He did figure out a few things about it that Q never bothered to tell me back in Langley.

After deciding on a simple search pattern, Jessica heads to the left to start searching and Trey veers to the right. I walk right down the middle of the crowded square and head for the Alexander Column. I have an odd feeling I will find her there.

Continually checking the face of any tall and thin woman I pass, I also keep my guard up. While I may not be able to sense Katarina's presence, she undoubtedly will sense mine. And I have no idea what kind of a greeting to expect when I find her.

It seems like half the women I've come across have been tall, thin brunettes, but none of them Katarina. By the time I make my way to the statue, I'm starting to wonder if I've misinterpreted the messages. After all, it would be uncanny for her to be here at the exact time … wait … is that? Could it really be her? She's standing at the base of the statue and she's the same height and build as Katarina. I don't see her eyes, but I think it's her. She's holding a small paper bag in one hand and a handful of seed in the other, and just as she tosses some of the seed, she stops, turns her head, and looks right at me. She lets all the seed simply drop from her hands and the pigeons scurry to get as much as they can.

I start walking toward her, keeping my eyes glued to hers. She smiles and starts to run in my direction, scattering the birds. This disarms me completely and I open my arms to accept her embrace as she nearly dives into me.

"My Maximo! You have *finally* come!" her voice is more mature, but it's Katarina's voice. I'm struck by just how much I've missed her in my life, even after all these years. I never did find anyone like her who could spark my imagination ... my very existence.

"Katarina, you haven't changed a bit in all these years!" I'm in awe at how beautiful she still is.

"I knew you would find me here, but I was not sure when it would happen. I come here every day, hoping it is the right day."

I pull away to look at her. "Do you know why I'm here now?"

"Of course, I do." she's as confident in herself as ever.

"I've been guided here to stop this catastrophe from happening."

Her eyes cloud over for a moment, before she says, "You've been guided here, yes, but *who* is your guide?"

"Nostradamus. He's left several clues that led us to you here. Just the fact that I found you tells me we're on the right path."

"We have both live long lives, Maximo. We have both sacrificed so much. Can't we leave that behind now? Can't we leave everyone and everything, and just live our last years in peace ... *together?*"

The rest of my life, *together* with Katarina. Nothing I can imagine would come close to making me as happy as that thought. But I shake my head. "I haven't come alone."

She takes a moment to search her senses, but cannot predict who might be with me. "Who is it, Maximo? Who have you brought with you?"

"His name is Trey. He is ... *our son.*"

She gasps. "He's alive?" I can't tell if she's more thrilled or furious, but I'm guessing she's more furious. "Tell me how this can be."

I sigh, having dreaded this conversation for decades, and knowing it would have to take place eventually. "I switched babies immediately after you gave birth. The baby I presented to you was my cousin's. He was stillborn, just hours before you gave birth to Trey."

"Trey," she calmly whispers and then I see the emotional flair coming before it even hits her. She glares at me, eyes trying to burn

265

right through my skull. "You *saw* what I went through … the loss, the depression … you were there. *Why* did you hide him from me?" She reaches out and grabs my jacket with clenched fists, pulling me closer and screaming in my face, *"Why?"*

I've always known that someday I'd have to explain my actions from Trey's birth in 1964 and today is that day. "You must understand – as surely as I do – that if *you* knew Trey was alive, then *Viktor* would also have known. And right now, Trey would either be helping Viktor destroy our oceans, or he'd be dead." I pause for a second, trying to gauge if she's accepting what I'm saying. There's some understanding there … some guilt … but that's not what I'm after. I smile at Katarina. "*Instead*, he was raised by my cousin and her loving family. He grew up with two sisters and a brother. He went to university. He played professional football. And he's been a wildly successful business executive. Katarina, it's been a life that *neither* of us could have provided for him. He is happy and he has found love."

Katarina drops her head to my shoulder. She slowly releases my jacket. "You … you are right. I can see that it was the only way for you." She then glares back into my eyes. "I need to see him. Where is he?"

I pull her in for a hug. "He's here. We were searching for you together. We need your help, Katarina. Viktor is involved with this crisis in some way and we need you to help us stop this before it happens … before our planet is destroyed."

———————

KATARINA KROSTOV

"I do not –" Before I can complete my sentence, I notice a man and a woman walking toward Maximo and me. *My son?* I want to grab him, to hold him and never let go. However, I sense some trepidation in them. Them? No, just her. I sense nothing from the man. This fact is

simultaneously frustrating and encouraging. I now *know* this is Trey …
my son. He has the same ability I have. Psychics cannot sense him.

I pull away from Max's embrace, tears flowing freely down my face.
I look at Trey and he examines me for a moment … no words … and
then his own tears come suddenly.

The woman, and I assume this is the love interest Maximo
mentioned, whispers in his ear. Her voice is still clear to me as she says,
"Go to her."

Trey moves closer and opens his arms wide. I leap at the
opportunity, holding him tightly and sobbing. When I finally catch my
breath, my voice escapes me. I can barely exceed a whisper. "Trey. My
dear son. I thought you were dead. I …."

"I know," he says, "Max told me everything."

"No, please." I shake my head and put my hands on his face. He's
a true mix of Max and me. Max's nose and bronze skin tone, but he has
my hair and my blue eyes. "Please call Maximo *Father* and call me
Mother."

Trey lifts his head, contemplating my request. He seems to be
gaining a measure of comfort with it.

"*Mother* …" He tries it out. "*Father* told me what he did and why he
had to do it."

"Please know, my son, I understand what Maximo did. It had to be
done." I look at him again and suddenly realize who he is. "May the
gods forgive me. You are Trey Tyson?"

He nods.

I almost killed my own son! I pull him in for another hug, not daring
to tell him about my past. I can only nestle my head on his shoulder and
cry. I've never been able to sense him, and it's been a curse and a
blessing. He *must* have inherited the same special gift I possess.

"Mother, this is my fiancé, Jessica."

I pull away from Trey and look Jessica up and down, measuring,
assessing … sensing. "This is a very special woman. She is right for you.
I can see it clearly in her." I embrace Jessica and she hugs me back.

Maximo places his hand on my shoulder. It's a compassionate touch. "Katarina, we need to find your brother and we can't do it without your help. This Somali threat is not going to end well."

I search with my senses, blocking out the outside world as best I can, reaching with my vision …. He is right. *This is not going to end well*, that much I can see. But, at least I can right one wrong. I can improve our chances. "I have much in my past to pay for. I believe I have a second chance. I will help you, but we must stop at my apartment first."

Chapter 51

Support for the greatly troubled criminals,
requires clarity for them to march.
The family will be nearly overcome by death.
The reds will take down the red one.
(Nostradamus, Michel. The Prophecies. C8:Q19)

JUDITH TYSON
ST. PETERSBURG, RUSSIA
2 HOURS UNTIL TERRORISTS' DEADLINE

The sky is so overcast I can barely tell that sunset is only minutes away. A fresh layer of snow covers the ground and the temperature is just below freezing. Standing behind a tall row of shrubs outside of a country estate east of St. Petersburg, I turn to Samantha and whisper, "This is it, Karl's home."

"Holy fuck. It's not a home, it's a *mansion*. One good thing. If he has neighbors, they won't hear a thing." Sam is assessing the situation at the same time I am.

"There'll be an alarm, some form of resistance inside, or both. We'll move in quickly, immobilize him, and keep him quiet."

Sam nods her agreement.

Before we can take a step, the front entrance pops open. An older man, seeming quite spry for his age, walks quickly down to the end of the estate's grand porch. He walks right past the tall shrubs, never noticing us.

He's off to get his mail. It's at least two hundred feet from the porch, but the man covers the ground quickly. He appears to be in his late eighties. I pull out my gun with silent efficiency. "We'll take him from behind right after he passes on the way back to the porch."

Samantha nods, readying her gun as the man returns from the mailbox at a quick pace. Not wearing a coat, he visibly shivers in the cold.

I'm prepared to pounce on a moment's notice. The man walks past the shrubs, still oblivious to our presence. Like two cheetahs, we spring on our prey. I hit the man with the butt of my gun on the back of his head. It was a measured blow, not meant to kill, or even hurt the man. It was more of a notice of our intentions. I then put one arm around his neck from behind and my other hand firmly over his mouth. Samantha instantly has his hands locked in her handcuffs. In the next instant, she has her gun back out. While I maintain control of Karl, Samantha stealthily leaps into action. She glides through the entrance, checking behind both doors for anyone else who might be in the mansion, then gives the sign that all is clear.

Karl is stunned, nearly out cold. He won't be causing any trouble, but with his girth it's going to be a hell of a lot harder to move him around than I anticipated. After almost having to drag him into the mansion, I position him on a chair in the huge dining room off the entry hall, keeping my gun ready as Samantha searches the place for anyone else.

I hear a scuffle upstairs and then a single gunshot.

"Talk to me, Sam. What's your status?"

"All clear. There was only one bodyguard." It only takes a minute for Samantha to cover all the rooms and return.

KARL
ST. PETERSBURG, RUSSIA

One bodyguard? They killed Ozzie.

V. RAY

My head is clearing quickly. My hands are bound, but they haven't gagged me. Samantha stands across the room, staring at me.

Ah, my rogue. At last we meet in person. The timing of this meeting could be fortuitous, but how will it turn out? Will my rogue be able to convince her colleague to join our side? Those are questions that will be decided in the next few moments. I'm quite comfortable, however, that my contingency plans will succeed – no matter the outcome of this encounter.

Chapter 52

KHAN

After all these years I can still clearly recall the image of my murdered father, a proud king taken down ... killed when I was just a boy. The life my family would have enjoyed would have been so different if my father had lived. We were royalty in a time and place where that meant something. *This time and this place* ... are so different. Karl became my family, saving me from a mundane life in Egypt – a life of petty crime and obscurity. The time for lying low, however, is drawing to an end. I can't wait for the oil rigs to blow ... the damage it will cause ... the starvation and the suffering. I lobbied hard with Karl to simply blow the rigs and be done with it, and Karl would have done it if it hadn't been for his colleagues. *Friends*, he calls them. Karl's friends wanted to make sure the world's leaders have someone to blame – a patsy, as Karl says. He let it slip that their group has survived millennia by being cautious and taking measures to ensure their anonymity. It was the most telling information I've ever been able to glean from Karl about this group of friends. Even though they're on the brink of the culmination of their generations of planning, they cling to their anonymity like a warm blanket.

I remember more than once when Karl told me that every great crime has a patsy. If you don't know who the patsy is, then *you* are the patsy. I suppose I should be glad that I know who it is.

The secure call I placed finally connects. My most trusted friend is on the other side of the call from the other side of the world. Paka had served as my loyal bodyguard when my father was still king. When the king was killed, Paka smuggled me and the rest of my family into Egypt, using his connections to scatter my family safely across the country. We'd have been easy targets to identify had we stayed together, Paka wisely argued. While my family scattered, Paka never left my side. And when our paths crossed Karl's, it was more than pure chance. It was providence; somehow meant to be. *I am meant to be here ... on this path ... with the world at my mercy!*

"We are secured – go ahead."

"Khan! How are things going on your end?" Paka sounds tired. There's a terrible storm in the background where he is, forcing him to yell into his phone.

"Just as we planned, my friend! Just as we planned! How are the men all holding up?"

"It is difficult to be certain. I can only reach four of the teams by mobile phone. The rest are either out of cell tower range, or possibly being jammed at their locations."

"It is as Karl told us it would be. Not to worry, Paka. Viktor can still reach all the teams through the satellites."

"Yes, but ..." Paka hesitates.

"What is it?"

"Our men – at least those I can reach – are getting anxious. We have no word about payment. They are becoming troubled with doubt. The other teams must be having the same doubt. Probably even more without any communication from me."

"We are only hours away from a resolution. They *must* remain vigilant. What can we do to help?"

"Tell Viktor to contact them ... to give them some sort of reassurance that all is well and that they will get their money." Paka's exhaustion is nearly breaking the strong and proud man. He's almost pleading.

"I will make it happen, my friend."

Paka regains his composure at this good news. "Destiny smiles upon you! You are the prince of princes, Khan. The king of kings!"

Chapter 53

TREY TYSON
PUSHKIN, RUSSIA
1 HOUR AND 52 MINUTES UNTIL TERRORISTS' DEADLINE

"*This* is the palace where the Romanovs last lived?" I ask, only thinly veiling my sarcasm. The last Russian Tsar, Nicholas II, along with the rest of his family last lived here in the Alexander Palace in Pushkin during the Bolshevik Revolution. The Bolsheviks executed Nicholas, his wife, and their five children in 1918. Pushkin had been a short drive from St. Petersburg, but the conditions here are so different. "It looks like it's been through a war or two."

The wing closest to the road has gone through some upkeep, but the condition of the rest of the exterior of the Alexander Palace is appalling. And the grounds appear to be completely ignored. A brisk wind gust causes me to shiver. A light dusting of snow fell before we landed in St. Petersburg, but it hasn't snowed since.

"Indeed. It has been through both the Bolshevik Revolution and Nazi occupation," replies Katarina. "It is kept just nice enough to attract some tourists, but not so nice as to attract large crowds." I'm not certain, but I sense a touch of sadness, perhaps a bad memory, when she mentioned the Nazi occupation.

Katarina led us through the main entrance to the Alexander Palace just before it was scheduled to close to the public. The woman at the door knew Katarina and waved us in without any questions. We're heading into a grand semicircular hall, ornately furnished.

"Viktor's lair is in the Alexander Palace?" Max sounds dismayed at the idea.

"Well …" Katarina looks at him with a raised eyebrow. "Not exactly. Just follow me and be quiet."

Max and I share a quick glance and an even quicker shrug. We're forced to trust Katarina as only she can get us in to see Viktor. We follow quietly as she leads us left through a massive columned opening and into another grand hall. From here, we must pass through wooden double doors and into a large room dominated by a huge wooden slide.

Jessica lets slip a small giggle. "How fun! All the Romanovs could have slid down that thing together as a family."

"I imagine that they did exactly that," Katarina says, as she leads us through two rooms that seem to have served as studies or libraries, then into a large reception room. We take another left and enter a long corridor.

When we reach the end of the corridor, we're forced to stop in front of a large metal door. Katarina holds up a hand and says, "Wait here." She knocks three times quickly, waits a second, and knocks once more. We wait a moment, then hear a metal click from a locking mechanism, and the door opens slightly. Katarina slips through the opening and closes the door behind her.

Max and I share a quick glance, hoping this isn't some trap we've just stepped into.

I hear hushed voices behind the door, all female, and all speaking Russian.

It only takes a minute before Katarina opens the door and says, "Come." It's more of a command than a request.

We all pass behind the door and into a small opening with nothing but two elevators. The opening is guarded by two women, each dressed in all white, and each carrying a submachine gun. They obviously know Katarina and allow the four of us to enter the first elevator.

Ah, this explains why only one part of the palace has been kept up. We're in that section now and they've done some renovations to add these elevators. I wonder what other surprises might be in store for us.

Katarina uses a key she has in her possession to provide access to use the elevator, presses a button, and we start to descend.

I estimate we've gone down roughly six or seven stories when the elevator slows.

"A hideout below a tourist attraction just outside of St. Petersburg," Max says, smirking. "Strange cars and people coming to and from the palace all the time. It's rather brilliant, I have to admit."

"It has served us well. But realize *this* ..." Katarina takes on a very serious tone. "Now that you know the location, there can be only two outcomes from this meeting. One, and the most likely one, is that we will all be killed. The other will require some very convincing arguments on your part."

Max looks concerned, but there's a level of determination in him beyond anything I've ever seen before. His whole life, it seems, has been destined to bring him to this time ... this crisis. "We've been guided here for a reason and we *must* find a way to succeed. There's much more at stake than just our survival."

And then Max's words from Paris stream through my consciousness, *the third Antichrist is here and I believe you are the key to stopping him*. Me? How am *I* the key? If I'm truly a descendant of Nostradamus, shouldn't I know how and why I'm the key to stopping an Antichrist?

The elevator doors open, and we are immediately greeted by two different women, also clad in white and carrying machine guns.

It strikes me as odd that all of Viktor's henchmen are in fact *henchwomen*, and each is young and attractive. Kind of like henchmodels. "Are all of Viktor's guards women?" I can't help but ask.

"Viktor has always believed it was wise," Katarina replies, seeming to have expected the question. "An attractive woman has an immediate advantage over a man. Almost any man will want to please her. It could be some information that is useful ... money ... even to kill someone – almost anything she wants as long as he thinks he has a chance to be with her. A man will almost certainly hesitate to shoot an attractive woman. It could be the difference in survival, just a moment's hesitation."

I see Max nodding at this, something important going through his mind.

The guards lead us through two dark corridors past several closed doors, and then into a bright and expansive room with a ceiling at least twenty feet high.

"This room looks like NASA's mission control room in Houston. Not that I've ever seen it, but it looks like the movie versions of it," I say.

"I have seen it and you're right," says Max.

A hulking figure of a man, nearly bald except for a pointy, white wisp of hair above each of his ears, scowls at us. This must be Viktor, one of the men Max believes is behind the terrorist attack on the world.

"Katarina, my dear sssister," Viktor hisses from across the room. "You bring to me an old nemesis. What is the purpose of this?"

From my football days, I've seen noses that look like Viktor's. It's been broken in at least two places and Viktor never bothered to have it straightened out before the cartilage set. It now forces him to breathe through his mouth. That, with the gap in his teeth and his broken English, causes his speech to be quite choppy. His sickly pallor tells me he spends too much of his time in his underground headquarters.

"He looks like a white bull," Jessica whispers to me as we're herded toward Viktor by his guards.

"Viktor!" Katarina walks over to her brother and kisses him on the cheek. "You know who Maximo Medici is. He needs to talk with you, *urgently.*"

Viktor returns his sister's kiss and then turns his attention to Max. He picks up a large handgun from the table beside him. "Medici. After all these years and all my attempts to kill you! You are *ssstill* alive. Tell me – why should I allow you to remain that way?"

"Viktor, haven't you caused enough damage for one lifetime?" Max's boldness while facing an armed enemy surprises me. It doesn't appear to surprise Viktor, however, who raises his gun and seems prepared to shoot Max.

Katarina deftly moves into his way. "*Wait*, my brother. You must listen to what he has to say."

"First, tell me who these other two are?" He uses his gun to point at me and Jessica, and then reluctantly lowers it.

"This is Dr. Jessica O'Neill. And this," Katarina points to me, "is *my son*. His name is Trey Tyson and Maximo is his father."

Viktor stands for a moment, square jaw agape, before saying, "You told me he died in childbirth. A child of *yours* and *his,* and he lives?" He reveals a sinister grin and walks over to me. "I know who you are, *nephew*. We were watching you closely when you were younger. I bet your abilities are quite impressive. Am I right?"

I refuse to confirm or deny Viktor's statement. Trying my best to ignore the man's offensive stench, I only smile back at him.

Chapter 54

KARL

ST. PETERSBURG, RUSSIA
1 HOUR AND 47 MINUTES UNTIL TERRORISTS' DEADLINE

My rogue assumed this would be an easy recruit, but it went in the wrong direction quickly. The two agents sensed simultaneously that they were on opposite sides and both drew guns and started shooting. The way they dodge each other's bullets is spectacular. Rogue had best win this battle. It would be a shame to lose such a valuable asset.

Samantha seems to sense Judith's next shot and dodges away from her shot just before it's taken. She rolls on the ground and takes two shots of her own.

Breathing heavily, Judith says, "We've trained together for years and we're nearly equal in ability. But, I'm the quicker shot," she squeezes off two shots that Samantha anticipates and dodges.

"Perhaps," Samantha is breathing just as heavily as Judith. "But I have better aim!" She returns fire and one of her shots grazes Judith's arm, drawing blood.

"That hurts, you bitch. But you'll soon find out for yourself." Judith rolls to her right, spins around, and returns fire. But she misses her target.

Samantha ducks behind a wall. She peeks around the corner and says, "That was your shooting arm, wasn't it?"

Judith winks at me, before replying, "It's okay, my other arm works just fine." She closes her eyes, taking several deep breaths. She's exerted herself greatly in the battle and must be exhausted. Keeping her eyes closed, she lifts and aims her gun. Then, with no sound or movement from Samantha, Judith shoots a burst of three bullets into the wall. First, there's a sliding sound against the other side of the wall, then a thud. I feel a quick jolt of horror when Judith then turns to me, aiming her gun right at the middle of my forehead.

Chapter 55

GREG RUTLEDGE
WASHINGTON, DC, USA
1 HOUR AND 38 MINUTES UNTIL TERRORISTS' DEADLINE

"It's 10:22 and we only have an hour and 38 minutes. I'm just heading into the Oval Office. Say again!" I pause outside the closed door. I thought I was heading into this meeting with nothing to report to the president about the Chinese. However, the vibration from my smartphone suggested that was about to change.

A huge portion of my budget is dedicated to monitoring and deciphering data and voice over the internet – and any public or private network we can tap into. Processing all that information requires the first level of analysis to be software-based, residing on thousands of the world's most powerful servers, all running in parallel. It helps immensely if you have a key phrase to narrow the search.

I step away from the door. "Stan, we're up against a wall. Tell me you have something I can use."

"Yes, sir. It's an email. The subject included the phrase *New Society*, so it was flagged for human analysis. I'm sending a copy to you now." It's my deputy director on the line, proving his competence once again.

"Who sent it?"

"Vladimir Radnikov."

"Chief of finance at Russia's FSB. Now that's an odd connection, isn't it?"

"Is that a question, sir?"

"No. Not a word of this to anyone! Understand?" I'm adamant.

"I certainly do."

After ending the call, I take a minute to read the content I just received and walk confidently into my meeting with President Sanchez.

"You look rather chipper, considering the circumstances." The president doesn't stand to greet me, but simply points to one of the chairs across from his desk. "I hope that means you have some good news for me. We have a little more than an hour before the oceans start turning black. The Russians are refusing to even discuss paying the terrorists and the Chinese still aren't budging if the Russians won't pay."

"Sir, I do have something that may prove useful when talking to the Chinese."

"I'm addressing a joint session of congress immediately after the Somali deadline, and our entire nation … who am I kidding? The whole fucking world will be watching." The president lifts two stacks of paper to emphasize his next point. "I have *two* speeches prepared. In the *first*, I'd have to explain a global tragedy, and how we must pull ourselves together and best move forward as a nation. That's *not* a speech I want to give …. In the *second*, I'd have to explain – because it will *all* be very public – how we had to pay a gang of terrorists to *avoid* a global tragedy, and how we best move forward as a nation. That's *not* a speech I want to give, either. But we at least need to do everything possible to avoid the destruction of our oceans." He frowns at me. "So, this better be good."

"What I have, sir, is an intercepted communication to the Chinese from Vladimir Radnikov, chief of finance at Russia's FSB."

The president turns his head to give me his full attention. "Go on."

"It looks like a copy of a bill drafted by you that somehow got into the hands of the Russians. They seem to draw a correlation between the current crisis and your bill. First, it's truly disturbing that they could get it and, second, even more disturbing that they have a reason to share it with the Chinese. Sir, the Russians and Chinese are working with someone very high up in our government behind our backs. It may even be someone close to you."

"Which bill?"

"It contained a heading called *The New Society*, Mr. President."

"Hmmm …. So, we caught them snooping on us. That may very well be the leverage I need. I have a couple of secure calls I need to make before I head to the Capitol building. I'll let you know if I need anything else." He then points to the door.

Chapter 56

MAX MEDICI

PUSHKIN, RUSSIA

1 HOUR AND 33 MINUTES UNTIL TERRORISTS' DEADLINE

Viktor is pacing back and forth, sometimes in control of his rage and sometimes on the verge of losing himself to it. The man is muscular, powerful in fact, but all the gracefulness in the family has fallen to Katarina. He turns and faces me, gun raised ominously. "Why do you come to me, Max? What can I possibly have that you want?"

"Viktor, you're working with a man we know only by the name of Karl."

"Karl is a common Russian name."

"*This* Karl is working with the Somalis."

"I don't know what you are talking about."

"We don't have time for games, Viktor. Do you know what will happen when the Somalis destroy all of those oil rigs?"

"I watch the news. I doubt it will turn to that. The terrorists and their leader are ruthless, yes. I give you that. But when they get paid, they will leave without harming the precious oil rigs."

"Viktor, you know both your sister and I have some special abilities. We're not the first and we won't be the last." I gesture to Trey.

"Your point?" is Viktor's coy reply.

We must win Viktor over to our side or we have no chance. So, I decide to try something new to the world of espionage ... complete transparency. "Okay, listen. I have a story to tell you. It's about the prophecies of Michel de Nostradamus. He foresaw three Antichrists, pointing at Napoleon and Hitler as the first two. The third, he didn't name. All three, in his visions, were men determined to mold the world to their own needs, even if it meant destroying the very world they intended to conquer. The third Antichrist is behind the Somalis. And your friend Karl is behind the third Antichrist. Viktor, I know you and I have been on opposite sides all our lives. On top of that, you probably will be paid an immense amount of money for your role in this threat. However, I don't think *you're* the third Antichrist. I don't get the sense that you're in this to destroy the planet and *that's* where this is headed. Nostradamus has foreseen the destruction of the oil rigs. He's seen the end of life in our oceans. And he has seen the great famine that will ravage our world."

I risk a quick look to Katarina, wondering how far she'll go to help me, then bring my attention back to Viktor. "You can't possibly want that, Viktor. I don't think that's who you are."

Viktor lowers his gun to his side as he turns to face his sister. "Katarina, my ssssister. You have been away for too long. What do you know of this?"

"Viktor, this is a very dangerous game you play," she replies warmly, sister to brother. "I can see the truth in what Maximo says. Please keep an open mind and hear more of what he has to say."

"Let us assume for a moment that you are correct." Viktor takes a few steps toward me, speaking with a tone that seems a bit more reasonable now. "Sssay there is a Karl and your claims about this Antichrist are true. And, they are working with the Sssomalis. What makes you think *I* have anything to do with this?"

"Because Nostradamus led us directly to you," I answer. "Centuries ago, he left clues that he knew we'd find. Clues that point the way here. The fate of the world is in delicate balance right now and you can tip the scale in either direction. Choose the wrong side and the world as we know it will end."

I suddenly recall the image from the lost picture book by Nostradamus. Viktor is the white bull facing the scale. *Who* is the woman holding the archer's bow?

"Medici, I am going to tell you this because I have nothing to lose. No matter how this turns out, I will be retiring to an island with a warm climate and lots of beautiful women. The only question for me is whether I am wealthy on this island, or disgustingly wealthy. For you, however, the ssstakes are much higher." He waves the gun once to remind me of my likely fate.

"What can you tell us about Karl?" I ask, hoping Viktor is truly done with his charade of not being involved.

"I can tell you that Karl gets what he wants and what he wants now is an enormous amount of money."

"But how will you ever get your hands on this money? Our government will be able to trace almost any reasonable portion from that amount. It can't be hidden. It can't be used. Only an entity the size of a major government could process such a sum without it raising red flags all over the place."

"Indeed, you are correct." Viktor turns on his sinister grin again.

"You have the Russian government helping you?" I ask, but already know the answer.

"Again, you are correct. It is the only way. They are quite happy with the deal, and why not, they are keeping 60% of it for themselves."

"Why do you think they will pay you your share once they have all the money in their hands?"

"It is simple, no? We hold evidence of their involvement. None of us wants any attention, so they will pay us. It is what you Americans call a win-win situation. Is it not?"

"Viktor, even 40% will be impossible to hide. Karl is setting you up. Think back to the Kennedy assassination. The only coherent statement we could ever get out of Oswald was that he was a patsy. And then Jack Ruby kills him before he can go to trial. Oswald may have pulled the trigger, but he was the patsy all the same. Are you the patsy this time? Karl must know that the money is the key for us to find who's responsible for this. You don't know who he really is or how to find him, so even if you talk, it doesn't matter …. Let me guess; the money flows from the Russian government to you. Correct?"

A quick look of concern appears on Viktor's face and I may have finally inspired the first bit of doubt in the beast of a man.

"This isn't a win for anyone if the world is destroyed." Trey adds his voice to mine.

"But why would that happen? The governments will pay our demands. There is no incentive for anyone to blow up the oil rigs. As a matter of fact, I have been given reassurances that this will not happen."

Viktor has no reason to lie to us and seems to truly believe that Karl has no intention of blowing the rigs. I must convince him otherwise. "The destruction of the oil rigs and our planet *will* happen if we do nothing. It's been foreseen by Nostradamus. There's a reason. We just need to figure out what it is. What we really need is access to Karl."

As if on cue, my ComWatch chirps. It's Judith.

"I should answer this. It's my colleague, Viktor. She's been trying to hunt down Karl."

Viktor aims his gun at me. "Go ahead. But if you give away our location, you will die now."

"Judith, what's going on?" I put her on speakerphone so everyone can hear the conversation … complete transparency.

"It's terrible news, Max." Her voice is raspy. "Samantha was working with Karl. She tried to recruit me to their side. Offered millions of dollars. When she saw I wouldn't join them, she tried to kill me! Max, I had no choice. I had to defend myself. Samantha is … dead." She's weeping.

Trey jumps into the conversation, "*What!* That's … that's just not possible. I should have trusted Max. It's all my fault." The devastation in his voice is clear to all.

"Trey, is that you?" Judith's tone is warm. "Oh, I needed to hear your voice. I know Sam was your best friend. I'm so, so sorry. I wish it didn't have to be this way."

"Judith," I need to know more and take over the conversation again. "We know you only did what you had to do. Where are you? Do you have Karl with you?"

She sniffles over the speakerphone and then takes a deep breath. "I do have Karl and we're near St. Petersburg. He's handcuffed and under control. I'm taking him back to question him."

"No, Judith! There's no time for that. You aren't far from us at all. You *must* bring him here." Looking to Viktor I ask, "Okay?"

Viktor nods, but holds a finger in front of his mouth. I take that to mean I must not divulge that our location is his headquarters.

"Where are you?" asks Judith.

"We're at the Alexander Palace." I think for a moment about how to make this all work with Viktor's consent. "Look for Jessica inside the palace. She'll bring you to us."

"Okay. We'll be there in twenty minutes." She ends the call.

"You!" Viktor points to one of the guards. "Take her up there and prepare for our visitors."

The guard nods and points her machine gun at Jessica. "Come with me."

Chapter 57

PRESIDENT SANCHEZ
WASHINGTON, DC, USA
50 MINUTES UNTIL TERRORISTS' DEADLINE

After dialing my secretary, her mature yet perky voice answers, "Yes, Mr. President?"

"Contact Director Rutledge and notify him that the Chinese have agreed to pay the terrorist's demands. All ten nations are in line. He needs to follow the Somali instructions for payment immediately. I have one more secure call to make before I head to the Capitol. Make sure the limo is ready to go."

Chapter 58

TREY TYSON
PUSHKIN, RUSSIA
48 MINUTES UNTIL TERRORISTS' DEADLINE

Viktor presses a button on one of his control panels and the largest of his monitors comes to life with an image of the room with the elevators leading to his underground lair.

We all watch as the guards push open the door and Jessica walks in. She's followed closely by an elderly man, head bowed, who is still wearing handcuffs. Judith is right behind the man. As they step closer to the camera, the elderly man looks up and smiles.

"Oh my God!" I can't believe what I'm seeing.

"What?" asks Max.

"I know who Karl is. I've known him for years."

"Who?" Viktor demands before anyone else can.

"I don't believe it …. It's Roy Starr!"

"The Roy Starr who heads up Starr Aerospace?" Now Max is incredulous as well.

"Yes." I think back to all the times Roy avoided having his picture taken. "He's one of the wealthiest people in the world, but he's so private that no one would know it." I pull my iPhone out. There was *something* in that quatrain ….

"What are you doing?" Viktor points his gun at me.

"Please, Viktor. I'm not calling anyone. I have some information on this device that may help us understand Roy's – Karl's – intentions."

Viktor moves closer. "Go on. But I'm watching you."

I find the quatrain and read it for all of them to hear. "This is from Nostradamus, Century 2, Quatrain 62." Clearing my throat, I read, "*Mabus* will come to cause horrible deaths of men and beasts. Then, suddenly one will see his vengeance. Vast numbers will suffer hunger and thirst when the comet will run."

"Who is this Mabus?" Viktor obviously isn't taking the prophecy from Nostradamus lightly.

Max begins to explain, "I believe he's the power behind the Antichrist. If Karl is as wealthy as Trey believes, he would certainly have the resources –"

"Mabus," I interject, shaking my head, "is not a person. Nostradamus isn't telling us *who* is behind the Antichrist, he's telling us *why.*"

Before I can continue, the guard leads Jessica, Karl, and Judith into Viktor's control room.

"Viktor, my old friend. I must admit that I'm a bit surprised to find you here with your arch-enemy, Max Medici. But I see at least you're in control of the situation. Have them release me. *Now!*" Karl confidently turns sideways to show Viktor his handcuffed wrists.

"Just a moment, my *old friend.*" Viktor motions to the two guards and they take flanking positions, each ready with her submachine gun. Jessica moves to my side, while Judith stays close to Karl. She seems to still be covering him, even though Viktor's guards are covering all of us.

"I told you to set me free, Viktor!" Karl o. "What the hell are you waiting for?"

"Katarina has brought these people to me," Viktor replies firmly, "and they believe you are going to *blow* all the oil rigs."

Karl assumes a look of rage. "Shut your fucking mouth, you fool! What? Are you telling them all of our plans?"

Viktor instantly ramps up to match the Karl's rage, "You told me we had *no* intention of blowing any of the rigs after the first one. Trey, here, was just about to explain to me why you might want to destroy them, after all."

"Trey, my *dear* boy." Karl turns on the pleasant persona of Roy Starr as if it's simply a switch he can click. "It's not too late for us all to win here."

I feel the beginning signs of a migraine coming on. But the amulet around my neck seems to warm a bit and instead of a migraine, my mind gains a new level of clarity. I can see Karl's plan.

"MABUS," I say, loud enough to draw everyone's attention to me. "Or, if you prefer, Modern Agriculture and Biofuels, US Division: it's a corporation, not a person. Karl uses it to collect vast tracts of the most farmable land in the US. It's the most fertile land in the country, perhaps in the world. He's also an investor in most of the international farming conglomerates. If he goes through with blowing the oil rigs and destroying the oceans, people around the world will be completely reliant upon farming – *his farms* – in order to survive." I recall the line the man I knew as Roy Starr would say to me all the time. I glare at Karl. "*People gotta eat,* don't they, Karl."

Viktor leans over to Katarina. "Is this all true? What do your sssenses tell you?"

"It is *all* true. He *does* intend to blow the oil rigs," she replies with complete confidence.

Viktor's rage grows, but now it's directed solely at Karl. "The US is going to *hunt* me down and *kill* me. Tell me why I should let *you* live?" He aims his gun at Karl's head.

"Because you need me." Karl speaks with amazing calmness, effectively causing Viktor to pause. "As long as I'm *alive*, the US government will always be our ally."

"What are you talking about?"

"Look. I can prove it, if you let me." Karl smiles a warm, grandfatherly smile at all of us.

"How?"

"We can talk to someone right now and I guarantee he will convince you … beyond a doubt. Open the connection to the satellite system and enter this code. 7, 2, 7, 3."

"Your friend better be convincing." Viktor goes to his keyboard and types a few commands. The large monitor comes to life again. This time it shows a blue screen with an empty data field in the middle. Viktor types in the code from Karl and we all hear a beeping noise, the unmistakable sound of a phone dialing. Almost a full minute goes by with ring after ring and no answer on the other side. "This does not look promising for you. What are we waiting for here?"

"Be patient, my friend. Our ally is a very busy man, and it can sometimes take a couple of minutes for him to get to a private and secure connection. Especially for a video call."

The ringing stops and for a moment nothing else happens. Viktor scowls at Karl, lifting his gun. Then a few audible clicks, the blue screen flickers, and then goes solid blue with no data field. A voice comes through the system. "I have a secure connection, Karl. What's our status?"

"Khan, my boy. I need to see you. Please turn on your camera."

Out of the corner of my eye, I see Max casually fold his arms across his chest.

The screen flickers again, then an image appears, and we can all see Lou Sanchez, President of the United States of America. "Karl, what's going on?"

"Our dear friend Viktor needs some reassurance that the US government will not be tracking him down and killing him after our Somali friends blow the oil rigs."

"Nice to finally meet you, Mr. Krostov." President Sanchez is as cordial as if he were meeting a foreign ambassador. "You can be certain that Karl has my full confidence and the cooperation of my country. We are close to the finish line. Blowing the oil rigs is a critical component to our overall plan. We all just need to stay the course and reap the rewards of our efforts."

Out of the corner of my other eye, I see Judith reach into her bag and draw two guns in a fluid and rapid motion that no one else notices until she pulls the two triggers. The shots echo throughout the entire control room and Viktor's two guards drop to the ground, both dead. She then swings around and has Viktor in her sights.

"Drop your gun!" she yells.

Viktor, completely caught off guard, acquiesces. He tosses his gun to the middle of the table next to him.

"Judith! We need Viktor's help. What are you doing?" Max cautiously moves his hand toward the gun that is still holstered inside his jacket to his left side.

Judith keeps one gun pointed at Viktor and turns the other toward Max. "Back down, Max!"

Max refolds his arms and holds his position.

Karl starts to laugh, sounding close to a cackle, with a hefty cough at the end of the laugh.

Judith keeps everyone else in check while he catches his breath.

"Meet my lovely *Rogue*, you fools!" Karl says, and then coughs again.

"Everything under control now?" asks President Sanchez from his large screen above everyone else.

"Yes, Khan, I believe everything is under control now. Your concern about Viktor was obviously warranted. Were you able to get the Chinese in line?"

"Yes, finally. *All* payments will be made to the Russian government. Now, I'm off to the Capitol building. I trust you two will *take care* of things there." His hand reaches to the side of the camera on his end, and the video and sound flick off simultaneously.

"You have the American President as an ally. You have proven that," Viktor is trying to sound reasonable. "And sssoon we'll have the money. We can end this now."

"It's not that simple anymore, my *old friend*," Karl replies with a gentle, yet subtly sinister tone.

"I understand your motives," Max interrupts, "up until the blowing of the oil rigs. I don't understand the necessity for it."

As he unlocks his own handcuffs with a key that he must have been holding the entire time, Karl checks his watch. Maintaining an unusually casual tone, he says, "We have 27 minutes to … *kill* … so I see no reason not to enlighten you. I brought Luis Khan to America as a young boy. Changed his name to Lou Sanchez, forged a birth certificate, adopted him, provided a home, an extensive education. He had everything: the finest clothes, the best cars, anything he wanted.

Nevertheless, there was no filling the hole in his *soul*. Khan aspired to be a leader. First a pilot, then off to space as a shuttle commander. I thought that was his ultimate goal for a while, but he had another plan."

Karl tosses the handcuffs on the table as he continues, "Khan wanted to go into politics. He's always been an educated and eloquent speaker, but it could have taken him decades to work his way up the food chain without my assistance. Therefore, we manufactured the space shuttle accident in 1999 to have him come out as a national hero. That put him on the political fast track and got him elected to congress. His success there encouraged him to aspire for more, even the presidency. As president, he knew he'd be in the perfect position to *exact his revenge."*

Karl smiles as though he's simply a proud parent describing how his child had won a spelling bee. "Khan was born a prince, destined to rule. However, the Americans stole that from him. They killed his father and forced his family into exile. Now he wants the whole country to suffer. Hell, he wants the whole *world* to suffer. He wants everyone to share in the pain he endured as a child."

I take a measured step toward Karl, but Judith waves her gun at me to get back, saying in an almost playful tone, "Ah, ah, little brother."

Karl faces Viktor. "The money will flow to you, Viktor, and we know the authorities will be following the money. To isolate ourselves from you, we must leave control of the communications through my satellites in your hands. It has to look like you hacked your way into the system and wrestled complete control for yourself."

"At first," Viktor responds, "I did not understand why you would come here. It was a risky move, after all. You did not think I would follow through? Ssso, you have come to contact the Sssomalis to make sure they blow the rigs."

"No, Viktor." Karl says and laughs again. "The rigs will blow on their own. I would never entrust you *or* the Somalis to get that done. The one area of vulnerability we have is here with us now. *Trey Tyson.* The fact that *he* is here is a threat. Each of you has information that, on its own, is harmless. However, the two of you together *become* a threat. Plus, the CIA discovered part of our long-term plans. It made Khan nervous. So, we are here to make sure the oil rigs do, in fact, get blown up. And that none of you make it out of here to share any of this with anyone else."

Karl takes three steps back, now behind Judith. "My dear Rogue."

I hold up my hands, palms forward, to show that I'm not armed. "Judith, you're in control here. Not Khan, not Karl. It's you. And you *don't* have to do this."

Judith is visibly assessing the situation. Comfortable that none of us are about to spring at her, she takes a moment to respond. "No, I don't *have* to do this, but I *want* to do this." There's a sparkle in her eye and the sides of her mouth curl up.

Max speaks without making a physically threatening move. "It was *you* who shot Reagan, not Samantha." He then takes on a sullen look, his shoulders slumping. He suddenly looks old and worn.

"Yes, old man!" Judith howls at him. "A drop of oil smeared on the security camera lens and a black wig were all I needed to outsmart the legendary Max Medici."

"You didn't have to kill Sam!" I can clearly see what happened between Judith and Samantha, and I suddenly realize I am – just as Nostradamus had foreseen – the cause of my best friend's death. Max would have left her with Italian authorities if I hadn't insisted upon getting Judith to intervene. "*Why*, Judith?" I shake my head, still holding out a sliver of hope for her.

JUDITH TYSON

"It's *you*, you arrogant ass!" I point one gun at Trey, while training the other on Katarina. They're the two biggest threats in the group and my first targets. "You were always everyone's favorite; valedictorian, football star, wealthy beyond any normal person's wildest dreams. My friends have only wanted to be *my* friend so they could get to know *you*.

Mom and Dad thought you were the best at everything. They thought you were the smartest – the one who always made the right decisions. It's disgusting, like you've *never* made a fucking mistake in your *whole life*."

I aim one gun back to Max. "And you! *I* listened to your bullshit! *I* joined your team! *I* became the best agent you ever had. And all you can *ever* talk about is how *Trey* is the chosen one. *He's* the one you need to save the world! Well, guess what, *jackass*. The world isn't going to be saved. And this is the end of the road for all of you!"

Even though I have two guns, there are five targets, and three of them with my same abilities. I can sense that Max is armed, but he's old and worn out, so much less of a threat. My hatred for Trey makes me want to take him out first. Plus, he would be the most adept at dodging and finding something to use as a weapon. There's a slight chance he might be armed and Katarina probably is, too. Reaching out with my vision I see … nothing. *Fuck!* I can't see how Katarina or Trey react to *anything* I might do.

Shifting my focus to Viktor and Jessica, I see that if I shoot the two of them simultaneously neither one will get hit. It dawns on me that Trey will take the bullet for Jessica. And Katarina is the only one close enough to Viktor, so she must be taking the bullet intended for him. Max might be able to return fire, but at least I can see that coming if he does.

I change my targets, left-hand gun to Viktor, right-hand gun to Jessica. I want Katarina and Trey to have barely enough time to react, so I pause, just a moment, then squeeze both triggers.

KATARINA KROSTOV

As Judith aims at Jessica and Viktor, I realize what her plan is. Viktor is the only one the Somalis will listen to. Only *he* can reach them all in time to convince them to not detonate the oil rigs. He *must* live, while I have much I have done in my past to pay for. With all the quickness I still possess, I leap in front of Viktor.

TREY TYSON

I sense my surroundings as if I have all the time in the world. Judith and Max possess the same abilities I have, but not nearly as powerful as mine. My vision can now reach far beyond anyone else's. I can even sense Katarina, understand the level of her abilities, and I know that mine are greater. Peering into the future, I can see the clock expiring on the automated detonators. Then comes the explosions at all the oil rigs. *Flames everywhere!* Oil spews into the oceans of the world and can't be stopped. Peering even further, this vision is ever shifting and ever more disturbing. I see death. *Death in the oceans … dead animals … dead people.* They starve to death in massive numbers. My vision shifts to Jessica as Judith takes aim at her. I can see her on the ground with a bullet wound through the base of her neck. *Bleeding to death.* I won't let that happen. Not Jessica … not now … not ever.

With a firm understanding that my death means there will be no hope to stop the oceans from being destroyed and no hope to stop the famine to follow and all that death, I leap in front of Jessica with hesitation and no regrets.

Judith squeezes both triggers and her aim is true. In perfect unison, Katarina and I are each hit in the chest and fall to the ground.

Chapter 59

The next cycle will come with a turbulent whirlwind.
Their faces covered by cloaks.
The new republic will no longer be ruled by its people.
The whites and reds will rule wrongly.
(Nostradamus, Michel. The Prophecies. C1:Q3)

PRESIDENT SANCHEZ
WASHINGTON, DC, USA
17 MINUTES UNTIL TERRORISTS' DEADLINE

"President Sanchez! So good to see you again." Reno extends his hand to me.

"Bruce, wait outside." Ignoring Reno's hand, I enter a private conference room in the US Capitol.

"Sir?" The young agent Judith assigned to me, Bruce Cullens, lingers in the doorway.

"Yes, Bruce?"

"I'm told they're waiting for your speech so they can load it into the teleprompter."

"My press secretary already has it. They can get it from her. Now close the goddamn door!"

"Yes, sir." Bruce closes the conference room door and takes a position just outside of it.

Once the door closes, Reno continues, "I can't tell you how difficult it was to line up Congress on such short notice. I don't think it would have happened without the crisis. Oh, and I saw the newscast. Congratulations on getting the payments to the Somalis, sir."

"Forget the pleasantries, Reno. Where the fuck do we stand?"

"We can't count on any of the Republicans, but we shouldn't need them. We're close with the Democrats to having the numbers we need. It's going to take some favors and possibly some coercion on your part to win over the last few we'll need."

"Who do we still have to convince?"

"It's too early to know for sure. I've spoken with the party leaders, and had them pass on the word about how important this is to you, to our party, to our country, *and* to their careers. I've told everyone who's with us to wear a dark suit, white shirt, and red tie today as a sign of unity."

Great initiative. I'm impressed. "What a bright move, Reno. We'll be able to see who's not in line right away and we can strategize on how best to get them in line. As a matter of fact, let's meet back here right after the speech and compare notes."

Now, at three minutes past noon, I make my way to the podium. The first report came in just moments after noon. Long-range visuals confirmed an oil rig had been blown in the Gulf of Mexico. Karl and Judith came through. They did what they had to do. Hurrying through the usual progression of small talk with reporters and loyal friends in Congress, I want to deliver the news before it can spread by any other means. Everyone in the House chamber with a joint session of Congress is in a somber mood. No one has been allowed to get close to the oil rigs, so everyone is waiting for me to provide definitive news. While there would usually be a loud round of applause for the president addressing a joint session, especially from my own party, there's no applause this time … only anticipation and concern.

My teleprompters light up with the speech I passed on to my press secretary about a half an hour ago. I can't help but scan the Democrats to see who isn't wearing white shirts and red ties before beginning my speech.

"Vice President, members of Congress, and fellow Americans. We meet today, facing a crisis not seen before in our history as a nation, or in the history of humankind." I'm aware that I'm an impressive looking man. I often practice my facial expressions in front of a mirror. My audience is somber, so I take on an expression that's even more somber.

"We made every effort to stop the Somali terrorists. Negotiation attempts failed. Military action was thwarted at the onset. We even took the unprecedented step of fully meeting the terrorists' demands. *Brave Americans*, fighting for all of us, have paid with their lives to prevent the Somalis from destroying our oceans. I come to you today, having just received word that it was all for naught. The Somali terrorists have just detonated their bombs, destroying 27 oil rigs around the world … 28 if you count the initial blast in the Aegean. The hostages they held on the rigs are all dead. Oil is spewing from the ocean floor from 28 newly made crevices. Every ocean and every major sea on the planet will be affected."

While the response from the members of Congress is mostly silence, waiting for some miraculous follow-up with how we can save the planet's oceans, others abandon protocol and embark upon frantic texting with the horrible news.

"I wish I could offer you hope. But, the truth of the matter is that we cannot hold back the oil," I continue. "With all the resources of every nation on this planet, we might be able to contain and control 3, possibly 4 of these oil spills, but the challenge of containing 28 oil spills is simply beyond our capabilities."

It's taking all my effort to keep from showing even a hint of satisfaction … redemption … *revenge* for my father and my family.

"This is a dark day indeed, but it's not our *last* day. We are still here. We must persevere! We must fight on! A crisis of this magnitude, creating a challenge of this magnitude, requires a response of even *greater* magnitude."

I look around the room and see shock and horror. Some are in denial. Some clutch to a sliver of hope. Many are in white shirts and red ties, though. "This is an opportunity. *Yes*, an opportunity to change …. We must get to the root of what inspired this terrorist act. So many people around the world despise America's very existence. They see us as greedy, they see us as selfish, and they see us as meddling in every other part of the world. They wonder why we would behave in such a way when *our* house isn't even in order. Well, it's time to get our house in order."

Applause erupts, but it's limited to Democrats wearing dark suits, white shirts, and red ties.

"I'm proposing a sweeping series of acts to do just that."

Again, applause, less boisterous, from the same Democrats.

"My conservative friends, here today, would tell you that competition has been the greatest force for good in our economy since our inception." I pause to allow the Republicans a few seconds to get their applause out of their systems.

"I think unnecessary competition can create huge inefficiencies. Now that our planet's most critical resource for our survival – *food* – has taken a major blow, we can no longer afford to be inefficient. We can no longer be wasteful. We must consolidate everything we can. I'm proposing several acts to do just that and I expect Congress to pass these acts quickly. I expect to have them on my desk and to sign them into law by the last day of business this year."

I take a deep breath. "The first act for our *New Society* is –"

Chapter 60

MAX MEDICI
PUSHKIN, RUSSIA
9 MINUTES UNTIL TERRORISTS' DEADLINE

Now wearing my amulet that we retrieved from Katarina's apartment, I'm able to draw my gun and return fire far faster than Judith can anticipate. My vision now surpasses hers and I can see her every move before she can even think it. I shoot high and right on purpose, knowing she'll have to duck to the left. Then I shoot even lower and more left, forcing her to dodge to the right. Every shot has a purpose. I'm boxing her in and keeping her off balance. If she dares try to return fire instead of dodging, I'll hit her before she has a chance to shoot. My next shot is low and right, leaving her no choice but to jump. Once airborne, and with no ability to change direction, I efficiently put two bullets into her chest.

Judith's guns hit the ground just before her body drops, spewing blood, motionless.

Jessica immediately goes into triage mode. She pulls the first-aid kit out of her backpack and dives to Trey's side.

"I'm fine," Trey coughs out. "Help Katarina."

"What do you mean, you're fine? Let me see your wound!" She tears at his shirt.

Trey quickly pulls his amulet above his shirt collar and shows her the bullet firmly embedded in the soft metal. "Please. Help my mother!"

Meanwhile, Viktor takes one look at his sister, laying on the ground, chest and neck covered in her own blood. He then grabs his gun off the table, and starts toward Karl.

"Don't kill him, Viktor!" I keep my gun aimed at Karl, but have no intention of shooting him. "We're down to seven minutes, and he's the only one who knows how to stop the automatic detonation system."

Karl drops to the ground and tries to push Judith's body to the side to get to one of her guns.

Viktor glowers over him. It seems to bring him great pleasure to see Karl scampering on the ground. He shoots him once in the middle of his back and watches for a moment as Karl rolls over in agony. "That is what I wanted – to see your face, old friend." Viktor walks closer, now standing over Judith's body. He aims right in the middle of Karl's forehead, waits a second to hear Karl's last whimpering cries for mercy, and then fires.

Jessica is kneeling next to Katarina, applying pressure to her gunshot wound. Trey and I both move to her other side, while Viktor approaches.

"How is she, Jess?" asks Trey.

"Put your hands here and apply pressure," she commands. When Trey does this, she reaches into the medical kit, quickly prepares a needle, and injects it into Katarina's arm.

"What was that? Will she be Okay?" I ask, but I already know the answer.

"Something for the pain," she replies. Tears flow down her cheeks while she gently shakes her head.

"My Maximo ...." Katarina reaches for and grasps my hand and I'm taken aback when I notice she's wearing a white gold ring with a small diamond. The emotions I've fought against since her betrayal storm their way to the surface. Katarina is the only true love of my long and lonely life. "I am sorry for the great wrongs I have done to you .... I have always loved you, but have never been worthy of your love in return."

"Rest easy, Katarina," I say, fighting a losing battle against the tears that come. "Today, we were finally on the same side. And because of you, we can still save the planet. We can still save our son."

Viktor stands over us, a single tear streaming down his face.

V. RAY

Katarina sees him, her breathing very faint now. "My brother ....
There is a good man in there, I know it .... You must help them ....
Promise."

Viktor nods.

"Trey, my son ...." She puts her hand on top of his, while he still
maintains pressure on her chest. "I wish we had more time."

Trey bends over and kisses her on the forehead.

"Trey ...." She's fading quickly. "You need to know about the
Oracle .... Stray sisters are not the same .... It's not our choice .... The
First Order ...." Her eyes close. Her breathing stops.

Jessica gently takes Trey's hands. "She's gone."

"*No!*" he wails.

"Calm yourself, nephew. We only have four minutes." Viktor points
to the time displayed on one of his computer screens.

"You best make your call to the Somalis," I tell Viktor.

"What's the point, Medici?" Viktor's resolve seems to have passed
with his sister. "There's an automated detonator that will set them off
anyway."

TREY TYSON

Wiping my tears, I force myself into action. I've lost my best friend,
my sister, and now my birth mother – all in the last hour. That's enough
death for one day. And grieving will have to wait. "Make the call while
we figure out how to stop the automated system. I need internet
access!"

"You can use this one." Viktor points to one of the computer
stations and then moves to another station to initiate his satellite call to
the Somali terrorists.

I enter a search query, *NOSTRADAMUS VATINICIA CODE*,
and hope the results show what I need. In less than a second, the screen

fills with search results … including the actual images from Nostradamus' Lost Book. Scrolling through, I look for the one from my dream.

"Ah, finally!" I open and enlarge the image, showing it on one of the large monitors hanging on wires from the ceiling so everyone else can see it.

"*This* is what you dreamt?" asks Jessica.

"Yes, *exactly* this. Nostradamus drew this and meant for me to find it. We must figure out these symbols quickly. I think it's safe to say that Viktor is the white bull."

"Aye, and now he's chosen our side of the scale," says Jessica.

"And the ship's wheel," Max jumps in, "typically represents choosing a major new direction. The crescent moon means the start of a new cycle. This correlates with the Bible and Mayan prophecies of a great change in the world just about now. While many have assumed it to mean the end of days, it's more likely a crux point in human history."

"Yes," I agree. "We need to figure out the center of the drawing. Who's the woman threatened by the arrow?"

"That must be Mother Earth, personified," answers Jessica. "The entire planet is at risk. What we need to know is who the archer is. Is it President Sanchez?"

Max shrugs and turns to me. Jessica sees him and also turns to me.

This is *my* question to answer. I've been guided by many forces beyond my control just so I can answer *this* question. It's about me. For *some* reason, it's about me. Max says that I'm the key. Nostradamus saw the future and chose *me* for this. Closing my eyes, I try to draw upon my own experiences to solve the riddle.

The woman is Mother Earth and she's *connected* to the bow.

Who is the archer?

My mind brings up a quick flash of the famine vision.

That cannot be our future. *Think!*

There's an automated detonation system embedded within the satellite software.

Starr Aeronautics created the satellites and the software.

Roy Starr. *Karl!*

"Karl was the archer, but that's not the problem. He's dead and the clock's still ticking. It's the bow and arrow!"

Viktor returns from his station. "I was able to reach all of the Sssomali teams except for one. I told them we have received payment in full. They are releasing their hostages and will take their designated escape routes. What is the point, though? We are down to just over one minute."

I hand my iPhone to Viktor with a phone number displayed on it. "I need you to call this number now!"

Viktor works the keyboard at the station I had just been using and we can all hear a dial tone followed by a phone number sequence over the sound system. The call is answered right after the first ring.

"Hello?"

"Paul, it's Trey. We're in the middle of a crisis and you're the only one who can help. Are you at your computer?"

"Accurate assessment, bro. You know I'm always at my –"

"Listen! You have access to Starr's systems, right?"

"Yes."

"There's a corrupt executable file for my algorithm to determine if a point is in a polygon. Find an archive from *before* Starr bought your company and upload it. This is life and death. You have 18 seconds!"

Nothing but silence for a full 2 seconds and then we all hear frantic keyboard typing on the other end of the line.

"10 seconds," I say as calmly as I can.

"Found the archive. Starting the upload. The file sizes *are* different. Uploading still …."

"3 seconds!" yells Max.

"… Aaaaand done," says Paul.

Viktor switches the monitors to multiscreen images of all the oil rigs. They are all still fine, except for one that had burst into flames, quickly blazing out of control. "One oil rig blew in the Gulf of Mexico," he says, smiling, "but it's the *only* one we didn't stop."

"You did it, Paul!" I yell ecstatically.

"Great, but what was the purpose of that?"

"Remember when we first discussed the algorithm back in Mom's class in high school?"

"Sure, I do. It was a stroke of genius. A ray stretching from a single point, passing through a polygon."

"Visualize it ... an *arrow* and a *bow!*"

"Yes, I can see that analogy, but what do a bow and arrow have to do with anything?" Paul still sounds confused. "I don't understand what I just accomplished?"

"You just stopped the destruction of the world's oceans, Paul! Listen. I'll call you later to explain in detail. But make sure that corrupt file can't get back into the system."

"Affirmative," answers Paul, and we end the call.

"You didn't want to bring up Judith or Samantha?" Jessica says, with a very concerned look.

"That's a conversation best to have in person."

She puts her hand on my shoulder and kisses my cheek. "Aye, of course it is."

"Max, what do we do about the third Antichrist?" I ask. "This Khan ... or Lou Sanchez is still the president of the United States of America. He's the Commander in Chief or the world's most powerful armed forces. That's not any easy thing to overcome."

"No, it's not." Max presses a button on his ComWatch and waits for a connection that comes quickly. He puts it on speakerphone.

"Max, I see you're still okay. What's your status?" It's CIA Director Greg Rutledge.

"Greg, we were able to gain access to Viktor's headquarters. Viktor agreed to call off the Somalis. He reached them all except for one team in the Gulf of Mexico. The others have released their hostages and are fleeing the oil rigs right now. That wasn't our only problem, though. We discovered, located, and halted an automated detonator system that would have blown all the oil rigs with or without the Somalis."

"We're aware of the one blown oil rig and have containment vessels headed there now. Having only one blown oil rig is a situation we can deal with. Bravo, Max! How in God's name did you do it?"

"I'm sending you something now." Max presses a few buttons on his ComWatch. "You need to watch this as soon as you get it, but then you're going to want to have the attorney general watch it immediately after that. And you'll need to explain the situation to Agent Bruce Cullens before any action is taken."

"Okay, good, I will."

"Greg, one more thing?" Max presses.

"Yes?"

"We couldn't have done this without Viktor's help. I think he's earned a … well, a quiet retirement."

There is a slight pause. "I can guarantee him immunity *if* he'll tell us where to find the Somalis."

Max looks at Viktor, who nods yes without hesitation. "He agrees."

"Then we have a deal."

Chapter 61

PRESIDENT SANCHEZ
WASHINGTON, DC, USA

After finishing my speech and New Society presentation, I'm headed back into the conference room. I've taken mental notes on exactly which members of Congress are with me and which are not. With Reno's help, I'm confident we'll achieve enough votes to pass the New Society package in its entirety.

"Bruce!" I'm in a jovial mood, having justly avenged my father and my family. My voice is electric with excitement. "What did you think?"

"Considering the news you shared, that was one of the more beautifully delivered speeches I've ever heard, Mr. President. It seemed as though you had weeks to prepare for it, even though that would *obviously* be impossible." Bruce opens the conference room door for me.

As I'm walking into the room, I nod. "Thanks!"

"Believe me, sir. It's my pleasure." Bruce smiles and closes the door.

Turning my attention into the conference room, I see Reno isn't here. Instead, it's Greg Rutledge, the attorney general, the chief of capitol police, and two armed capitol police officers. On the far wall, there's a large flat-screen TV playing a recorded video from Viktor's headquarters. In addition, my own image can be seen in the background. The audio is just loud enough to hear my own recorded voice.

"Blowing the oil rigs is a critical component to our overall plan. We all just need to stay the course, and reap the rewards of our efforts."

1ST VISION

"President Sanchez," the attorney general begins, "CIA Director Rutledge has brought this video to our attention. Former AI Director Max Medici was able to capture and transmit this to him. I hereby place you under arrest."

Epilogue

Seated at night in my secret study,
alone, reposing over a brass tripod.
Cramped flames come out of the solitude.
Facts uttered that one would be vain to believe.
(Nostradamus, Michel. <u>The Prophecies</u>*. C1:Q1)*

TREY TYSON
LONGBOAT KEY, FLORIDA, USA

Max and I watch as the last rays of sunset fade across the Gulf of Mexico. I found the perfect property with a western view on the gulf that was large enough to build a main house and two guest houses. Helen, my mom – at least I've always known her as my mom and she *is* the woman who raised me as her own – moved into one of the guest houses for the winter months. Max has moved into the other guest house fulltime. Someone who's done so much for his country and the rest of the world deserves to retire comfortably, surrounded by loved ones. At Max's suggestion, I don't call him Father or Dad. It would be too weird to suddenly make that change and neither of us wants to make Helen uncomfortable.

We go sailing about once a week on the one possession Max owns – a small sailboat named *Tinef*. We also play a round of golf together a couple of times a week. Our relationship had always been great, but now that we've been through a major crisis together, it's even better.

Once the skies fully darken, Max breaks the silence we've been enjoying, "You sure seem to have it all, Trey: an amazing wife, a child on the way, a beautiful home that's finally finished, your golf game is coming around nicely, and you'll have access to me or Helen whenever you need a babysitter."

"It's so nice to have you here, Max …. I'm very curious though."

"About what?"

"We've had a few funerals, then everyone took a while to digest what we went through. Well, we really haven't talked about this yet. Before Katarina passed, she mentioned the *Oracle* and the *First Order*. It was obviously important for her that I know something about both, but she never finished what she wanted to say."

"Yes," Max says in his serious, yet understanding voice. "I've been thinking about that often."

"You knew her. What do you think she meant?"

"I've had some experience with a stray sister very early in my career. The part of what Katarina said, that it's not their fault, but the Oracle's doing … well, I've seen it myself. The First Order, however, is as much a mystery to me as it is to you. I've always suspected Karl was part of some sort of secret society. His resources were seemingly endless. But, I'm afraid that secret may have died with him."

"What about the Oracle?"

"I imagine the Oracle refers to the Oracle of Delphi. It's hard to believe, but Katarina may have descended from the family line of the Oracle. One of the stray sisters that left the sisterhood of the Oracle centuries ago. Her abilities far exceeded my own."

"You descend from Nostradamus. So, why is it hard to believe she comes from the Oracle?" I ask.

"The line of the Oracle of Delphi was supposed to have ended."

"Ended? How?"

"The Oracle," Max begins, "was represented by a lineage of young women with prophetic abilities they claimed were granted by the Greek god Apollo. Their influence spanned the last six centuries of ancient Greece through the first four centuries of the Roman Empire. Think about it …. The Oracle was in a position of prominence for a *millennium* in which kings and emperors bowed to them, seeking their prophetic guidance, and paying them handsomely for their services. With the Roman adoption of Christianity, however, all pagan religions —

including the Oracle – were disbanded in the 4th Century AD. It had long been believed that the line of the Oracle had been wiped out, but *perhaps* there were survivors."

"Max, you and I have never really discussed the religious aspects of our abilities."

"I've always thought you were an atheist. So, what religious aspects do *you* see?"

"What Sam did in Detroit years ago, where she experienced the past to learn about the Presidential Curse. How do you explain that? Was it her *spirit* traveling through time? Her *essence?*"

"*That* is a very good question. Was she guided by a higher being? On the other hand, is there a scientific explanation that makes sense? I don't know for certain, but I can tell you what my mentor, Albert Einstein, would have said."

"What?"

"He'd have told you what he told me on several occasions. Time is the 4th dimension and all of time has played out. We reside at a specific point in three-dimensional space at a specific point in time. Physically traveling back in time is impossible, according to his Theory of Relativity. But quantum physics experiments point to the possibility of perceiving the past and the future. Yet, *how* do we perceive past and future events? Is it spiritual? Or is it an ability of the human mind?"

"Those are more questions, not an answer!"

Max laughs. "True, but Einstein *would* define the question better. Then he'd let you decide for yourself."

I nod, feeling unfulfilled by his answer, but knowing he wants me to come up with my own answer.

Max had spent a year after the Somali terrorist crisis consulting with AI and training Bruce Cullens to take over leadership of the division. He brought me into the fold with AI before he retired again. We've both gone to DC often and we both became good friends with Bruce.

Jessica left the Detroit emergency room behind to focus on gerontology in Florida and is building a highly respected practice. I've been able to golf as often as I want, and my consulting with AI has turned out to be far more rewarding than I ever imagined it would be when I was young.

"Are you sure you want to go through with this?" Max positions the brass tripod in front of where I sit. "What happened to Judith was her own doing. Katarina made her own choices as well. And, you can't blame yourself for Samantha. She sacrificed her life for our country … for the world. We can honor her, but using the tripod can't bring her back."

"I think I need to do this for some sort of closure."

"Look, Trey. It will help if you think of this as opening a new door, instead of closing a door to a past you know. Your world is about to get much bigger. Are you comfortable with how to proceed?"

"Quite comfy indeed." I put on my amulet. Since I first came into contact with it, I haven't had a single migraine. I light the candle and lean back comfortably into the chair.

"Clear your mind and focus on the flame."

The flame dominates my vision. The stars fade to blackness. I feel my amulet warming to my skin and feel myself falling into a trance state. My eyes are closed, but I still see the flicker of the flame. Calmness settles over me. A noise emanates from the darkness. It's a voice and I think I can make it out.

"I can finally communicate with you, my son of many sons. You are the first in my line to share this ability." The voice is speaking French, but everything converts in my mind to my native English.

"Who are you? Nostradamus?"

"Yes …. Unfortunately, we must keep this conversation short. This is your first time and you will not be able to maintain your focus for long. Wear the amulet as often as possible. The more you wear it, the greater your strength becomes."

"How did you do it? How do you keep doing it? It's the 16th Century for you, and you've had this grand design for centuries into your future. And how can we be communicating?"

"Communication over time is a rare ability. Since the 1st vision, our family line has sought to use our prophetic abilities to protect the future."

Trying not to laugh, I say, *"I read about your 1st vision, and it sounded like you were shocked, to say the least."*

"It was not my 1st vision I meant, Trey. There have been psychics and visionaries throughout history. There are few within this group I would call prophets. Truly rare are those who can act as a guide. You will be such a guide."

"A guide, like you? I can't do what you have done."

"You combine the bloodlines of two separate and powerful families. I cannot see a limit to your abilities. I will teach you to reach further than you can imagine. To see future events so far beyond your own time that the civilization in your visions will look as foreign to you as yours does to me."

"I simply can't believe that. You have influenced the centuries and saved humankind from three Antichrists. How can I possibly do what you have done?"

"The three Antichrists I foresaw will not be the last to threaten the world. The future still needs safekeeping. This is your fate, Trey. You have a great gift and you must choose if you are to use it. The planet and all its people depend upon you. The third Antichrist represented a crux point in time. I could only see glimpses past that time because fate had not yet been determined and time could have followed two very different paths. You must look to both the near and distant future to protect your family ... to protect the world. There will always be evil attempting to dominate or destroy everything. It is a sacrifice, no doubt, but one that must be made. My time is near an end and my strength ebbs. I will teach you to look forward and to guide others."

"I've lost so much already: my sister, my birth mother, and my best friend. I fear if I follow the path you are laying out, I will put the lives of my other loved ones at great risk."

"There is risk involved with any choice. But which scenario presents the greater risk to your loved ones? When you are looking to the future ... or when you are not?"

Damn. He can see the future and debate with logic.

"I see your point. When do we start?"

"Time is ever lasting, yet my time is short. We must start immediately. You shall be my greatest legacy.

Extras

Fact with Fiction

Much of the history within this book is accurate, and there are probably far more facts and actual events included than most would imagine. I invite readers to visit www.facebook.com/vrauthor to ask questions and learn more.

Kindly Help a First-Time Author

Did you enjoy the book? If so, please give a top rating and/or write a positive review. Any positive feedback and word of mouth from readers greatly helps and is mightily appreciated!

Special Thanks

To those brave people who risk their lives to defend and protect our great nation, our people, our interests, and so often other parts of the world – you can't be thanked enough!

About the Author

V. Ray was born and raised in the suburbs north of Detroit, and now lives and works in Florida. He has a bachelor's degree in computer science with an emphasis in artificial intelligence, and is immensely intrigued by history, religion, politics, science/technology, and philosophy.

Visit his page at www.facebook.com/vrauthor.

V. RAY